KT-489-252

Praise for *Freight Dogs*

'*Freight Dogs* is an ambitious and intricate novel. Foden's understanding of the nature of war, and of this war in particular, is
exemplary . . . *Freight Dogs* is also a fast-paced adventure yarn
featuring battles, exploding volcanoes, buried secrets, a deathbed
revelation, daredevil flying and an elusive love interest. In this
Foden has cleverly reworked the grand African adventure novel
epitomised by Rider Haggard and Wilbur Smith, or later, John
le Carré's *The Constant Gardener* or Michael Crichton's *Congo*
. . . This book is a testament to all those civilians, in Congo,
Afghanistan, Syria, Colombia and elsewhere, whose lives have
not so much been touched by violence as tossed round like flot-
sam on the waves of history and conflict'

Aminatta Forna, *Guardian*

'Sharp and fast-paced . . . Foden does a fine job of locating the
reader in the maelstrom of this brutal period in Congo's past . . .
he takes us deep into the heart of a complex conflict, showing
how even the innocent can get caught up in acts of horrifying
violence'

Alex Preston, *Observer*

'Underpinning and directing everything are ever-restless time and
history, the biggest characters of all. At one point Manu "senses
the rub of history, of past events . . . jointly seeking form, seeking a stable meaning". That's a pretty good description of what
a novelist seeks too, and in *Freight Dogs* Foden makes a damned
good job of it'

John Self, *The Times*

'Full-throttle adventure'   Anthony Cummins, *Mail on Sunday*

'Foden is a brilliant voice and African observer'   *Spectator*

80003765893

Giles Foden was born in 1967 and spent much of his early life in Africa. He was educated at Cambridge University. He has worked as a barman, a builder, a journalist, an academic and as a *rapporteur* for the European Commission. For ten years, he was an editor and writer on the *Times Literary Supplement* and the *Guardian*, and his writing has since been published in *Granta*, *Vogue*, *Esquire*, the *New York Times* and *Condé Nast Traveller*, where he is a contributing editor. His fiction includes *The Last King of Scotland*, *Ladysmith*, *Zanzibar* and *Turbulence*. *The Last King of Scotland* was made into an Oscar-winning feature film in 2006.

FREIGHT DOGS

GILES FODEN

WEIDENFELD & NICOLSON

First published in Great Britain in 2021 by Weidenfeld & Nicolson
This paperback edition published in 2022 by Weidenfeld & Nicolson
an imprint of The Orion Publishing Group Ltd
Carmelite House, 50 Victoria Embankment
London EC4Y 0DZ

An Hachette UK Company

1 3 5 7 9 10 8 6 4 2

Copyright © Giles Foden 2021

The moral right of Giles Foden to be identified as
the author of this work has been asserted in accordance
with the Copyright, Designs and Patents Act of 1988.

All rights reserved. No part of this publication may be
reproduced, stored in a retrieval system, or transmitted
in any form or by any means, electronic, mechanical,
photocopying, recording, or otherwise, without the
prior permission of both the copyright owner and the
above publisher of this book.

All the characters in this book are fictitious, and any resemblance
to actual persons, living or dead, is purely coincidental.

A CIP catalogue record for this book is
available from the British Library.

ISBN (Mass Market Paperback) 978 1 4091 3742 9
ISBN (eBook) 978 0 2978 6802 6
ISBN (Audio) 978 1 4091 6112 7

Typeset by Input Data Services Ltd, Somerset

Printed in Great Britain by Clays Ltd, Elcograf S.p.A.

MIX
Paper from
responsible sources
FSC® C104740

www.weidenfeldandnicolson.co.uk
www.orionbooks.co.uk

I

The Aftermath

June–November 1996

Chapter 1

Even though other tall boys were at his side that evening, Manu felt lanky — arms sticking out of cuffs, legs encumbered by pews. His school choir was singing in the cathedral, jostling elbows as they bawled it out, under a blue-toned cupola. A prize event was taking place, as well as a Mass. All the schools in Bukavu — a lakeside town in eastern Zaire — were competing, in the presence of the archbishop himself. A girls' school won, integrating handbells into their performance. Looking glumly on, Manu was struck by the intense concentration on the faces of those pig-tailed girls as they rang their bells in a synchronised manner, one choreographed by their music teacher, no doubt.

The girls, they were simply better. They deserved victory and his school's lusty rendition of a French hymn, '*Seigneur, je vois*', deserved failure. Was it his fault? He'd sneezed at a crucial point. It might equally have been the fault of Clement next to him, who cawed like a crow; but anyone, in fact, in his thirty-strong choir of school leavers (all between seventeen and nineteen) could have been the cause, many struggling to keep time, despite the attempts of Don Javier to improve them in practice sessions.

Manu was downcast not by natural adolescent gloom, but by events: by now, after all, his father had sent his fateful message, summoning him back to the farm, and this had plunged him into despair.

In his address afterwards, the archbishop mined more solid ground for that emotion, saying, 'There are things that can be seen only with eyes that have cried,' but that no one should lose hope. He pleaded that the congregation avoid ethnic dispute. He pleaded that they refer to God and his angels, not tribe or clan. If, he added, 'this country only could work with mutual understanding, singing in time from the same song sheet, like these fine young women with handbells, then through grace of *Mungu Baba*, Zaire will be preserved from the crimes that have befallen our neighbour, and life will go on'.

The archbishop spoke of the killings by Hutus in neighbouring Rwanda. He spoke of the following invasion there by Tutsi exiles – notionally people with whom Manu's family would be in covenant, being Tutsis themselves, albeit Congolese rather than Rwandan. And then he spoke of the invasion's consequences. One was a refugee crisis in Zaire itself, now fomenting hatred among other tribes against both Hutus and Tutsis, but mainly the latter.

The genocide in Rwanda – the border was very near to Bukavu – occurred two years ago. So Manu and his schoolfriends knew very well, as they sang their guts out, that the killings were triggered by a missile attack on a small jet containing the Hutu President of Rwanda and his Burundian counterpart.

They knew, too, that the Rwandan Hutu government, long before that Falcon 50 fell from the sky, had already planned the programme of death that it ignited. For months before, elements in the Hutu leadership had been readying the kindling through messages in the media, shrill and demented. As with spiders producing enormous webs from tiny bodies (there were some of these above Manu, crossing the curved spans of the cathedral roof), these messages worked insidiously on the minds of the populace, bringing forth a platform of communal hatred.

Suspicion about who fired the missiles fell either on the Tutsi army in exile that invaded, then called the Rwandan Patriotic Front, now designated the Rwandan Patriotic Army, or RPA; or on Hutu Power, an extremist element of the former Rwandan government, opposed to negotiation by more moderate Hutus.

The truth remained unknown to Manu, to nearly everyone. Maybe that even included the leader of his own country, Joseph-Désiré Mobutu Sese Seko Kuku Ngbendu Wa Za Banga, President of Zaire. Indeed, the downing of the jet could turn out to be 'one of the great mysteries of the late twentieth century', according to a reporter for the BBC World Service.

This was the station to which Manu and his schoolfriends mostly listened, along with Radio France Internationale. Short-wave transmissions seemed so important in those long-ago days, dispersing among millions with all the apparent power of the drops of holy water that the archbishop flicked at doomed youth with a little, silver-handled brush, as he processed down the aisle and out of the cathedral.

In their dorm afterwards there took place, courtesy of Clement's dinky radio, the customary audience of successive news broadcasts on the Africa services of the British and French national stations. Both happened that night to examine the links between the genocide in 1994 and the following influx of Hutu refugees into Zaire, and how these two events had become bound up with attacks on Congolese Tutsis. This designation included two main groups, Banyamulenge and Banyarwanda; Manu was one of the former, but his situation was complicated, because his family had migrated away from the main Banyamulenge area in South Kivu, fleeing earlier inter-tribal violence.

In the wake of the broadcasts, an argument developed. Jerome, the school's soccer star, said from his bed: 'It's obvious as fuck the British blame the Hutus for the jet attack and the French blame the Tutsis. They're like fans when a fight breaks out after the game. The French support the Hutus because they think they own us, like they really do own other Francophone countries in Africa. Just pissed off the Belgians beat them to it here, and the Brits have kept interfering ever since.'

Emile, a boy from Baraka, a town in Fizi district, was lying on his back, bouncing a tennis ball against the opposite wall. 'Maybe, but it's nothing to do with the actual cause, which was that the minds of stupid Hutus in Rwanda got poisoned by those broadcasts from Kigali. What do you think, Shitshoveller?'

This was Manu's unfortunate nickname, born of him being of cow-herding stock, and coming from a poorer family than the others.

'I heard the haters all right. But it's not about what a few *blancs* say, it's about what happened. So I agree with you, Emile.'

'Typical,' said Clement. 'You always take his side. I'm with Jerome.'

'All part of the same thing anyhow,' said Jerome. 'How the story's told gets mixed in with whatever it's about.'

'Doesn't mean committing an atrocity is the same as having an opinion about it,' Emile countered. 'What d'you know, anyway? You're only good for kicking a ball!'

Jerome leaped from his bed and started laying into Emile with a pillow. Clement joined in the assault, but Manu didn't get involved. This kind of thing happened every night, and he left it to other boys to come to Emile's aid.

The pillow fight and the argument were no more conclusive than the voice of Don Javier, who arrived seeking to quieten them down.

'Settle boys, settle,' he said, and so they did, but only for a while.

Once Don Javier went back to his quarters, Jerome turned the conversation to Roger Milla, the Cameroonian footballer, who in 1994 had become the oldest scorer in World Cup history. Most of them, though none anywhere near being Cameroonians, held Milla in as much reverence as Don Javier held the Pope.

It was, everyone concurred, not so fine a performance as Milla had given in the 1990 World Cup, when they were new boys and all Africa swelled with pride, but still something good to have held on to in a time of gloom four years later, when images on the television – of the last phases of the genocide next door and soccer matches in far-off America – had competed for attention, the one producing horror, the other joy, at least until Nigeria got knocked out, Cameroon having failed to progress, this time, from the first round.

And now, in the dorm, the blunted stub of that joy manifested in the boys singing an anthem to Milla written by Pépé Kallé, the elephant of African music. Clement jigged about on his bed, trying to somersault, and Jerome did back kicks and keepie-up-pies with the tennis ball, the former playing the role of Emoro, the dancer in Kallé's band, the latter Milla himself, as the rest of the boys chanted:

I am Roger Milla Milla Roger Milla Roger Milla
I am Roger Roger Milla Milla Roger Milla
Motherfucker what you saying yo?
Gimme my fucking respect tho!
I am the Green the Red and the Yellow star shining above yo!

It was a fantasy, this part-remembered praise song. As the dorm mates acted their roles, Milla was past his best and Emoro dead already – Emoro the dwarf, with whom enormously fat Kallé used to duel in jerky, frenetic dances, along with singer Papy Tex and three virtuoso guitarists dubbed Elvis, Doris and Boeing 737.

This night of singing twice occurred in June 1996: the end of Manu's final term, by which time he'd turned nineteen, having been late to start school.

Despite the elation of singing the Kallé song with his friends, he fell asleep depressed that night, thinking again of the letter he had received from home. In it, his father said that he had decided that events in the Great Lakes meant that Manu would be unable to pursue the other life for which his education had been preparing him.

Zaire's falling to pieces, his father had written, and there was no chance of Manu going to university in Kinshasa, as he'd planned. Doubly galling because he originally wanted to go to Europe, not the Zairean capital, but his father had already ruled that out on grounds of cost. Now all options were closed. Further education was not necessarily going to protect him from the violence that was growing. Those were his father's feelings and perhaps he was right.

It was good, though, the education Manu had acquired – one his family could not have afforded had he not won a scholarship as a boarder – if a little old-fashioned and Jesuitical in nature. Don Javier was a hard taskmaster, often switching between different languages to keep the boys on their toes. In maths, he was insistent that all sums were done in pencil, so that wrong answers could be rubbed out and replaced with right ones. Manu was quite good at maths, calculus especially, though there was one embarrassing incident when he kept getting the remainder of a long-division sum wrong, which Don Javier said was just silly, as calculus is harder than long division.

He got his best marks in English and history. Don Javier liked to discourse on a statue of Clio, the muse of history, which he had viewed at the Vatican Museum during his time as a seminarian in Rome; he sometimes mentioned the half-smile manifesting on the lips of this particular statue, suggesting it indicated a blind spot in understanding of the ongoing present of human affairs – that tawdry template of repetition about which, the priest would invariably say, 'we so often do not know whether to laugh or weep, but God just weeps' – before going on to sketch the principal phases of whichever period the class was studying.

Whatever patch of time was involved, Don Javier was always keen to stress that each one was always subject to the effects of earlier parts in a longer series – and so on to the present era, he once gloomily added, 'and the kind of viscosity you see when windscreen wipers in a car are rubbing against glass that's too greasy to make out much on the road in front'.

Rarely did these eras that they studied include ones in Zaire's own historical journey: not when the Kingdom of Kongo held sway over much of the country, eventually falling under Portuguese control; not during the following chapter of the Congo Free State, later in the nineteenth century, when the country was ruled by the King of Belgium as his own personal estate, nor its time as an official Belgian colony, or even after independence in 1960.

Don Javier did once, however, mention the Chwezi Empire – the mysterious, Europe-untrammelled 'Empire of Light', as it was also known. Said in oral tradition to have been founded by a man called Kintu, it stretched throughout the Great Lakes and well beyond in early medieval times, so long before the tide turned in Rwanda: spread itself as blood – red, sticky goo – on Don Javier's windscreen of the present.

Manu learned about this ancient, shut-off past mostly from his mother, who also spoke eloquently of the traditional wisdom she'd acquired: such as sansevieria, or *irago* as she more properly called it in Kinyarwanda, being the right plant to counter snake-bite, or when to sow maize or harvest mushrooms – matters for once paid heed to by a husband mostly liable to tell her to stop babbling. Though he never did when she talked of *abadayimoni*, the demonic imps that haunt guilty people.

There was a large, out-of-date map on the white-plaster wall of the classroom, a remnant from the Belgian colonial period that, despite its antiquity, Don Javier used for teaching. Don Javier himself was not Belgian but Spanish, though he did speak French well. He was equally (not remarkably for a Jesuit missionary in that region) fluent in Swahili and Lingala. He had a theory that each language had its own animating spirit. The spirit of French was respect, the spirit of English was aggression, the spirit of Swahili was combination; Spanish, he said, was imbued with the spirit of infuriation.

Employing a short cane of bamboo, as pointedly focused on the country's geography as he was neglectful of its history (as if space could ever be free of temporal form!), Don Javier would trace the borders of Zaire with Uganda and Rwanda in the east and also where it hit the Atlantic in the far west, at the ports of Banana, Boma and Matadi. Nearby to these was the throbbing metropolis of Kinshasa, where he'd served previously, after an interval in Macau in China. That was his first posting in the order, after graduating from the Gregorian University.

He was, all the boys agreed, a rather unusual teacher, full of surprises, sometimes seeming quite disciplinarian, at other times almost louche. He was very fond of his car, an old Ford Zodiac, its chrome bumpers much polished, and now and then he was spotted in bars in town. Once in class he compared the liveliness of nightclubs in Kinshasa with the liveliness of nightclubs in Macau, which is not your usual priestly prattle.

Kinshasa won. Don Javier represented Zaire's capital city with desire, in fact, as if he were desperate to go back there; but he was now tied to the archbishopric of Bukavu. He would have been a better university professor than schoolteacher, probably, for he had a remarkable ability to bring science and religion together, speaking of black holes in one breath and negative theology in the next. He described both these as involving unknown dimensions resting on the interference pattern of known ones.

'What the fuck?' Jerome whispered to Manu at the time, a sentiment repeated a few seconds later, but with more vehemence, as gravity was explained in terms of the force needed by Adam to spring up with alacrity as soon as God first put breath into him.

When Don Javier was teaching, God always came into it somewhere, whether the subject was the transient evolutionary nature of prehistoric animals, the difference between Luxor and Athens as civilisations, the wanderings of Odysseus, or the system of categories in human cognition. Sometimes it was just all too hard to follow, and what use was any of it now, anyway?

With Jerome and Clement and Emile, one day in May, before his father delivered his ultimatum and before the singing competition, Manu and his chums had made wild plans for the future, sitting by Bukavu docks, swinging their legs over the stagnant water as they passed a stick of sugar cane between each other and watched dockers load ships.

The boys were using up time, waiting for the school church bell summoning them to vespers, where Don Javier would be waiting in his white cotton surplice, signifying innocence, he once said, and the clothing of immortality given to us in baptism.

Meanwhile the bare-chested, muscle-bound dockers sang ancient Swahili songs as they laboured, half immersed in foamy water while gunning in rivets or loading crates. Brought to the region by slave caravans of the past, so knowledgeable Emile said on this occasion, the old songs filled the chests of the friends with the untrustworthy romance of escape. Jerome wanted to be a professional footballer; Emile wanted to be a professor; Clement wanted to follow his father into diplomacy.

Something technical to do with machines was what Manu hoped for. But now he had to return home to tillage and herding, the only good thing about this plan being, to his mind, that he would see Joséphine, his favourite cow. The best of the family herd, sarcastically named after the great leader Mobutu, Joséphine was a clever beast with distinctive markings: a series of small white boxes, like cigarette packets, running across both flanks.

Chapter 2

Manu's family lived over 100 kilometres away from his boarding school, near a village called Pendele in the adjoining Zairean province of North Kivu (Bukavu being in South Kivu). At some distance from the provincial capital, Goma, Pendele lay in a rural area, and the Kwizera homestead was itself a couple of kilometres from Pendele proper.

His home sat in a place where tracts of forest and semi-alpine meadows collide with the jagged cinder blocks of Mount Nyiragongo, one of eight volcanoes in the region – of which it may confidently be bet, across the long X-axis of geological time, that some are active to this day.

The Kwizera compound stood on the grassy slopes of a hill under the volcano. Two hills away, in the main part of Pendele, lived a couple of uncles – Banyamulenge, like Manu's immediate family and the rest of the Kwizeras down in the south – but settled in a village of Banyarwanda. This was a group with which Manu and his relatives were kin only in so far as they were both peoples of mainly Tutsi descent, living in Zaire but originating in Rwanda.

Three hills away, hidden in a forest clearing for reasons of superstition relating to the volcano, stood the forge with which his father supplemented the family income, working as a blacksmith, as had long been the role of Kwizeras down the male line. It was said in family stories, clan legends, that this occupation should never be abandoned; but Manu, who had a modern mind, for the time being still well able to make a caesura between past and present, didn't believe in these vain prophecies, these time-thrashed family curses, however common they were in the region, among people not enlightened by Don Javier about caesura. *Caesurae*, he'd typically correct, causing Jerome to mimic pulling out an eyeball, a manoeuvre that sometimes ended with him lying on the floor by his desk, the fake eyeball (a scrumpled-up piece of paper) sitting in his outstretched hand, as Don Javier approached with the cane.

On the far side of the mountain was another grove, in this instance of ancient, orange-flowered flame trees, within which Manu's initiation ceremony took place. Along with other Tutsi boys, all about fourteen, he had submitted to various rituals amid that circle of trees, their spiky, sticky flowers seeming like bushels of fire.

These rituals included: making meaningless growls (intended to become intelligible when ancestral spirits were reached); wearing a necklace of dried grass smeared with goat blood while sitting on a wooden stool; ingesting water channelled from the base of a termite mound (thus absorbing the spirits of ancestors); being subjected to a mud massage and the covering of his body by the burnt residue of groundnuts; falling over backwards deliberately and banging his head – all to an accompaniment of incantations, rattle-shakes, drumming . . .

At the heart of this milestone of maturity lay an expectation – of spirit possession. During the ceremony, he was told by one of the elders: 'If you pretend to be possessed, you will be destroyed.' By another all the initiates were warned: 'If you make a copy of being possessed, another one of you will be taken at random to be sacrificed.' Manu pretended all right, but the silly business went off OK, and at last he was permitted to go home – feeling oddly, as he made his way down the paths, as if the pretended thing had been authentic all along.

The Kwizeras' complex of huts was surrounded by four agricultural storehouses with conical roofs. Their straw eaves were plagued by avaricious birds that, as a boy, Manu used to exterminate with a catapult, developing significant skill in aiming and firing at the exact right time and on target. These storehouses, making one circle, in turn were surrounded by the circular thorn hedge of the *boma*, a fence behind which cattle, the main source of the family's livelihood besides the forge, were corralled at night; such that the last thing he used to hear before falling asleep, and the first thing he would hear on waking, was the note of their lowing.

These cattle felt like family too, part of a wider natural order, but the Kwizera family's human members consisted besides himself only of his flinty-faced father, his cloudy-faced mother (they often argued), and his elder sister Beatrice, whose face would have been pretty were it not for an over-prominent nose. She liked clothes, his sister, carefully washing the one or two finer frocks she owned.

By the time Manu came home, a few weeks after the singing competition and in a disconsolate state, large camps of Hutu refugees had been established within Zaire's borders for two years. He had to pass near some of them during his journey; in his letter, his father had told him to be careful about those places. There had already been significant attacks on the main Congolese Tutsi settlements down in South Kivu, where he was coming from.

So far, his homestead outside Pendele had escaped, but security wasn't the only issue. Money was very tight. The whole economy was collapsing. Accordingly, out of financial necessity, and somewhat in contradiction to his concerns for his son's safety, almost the first thing Manu's father did, as Mrs Kwizera served her son a welcome-home meal of beef, beans and *ugali* maize, was ask that he begin selling milk in the nearest Hutu refugee camp.

'You will have to use a lad from another tribe to go in there,' he instructed, dipping his hand into the *sufuria* containing the maize, which stuck like glue to the edge of the saucepan.

No one said anything for a few seconds, but Manu could feel the eyes of his mother and sister upon him, jointly willing that he give the negative answer that he knew he could not. For what his father meant was that if Manu went in himself, the Hutus would kill him, counting him as a Rwandan Tutsi, pure and simple (not that this question of ethnicity, which had already caused so much bloodshed, could quite so easily be calculated).

There was no option of refusing; or so it seemed at the time. This instruction came from a man who, though broadly kind, was also very rigid, dealing out beatings to Manu in the past using one of the ropes employed to tether cattle, usually the more restive bulls, within the *boma*.

After the meal, Manu took up a musical instrument and went to find Joséphine. She was roaming free in the *boma*, its enclosure heavy with odour and a sound of stamping hooves. Some time passed, during which night fell on Pendele, and Manu tumbled into his own version of that trance-like stasis which has ever been the cowherd's lot in myth.

The cowherd's lot in life, too, it had often seemed to him, when younger and bored, though this paralysis was more likely to strike in the sunlit meadows, product of a parched tongue and burnt forehead, than down in the *boma* in darkness as he was now. Here it came again, all the same, that precious monotony which children know as well as cowherds: that time of summer's lease, before life exacts its price with winter after winter of events.

As Manu was stroking the cow's silken flanks, like he used to every night before he went away to school, Beatrice came up and joined him, jogging his arm. A few moments before, Manu had begun playing Joséphine some notes on the instrument he'd brought with him from the house – a wooden flute, in the playing of which, during those upland hours of watching over cattle, he had made himself adept. The flute itself had been handcrafted by a master, now sadly dead, his work stopped by TB. All those old skills are going anyway, Manu's father had commented when they heard the news.

'I've missed you,' his sister said. 'Tough about university – and going into the camps like Dad demanded.'

'Has to be done,' he replied shortly. 'We all have to behave differently now.'

'Why?' she asked.

'Life has become more serious. There might be fighting, sis.'

Joséphine gave a low moan, as if she too were feeling the pain both humans were experiencing; as if that quantity, like love, circulated telepathically through all species, all parts of the natural world, from subterranean depths to the stars above. But there were no stars that night, and the moon too was obscured; the only light came from the glow of the fire over which their mother had cooked supper, using an iron spit and a tripod for hanging the *sufuria*, both of which their father had made in his forge.

'I'm glad you're back anyhow,' Beatrice said. 'But look, you don't need to only think of the family.'

'There isn't anything else left. What about you? You should be married by now.'

'Nothing in view. All the young men round here see me as a southerner. Or their fathers do. I suppose I better get a move on, but I can't seem to find anyone suitable.' She jogged his arm again. 'What about you anyhow, any girlfriends down in Bukavu?'

'A couple.'

Not quite true. In fact, there had been rather a lot of action in that department, if secretively, which was why he'd sometimes inwardly laughed at the attempts of Jerome, Clement and Emile to get girls from other schools in Bukavu to kiss them. They didn't understand that you actually had to talk to girls if they were to be the slightest bit interested.

His sister touched his arm again, very lightly, and stole back through the darkness. As she went, he heard a noise – perhaps her tripping over one of the gourds used for curding milk that often lay around the compound, their interiors waiting to be smoked with fire coals the next morning, which was a process of sterilisation.

That night he lay within the clay walls of his sleeping hut – permeated with smells of soot and cow dung – desperately missing the camaraderie of his dorm friends. He was suffering some sort of reverse homesickness, perhaps.

The very next day, acting on his father's instructions, he found a Bembe accomplice, someone he'd been to primary school with, whose name was Daniel. Together they began carting buckets of milk through the forest to the outskirts of the nearest Hutu camp.

On his return from the camp this first time, Daniel brought strange news. These camps, apparently, had many bars and shops of every kind.

'Today I counted thirty hairdressers!' he said, as he and Manu squatted on the ground, splitting what felt like dirty money.

But although everyday services of all kinds had sprung up in these camps, they were also vicious places where dissent against Hutu Power leaders was violently suppressed.

'You could be beaten, even killed just for speaking to someone from a human rights organisation,' Daniel told him, after a second trip a few days later, having witnessed several beatings.

Daniel was a wiry little guy whom Manu was quickly starting to really like – after the usual hiatus of understanding that often happens when meeting again someone you knew when you were younger but have not been in touch with since. In another world and another time, the two of them might have become friends for a longer span. But their fathers, both still inured to tribal atavism, would have disapproved of this, so they kept everything on a professional level, refusing the authentic connection that they both knew was there in embryo.

'It's weird, as the perimeter is guarded by international peacekeepers while all this violence is going on inside,' continued Daniel on the day of the second trip, thumbing his stack of grubby notes. 'And NGOs supply them with food aid. We should try to get some of that in exchange for milk.'

The plan never came off. For on meeting up with him a few weeks later, Daniel announced that he would not go into the camps any more, having seen a woman stoned to death following accusations of being a Tutsi. 'I can't tell the difference, and they can't either, those crazy Hutus. She was just an ordinary woman selling beer. I think Kagame's right, the RPA should go after them. Clean out the rotten ones.'

Manu didn't say so, but at the time he half agreed, like so many others did back then, misunderstanding what was happening.

17

What was happening was the start of an invasion of Zaire by Rwanda. Orchestrated by the new Rwandan president, Paul Kagame, it would later be presented as a measure to prevent exiled Hutu *génocidaires* mounting their own invasion back into Rwanda. This was a real risk, so perhaps it was true at the outset.

In Manu's community, there were lots of rumours during this period about Kagame's soldiers slipping over the border in disguise. That was something his father and the other Congolese Tutsi elders would have welcomed, still assuming an ethnic amity with the potential invaders that could be carried onwards in trust. Dressed in civilian clothes, many of this RPA forward column were said to hide in wagons carrying timber, their objective being to spy on the Hutu refugee camps and to link up with local political groups aligned against Mobutu.

It was plainly obvious that as a place to sell milk, at any rate, the camps were now out of bounds, as even Manu's father grudgingly agreed. The whole region, in fact, was beginning to feel as dangerous as the volcano that towered over it.

Over the next four months life at home became almost unbearable, as his father's temper worsened, cash became scarcer and Beatrice grew more irritated that her own prospects seemed even more limited than they were before. His mother showed more signs of the depression that had always been with her. All these frustrations were intensified by an outbreak of rinderpest among the local herds.

The ethnic hatred brought by the Hutus seemed to be spreading, as if it too were some sort of virus. The other tribes around Pendele began to treat Manu's family and other Rwandan exiles like pariahs. They blamed the Hutu camps for the upset in the local economy and Tutsis – lumping together Banyamulenge, Banyarwanda and the Rwandan government over the border – for causing the camps to spring up in the first place. In a sense some of this was, as so often when hatred is politically exploited, true in the crudest way. But it ignored crucial historical details.

By the closing weeks of October 1996, local politicians from other tribes were tearing into Pendele in vans with loudspeakers, telling locals of Tutsi origin that they should leave or risk death. On 28 October Mobutu announced military rule in the region, warning Tutsis they were legitimate targets of the *Forces Armées Zaïroises*, or FAZ as the Zairean national army was then known.

It was in November, shortly after this announcement – as Manu's father was tilling his parcel of ground, his mother grinding maize kernels, and sister Beatrice flailing bushels of millet – that conflict first came to the Kwizera family in deadly earnest: itself precursor of a much greater conflict that would claim millions of lives and change other lives forever, turning over their fates like the blade of Mr Kwizera's mattock turned over volcanic soil.

Chapter 3

The mist that cloaks the valleys and the hills of the Kivus at dawn cleared quickly that day. As the rest of his family bent to their agricultural tasks down in the compound, Manu was in the upland meadows with his cows and his flute. He was in the midst of playing his tune, his eye hooking on Joséphine, who was seeking flowering clover, when a group of Mobutu's FAZ soldiers appeared round the bend of a track. They were in a column of jeeps and APCs, followed by a truck carrying plunder from Pendele village itself.

They were grim-faced, these soldiers, wearing camouflage and round helmets, and bearing sub-machine guns or rifles. Manu had scarcely got to his feet when one of them grasped him by the arm and flung him into the cab of a jeep, injuring his cheek on the metal of the door. His flute, which had fallen to the ground when he was grabbed, was picked up by another soldier and tossed into the branches of a nearby tree; through the grimy glass of the jeep's windscreen he watched it spinning through the air.

Other soldiers then began the work of shooting some of the cattle. They butchered them on the spot with their bayonets, tossing huge sides of meat on to the flatbed of the lorry that accompanied the column.

As the row of vehicles reached the Kwizeras' compound, looking up from where he cowered in the footwell of the jeep Manu expected his parents to come out to greet the visitors in supplication; but, perhaps knowing that Mobutu's men had no mercy, his mother and father simply ran out of the back gate of the *boma*, followed by Beatrice, who dropped her jointed wooden flail – a little chain, forged on their father's own anvil, connecting its two pieces – on to the pile of millet seeds she'd been thrashing on a woven mat.

Some of the soldiers chased after them, while another ordered Manu to begin roasting one of the sides of meat, by means of the spit set up above the still-smouldering fire of the previous night. Usually Beatrice would have thrown the water from her laundry bucket on it, but she must have forgotten, for here the bucket was, still by the fire, a mousse of suds remaining on the surface of the liquid inside.

Prodded by a bayonet, terrified for his own fate, for that of his parents, and that of Beatrice, Manu blew on the embers and got the fire going again. The joint of meat, however, was much too big for the spit. It kept falling into the flames, burning his hands each time he picked it up, often being kicked by the soldier for letting it drop.

At first, perhaps irrationally, considering what was going on – how human lives so close to his own were under threat – he feared that Joséphine was among these slaughtered cattle, but he didn't see her killed.

Did she escape? He didn't know.

Soldiers began going through the main family hut and adjoining sleeping huts and storehouses, taking everything of value – even old clothes – and loading items on to the truck of swag. Recaptured, his mother and sister were taken into one of the storehouses by some of the soldiers.

He saw another soldier tugging at his father's neck, pulling him by a necklace that he wore. It was a leather thong attached to an old Belgian coin, to which his father had a sentimental attachment; it had been given to him by Manu's grandfather. As all this was happening, his father turned his head to look at Manu, his eyes wild and staring.

From the storehouse, anguished cries in familiar female voices penetrated Manu's ears. Hunched over the fire, too scared to move with a FAZ trooper standing over him, he listened in torment to the screams of his mother and sister. What was happening to them in there?

Gunfire sounded from the storehouse. At the same time, Manu saw the thong round his father's neck snap as he stumbled, his full weight pulling suddenly against the thin strip of leather. His captor stuffed the thong and its coin into the pocket of his camouflage jacket, before pulling his father by his shirt and tying him to a post with one of the ropes normally used to tether cattle.

Beatrice came tottering out of the storehouse, shouting in Manu's direction over her shoulder. 'They killed our mother! Run!'

Wearing only one shoe, she stumbled out of the *boma* again, in the direction of the forest. He jumped up, meaning to follow her, but the FAZ soldier at once knocked him down and, raising his rifle, shot Beatrice in the back just as she reached the forest edge. She fell like her own flail, collapsing like a puppet whose strings have been released.

The soldier kicked Manu several more times, making him roll over, until his face was very close to the fire and the roasting flesh of the cow. The other FAZ, the one who had tied up his father, came over and said something in Lingala to Manu's guard. He then reached down into the pile of wood by the fire for a stick and returned in the direction of Manu's father, whistling as he walked.

At that moment, Manu's guard was called away by an officer and Manu was suddenly alone, half choked by the fumes from the fire. Numb with shock, unable to move for fear of being shot, he lay there for some minutes. Hearing after this interval a cry, he got up into a crouch and slowly edged away from the fire.

On the other side of the *boma*, his father was kneeling, bare-chested now. The look of terror in his eyes had intensified and he was letting out gasps of pain.

The FAZ soldier who had pulled off the necklace was now engaged in applying the stick fetched from the woodpile to his father's back. He was shouting at him in Swahili, in the hope of getting him to divulge details of the family cash hoard. It was the custom to bury this somewhere on the family plot. But the family had spent everything in that tin long ago, mainly on bus fares to Manu's school down in Bukavu – which was one of the reasons he'd obeyed his father when he'd said he must sell milk at the camp, feeling guilty that the family was short of money.

While Manu's father continued to insist there was no cash to be had, the soldier took the long length of rope with which he was tethered and began twisting it round his neck, using the stick as a lever.

Again Manu started forwards, hoping to save his father despite having failed to save his mother. He ran across the *boma* but was soon restrained by another soldier, who put his boot on Manu's neck.

So it was, scorched by flames, in an agony of distress and with a boot on his neck, that Manu watched his father die by strangulation – his face turning in the dust, his breath pattering out. The soldier bundled his body to the edge of the *boma*, after which other soldiers dragged Manu back to the fire and made him cut chunks of meat off the roasting joint for them to eat. This caused him to burn his hands even more, and he took to dousing them in Beatrice's laundry bucket, until one of the soldiers kicked it over, sniggering.

The soldiers ate quickly, like dogs, shoving the steaming, half-cooked meat into their mouths. Next they set fire to the hut and outbuildings, before fastening a length of rope to Manu's own neck. At first he thought they meant to kill him too, and in the same way, but instead they began dragging him towards their truck.

It seemed, so far as he could gather from their talk in Lingala and rough, western-dialect Swahili, that they intended to conscript him into Mobutu's FAZ. Using his legs, he tried to push away from the truck, but the soldiers pulled harder. And in a way, this is where it all began, the push and pull between Manu being controlled by others and trying to exert some control over his own life – or at least trying to throw down some kind of anchor to prevent being dashed away.

From the flatbed of the FAZ lorry, as its engine was started, he watched as flames began to consume the buildings of the compound, including the storehouse where his mother's body was. The body of his sister, out by the perimeter of the forest, he could not see, nor that of his father – only the smoke and heat waves rising into the ripples of sunlight on the hills beyond.

As the lorry revved up, he had already resigned himself to becoming part of the FAZ. Yet it didn't actually happen like that, and Manu will often look back at it, this moment in the past when he projected what he thought was his own future, hapless absorption into Mobutu's army.

In fact, no sooner had the FAZ truck begun moving than another swarm of armed individuals – much larger in number – appeared out of the forest, running into the burning homestead. They belonged, Manu realised, to one of the anti-Mobutu rebel forces that the RPA forward columns were said to have been connecting with, slipping out of their timber wagons for clandestine meetings in the hills with the likes of these.

This body of new attackers, many of them hardly more than teenagers, began shooting wildly at the FAZ, who started to run or drive away at speed, dropping much of the booty they had collected. The haste of their flight caused Manu to fall off the truck to which he was tied, tumbling him on to soil soaked with the blood of cattle.

At first he could not disentangle from the uncoiling rope, the other end of which was still attached to the fleeing truck. Frantically scrabbling, he feared his neck was about to be broken, but he was saved by one of the newly appeared rebels who, producing a knife, cut the rope at the last minute.

Several of the FAZ soldiers, not managing to jump on the truck or into a jeep, were captured by this other gang. In a stupor, Manu got to his feet in the middle of the flaming compound, watching the newly arrived rebels lay down a perimeter guard lest the FAZ redeployed. He tugged at the piece of rope that remained round his neck, eventually managing to undo the knot.

The chief of these rebel soldiers turned out to be none other than the famous revolutionary leader Laurent-Désiré Kabila. He was well known throughout the region, but this was the first time Manu encountered that strange, plump, bald-headed mixture of bluster, cunning and self-aggrandisement.

His jowls wobbling above the collar of his paisley shirt (he was dressed in civilian clothes), Kabila called him forwards. 'So, young man, tell me what happened here.' He paused to cough, because of the smoke. 'Tell the truth, from the depths of your heart.'

After listening, Kabila said, 'Aha, so that is how it was? Well you must determine events and exact your revenge, young man. Perhaps you would like to twist off the head of each of these we have captured, in the way your father's head was twisted?'

Manu shook his own head, feeling sickened and terrified, already full up with violence.

'Or maybe cut off the noses and ears of each of these one by one? I have heard these FAZ bastards do that.'

Manu wiped his eyes, which were streaming from smoke and tears, and shook his head again, more forcefully this time.

'Or make them lick your arse clean? That too they have made others do, so rightly they should have it done to them. You know there is an inescapable logic to these matters?'

A third time, Manu shook his head.

'In that case, we must punish these wicked rogues ourselves. Ho, let's move away from these flames!'

The rebels moved closer to the forest. As his men were short of ammunition, Kabila ordered the six Mobutu troops who had not escaped to be lined up, back to back, so that they could all be shot with just a single bullet. The bullet lodged itself in the fifth man's skull, leaving the last soldier still standing; it was the very fellow who had strangled Manu's father.

This sixth man fell to his knees. 'Please, please, don't kill me,' he said in French.

'What is your name?' the great revolutionary asked the soldier, who had traces of a beard round his chin.

'Jean-Baptiste Musengeshi.'

Kabila glanced at Manu, eyes gleaming in his big bald head. Then he took a pistol from the holster under his paisley-draped paunch and handed Manu the weapon.

'Kill him if you wish,' he said. 'It is a simple thing. But be warned, once you do this, life will never be the same again; you'll spend your whole life waking and worrying about friend and foe, just as I have done.'

The fat leader of the rebels suddenly looked melancholy. 'Even those, like Che, whom I thought was my friend, turned out not to be, calling me unreliable – as if the name Guevara were itself synonymous with reliability!'

At the time, Manu did not know what in hell's bunghole this oddly ostentatious but also self-pitying man was going on about. The point, he would eventually realise in time, was that Che Guevara briefly fought in Congo in the 1960s, later writing disparagingly of this same Kabila, his unsteady comrade in revolution, then a young man.

Compelled by an inward-turning force that he did not then understand either but would later come to see as a grub of grace tossed in his direction by destiny, Manu found himself saying: 'Let him go.'

The soldier, still on his knees, turned and stared at him for a long time. Manu looked back at him – his father's killer, Jean-Baptiste Musengeshi, who muttered something in Lingala that Manu did not understand.

Kabila laughed. 'He wants to know your name.' He kicked Musengeshi, and said, 'Ask in French, *con*.'

The soldier was about to reply when Kabila kicked him again and said, 'What about English, do you speak that other language of oppressors, you wretch?'

Surprisingly, Musengeshi did. 'What is your name?'

'Manu Kwizera.'

Kabila grabbed the pistol from Manu's hand and held it to Musengeshi's forehead.

'I could kill you now,' he told him in an icy whisper. 'But I am going to let you go, just as this young moralist instructs. When you get to Kinshasa, tell them that Kabila is coming like a wind from the mountains, Laurent-Désiré Kabila and his *maquisards*!'

So instructed, Jean-Baptiste Musengeshi fled into the bush. All this Manu watched in stupefaction.

A little later a Rwandan Air Force helicopter landed, taking off Kabila and a couple of senior aides-de-camp. The rest of his soldiers began preparing to leave, intending to march through a mountain route down into South Kivu, where they'd join him again. As Manu had nowhere else to go (informed that Pendele, where his relatives lived, had also been razed, and everyone killed), it was determined that he should go with them. He did not remember anyone asking him if he wished to join this rebel force, which had the grand name of the *Alliance des Forces Démocratiques pour la Libération du Congo-Zaïre*, or AFDL; but that, in any case, was what seemed to be happening.

Before departure, he asked permission to bury Beatrice and his father, assuming that the body of his mother was being irrevocably consumed by fire. And to this, at least, they assented.

The worst of it was collecting his sister from the edge of the forest, where she lay sprawled amid glossy green leaves. Bringing Beatrice to the burial pit, carrying her limp, heavy body over his shoulder, he became aware of blood dripping down his back. His father's body was also recovered and committed to another shallow grave.

As it left, this AFDL column of which he was now a part, Manu turned to look at his old homestead, now more or less destroyed, except for the storehouse where his mother's body lay, around the thatch of which flames were still billowing.

Chapter 4

During the ascent into the mountains, Manu reacted almost mechanically to orders as they were given. One of Kabila's lieutenants – a young man called Recognition – comforted him during the climb through rocky defiles and clumps of giant fern. Manu realised, as the man spoke to him, that it was Recognition who had cut the rope when he was struggling to free himself from the FAZ lorry.

'Thank you for what you did,' he said, ducking under a vine-enshrouded branch of cedar.

And then this guy, Recognition, told him: 'Look, my own father was killed by the FAZ in a similar manner, but objectively speaking, it's too common a thing to happen to people in this region to personalise it. That is exactly why we must take direct action as group.'

Objective knowledge of death, of your family? No way *bwana*. But he didn't say anything back.

The name of this guerrilla intellectual, for so Recognition seemed to Manu partly to be, is not such a strange one. Many in the Great Lakes have old-fashioned names, borrowed from the classics or Christianity, or from the period of the Renaissance, which, Don Javier once said, sought to meld the previous two categories: Boniface, Innocent, Martial, Deogratias or Erasme . . . names of that type. There was even someone at his school called Redeemer, who despite his name was the main purveyor of weed and pornography.

Indeed, Manu's own full name, Emmanuel, which Don Javier

once told him meant 'God is with us' in Hebrew, came from the same old order – a product of the influence of too many over-educated European missionaries in the territory, past and present. Don Javier added that Manu itself meant simply 'human' in many other languages, for instance Sanskrit, often being used to describe the progenitor of the human race.

Your name was chosen by the priest who christened you, Manu remembered his mother saying, on a different occasion of enquiry: she was pounding maize, as he now recalled, shivering as if about to be struck by the pestle himself.

Birds flitted between mossy branches as they ascended what seemed like a vast flight of basalt-rock stairs, finally reaching the flat top of a mountain range, the expanse of which seemed to fill the cavern of the sky. By now the moon had begun to show.

The next day, further along on this way south across mountain tops, Recognition told him something more about his own life, principally how he came to have joined Kabila's forces. He spoke not in Swahili but in Kinyarwanda, the language of Rwanda and its diaspora in Zaire.

Recognition explained that he was Kivu born and bred, with a Munyamulenge father but a Ugandan mother, an Ankole from Uganda. His father and several forefathers before were hunters, thus his surname of Gahiji. He seemed very familiar with the peculiarities of both North and South Kivu, and clearly knew how to move as smoothly as an eel amid their complex conflicts.

Reaching the following day their destination in South Kivu, night again having fallen, the AFDL rebels lit torches, flaming brands of timber soaked in kerosene. Eyes itching from the smoke, Manu and the others went by these until the lights of a large encampment were suddenly revealed.

Slowly, he began to discern the serried shapes of tents, plying out in lines between metamorphic outcrops under a scurry of moonlit clouds, clouds that scarcely seemed to remain in the sky for a minute. As they got closer to the camp, a hiss of hurricane lamps could be heard, the sound itself seeming to part the darkness as they approached its source.

Recognition took Manu to a tent. There he gave him some food – dried bread and milk curd. After Manu had eaten, Recognition showed him by his torch to a sleeping bag, then lay down in an adjacent one.

At some point during that night he must have whimpered or called out, because he woke to Recognition shoving him and saying, 'Shut up!'

Grey moonlight was filtering through the seams of the tent. After waiting over the next few minutes for Recognition's breathing to calm again, Manu looked across at the long face of the sleeping man next to him, wondering if he was to be trusted. His personality seemed strangely self-chafing, care and brutality, intellect and practicality all mixing in the same cup.

In the morning, Manu was sitting on a canvas camp stool, eating boiled eggs (two each, in wooden bowls), with a view of green peaks down to the lake. Recognition had some binoculars and kept putting aside his own bowl of eggs to gaze down the escarpment. He eventually handed the binoculars to Manu.

Far below, on one side, the forest stretched in emerald-green continuity. On the other side were less forested slopes, leading down to the blue gleam of the same Lake Kivu on the shores of which he had spent his schooldays. On these barer declinations, large camps of refugees could be seen. Shining in the dewy dawn, the camps consisted of roughly constructed shacks of wood and tin, along with some blue-and-white plastic tents supplied by the United Nations.

Between two of these refugee camps – a gap of about five kilometres – moved a long green column of soldiers. Winding to and fro, it had the appearance of a giant grass snake.

'That is the RPA shifting to rendezvous here with us,' explained Recognition, still speaking in Kinyarwanda, before suddenly switching into French and a voice of low bitterness, 'misérables vengeurs d'une juste querelle' (wretched avengers of a righteous quarrel).

'What's that you say?' Manu didn't understand.

'It's from a play I acted in, at university. I think they're right to chase the Hutu bad actors but . . . well, never mind now.'

'What's the rendezvous for?' Manu asked, puzzled by this revelation of Recognition's past.

He continued, in any case. 'There's going to be a meeting. The new Rwandan army and the Ugandans are coming together to spearhead the invasion of Zaire, and now everyone's going to get some sugar for their trouble. We're going to chase down the murderous Hutu leaders, and we're also going to kick out Mobutu!'

At this, Recognition broke into an unexpectedly huge smile. 'And it will happen soon.'

'Everyone's going to benefit?' This seemed unlikely to Manu, even though he was far from being an expert in the tangled politics of the situation.

'That's the idea.' Recognition's smile disappeared as quickly as it came. 'We are hopeful that Kabila will prevail,' he added; and then, lowering his voice to a whisper: 'Though the truth is that the Ugandans, and the new leader in Rwanda, General Kagame, need a Congolese proxy for their actions.'

As Manu absorbed this, not before having realised how much the invasion was such a dirty game of cross-border politics, Recognition stood up, now seeming as proud as a cockerel: 'I myself am to be full leader of one of the groups. Maybe you shall become one of my deputies in time!'

Looking again through the heavy binoculars, Manu saw parts of the Rwandan column begin to break off and go into the camps, seeking out Hutu leaders, no doubt. It was too far away to hear shots, but he later learned that over 300 Hutus were executed that morning in one camp alone. It was the beginning of a cataclysm.

And so he began to understand, during that morning above Lake Kivu, as nearly 1000 Rwandan troops arrived on the plateau, that it would be his fate to join a force of killers. A different force from the FAZ, but killers all the same.

Above all, Manu knew that wasn't what he wanted to do: kill.

But after breakfast, he seemed to have no option but to go along with Recognition and all the rest. He was assigned to a group of several hundred Banyamulenge boys and young men, all of whom were roughly collected under the label *kadogos* – meaning 'little ones' in Swahili – who were to be turned into soldiers, to assist in the invasion of Zaire. Many having lost their own families, they had apparently found another family in the new force that was so quickly being assembled.

Well, mostly *kadogos* was how they were described; ambling by one moment during the preparations, Kabila shouted: '*Bon travail, mes jeunes lions!*' Good work, my young lions.

The youngest of Manu's pride of lions were about nine, the oldest in their early twenties.

He was given a coarse green uniform and boots. Green rubber boots. Wellingtons, as the English call them. He was also handed a wooden replica of a rifle.

The first exercise his group took part in was just running along in a group, carrying these replica weapons. Then they did crawling on their bellies. Then running along again. Afterwards, real bayonets were distributed, which Manu and the others affixed to the wooden weapons, binding them on with strips of inner tube from bicycle tyres.

With these attachments, they had to charge at piles of sacks filled with dried banana leaves and old maize cobs, in order to stab them. Some of the recruits had not tied on their bayonets properly and they fell off or got stuck when they stabbed the sacks. But Manu had tied his on well.

This business took up all the first day. On the second, crates were broken open and real rifles were handed out. All the young lions lined up and went to a table, where Recognition and others showed them how to take the rifles apart and reassemble them. Also how to fix the curved magazines, which made a click as they went in.

Later in this week, his group was marched off to a rocky part of the plateau and attempted proper shooting for the first time. At first it was difficult for Manu to connect the feeling of recoil – like someone hitting his shoulder bone with a hammer – or the sound of the report to the splintering of rock on the cliff face, which was the target. Someone had drawn outlines of soldiers on it with white paint, but so many bullets had already been fired at that cliff face that it was hard to know whether one had hit a target or not.

And that, give or take, was the end of his crash course in becoming a soldier, except for the taking of new names, which was part of an indoctrination process that Kabila was very keen on. Many of these were the names of famous African figures in liberation movements: Manu was given the name Sankara.

Marxist revolutionary, pan-Africanist, Africa's real Che Guevara (much more so than Kabila, who had only honoured himself as a smuggler and brothel owner), President of Burkina Faso: Manu didn't feel as if he fitted this new name of Sankara. But already he was starting to feel that he didn't fit his own name any longer, either.

One evening, from a wooden platform, Kabila spoke to all the *kadogos* in French. He said that the future of Zaire was in their hands, and that with their Ugandan and Rwandan brothers they would make the country free again. Zaire was also to revert to its old name, Congo.

First, however, Kabila added, they had to get rid of the Hutu who were aiding Mobutu. His exact words were: '*Les Hutus bloquent le chemin.*' The Hutus are in the way.

Then a Rwandan officer climbed on to the platform. My name is Gustave Rusyo, he told them, introducing himself as a major in the RPA. He addressed the recruits in Kinyarwanda, which of course the Banyamulenge understood, but he spoke with a strong English accent, a product of his own exiled upbringing in Uganda. Like many of the Rwandan officers, he was tall and extremely well turned out, in pressed khakis, fawn desert boots and a Sam Browne belt, in which was holstered a Heckler & Koch pistol.

What Major Rusyo said was that he was the Banyamulenge's closest cousin and that at long last all Tutsi people could be free in Congo, as they had become free in Rwanda, thanks to the RPA. He held out like a new Jerusalem the prospect of Greater Rwanda, an ethnic homeland that would return the country to its former size and influence before colonialism, in the days of the Chwezi empire, concluding with the statement: 'Tomorrow, with you Banyamulenge, sprung from the same soil as my father and all his forefathers, we will together engage in a refugee management programme that will secure the future not just of Rwanda but of eastern Congo, too.'

The morning after these speeches, the plan was that all the boys would go down the mountain with Rusyo's RPA to the refugee camps and begin to clear them.

'How are we going to clear all that?' Manu asked Recognition, looking out at the shapeless mass of people and tents below, over which a blue-black cloud of rain was now sweeping.

'With this,' he said, brandishing a pistol, as if it were an instrument of enlightenment.

Chapter 5

By the time they reached the camps, the storm had taken hold in earnest. People began fleeing, moving in waves from tents and shanties into the slanted forest. Whipped by rain, they ran towards the leathery trees, which had grown up in such a regular pattern that nature seemed to have planted them deliberately to create an area of shelter from the elements. But nothing about those dark hillsides was natural now.

Ostensibly, the purpose of the clearing force of which Manu was a part was to root out Hutu *génocidaires* and persuade the innocent to return to Rwanda. In fact, they were all mixed together, the people in those camps – the guilty, the innocent, and all in between.

What happened was partly done by Banyamulenge and other members of the AFDL, but more efficiently by the Rwandan troops, who followed their victims with grim determination. In glistening green plastic rain cloaks, which fastened at the neck and seemed to hiss when a body of men moved together, they streamed after those Hutus like mysterious priests.

It was clear even to Manu that there was a definite RPA plan to reduce the number of potential returnees, and that the AFDL, of which he was now a member, was a willing partner in this. But he just could not do any of it. Every time he lifted his new rifle, it shook in his wet hands. Bullets yipped and yowled above him, and bayonets drove and disembowelled below; but his bayonet remained clean and his gun, that day at least, kept its silence.

He hid in a vast kigelia tree, the bole of which curved inwards

35

in a series of large flanges, in between two of which he was able to lie back at an angle, hiding in their buttressed grasp. The tree's sausage-like fruits swung above him in the wind of the storm, ghoulishly aping the tubular kitbags on the backs of passing Rwandan soldiers.

And so he watched, Manu Kwizera, as flashes of sheet lightning illuminated the simultaneous and successive acts of murder taking place around him, praying that the latest fugitive, scrambling on wet roots and undergrowth, would escape. Dodging his head in and out of the tree, he ducked whenever one of the green-caped pursuers flowed past.

Though they did not seem to notice him, the face of each running Rwandan soldier nonetheless appeared to Manu to fasten on his own as it passed. He felt collapsed, as if every particle of moral sense was one by one being sucked out of him just by witnessing the *danse macabre* of these soldiers and their victims, whose cries by the end became routine to his ears.

The rain grew heavier, falling in unforgiving gouts from the bucket-like leaves of the tree above. At home, when he was younger, he sometimes used to go out and wash in the midst of these tropical downpours; but not now, not today.

When the execution but not the storm was done, he slunk out to join, fearful and disgusted, what was left of the 'refugee management programme', as Rusyo had duplicitously termed it.

This mainly meant superintending burials, for which the remaining living Hutus, under Rwandan and AFDL guard, were being forced to dig pits in the forest. These holes – their wet, collapsing sides glistening in the lightning like the pestiferous jaws of a monster – seemed to champ at each new body as it was thrown in, robbing the victims of their last dignity.

Manu was wrong, it turned out, in believing he was unobserved. Major Rusyo had spotted him hiding in the tree. That night, once the storm was finally over and the whole detachment had returned to the camp on the plateau, he beat Manu with a cane until his buttocks bled, cursing his treachery to the Tutsi cause with every stroke.

36

As he thrashed, he spoke in English, not Kinyarwanda, timing – as if they were active rests in a bar of music – the lashes with the pauses in his speech.

'Do you think I have come through them, all the troubles of my country, to allow cowardice under my command? Do you think I have spent years training – living in exile under other tyrannies, skulking over the border – teaching myself to be hard – to see others skulk when they need be bold? Do you think I have done all this and will allow you to do as you please on the battlefield?'

Afterwards, Manu curled up in agony in Recognition's tent. Later he came in, saying, 'This must stop. If you do not act properly tomorrow, you know you will be killed?'

With these words, Recognition turned on a little portable radio he had by him, tuning it to the BBC World Service.

As he found the station, the announcer was saying: 'Foreign media continue to implicate Rwanda in the crisis in eastern Zaire, but today President Kagame said the conflict was just Congolese fighting Congolese.'

The bigger picture of which their actions that day had played a part snapped into focus in Manu's mind, as a spokesman from the US State Department declared: 'The mass return of nearly half a million Rwandan refugees from Zaire obligates the United States to review its plans in the African Great Lakes crisis.'

According to the newsreader, there was expectation of foreign military intervention, but another deep-voiced American man said, 'We might not go, we're not the Salvation Army.'

'Ha! They're already here,' Recognition said, into the darkness, 'Lockheeds of the US Air Force are supplying info on refugee movements to Kagame's guys.'

'To help kill them?' Manu asked. 'Why would they do that?'

'Go to sleep, Sankara.'

He pretended to do so but continued listening. A commentator with a Scandinavian accent opined that the West was paralysed because of guilt about the Rwandan genocide; he called on the Western powers to assist, having failed in Rwanda itself two years ago, in order to avert another disaster. Someone else said the West just wanted to keep Kagame happy, at whatever cost, for the very reason that they wouldn't have to intervene.

The next voice came from very close, though in reality it was being piped back through the airwaves from Cyprus, or wherever the BBC Africa service transmitter was. The same Archbishop of Bukavu who'd given the sermon at the singing competition in which Manu participated – only a few months ago, it already seemed like a lifetime had passed – was now calling for Rwanda to cease 'its lying discourse on refugees'.

Recognition turned the radio off at this point, falling into slumbers. But Manu still could not sleep, as much because of the tumble of his thoughts as the pain from the beating by Rusyo. When Recognition was fully asleep, he crept out of the tent and lay on the wet ground, letting it numb the weals on his buttocks and back.

Chapter 6

Dawn found Manu still outside the tent, fragments of cloud entering his consciousness as he woke. For he must have slept a little, after all. Through bleary eyes, he watched a large aircraft fly slowly over the slaughter zone, passing to and fro like an iron on an ironing board. Maybe it was one of the US reconnaissance planes referred to by Recognition.

Then Recognition came out of the tent and asked, in frank perplexity, 'What are you doing down there, fool?'

Sitting upright at once, Manu said: 'Preparing myself to act properly.'

'You'd better,' Recognition replied, yawning. 'We're attacking Bukavu.'

When leaving school, Manu had always thought he might return to the town, but he didn't think it would be like this. There was no choice, however. Recognition stayed by his side like a guard, perhaps feeling that Rusyo's ire would next be directed at him if Manu did not perform as expected.

The journey was made in an RPA staff car, a dark-green Toyota Land Cruiser with a large VHF aerial spring-mounted on the bonnet and a long impact mark down one of the wings. Manu sat in the back with Recognition, Major Rusyo being in front with a driver.

Wondering what he'd done to deserve this dignity (for all the other AFDL recruits were marching on foot), he remained silent, watching the armoured personnel carrier containing RPA troops that preceded the Land Cruiser, or looking at the upright steel of his bayonet. Attached to the rifle between his knees, it was just a few inches from his own face.

On the way down into Bukavu, the two vehicles passed many dead bodies of refugees who had been killed by the RPA and by his fellow AFDL Banyamulenge, and also hundreds who had somehow managed to stay alive. Most were now fleeing in the opposite direction to the flow of troops, making further mockery of the idea that all this was anything to do with an orderly return of refugees.

Now and then, some of the RPA soldiers in the personnel carrier in front would loose volleys of bullets into the crowds. 'The troops are impatient,' remarked Rusyo on one of these occasions, 'they want to shift quickly to Bukavu, where there are real Mobutists to counter!'

When they reached the lake town, it was about five-thirty in the afternoon. Manu recognised some of his schoolboy haunts but many of the buildings and streets were damaged. The place had obviously been under bombardment by cross-border Rwandan artillery. There were bodies lying in the streets. He saw two men shot, and another set free after a heated discussion with the RPA men in front. There seemed to be no logic as to how sheep and goats were being separated.

In time the Land Cruiser arrived at the Nyamwera market, a location to which Manu had often come when younger, bunking off school. The place was deserted now, but after a few minutes two cars approached.

Rusyo said, 'Tell him to shoot at the tyres – the boy needs hardening.' In that moment, Manu realised the purpose of his role in this expedition.

Recognition reached across and wound down the window, gestured for him to lift his rifle on to the sill. He said, 'Shoot!'

When he didn't, Rusyo twisted round in his seat and, leaning over, pressed his pistol into Manu's neck.

Manu shot.

Just did it, fearful of the muzzle on the skin of his neck. His aim was not true, which was not surprising considering the pressure of Rusyo's pistol. Aiming at the tyres of one of the cars, he hit its windscreen, turning it instantly into a star. The Rwandan soldiers in the personnel carrier also shot, hitting tyres. Both vehicles were immobilised.

A man in white clerical garb flapped out of the front vehicle and came towards the Land Cruiser. This figure looked like a large bag of milk – milk is often served in bags in this part of Africa.

The man was holding out a cross. Manu recognised him as the Archbishop of Bukavu, the same who had been calumnising the RPA on the radio the previous night, also the same who had officiated at the Mass at his school.

The RPA soldiers jumped out of the personnel carrier and took the archbishop by his arms – Manu saw the cross fall to the ground. The soldiers pushed the cleric against the fence of SINELAC, which was the town's electricity-generating station, though it was not working. It was beginning to get dark by now, the white reflections of the moon playing on the buildings behind the fence.

Manu heard the soldiers shouting at the archbishop in English, saying that he had been helping those who had committed genocide in Rwanda. The priest protested in French that he had just been helping some Tutsi nuns. Not so many of these RPA soldiers spoke French as a lot of them had been brought up in Uganda.

'Let's get on with it,' Recognition said.

When Manu did not move, Recognition took him by the ear and pulled him out of the Land Cruiser. Carrying his rifle, he followed Recognition over to the fence of the generating station, to which the soldiers had now shackled the archbishop with plastic cable ties. They began to poke their bayonets into his thighs and arms, moving them in a coring motion, not really stabbing, more like stirring.

The archbishop cried out. Red stains advanced across his vestments.

'So now you prove,' Rusyo spat at Manu. At the same time, Recognition put his hand on his arm.

Yelling, not quite knowing what he was doing, Manu raised

his rifle – shot once more. Missed, he thought.

The Rwandan soldiers reared back in surprise from the report. The body of the archbishop sagged, hanging there as he was from wrists still attached to the SINELAC fence, and the red badges on his clothing began to merge with one another.

Recognition shook his head, saying, 'You weren't meant to shoot yet, you fool! Just to do the same as the others. We need to interrogate him first.'

Major Rusyo began slapping Manu about the face, reiterating Recognition's point, unclear as it was. 'Idiot! I meant you to use your bayonet like they were.'

Recognition looked on as the second beating Manu then suffered was conducted. It was fairly minor in comparison to the one he had received the previous night – almost as if, deep down, the major approved of what he had done.

After that there were some questions addressed to the archbishop, dying as he already clearly was before Manu's rifle discharged . . . and then more shooting, though not by Manu. Once this was done, Rusyo and the RPA soldiers who administered the *coup de grâce* walked back to the vehicles. Manu and Recognition followed them like dead ringers, progressing over the beaten earth of the deserted marketplace, which was strewn with fragments of glass from the windscreens of the two cars.

Rusyo and Recognition, when he caught up, climbed into the Land Cruiser. They sat there for a while talking, Rusyo now and then making calls on the radio. Manu sat on the ground outside, sobbing and trembling. In the distance, he could hear the crump of mortar fire.

After some minutes, Recognition came out of the vehicle and squatted down next to him, his voice surprisingly solicitous. 'You must learn to follow orders. The archbishop has been supporting the Hutu and we needed information from him before he was killed. You're lucky that the RPA got it and did not shoot you too.'

'But I thought the major was going to kill me if I didn't shoot!'

'Well, Rusyo's angry, Manu, and will not let you back in the vehicle, so now you must walk back up to the camp with the other *kadogos*. You'll find a detachment of them at the docks. Go there, and I shall see you up at the camp.'

With that, Recognition turned and got back into the Land Cruiser, which promptly drove off. After a while sitting there, hugging his knees, Manu got up, supposing to make his way to the docks as instructed.

The two cars which had been shot at were nearby, the first with the body of the driver hanging out of the open door, his fingers touching the ground. He was an ordinary civilian, wearing a white shirt, black trousers. Manu guessed him to be an employee of the cathedral.

In the back of this first car, the metal of which was punctured with bullet holes, were two other bodies, both priests, one a *muzungu*. He slowly realised that one of them was his former teacher and housemaster at the Jesuit mission boarding school, Don Javier.

His teacher's mouth was open, a trail of blood dribbling from one side. Manu could see no wound and darted forwards, hoping to help him. Could he just be alive? When Manu lifted him, however, he realised that there was no back to his head; the bullet had passed through Don Javier's mouth and carried away half his skull, into the boot of the car. It isn't his car, though – Manu plaintively thought, unable to comprehend – it isn't the Ford Zodiac with the chrome bumpers . . . The shadow of a kite, circling overhead in the dim moonlight, made him look up and shudder, as if its talons could take him down to hell in one fell swoop.

Guilt took root in him that day. He began slowly making his way in the vague direction of the docks, wandering like a wild beast strayed into human zones. It was by now fully dark; with SINELAC out of action, no lights were working. Even though he knew Bukavu from his schooldays, it suddenly felt impossible to choose which way to take.

He was at a moment of limits, tripping over kerbs and the broken parts of buildings destroyed by munitions, over belongings dropped by fugitives, over the bodies of those who had failed to flee. He stopped and sat on his haunches, wondered what to do.

Carry on to the docks as instructed? Desert? Go home? But there was no home any more.

Eventually, though, throwing away his rifle because it disgusted him, he decided both to desert and go home. To head for whatever was left of his past, at the other end of the Kivus. He made this decision because he wanted to fly to where he could be clean, even as his body stank, stank down to the slick of rank sweat that develops between men's balls and their thighs, stank down to a fear of discovery and certain execution if discovered. But he knew he had to shift: change, move – follow the destiny that this moment of limits had presented.

All this apparent cogitation was in truth too unwilled to be called a decision. It was more like he was a plane on autopilot, as he began what would become a hard journey, walking through mountainous forest, up from South Kivu to North: back along the geological spine that led to Nyiragongo, the volcano that glowered above Pendele like a watchful dog. En route he sustained himself on forest fungi, stolen maize and bananas, water from streams. Driven by fear, he headed to the home that was no longer home in this way, taking more or less the same route he'd taken with the AFDL in the opposite direction, but looking out for them, or other troops, all the way.

It was raining when he finally reached what remained of the Kwizera compound, finding only a circle of wetted ashes, lumped about with broken mud blocks, pieces of blackened straw and the scorched remnants of household utensils. Picking up a *sufuria*, he suddenly recognised what perhaps he'd already known at that moment of limits in Bukavu four days ago (but only in an uncanny, subconscious way): that the reason, the real reason, he'd come back to Pendele was to bury his mother.

He scooped the handle-less saucepan in the sodden cinders, again and again, until he found her body, eyes sunken down into a head that hungry insects had already begun to strip back. It took a long time to dig a deep enough hole to cover what was left of her form, because at first he had no tool apart from the *sufuria*; but then he found the metal end of a shovel – its wooden stock burnt out in the fire – and set to again with revolted vigour, stopping from time to time to vomit.

Before night fell, as if it hadn't fallen comprehensively enough already, he piled what bits of rock he could find on top of the makeshift grave, determined that after the gross indignity of her passing, his mother should not be dug up by hyenas or wild dogs.

He slept not far hence from this accursed plot, feeling nonetheless like he had fallen into it, along with his burnt mother and the nearby bodies of his father and sister. Their burial places, like the one he'd just dug, he'd marked with makeshift wooden crosses.

In the morning, after gnawing some cobs of maize that hadn't been consumed by the fire, he decided that he simply had to get out of this country that was tumbling into war – flee as far away as possible from the FAZ, the AFDL, the RPA – all those confusing agglomerations of initials which had, in so short a time, brought down such calamity on his own life. Uganda, even though it was already involved in the conflict, seemed like the best haven.

More marching across further ranges of mountain brought him by chance one evening to the edge of an airfield at Rutshuru, on the border between Zaire and Uganda, a country where he was still hoping that the torture of the past few weeks might be cancelled; and their limbo, so he also hoped, wanting the bliss of certainty almost as much he lacked food, water, shelter. Basic needs, bodily needs, but he was by now so delirious with exhaustion that, as well as manifesting physically, these needs and hopes contended like arguing voices in his mind. As he approached the airstrip, the declining sun itself adopted one of these peculiar inward voices, thin-lipped as an angry spouse as it slipped beneath the burnt-orange peaks of the mountains: *so you've got this far, Manu Kwizera, but you think you'll find certainty here, in this time, this place, this world that turns half its face from me, as far from bliss as its other half tomorrow?*

II

Seven to Heaven

November 1996–May 1997

Chapter 1

What summons him forwards is a chime of crickets, a chorus of tree frogs – resuming in concert, after the plane's whoosh. Filling the night around the airstrip, these familiar sounds of the bush give Manu temporary courage. Crouched behind a thorn tree, he looks about.

There's no tower – just a hut and a clutch of paraffin drums, which burn with a blue light. He wonders who lit them; the strip doesn't seem to be staffed in any way. His stomach's clenching from hunger, his throat is still dry with thirst, but he dare not move any further forwards from the scrub on the edge of the strip.

The drums illuminate an aircraft, ghosted by the burning drums. Three men in military uniform are descending the passenger steps at the rear. Manu's near enough to hear their voices, and to identify them as Ugandans.

A doughy white hand appears from inside the plane, followed by a forearm on which is tattooed an image of a woman in a cocktail glass surrounded by dice, cards and a dollar sign. The hand winds a rubber-covered chain. The whiteness of the hand, intensified in the electric light from the plane and the blue light of the flames, seems closer than it is – as if it's Manu who's being wound in, not the steps.

The passenger steps retract, housing themselves under the fuselage. The rear door of the plane closes.

One of the Ugandan soldiers has a brigadier's insignia on his shoulders. As big as the old wardrobe in which Don Javier kept his teaching materials, he looks like a tough sort of guy. For all that, he carries his briefcase like a businessman.

A vehicle draws up. With a jolt, Manu becomes aware that this is the same Land Cruiser – green with a VHF aerial and a black impact stripe on the side – that conveyed him to Nyamwera market that day in Bukavu. Major Rusyo, a pistol strapped to his thigh, steps out of the vehicle; Manu's stomach clenches again, and not from hunger this time. It seems like his escape attempts have been in vain, for here Rusyo is, this man who would (he has no doubt) kill him without a second's hesitation.

Should he retreat further back into the scrub? Once more he dare not move, for fear of being heard or seen.

Rusyo shakes hands with each of the Ugandans in turn. Towards the Ugandan brigadier, he seems a little subservient – something canine in his posture, is that what Manu's picking up? But he can't see his eyes. Rusyo is followed out of the vehicle by a couple of other Rwandan officers who are also familiar. Recognition there's no sign of.

Manu trembles, but Rusyo and all these men are consumed by their business. Their appearance seems manifestation, now made flesh, of *abadayimoni*: the demons that have been flitting in his head since the incident with the archbishop and Don Javier, for which he does not know whether he was to blame or not.

He is so frightened that he hardly hears what Rusyo says to the Ugandan brigadier, which is: 'It's all going well, Faithful. So long as Kabila can control his elements, we should not deviate from the objective. The Banyamulenge are the most troublesome factor. Despite our Tutsi kinship, they're unsteady.'

The big-shouldered brigadier mutters something in assent. Then all the men get into Rusyo's Land Cruiser and drive off.

Manu's heart crashes in his chest, almost drowning out the crickets and the frogs from his hearing. Not knowing what to do, he continues for a while on his haunches, trying to control the panic of the now, the pains of hunger and thirst, the pulse of blood in his neck.

He stares at the aeroplane, still bathed in light from the burning drums. It returns him to the candles in the cathedral where the archbishop gave his address, and also those in the Catholic church in Goma that he sometimes used to go to with his parents, on special occasions, before he went to boarding school. These memories must be snuffed out. Too much of the archbishop, or Don Javier, or his parents, or sister, and he will break down.

Grabbing a sod of earth from the edge of the strip, he holds it as if for comfort. What to do? Banish the panic of the present, which doesn't seem deep or wide enough to exist in. Do what he's bid by necessity, which feels like a chronic disease. Survival is a narrow tunnel that must be crawled through. But he can't see any way in, never mind through, though it's like he's been through this tunnel fifty times already since that day the FAZ came.

While he's enumerating options, the pilot door of the plane opens. The same tattooed arm drops another set of steps. A tall, fat white man lumbers down. His grubby safari suit is blue-ghosted, like most things, by the drum lamps. Its multiple pockets bulge with objects.

The man's sporting a Stetson. Its broad brim and high crown make his head seem as big as a jackfruit. This *muzungu*, in his early fifties maybe, shambles to a barrel by the side of the runway, extracts a brush that drips with water.

Carrying the brush, the white man returns to the aircraft. He begins rubbing at the base of its hull, which is covered with a muck of accumulated dust. After making several journeys to and from the barrel of water, cursing all the while as he sweeps the sodden brush against the underside of the plane, he throws it aside.

He walks back to the water barrel, tries to haul it towards the aircraft. But it is too heavy and he gives up.

Sighing, the man returns to the aircraft, mumbling something which sounds like: 'That dog don't hunt.'

He mounts the steps. A few minutes later, he reappears with a trestle table. He sets this a little way from the plane, then climbs the steps again, next time coming out with a folding stool in one hand. In the other is a Thermos flask with a glass perched on the lid. He unfolds the stool. Settling on it, he pours some liquid into the glass. There is a clink of ice as it tumbles from the Thermos. The man takes a sip from the glass, delves in the top pocket of his safari suit and produces a cigar, which he lights. Then pulls out a small plastic bottle of water from a side pocket, opening it and pouring a little into the glass.

As Manu watches the cigar glow each time the man sucks, the idea comes of offering to help him clean the plane. Could this *muzungu* in turn help him get out of the country? The Ugandan border is only about twenty kilometres away, but he worries what he might face, crossing on foot.

Manu's torn, fearing it will put him at risk to volunteer his presence. This man brought Ugandan military to meet with Rusyo, the Rwandan major; are his allegiances with the Ugandans or the Rwandans? Or both? Ugandan and Rwandan interests have long been aligned, now more so with their joint invasion of a third country. It's risky, yes . . . but what other choices does he have?

And so he approaches, materialising out of the darkness into the pool of light around the plane.

The man gives a tremendous jump, knocking over the stool. He looks at Manu for a second, then runs back to the aircraft, sprinting up the rattling steps – amazing agility for so fat a fellow.

Presently, the man is standing in the doorway of the aircraft, levelling a pistol.

'Who in hell are you?' he shouts, the cigar clamped between his teeth. 'What do you want?' He speaks with an American accent.

'I am just a youth,' Manu shrugs, standing there in his green gumboots and army gear. 'I saw you cleaning and I came to offer my help.'

'Help?' the man repeats, as if such a commodity is unlikely to be found in this part of Africa in wartime. 'What's your angle?' he demands, coming down the steps, still pointing the pistol at Manu.

This is a question he doesn't know how to answer, as the white man comes towards him.

'Well?' says the man, halting his advance on the ladder, but continuing to point the gun at Manu.

'Mobutu's troops attacked my homestead. Then were attacked themselves by AFDL rebels, who conscripted me.'

'Yeah?' the man says, as if all this were now just a trouble of ants in a school locker full of stale food.

'I was not a good soldier.'

'You and a hundred others.' He's still got the pistol on Manu. 'So what happened, kid?'

'The Rwandans affiliated with the AFDL . . . the RPA,' he adds.

'I get you,' the man says, a little less suspiciously. 'But affiliated's a Frenchy kind of word, kid, and though I guess you speak that lingo better than me, I reckon you got it plum wrong. The RPA are the silverbacks, it's them Kabila's cockamamy outfit's affiliated to. How'd you end up here anyhow?'

'I deserted in Bukavu earlier this month and came up through the mountains. *Afande*, I'm really thirsty.'

The *muzungu* nods at the plastic bottle on the table. 'Help yourself.'

After he has drunk some of the water, Manu says: 'I'm sorry, also hungry; do you have any food?'

'For fuck's sake.' He pulls a packet of biscuits from one of the pockets of his safari suit, tosses it to Manu. 'No wonder you were no good as a soldier.'

Hands shaking, Manu opens the packet. Must eat. He begins stuffing the biscuits into his mouth.

The man seems kind, but despite this he's still got the gun on him. 'I dunno, kid,' he says. 'How can I be sure you're telling the truth? You could be FAZ, or one of those Hutu *génocidaires* who's drawn the damnest short straw in looking like one of them Tutsis he wants to kill.'

'Look at my boots,' Manu mumbles through a mouthful of biscuit.

He holds out one of his legs with the gumboot on it as proof, for everybody knows the RPA and AFDL wear green rubber footwear, Mobutu's FAZ having leather army boots, not green rubber.

The white man chuckles at this, puts the pistol in one of his voluminous pockets, clomps down the steps. 'Maybe you're not as dumb as you look,' he says. 'Pick up that stool, will ya?'

Manu does as he says, and the man sits back on the camp stool. He recommences drinking from the glass. The ice in the glass has melted. Manu smells alcohol, reckoning the liquid as whisky.

He stands in silence as the man tries to relight his cigar, shaking the lighter. 'Gotcha!' he says, smiling at Manu with raised eyebrows over the flame when it finally flares. 'So you're one of those Banyamulenge kid soldiers, I guess. Out for kicks and 'bout as useful as tits on a bull.'

'Yes, that is correct. I am Banyamulenge. But please *afande*, not so much of a *kadogo* as some of the others.'

'OK, OK, I'm not insulting you. Sure as hell you've got a party downstairs in those dirty fatigues and plenty of scalps to your name. But you don't have a gun, do you? And speaking as a guy who's seen a lot of soldiers, I don't reckon your thousand-mile stare comes from combat either.'

Vile memory pours through Manu's head. How can he explain to this *muzungu* the sound made by the rain-slicked plastic cloaks of the RPA, sweeping down on the Hutu camps? Or the sight of livid-flickering forks of lightning, illuminating gashes in flesh?

'Yeah?'

'Some. I have seen some combat. That man who arrived in the Land Cruiser, the Rwandan major, is he returning?'

'Nope, that's one thing you don't need to worry about. All the same, you should be returning to your unit, right?'

He hesitates. 'I do not wish to, *afande*, I am sorry for having alarmed you.'

'And I'm sorry I pulled the gun on you. Thought you'd come to put me out of commission! But you seem OK, kid.'

Manu gives a sigh of relief. Has to chance it. '*Afande*, please, can you take me with you?'

The man just laughs. 'The last thing I need is a deserter. And bucko, I ain't your *afande*. I was a rank holder once, but that went down the Swanee.'

'Sir, I have nowhere to go. I could be your servant.'

'Servant? I fucking hate that word. Most of the world's

problems come from one bunch of loonies reckoning they're masters and another bunch of losers thinking of themselves as servants. You wanna pull yourself outta that right now, kid.'

'Please.'

He takes a suck on his cigar, seems about to relent; but all he says is: 'You can clean the bird for me while I think about it. Everything gets covered in crud from the fucking volcano. Drives me crazy.'

'Clean the plane?'

'That's what I said, didn't I?'

Manu begins washing the plane, dipping the brush into the barrel, sluicing off the volcanic dust. As he does so, the pilot becomes more talkative. 'What's your name, then?'

'Manu Kwizera.'

'Manu?'

'Emmanuel.'

'And your background?'

'What do you mean?'

'What do your folks do?'

'I'm sorry, kid,' the man says, understanding, after silence from Manu. 'Lot of it about. My name's Norm Cogan, by the way. Cogan to most folks. Say, you serious 'bout getting on the bus?'

'Yes, *afande*. You have seen how hard I can work.'

'Just call me Cogan.'

'Cogan.'

'You're an A-grade student!'

'Yes sir, at the Jesuit school in Bukavu.'

A smile passes over the man's puffy lips. 'So, you're really looking for a job? I am in need of a gofer, that's for sure. My last one ran away from Entebbe. Asshole took a fuckload of shillings out the till. Looks like you're done there.'

'I do want to get away from here,' Manu says, jumping from the wing.

'Not surprising! But if you work for me – I'm looking for someone to watch over the planes, this Cargomaster . . .'

'This what?'

'Cessna Cargomaster, that's the type of plane you just cleaned.

Others sometimes . . . plus do a bit of work in Entebbe. I've got a bar there as well, you see.'

He gives a reflective pull on the cigar. 'There wouldn't be much of a salary. Forty dollars a month OK?'

Manu nods.

'Cool. This old warrior needs to take a dump. Brave the long drop!'

Taking a torch and a flattened roll of toilet paper from another pocket of his jacket, he goes into the hut. While he's in there, the flames in the drums begin to gutter then go out, one by one. There is silence; even the insect-frog concert falls quiet. Tiny cracks of light show from Cogan's torch in the hut.

In the darkness, a great desire for companionship cascades through Manu. Half there in Rutshuru, half elsewhere, he remembers walking through the jungle with his Bembe friend Daniel, himself carrying a *panga* – its machete-like blade slashing at obstructing vegetation – and Daniel bearing two milk pails with wire handles, both brimful . . .

He remembers also – was it another day? – swishing the *panga* at the eggs of an insect that hung by a thread from a giant fern. Gossamer strand, innocuous-looking to the unwary, that Daniel could have walked into if he wasn't careful.

'Giant hornet,' he said then. 'Very bad sting.'

'*Nakotcha*,' Daniel replied, thanking him in KiBembe; and the two of them plied on, further up a path that he could not have known would lead here, to an airstrip on the Congo-Uganda border – where, emerging from the hut with his torch and trailing roll of loo paper, he utters, this white man, Cogan, four words that might change a life: 'Jump right in, then.'

Chapter 2

What's at stake in flying involves two wonderful structures: that of the sky (if pressure, altitude and fluid dynamics may be spoken of in such a way), and the structure of the machine that is being flown. Technical knowledge of these two structures (adding a third element, the capability of the pilot) has its own wonder, too; but all these are nothing to the wonder that Manu experiences during his first ever flight, rising above Rutshuru. Wonder mixed with fear, elation, relief . . . feelings that together have something of the physical power of the turboprop engine that's hauling him out of hurt.

Issuing rattles, quivers, vibrations, the Cargomaster lifts above the sporadic lights of rural settlements. Cogan banks, routing for the Entebbe beacon, he says, sweeping over the moonlit lustre of the mountains, amid which the fiercer glow from the caldera of one of the volcanoes is visible.

In time the American turns his hot, heavy head from the instruments to glance at Manu. Cogan has pale-brown eyes – set under flaking brows, sweat shining on the lids. He has by now replaced his Stetson with headphones (clamped on sticky hair, grey but glossy) and finally passes Manu a pair.

The headphones press on Manu's ears, pouring in static. The plane snags on a tooth of turbulence. He feels a soulful sensation, akin to iron being drawn by a magnet, of becoming detached from his own body; the aircraft continues pulling from the surface of the earth – fighting the force of gravity, fighting the friction of air itself.

The plane pierces the cloud cover. Slate-thin, lucent strata the Cargomaster tilts upwards through, lifting further from the landscape beneath: dark circle shapes of cattle-filled *bomas*, glimpsed through moonlit gaps in cloud. Cogan increases the pitch and rate of climb. A tremor passes through Manu's arms and legs.

After levelling off and going some kilometres on, Cogan says into his radio mike, 'Entebbe Centre Special HF, this is Echo Lima Sierra Alpha Alpha, entering the Mbarara deconfliction zone.'

'Roger, Echo Lima,' comes the reply. 'Corridor is your present bearing.'

To Manu, Cogan explains this term of aviation art: 'deconfliction zone'. 'The Ugandans have got Tutsis, Hutus, Yanks, French, Mobutists – plus business folk like us, all flying through here, to and from Zaire, not to mention their own air force. So they set up this thing called a deconfliction zone to stop us snapping at each other – you just keep to your own corridor and leave everyone alone – good way to save trouble and lives.'

The turbine hiccups. As Cogan fiddles with a lever, muttering something about adulterated fuel – 'full-rich mixtures that ain't no richer than me' – Manu is already reinventing, becoming someone else, despite constantly thinking back to the someone he was before.

Further into the journey, Cogan says: 'So tell me a bit more about what happened to you, kid.' Manu reluctantly does so, his voice breaking in the course of his account.

Cogan gives a low whistle when he mentions the camps, then says, 'You were part of all that, down in South Kivu?'

Manu shakes his head. 'I refused. I got beaten with a stick for doing so, by an RPA officer called Rusyo, the one who was in that Land Cruiser.'

'Rusyo, eh?'

Clouds flit by. Talk issues fitfully from Manu's panicked lips, the death of his family, the massacres in the forest, all still living in his head. Cogan pats his own sweating head with a cloth as he listens. Trying to anchor himself, Manu does not mention anything to do with the archbishop, fearing that this will raise a prejudice in the *muzungu*'s mind, instead wheeling erratically back to his first meeting with Kabila.

Staring through the cockpit window, Cogan responds mainly with grunts and windy sighs; it's as if the small saw of conversation, going back and forth between them, is missing a few teeth.

'I've met Kabila coupla times,' he does say, at one point. 'Did you notice how his head's squashed into his shoulders?'

'I don't understand.'

'No neck! My momma always used to say, never trust a man without a neck.'

'Maybe you're right,' Manu says, thinking of Kabila, but also looking at Cogan's neck.

He's fiddling with the fuel mixture again. 'Politically anyhows, Kabila's all hat and no cattle – but so far he's paid me, mainly in gold, and I reckon he'll dole out a bit more. For a while, anyhows. Nothing sticks forever, kid, that's a fact. But it sounds as if you've already learned that.'

'What is your business, sir?' Manu asks.

'I'm a cargo pilot – freight dog, as we get called back home. And right now, we're mostly freighting weapons – that's what mainly seems to be required round here. One day our clients might realise they're too late to go back on the decisions they've made . . .'

He suddenly starts singing, 'And it's too late, baby now, it's too late. Though we really did try to make it. Somethin' inside has died . . .' He pauses, adding, 'Some people call us mercenaries – mistakenly, we're not butchers, just carriers. You OK with that? If you hang with me, your allegiance will have to be with freight dogs, not any tribe or nation.'

Manu says nothing, doesn't know what to say.

His silence provokes another burst of song from Cogan, sarcastically put: 'Go now, go now, before you see me cry!'

There's a squawk from the radio. Next Cogan's replying to Entebbe Centre, confirming that the aircraft is leaving the deconfliction zone.

'Well?' Cogan says, picking up the conversation as the plane goes steadily on, the landscape below lit by the cloudy radiance of the moon, spots of starlight and the occasional bright scattering of a town or village below.

Manu doesn't reply again. What's he supposed to say?

'Reckon I was asking you, Manu, about hanging with freight dogs who ship guns and ammo? How would you find that, d'you reckon? This ain't gonna work otherwise, kid.'

He finally says, 'When I was younger, I used to lie in the North Kivu mountains, watching planes pass overhead, their trails . . .'

'Contrails.'

'Is it? Yes, making lines in the sky. Doing that, I must tell you, sir, I always hoped I could work with machines, maybe planes even. And now, thanks to you, here I am flying. So yes, it is OK with me what you do.'

As Manu speaks, knowing that the answer he has given doesn't quite fit with Cogan's question about being involved in the arms trade, he looks out of the window. On clouds below, caught in a drift of moonlight, the miniaturised shadow of the plane shows.

'Every pilot has some kind of memory like that,' Cogan says. 'Sounds to me like you do wanna be an airman, rather than a landsman,' he adds with a chuckle. One of his eczematic eyebrows jerks upwards as he speaks, as if filliped by appreciation of his own good humour.

The plane speeds eastwards, towards Entebbe and escape, Manu sitting next to his bulky saviour, still in deep shock. Odd phrases fall from Cogan's mouth as he flies, snatches of half-sounded tunes. *La la, lala salama.* Cigar ash drifts on his chest and belly. *She take me money and run Venezuela.* A loose smile plays across his lips as he constantly shifts, his safari-suit top making a noise like chewing gum as it unplasters from the plastic-upholstered seat.

Spume streams past the window, obscuring the moonlight that's been raying into the cabin. On Entebbe approach, other lights flash on the instrument panel. Cogan whips off his headset, sleeks back his hair, just humming now, humming exultantly, as the plane slides through cloud-wagged darkness, rushing giddily down.

Chapter 3

Cogan leads Manu to a red Cherokee in the pilots' parking lot and begins driving him to the bar that he mentioned. The windows of the Cherokee are down; smells of diesel, woodsmoke and dried fish fill the cab. The vehicle passes bars and restaurants, lit up by paraffin lamps and busy with people. He screeches to a stop to buy Manu a roll at a place called Pork Joint, next to a hoarding advertising the DIVINE BROTHER DEFENSIVE DRIVING SCHOOL.

'Well you said you were hungry, didn't ya?'

As Manu eats, Cogan begins outlining the work he has in mind for him in the bar. 'You're gonna be a pot boy, most, washing glasses, wiping tables, stuff like that. When you've got the hang of it, you can serve drinks. I'm away a lot and my wife needs help. A lot. And like I said, there'll be a few trips for you too – sometimes I need a body to hump cargo or wash the bird like you just did.'

'I am indeed very grateful for this work, sir,' Manu says.

Cogan manoeuvres the vehicle over a pothole. 'It's a dive, the bar, so don't expect too much!' He lets out a sound, halfway between a belch and a laugh. 'But I guess you wouldn't . . . it's called The Passenger. I won it in a poker game, pretty much run the air firm from there, though we have an office at the airport too.'

They park on a little concrete square, piled with empty crates and rubbish. Manu trails Cogan out of the Cherokee, round on to the main street – passing through a narrow gap, his feet slide

61

on curls of rotten fruit, coils of wiring, broken bottle heads, shards of clay pipe and concrete; amid all of which the ripped foil packets of condoms gleam.

Boxed in between two shops, The Passenger has a tiled roof, a wooden staircase and a veranda. On this stand some bamboo stools with padded seats, and barrels with the logo NILE BREWERIES painted on them. Behind the stools, a window, divided by smears and struts, looks on to the street. A radio aerial rises high into the air above the building.

Skipping guitar music filters through a wire-mesh door. Following Cogan inside, Manu sees a table with a group of mainly white men huddled over it. One of them gives Cogan a shout of greeting, and he raises a beefy arm. He leads Manu towards a dimly lit wooden bar, behind which stands a tall woman, under a big zinc-framed clock. Even from across the room, the floor of which is covered with treacly lino – nailed down at the edges – Manu can see that she is a powerful personality.

'Give this guy the sweetest Coke; he's had a rough time. The usual for me.'

The woman gives Manu a condescending look. Behind her, on the back of the bar, sits a squat, grey radio, frequency numbers showing on its digital dial, their red lights winking. It looks military but is maybe tuned to a civilian station, as that seems to be what's producing the music, with a wire from a jackplug in the front looping up to a tannoy.

'This is Aisha,' says Cogan, introducing him to the woman behind the bar, 'my squeeze, and too beautiful altogether.'

Manu watches Aisha as she levers open a bottle of Coke and pours it into a glass. He can see for himself that Cogan is right about his wife; she is certainly someone to gawp at. Her hair bounces in stiff curls round a wedge-shaped face, before flowing over large, hooped-metal earrings. As she moves, bangles jingle on long brown wrists; they draw his eye along her arm to her breasts, tight under a dress of coloured stripes.

Raising them, these bared arms – to get the whisky from the optic, which has a half silhouette of a walking man on its attached, upturned bottle, and the legend JOHNNIE WALKER

RED LABEL — she looks, with what seems like deliberate magnificence, across her shoulder and says, 'Where did you pick him from?'

'Rutshuru,' Cogan says, prospecting the swirling, oily fluid in the glass that she has by now placed in front of him. 'Thought he could give you a hand.'

She purses her lips. 'He'll probably run off like the last one.'

Cogan says nothing. Manu sees what looks like a hint of sadness in Aisha's eyes, but her words, as she pushes over his Coke, are spoken harshly. 'I suppose this is on the house, Cogan.'

'You betcha,' he replies.

'Thank you, Aisha,' Manu says, inadvertently touching her hand as he reaches for the bottle.

'Mrs Cogan to you.' Snatching away her hand from his polluting contact, she tilts her head towards her husband.

'Ice?' Cogan says, nodding petulantly at his own glass. 'You know what I like, but you never do it.'

She grabs a handful from the bucket and flings it into the glass. A few cubes hit their target; others skitter across the top of the bar.

Cogan looks at Aisha from the depths of his fleshy face. 'Don't waste the ice, babe.'

This time Aisha does not reply. She simply regards him in stony immobility. Even the large steel rings hanging from her ears seem frozen.

Cogan turns to Manu, saying — as if to himself — 'Come and meet the freight dogs.'

Conscious of his ill-fitting army greens and rubber boots clumping on the floor, he follows Cogan over to the table of men. There is only one African among them, and Cogan introduces Manu to him first.

'Gerry, this is Manu. He's a Munyamulenge guy I'm taking on. Manu, Gerry Magero, from Kenya.'

In a white linen suit and crocodile-skin shoes, Gerry sports a half-Afro hairdo, cut sharply at the sides. As Manu sits, Gerry looks at him with the same sort of disdain as the woman at the bar.

'Almost think you were gay, Cogan, the way you keep bringing these waifs and strays to The Passenger.'

'Fuck you, Gerry. Ask Aisha.'

This brings a peal of laughter from the assembled company. Cogan flinches, as if the jibe has touched an already fissured wound.

An angular, wiry *muzungu* with thinning hair and sad-old-man glasses reaches across and takes Manu's chin in his boney hand, inspecting his physiognomy.

'As you all know, this is my speciality.'

Manu freezes, feeling like a specimen with the man's claw on his chin.

'And I can say, with all my expertise, that this boy is not homosex. Sorry to disappoint you, Gerry.'

They laugh, but Manu cannot speak for astonishment.

As the man with glasses drops his hand Cogan grunts, then introduces him, saying: 'This is Max Chénal. From Belgium. We call him Papa. He's one of my pilots. Used to be a missionary, flying aid into Ethiopia.'

'Jesus Christ Airlines!' says the old man. 'But I decided the priesthood was not my vocation after all. Welcome to our team, Manu.'

'*Nyet*, not *compleeetely* a team,' says a man in a flat leather cap. His cut-off white T-shirt reveals impressive biceps. Speaking with an Eastern European accent, from a mouth half covered by a thick moustache, he's smoking ferociously, as if trying to suck the cigarette smoke into his very core. 'My name is Evgeny Blok.'

'Sometimes,' smirks Gerry.

'He jokes about our *biznes*, meaning trouble – my name really is Evgeny Blok,' explains the smoking muscleman, smiling. 'And I am not part of this cosy little company. In fact, I am your main competitor, is that not so, Cogan? That is when I am not bailing out you shitholes. Talking of which, Norm, you better have my money on the table for today's job, or I'll fry your balls in hot oil.'

Cogan looks across at him, speaking coolly. 'Evgeny, our catering service at The Passenger will always provide you with a balanced meal.'

After this retort, which produces another round of laughter, Cogan grunts again, but once more there's an air of anxiety; as if he might not, in fact, be able to give Evgeny his money.

Manu sips his Coke from the bottle, and the others slug back their beers and spirits. It seems they all run on heavy fuel, these so-called freight dogs. The only one who doesn't drink alcohol is Papa Chénal, who's nursing a glass of milk – on account of a peptic ulcer, he explains.

The man called Gerry begins discussing a new Nigerian singer in the Sheraton Hotel band in Kampala – a Yoruba import, as he puts it, going by the stage name of Michelle Tikoto. 'Amazing dancer,' he says. 'She's got two sisters too.'

'Yeah right,' says Cogan.

Manu notices, during this exchange, Aisha's gaze on them. She's in front of the bar now, polishing the brass rail that runs along its edge, and again looking back over her shoulder.

Cogan gets up from the table to go behind the bar, passing what seem like a few apologetic words to Aisha as he fetches down a bottle of Chivas Regal. He next reaches up to change the frequency on the radio receiver. The music stops as he wheels the dial through, until static and garbled voices fill the room.

From the mouth of Gerry, now smoking an enormous joint: 'Guy got there in the end.'

Papa Chénal explains. 'What Gerry means, Manu, is that Cogan has found VHF 118.2, the general channel for aircraft information when not talking to air-traffic control. In Europe it remains straight talking, but here you hear every kind of nonsense.'

And so it proves, as Cogan returns to the table. Manu hears successive bursts of transmission, including *Maputo beacon has moved to 132.7* and *If anyone sees Zeb Zinika, tell him to call his wife asap*.

'I once did mines to Maputo,' says Evgeny, stowing away his phone. 'Came back the next year with artificial legs.'

'That,' says Papa, 'is just not funny.'

'Wasn't being funny, priest. One of the worst cargoes I've carried – those limbs weren't properly packed, rattled in their crates the whole way.'

Papa looks morosely at the collection of glasses on the table, next to assorted cigarette packets, lighters, an overflowing ashtray and his own half-drunk glass of milk. His lens-covered blue eyes glance at Manu, as if appealing for solidarity.

'Live animals are the worst,' Gerry says. 'Eldoret to Frankfurt. Hopping in a Bristol. PAX three Rothschild giraffes. Was gonna be four but one died of heatstroke in the pen before we loaded.'

'Worms!' shouts Evgeny. 'Over a million from Minsk to Muscat, in two hundred boxes. Do you know, worms make a noise if you have enough?'

'That's just the sound inside your head,' comments Papa. 'A place I would not like to be.'

Evgeny's moustache twists into a grin, as if acknowledging a point well scored.

Manu sits in silence. Two persons: the one who's here, still becoming, the one that got left behind in Zaire. Neither quite brave enough to ask for another Coke.

'In the US Air Force,' muses Cogan, 'we had a special training module on flying animals.'

'Green Berets,' says Evgeny, and Cogan laughs.

'Can't believe they're doing PPL training for twenty-five thousand US in Joburg now,' says Gerry. 'Fifty kay for commercial. Another fifty kay for each type rating. I paid a lot more in Peoria for all these, even if I did have the privilege of flying over beautiful Illinois.'

'Much of this civilian training is substandard,' says Evgeny. 'You agree, Cogan?'

'For sure,' says Manu's saviour. 'For instance, I could take this young guy, who's expressed an interest in planes, put him through air force-style training and he'd soon be flying far better than if he went through any profit-led flight school.'

'No chance,' says Gerry. 'He'd have to be able to do maths for a start.'

Manu shrinks into his chair, feeling oddly as if the chair itself is rubbing his buttocks away. Don Javier taught him well in maths. The memory of his teacher's open mouth, in the back of the punctured car, makes him grip the empty Coke bottle hard.

'Wanna take a bet on the kid getting trained?' says Cogan,

levelling his pouchy face at Gerry.

'All right,' says the Kenyan. 'Let's make it a grand. Dollars. Commercial licence in eight months.'

'That's tight, man,' says Cogan, shaking his head. 'That's flying even when you are asleep, that's flying when you are in the shower or taking a shit.'

'In Russia this is normal,' puts in Evgeny.

'Flying while you're on the crapper?' queries Cogan.

'Don't be baby,' admonishes Evgeny. 'In military, training is intense. You know this yourself.'

Cogan pulls on his cigar, makes a decision. 'OK. Manu trained to commercial pilot level within eight months. One kay.'

'*Ndiyo bwana!*' shouts Gerry, and they shake. 'Aisha! Bring drinks!'

Neither Cogan nor Gerry have even looked at Manu during this exchange, still less asked his opinion about whether he is happy to be traded in this way.

'I'll help,' says Evgeny, just as oblivious of him as the others. 'My own mentor, Anatoly Anatolyevich of fond memory, was an instructor of genius.'

'Hey, that wasn't part of the deal,' Gerry protests as Aisha appears, lightly resting her hands on the adjacent shoulders of both Gerry and Cogan, then reaching over to pick up the bottle of Chivas.

'Enough of that I think, Norm, if no one's paying for it – all you fellows are very noisy tonight,' she says, her eyes darting swiftly over Manu, as if she's determined the subject of discussion. 'Can I get you all something that isn't on the house?'

Once everyone has given orders, even Manu asking for another Coke, Cogan says: 'Sure is kind of you, Evgeny. Can't think of anyone else whose experience I'd like the benefit of, if I was a young fly boy.' Manu wonders if he is being sarcastic.

Papa points his azure-sharp eyes at Manu, who's faint with tiredness, his mouth gaping. 'I think I, too, might have something to teach this young man.'

Gerry sighs. 'What's the plan, then?'

'All except you take our turn in giving him a series of training flights, but me doing a few more,' says Cogan. 'Seven to-and-fro missions, seven to heaven we used to say in the air force: that should just about do it, so long as the hours are enough.'

The other white men appear to think this a good idea, but Gerry says: 'Yeah right, all you *wazungu* lined up against me again . . . anyway, what do you yourself think about this, country boy?'

Manu assents with a firm-seeming nod to the terms of the wager – and so it's summarily agreed, his yet-to-be-unfolded future, over which the freight dogs clink their glasses. 'But are you sure?' Cogan asks, once it's too late.

'I'm very happy with this idea, sir,' Manu says, and it's true, but he finds himself yawning again, even as he speaks.

'Cool,' Cogan replies. 'Looks like you're tuckered out. Say good night to these ladies and follow me.'

Cogan ushers him past a pool table to a room containing a bed, a basin, and a battered chest of drawers with brass handles. A small window's wedged high up in the yellow wall. Under the bare bulb, Cogan eyes Manu's dirty army greens and rubber boots.

'I'll get Aisha to buy you some clothes: what shoe do you take?'
'Forty-six.'
'Tell me that in American.'
He looks at Cogan blankly.

'Never mind. We'll work it out. Good night, Manu. Look, I'm away on a flight tomorrow, but I'm dead serious about you training up. You too?'

'Yes, sir,' he says, but wonders why he has so soon pledged himself like this, given his acquaintance with Cogan is so recent, so superficial and, so far, untested.

A smell of rotting garbage wafts in as he tries to sleep, along with the sound of the lake washing against the Entebbe shore. Car headlights illuminate the ceiling. A lizard dodges between the beams. He slaps at the sonic whine of mosquitoes near his head, broods on his father's ability to move his anvil as if it were made of air, not iron. Something of the sorcerer about the way he did it. Like this Cogan, Manu determines as he finally dozes off, this one who is offering me the power of flight.

Chapter 4

Woken by the call to prayer echoing across the town, he finds himself with an erection. It's because he needs to pee, no doubt, and he's just getting up to do so when there's a bang on the door. With the knot of sheets, he covers his nakedness. Aisha, already immaculately turned out in spite of the early hour, is standing in the doorway. 'Get yourself up and dressed,' she says. 'We have to work here, you know.'

He pees, washes, dresses – goes through to the bar. Aisha's sitting at a stool, smoking. There is a cup of coffee, a bread roll and a branded jar – Not Tonight Honey – a little further down the bar.

'Eat,' she says, not looking at him, fiddling at her upturned calf.

'Thank you, Mama.' He sits on one of the other bar stools.

'Mrs Cogan.'

'I'm sorry.' But it was a perfectly respectable form of address for the region, the one he used.

She takes a pot of ointment from her handbag, begins applying it to her calf, explaining, as she rubs it in, that her car broke down on the way in this morning; she had to ride in on the pillion of a *boda*, and burned her leg on the exhaust.

He sips the coffee, which is lukewarm, but very strong, and puts some honey on the roll.

As he eats, she gets straight to the point. 'I need help in this bar: what me and Cogan have agreed is that when you're not learning to fly, you'll help with jobs here, which is what he originally hired you for. Understood?'

'Yes, Mrs Cogan.'

'Good, because this bar might be called The Passenger, but we cannot afford to have any on board. Got it?'

'Yes.'

'Today I will give you some money and you will go to the market.' She gives him a list of purchases that he needs to make: fish, meat and veggies, plus cleaning products and clothes and shoes for himself – adding that the cost of these will be knocked off his wages.

It's a hot and humid day already. Entebbe's an attractive town, he discovers, spreading out haphazardly by the lake, with gardens of bougainvillea and white-flowered moringa trees. He enters a street full of clubs, bars, *dukas*: small stores packed with products. He buys the cleaning products Aisha asked for at one of the *dukas* – Twinkle, Jireh, Spic-Span – then finds the informal market.

Women stallholders are laughing joyously, cracking jokes with each other. Men are dozing on mats or playing *bao*. Infants are dabbling in puddles with home-made toys or are tied snugly on their mothers' backs.

Wandering through, he weighs Cogan's offer of pilot training. Doubt assails him. Is he up to it? Is it even real anyway, this wager-promise made among drunk men of questionable character, jousting with each other in a bar?

Distracting him from his thoughts are piles of homely plastic ware, and pyramids of fruit and vegetables. 'Irish, Irish!' a vendor shouts over a pile of potatoes. He buys some of these, and some beans, both being on Aisha's list, along with mangoes and bananas.

He next makes for the shoes-and-clothes area of the market to fit himself out for his new life. He looks over a pile of trainers, knotted into pairs on a papyrus mat. Still a nineteen-year-old, despite everything, he loves the red Nike Airs that he spots there, counterfeit or not; the little windows in the soles seem like a portal to somewhere better. But there's not enough money to buy those and much else on top, so he buys some cheaper blue trainers – and, at another stall, a couple of T-shirts, a pair of jeans, some shorts, socks and underwear.

Dumping his green army boots in a bin and putting on the

trainers, Manu knocks along with his plastic bags to another part of the market to buy the fish and meat Aisha wanted.

He buys the tilapia first. Fish guts around the stall are enticing Marabou storks. Swooping in with enormous wings, and ungainly legs, white with excrement, braced for a swerved landing, their beaks rattle as they squabble over stinking scraps. The stall extracts a mental image of his mother, who loved to cook fish and was very good at it too, crusting the skin with spices.

In the butchery area, great slabs of cow swing from hooks. Chickens, crammed into tiny cages, peck at the wooden edges of wire-strung doors. He asks for the steaks Aisha wanted, watches almost hypnotized as the butcher hacks them off, thinking of the ceremonial way his father killed cattle back home.

On the way back to The Passenger, he notices a tradesman's bicycle, ridden by a man selling Snow-brand ice creams. As the man turns the pedals, a melody plays – its predictable electronic chords advertising, haltingly, his melting wares.

Further on, Manu passes a pretty, green-eyed young woman eating one of this fellow's ice creams. She has straightened hair and trendy clothes, and is arm-in-arm with an athletic-looking guy in a suit – to whom she says, in English, as she passes: 'Look, if we don't get engaged, how will it ever be real?'

The young man with her, who seems uncomfortable in his square-shouldered suit, says, 'I'm not ready, let me get this one job.'

Except for unemployment – is the boyfriend on his way to an interview? – he looks exactly the sort of business-inclined person of whom her evidently prosperous parents might approve; her English accent suggests she was either educated or grew up in the UK. Manu watches as the girl hails a *boda boda* and the couple drive off, both sitting on the pillion – the young woman's glossy hair streaming out in the wind behind as she continues licking the ice cream, holding her boyfriend round the waist.

As he trudges back to The Passenger, Manu's mood plunges. The cracked pavement under his feet displays with each step shattered fragments of memory. His sister Beatrice – tottering out of the storehouse shouting his mother's been killed – the look of terror in his father's eyes, when he knew he was going to die — and all that followed, all that followed, just as if those events, too, have become in tormented retrospect the chords of a predictable melody . . .

He becomes very familiar, during his first day of work at The Passenger, with the particular scents of Twinkle, Jireh, Spic-Span. Their odours are foreign to him, used to only Omo for soap powder (if it could be found, and usually Beatrice did find it) and the ubiquitous bars of Imperial Leather, on sale in almost every African market, for washing bodies. He couldn't, across his whole life so far, recall Beatrice or his mother cleaning anything with a substance that came from a spray-bottle.

Aisha barks, 'There!' and 'There!' as he rubs the gritty bar with a rag; clicks past on high heels as he wipes dead flies from the slats of the louvred windows; stands with her hands on her hips as he shakes out the dusty, stained cushions of the bamboo stools on the veranda.

All this, he silently supposes, as the zinc-framed clock above the bar ticks along, Aisha once did herself, or his runaway predecessor did. Despite her harangues, he's very aware of the soft rustle of her dress; he's aware, too, of her perfume, which overlays with a passionate invocation of cheap romance the acrid smell of the cleaning products he's been applying. What's invoked by the perfume is not Aisha herself, however, but the young woman he saw this morning, eating an ice cream as her glossy hair streamed out behind her in the *boda* breeze.

Later, Aisha teaches him how to use the till and serve particular drinks. Beer and sodas are easy, he finds, spirits with mixers harder. Cocktails? Almost impossible.

That night, a Friday, an air of grim carnival develops as revellers pour in from the nearby clubs and bars he noticed on his walk, all whooping by in crazy rushes as they seek out drink, sex and trouble. Aisha tells him to wedge open the mesh-screen door on to the veranda, else it breaks the hinges, with so many people coming in and out.

The centre of activity in The Passenger is a cluster of camouflaged men occupying three tables. Each of these officers of the Ugandan People's Defence Force has a sidearm, which they wear in brown leather holsters or place ostentatiously on the tables.

The bar is also filled with young women with designs on the military visitors. They wear short skirts or shiny slitted dresses, and perch on stools. Low-browed with anxiety, these girls – many of whom, he gathers, have other, real, daytime jobs as secretaries or teachers – are waiting to be bought Fantas or mango juice by the soldiers, who make their orders by banging on the bar with the flat of their hands.

After an hour or so, Gerry, the Kenyan pilot, appears, catching Aisha's eye, Manu notices. Gerry sits down next to the senior ranking officer of the UPDF, an extremely tall and imposing man with a grin on his face, and shoulders so wide it looks as if they'd hardly fit through a doorway.

'Brigadier Faithful,' Gerry says later, making introductions at the bar, 'this young man is Manu, a Munyamulenge lad who Cogan's training to be one of us; me and the Yank have had a bet on whether he can get his commercial licence within eight months!'

'Is that so?' says the brigadier, sizing Manu up. 'There should be a proverb about you Banyamulenge – something like, the reed that shivers when the wind blows! Are we going to get these drinks or not? Mine's a whisky and Coke.'

'Same for me,' Gerry says. 'Doubles, Manu.'

'Well you're going to be busy if you succeed in becoming a pilot,' the brigadier says as Manu makes the drinks. 'Kabila has just taken Goma with all your Banyamulenge mates.' He doesn't seem at all perturbed by Manu's patrimony or how he got here.

'My forward scouts,' the brigadier continues, 'are flying into Zaire tomorrow, with Gerry here, to begin giving the FAZ and their new white mercenaries, who are Turks, or Serbs, or Bashi-Bazouks or something, the whipping they deserve! Then we'll march on Kinshasa. We can't let Kagame and Rusyo and the other RPA high-ups take all the glory.'

73

Manu swallows, hearing Rusyo's name.

Brigadier Faithful, oblivious to the effect his words are having behind the bar, continues. 'When I first knew them, when they were in the Ugandan Army, all those Tutsi lordlings were just anxious teenagers; they looked just like this fellow here!,' he says to Gerry – referring to Manu, who's shakily spooning ice into the drinks. 'Back in the day, Rusyo in particular constantly needed his bottom wiping.'

They take away their orders, go off to play pool, but Manu can hardly concentrate, because he's hearing Rusyo's caustic voice as he thrashes him.

In a lull at the bar, Manu looks over at the pool table, belatedly realising that Brigadier Faithful is, in fact, the same wardrobe-sized man that he saw coming off Cogan's plane to rendezvous with Rusyo at Rutshuru. The memory causes him to want to burrow back into himself, worrying again for his safety. Between bouts of service – Nile Specials, Bells and Club, Amstel and Tusker, spirits with every kind of mixer – other events of the recent past flash again into his mind.

Laughing, their game of pool over, Gerry and Brigadier Faithful return to the UPDF tables, and Manu's mind purls further back, to Pendele in peacetime – where his father's showing him how to plant millet, using the leg of an old table (the rest lost to woodworm) to draw a furrow in black volcanic earth . . .

Later, when Gerry leaves with the soldiers, he blows a kiss at Aisha, in the same movement resting his other hand on his hip and doing, in his white suit, a kind of disco twirl.

Aisha shouts, 'For God's sake, look where you are going!' She and Manu have bumped hips at the bar, causing her to drop a bottle of vodka on the floor. 'No problem, I'll pay for that, and two glasses of milk too,' intones a French-accented voice. It's Papa Chénal, winking at Manu as he hands over grubby notes.

'Don't give him such a hard time,' the former priest continues, 'he's got to start being a pilot in the morning. Each of us losers is going to do some hours with him, seven missions in all. I passed Cogan in the air, Aisha, if that is what's getting you angry; he should land at Entebbe in about an hour.'

'What's getting me angry is not Cogan not being here, he's hardly ever here anyway, it's him expecting me to work with *washamba* like this one.' Manu bridles at being called a country boy, but it is partly true.

'That's why he is just right for us! For aren't you always complaining, my dear, how stupid Cogan and the rest of us pilots are?'

She shakes her head but smiles a little all the same at the tight-faced old man in his oversized specs. Balancing his two glasses of milk, Papa wanders outside on to the veranda.

At closing time, Manu finds him there on one of the bamboo stools, staring through his thick lenses into the darkness of the street, the revellers having finally dispersed.

Papa says, 'How're you getting on, Manu?'

'She, Aisha, Mrs Cogan, is very strict on me.'

'Nothing to do with you. Her anger is because Cogan cannot satisfy her in bedroom aerobics. He buys drugs to increase his potency. You ought to be careful round that one.'

Manu wonders if 'that one' means Aisha or Cogan; Aisha, he reckons.

'Did Cogan say anything more to you on the subject of your training?'

'He has not been here.'

'Well, don't worry, he'll keep his promise. He's loyal in that way at least.'

Manu summons up the courage to ask, 'Why do you think he is doing it?'

'Taking you under his wing, you mean?'

'Yes.'

Papa laughs. 'I'm tempted to say it's just the bet, because that is the kind of risk-taking people we crazy freight dogs are. But he actually does need pilots, and African ones, too: some of the situations we get into need a black face at the front. So there's no need to doubt his motives.'

Manu doesn't say anything.

'And you should not doubt me, either.'

'Sorry, sir, I do not understand.'

'I mean I will also keep my promise – help teach you to fly.'

'Do you often work together, all you pilots?'

Papa shakes his wizened head. 'Well I work for Cogan, but Evgeny has his own show. Gerry works for both of them, and himself. But yes, we work together in a way, depending on the scale of the jobs. Right, I'm off. Need my beauty sleep. Take care, young man.'

Chapter 5

At about nine-thirty the next morning, as Manu's pushing a mop across the floor of The Passenger, the mesh-screen door bangs open. Cogan thunders across the lino, heading straight for the lavatory, where he begins vomiting copiously. Manu glances at Aisha, again sitting on a bar stool, putting more ointment on her *boda* burn. A high-heeled shoe's dangling from the end of one of her crossed legs as she says to him, 'Get on with your work.'

Without overmuch urgency, she places the ointment tub on the bar and follows Cogan through to the toilet. Still pretending to mop, Manu glimpses her kneeling beside Cogan, a hand on his back, as he continues heaving – in between bouts making a hoarse, sobbing noise through his nose.

Afterwards, as Cogan washes his face, Manu can hear Aisha murmuring to him. They seem an affectionate couple in that moment, despite what Papa said last night. From his parents, Manu knows enough about marriage to understand it as a state of punctuated emotions.

'Hi kid,' Cogan calls over to him, rolling back into the bar, looking drawn and grey. 'Sorry 'bout that. Saw some bad stuff on my trip. Got stuck on the other side of the border. Rusyo and his boys driving refugees like cattle or doing turkey shoots, depending on whether the UN is watching. You're so well out of it, kid.'

He pours himself a Nile, and Manu watches how the movement in Cogan's muscles animates the tattooed woman on his arm. 'At one place, I saw more corpses than I've ever seen in my whole life. Worse thing is, I have to go back into the war zone again tomorrow. Guess you better come with me, begin your hours.'

As Cogan glugs his breakfast beer, sighing with satisfaction, Manu grips the mop handle, trying not to let what Cogan has painted fill his mind. Convinced that he must never see piles of bodies again, he frantically wants to pedal back on decisions that he already appears to have made. 'It's OK, sir,' he says, 'there's no need for you to fulfil your bet. I'm happy to continue my work in the bar.'

'What the fuck?' Cogan's sweating heavily, eyes bulging out of his head. 'I'm your employer now, I say what type of work you do.'

'You have been very kind to me.' How this *muzungu* looks like a white version of Kabila! 'But now I feel becoming a flyer is not the best thing for me.'

Cogan takes a gulp from his glass. 'Don't be a jerk. If I'm to grow this goddam company, I need new pilots.' Confirming Papa's suspicions as to his motives in hiring Manu, he adds: 'And I need black ones because . . . some of these governments, well they like to see that. And this is a real chance for you to progress personally, kid.'

He grabs Manu by the shoulders, puts his big face very close – the deep furrows in Cogan's brow and cheeks seem like chasms carved in rock over many years. 'Look, I know you've been through the mincer, but what I'm proposing will give you a profession. So no more bullshit. Any more backsliding and you're out. Period. Today we're gonna go for lunch at Aero Beach, then sort out your certifications, OK?'

'What is that, Aero Beach?'

'Kind of a leisure place by the lake, with a restaurant, animal enclosures and a sorta aviation theme. Reason we're going, it's 'cos there some wrecks of old birds there. Most non-pilots who board aircraft are blind as eggs: you need to see an airframe in the raw to really understand.'

Aisha, who has lit a cigarette, blows a cloud of smoke into the air. It dances under the spotlights, keeps its identity for a few seconds, then separates. 'How exactly is this going to work, Cogan? Can he really still work in the bar?'

'I'll lose money if he isn't flying intensively,' Cogan growls. 'He's off the bar work now, I've decided, except in emergencies.'

'I want the air conditioners cleaned before he goes,' Aisha says, setting her painted face.

'OK. I'll pick him up at one.'

'You're going to have to find me more help! Like you promised.'

'OK, OK.'

Manu spends the next hour or so scooping out the congealed, mouldy paste that gathers in the guts of air-conditioning units. It's revolting, but as he flicks the furry white worms off his fingers into the sink, he senses excitement that his education as a pilot is finally beginning. The worries of earlier dissipate, running away with the muck down the plughole; what replaces them is a strong desire to succeed in the plan that Cogan has laid out for him.

It's busy, Aero Beach, packed with Ugandans having fun. Manu and Cogan make their way through the throng to a restaurant within the complex, where Cogan orders *piri-piri* chicken and chips for both of them, without asking what Manu he wants. Under red umbrellas, sipping drinks − Manu a Coke, Cogan a Nile Special − they watch some boisterous boys shouting and splashing about in the lake, some even shampooing their hair.

The airframes of three passenger jets, damaged and stained − one almost burnt out − dominate the scene. The planes are from previous Ugandan wars, Cogan says, brought here as tourist attractions and now standing amid volleyball nets, trampolines and a number of colourful statues of African statesmen.

These include ones of the Ugandan president, Yoweri Museveni, and Paul Kagame, his Rwandan counterpart. 'Looky here,' says Cogan, casting his eye over the statues. 'The way things are going, they'll soon have to get a statue of Kabila, too. His invasion forces are heading for Kisangani. All the Zairean cities will fall like dominoes in my opinion, except maybe Lubumbashi, where they'll fight to protect the mines, I expect. I heard Kabila wants to go back to calling the country Congo.'

'Yes, he said that when he came to the AFDL camp. In my mind it has already happened.'

'Well don't be too hasty, kid. It ain't necessarily gonna be better. Kabila has a lot of work to do. And so do you.'

Cogan begins explaining that if Manu really wants to be a commercial pilot, it will mean committing for a long time. 'Easy the eight months we said. Possibly more, in which case I'm out of pocket and lose the bet. Too bad. All the time living, breathing, shitting aviation. And, if you're hanging with me, possibly dying. You'll have to get your private pilot's licence first, which involves practical flying experience, getting your hours. And theory – seven exams! – sucks. And then do more exams, but harder, to go commercial. Mind you, if you get enough hours, you might be able to do both exams at once.'

Putting down his beer, he starts numbering the exam segments on his fingers. 'Air law. That's learning about airspace . . .'

Listening to Cogan, Manu spots the girl he saw yesterday on his trip to market, eating an ice cream as she mounted a *boda*. She's wearing a yellow bikini now, a matching spotted wrapper on her head as she makes her way down to the lake. He watches entranced as she moves elegantly into the water, up to her waist, before allowing herself to fall forwards into the lightly lapping waves, as she does so looking askance at the rough young boys, now throwing a football between each other, amid the dispersing foam of their shampoo. In a delirium of mental time shifts, he suddenly thinks of the froth round the workers in the Bukavu docks, as they gunned in rivets or loaded crates, singing their old Swahili songs, and then of the suds in his sister's laundry bucket.

'Hey, you paying attention?' Cogan says, chuckling. 'Here I am telling you 'bout flight performance, and you're looking at that chick aren't you, you dirty devil? If you wanna get women, you can't just look, you have to perform before they'll let you go the whole nine yards. But sometimes haughty hotties like that prefer you to ignore them totally at first, not even looking. I'll show you one day, but today we gotta do our business.'

'I am with you,' Manu says. But he's not really. As the girl progresses to and fro – using a stately breaststroke, the wrapper moving through the water like a crowned head – he asks himself: is this the life I can have if I become a pilot, is she the kind of girlfriend I can have?

'What's next?' says Cogan. 'Human factors: keeping your head straight, mainly. Also pilot actions when there's no engineer: tying down, dressing out – that's filing damaged prop blades till they're smooth again. No hope with these, anyhow . . .'

He gestures at one of the damaged planes, its propellers as marked by incisions as the old tools that local farmers would bring to Manu's father's forge to be fixed.

'Well whaddya know, here's Evgeny.'

The muscular Russian is coming in the direction of their table, carrying a bottle of beer. Sitting down, he reaches over and takes one of Cogan's chips, dipping it into the puddle of tomato sauce on the plate. 'Thought you might be here, Cogan. So, Goma, what did you make of it?'

'Grim's not the word.'

'You know I passed over you in the Antonov on the way out?' He gives his moustache a little lick, removing misplaced tomato sauce.

'Yeah, I saw, but was keeping radio silence. You got them out, then?'

'Yes, Nairobi. All gibbering and shaking till we left Zaire airspace. And a bit after, during a storm on approach. Bunch of murderers transformed into whining puppies, frightened by a little bit of turbulence.'

Cogan doesn't reply for a moment, then swallows. 'Well,' he says, 'the following morning the RPA went in and killed most of those left behind, in camps outside the city. I've seen a lot in my time, Evgeny, and so have you. But this was the worst, bottom of the barrel.'

Watching Cogan warily, Evgeny lights a cigarette. 'We can't get involved in the details, Cogan. You know that.'

The Russian gives a big sigh, as if even his moral compass has been tested by what's been happening. Then drinks from his bottle of beer, swirling the liquid around in his mouth, as if to clean both his teeth and the ethical ground.

Once the meal is over, they climb into the old Boeing 707 that's outside on the yellow grass. Evgeny and Cogan go through the fuselage with Manu following behind, the two middle-aged men calling out like a couple of kids as they show him where the spars attach to the wings, the lines coming from the fuel tanks, and what's left of the internal system of hydraulics that operate the rudder and elevator, ailerons, brakes and landing gear.

On tired old seats, ripped and showing metal in many places, the pair sit in the cockpit, pointing out amid a bewildering array of instrumentation the gyroscope and the balance indicator, which is a ball in a curved glass tube.

'If there is a yawing movement – that's a slide when you turn – the ball will be on the low side,' explains Cogan.

'Ball to the left, left rudder!' shouts Evgeny, stamping his foot on one of the dead pedals, and the two men laugh over their respective control columns.

They show him some other things, too, but the lesson is limited in extent, because so many of the instruments have been smashed or removed. The airspeed indicator is still there, though, Cogan pointing out a red line on it, saying 'That's the VNE, the never exceed speed – what you shouldn't go over.'

'Unless someone is shooting at you!' says Evgeny.

'The main thing to remember,' says Cogan, as Manu climbs down from the airframe, 'is that there are four main forces that act on an aeroplane: weight, lift, drag and thrust.'

'And these we call,' intones Evgeny, as he follows, 'the principles of flight.'

At the foot of the steps, they all stand in silence for a second or two, absorbing the unexpected sight of a small Ugandan boy on a camel. A groom in a riding helmet is leading it down to the beach. Manu notices the ice-cream girl taking a picture of the boy; perhaps he's her little brother.

As she lowers the camera, she slants her green eyes at Manu. Feeling a kick of desire, he wonders if she recognises him from the street, despite his new clothes and the company of two *bazungu*.

Later in the day, Cogan takes him to the Uganda Civil Aviation Office at Entebbe Airport, or EBB as Cogan calls it, using the system of airport identifiers employed by aviation professionals. He signs Manu up with the authorities, pays a fee. At another place, he buys him a pilot's uniform together with all the training manuals and other kit he'll need to do his exams, including some sunglasses and a flight bag.

After all this business, he takes Manu to a little kiosk to get his photograph taken. 'We're gonna have to get you a new passport; Kwizera right for the second name, Emmanuel first?'

'Yes.'

'Any middle names?'

'Faustin. Emmanuel Faustin Kwizera.'

'OK. And date of birth?'

'Sixteenth of May, 1977.'

But a few seconds later, sitting in the photobooth, Manu's wondering who the hell he is now, in fact, and is really none the wiser when four small square images slide out of the slot, slightly wet to the touch.

During the journey back to the bar, Cogan turns on the radio. It's the news. A spokesman for an NGO, Refugees International, declares: 'Of the million-plus Rwandan and Burundian Hutus who fled to Zaire in the post-genocide period, hundreds of thousands have not returned home and are missing. Questions need . . .'

'To be asked about math,' says Cogan, promptly switching the station to one playing the high-tempo guitar of *soukous*, tapping his hand on the wheel in time to the music. Again Manu watches the half-naked woman jiggle in the cocktail glass, moving on Cogan's bare forearm with the dollar signs and the dice.

As the Cherokee continues along the highway, Manu asks, 'Who was Evgeny talking about, the murderers who became puppies?'

Cogan at once stops tapping his hand. 'Well he didn't want to say, he's a secretive kinda guy, but I will tell you, Manu, because this ain't gonna work unless I can trust you, and you me. Evgeny flew some of the Hutu leadership out of Zaire to Nairobi just as I was flying ammo in for the RPA who were seeking the same guys. Basically kid, it's a sorta brotherhood . . . we have this tacit agreement that he does for one side, I for another, until it becomes too hot, then we switch.'

'It's not a problem?'

'No, well, no more than it is for a girl who goes with other boys. Just gotta stay organised and ready for love. But we don't need to worry about that now, 'cos tomorrow we're picking up an industrial generator that the RPA have liberated from the Congolese – they've been lugging it on the back of a pickup truck, but now need to move more quickly. Fucking heavy, those generators.'

Mention of the RPA throws Manu into a panic. He cannot bear to allow what happened at the Nyamwera market, so recently, to resurface – coming up like the snout of a crocodile in a lake; but he doesn't say anything about this to Cogan. Instead, trying to keep his voice as neutral as possible: 'We're going to Bukavu?'

'No, the Tuts are way out of there – they don't need to stick around, they've taken a town deeper inland – some place called Kamituga. That's our destination tomorrow. In the Cargomaster, same rig I picked you up in. Kamituga's about two hours' flight from EBB. Listen, I gotta go into the capital this evening, so I'll just drop you at the bar. Read the flying training section of the first volume of the manuals tonight. And hey, bring that tomorrow!'

Chapter 6

They're on the way to EBB for Manu's first flight, beginning the planned seven missions from which he's expected to absorb the hours and knowledge needed to pass his exams. Yvonne Chaka Chaka's 'Umqombothi' is playing on the car radio and Cogan's storming through the meteorology segment of the training modules. Already sweating heavily, he's wearing the same kind of white pilot shirt as Manu's new one, though it has a captain's epaulettes and is straining across his chest.

'We'll go over it in more detail later,' Cogan says, over the music. 'But remember, always different near the equator, kid! Main thing is, wherever you are, make your own decisions in bad weather. Loadsa times I've had to make my own judgements against the weatherman. Never subscribe to what others say, else you're just a catspaw.'

'A what?'

'Somebody's dupe, somebody's tool.'

'Oh.'

Swelling in volume, Mama Africa's song about magic beer fills the vehicle like a rising burp.

On arrival at EBB, Cogan tells Manu to study the flight plan to Kamituga, the place in Zaire they're headed for. He does so in one of the fly-blown rooms off the old Entebbe Airport hall, famous from the raid of Israeli commandos in 1976, which Cogan's outfit now rents from the military. It's messy, this so-called office of Normair, full of old grey filing cabinets and bins overflowing with crumpled coffee cups. Pinned on large corkboards, almost floor to ceiling, are maps of different African countries at 1:250 000 scale, interspersed with *Playboy* and Pirelli calendars, all withered by heat.

Cogan goes for a leak, as he calls it. Manu looks at some of the half-clad, sun-faded women on the calendars, then – turning to the window, its mosquito mesh torn almost to shreds – watches engineers preparing the Cargomaster.

Then it starts, his face-to-face education in aviation, with a three-hour classroom session. Sitting on a chair, legs up on a table, Cogan yacks away, licking his thumb each time he turns a page in the manual. As about the last working fan in the half-wrecked building spins above them, Manu tries to concentrate on the technicalities of weight and balance, airworthiness, weather and navigational track.

When they are done, Cogan stands up, puts a hand inside his shirt to scratch his armpit. The hair on his chest, exposed by this movement, is the colour of rusty steel wool. After moving his hand vigorously to and fro, he withdraws it and smells his fingers, remarking: 'Heat rash, or something. Can't get rid of it. Feels like two rats screwing in a sock.'

'Maybe clip your nails?'

'What?'

'Clip your nails. My mother always used to say most rashes come from itching with dirty nails.'

'She did, did she! You for real? Lessons in hygiene from a boy straight out the bush!'

'We still wash.'

'What?'

'We still wash in the bush.'

'Watch your fucking place.'

Cogan walks out of the room, leaving him standing under the circulating fan. Has he just got himself sacked?

'Come on!' Cogan shouts from outside. 'Let's have some lunch and get moving.'

Manu follows him into the corridor, the dirty paintwork of which is blistered, here and there showing places where bullets have penetrated through to the pink plaster beneath. Cogan's scrutinising the black nails on one of his big paws, nodding to himself. 'They are pretty gross. Maybe you're right, Manu. I'll do them when we're back. I'm not so old a dog I can't learn new tricks!'

Having eaten samosas at the airport café, the two of them walk out on to the apron on which the aircraft is parked. On the apron, Cogan does what he calls a walk-around, telling Manu to look for things on the fuselage such as buckled skin and popped rivets. There are plenty of these on the Cargomaster. Running his hand over its steel skin, Cogan says they are not such a problem. 'Lot of this is just cosmetic,' he says.

'What's that for?' Manu asks, pointing at a ring protruding where the strut meets the wing.

'For anchoring the plane, case things gets windy.'

Next, Cogan goes down on one knee, reminding Manu of being in church. 'You also gotta make sure there aren't too many cracks in the tyres, too, though there are always some on these old planes.'

He goes on to explain how to check the nose oleo strut for extension, the shimmy damper for security, and the air intake of the turbine for birds' nests or rags.

And a whole lot of other things there are to be checked and told to Manu. It's almost four by the time he mounts the steps to the aircraft, his head spinning with information. And there's more to come when he takes his seat: battery checks, fuel-pump checks, flap checks, so much it's overwhelming.

He has only just absorbed all this other information when Cogan says: 'Control is with me, but – put your hands and feet on the controls on your side, feeling and following, repeating whatever I speak, except when to the tower. Don't do anything to the controls yourself, just feel them move. OK?'

'OK.'

'I'm gonna clear departure with the tower first. You keep quiet. Notice I say Kigali, though. That's where our flight plan's for. Nobody wants to know jackshit about Kamituga!'

He hits the press-to-talk button, the mike's black plastic retractable cord swinging under his chin like a satanic rosary.

After take-off, the plane keeps its upward attitude till Cogan says, 'Twelve thou, that's about ten below her service level. And now she's yours!'

'Mine?' The feeling of lift has lulled Manu into a kind of dream.

'Your control.'

His hands begin to tremble on the horns of the control column, but then Cogan says, 'Relax, kid, make your hands like a feather, but always be ready to act – think of the sky as a pathway for your own will, but don't exert it unless you need to.'

Frowning with concentration, Manu is aware of the power of the machine rumbling through him, envisions it blazing towards the ground at over 200 miles an hour. But nothing happens; it just continues gliding forwards. After a few minutes of terror, he relaxes a little; and as the minutes pass into a quarter of an hour, he feels the stress running out of his body.

To his great surprise, Cogan gets a newspaper out of his flight bag, the Ugandan *New Vision*. He spreads it over his control column and starts reading. The two headlines on the front page read UPDF CROSSES INTO ZAIRE and MASTURBATION BAD FOR MARRIAGE.

'But . . .'

'Chill, kid. I've set the nav, just keep her in straight and level flight.'

Slowly, as the plane makes its way westwards, he begins to enjoy the experience of cruising at 12,000 feet above the Ugandan countryside, deep in the moving now of flight. They more or less follow the Mbarara road, flying over Lyantonde, Lake Mburo and other places – till they pass over Bwindi Forest, heading in the direction of the sun.

Inside, as the plane transits above a glittering green mass of trees, something like desire leaps inside him. Its source is sudden pure joy in the flow of what he is doing in each successive moment, making him feel at one with the air that's moving across the windshield.

I can fly! I can fly!

Cogan looks up from his newspaper, grunts. 'The so-called impenetrable forest. It isn't. That's where I first flew to most, when I came here after leaving the air force – flying fuckwit tourists to see the gorillas. I had two options after I got kicked out: a freight company in Kazakhstan, or here. Made the right choice. Evgeny says I wouldn't have lasted five minutes in Kazakhstan. He goes back there a bit because all his planes are registered there. Me, I use Liberia.'

'I thought Evgeny was Russian,' Manu says, keeping one eye on the artificial horizon, which from this morning he knows provides guidance on pitch and bank.

Cogan laughs. 'He's Russian all right. But Kazakh-reg planes have the call sign Unicorn November and that's handy because it comes out as Flight UN-1234 or whatever. Officials at small airports sometimes assume it's a UN flight – handy for people who have become *biznesmeny* like him.'

'He wasn't always that?'

'No, he was air force like me, but on the other side. That's one of the reasons we do OK out here – on this kind of mission, this kind of life. Me, Evgeny, we think like military. Gerry and Papa, they're a bit different.'

Manu glances at the newspaper draped over the other control column, before venturing to ask, 'Why did you come out of the air force?'

Cogan sighs. 'I was stationed in the UK, in the east of the country. Lakenheath – boring place, flat as fuck. I went off-base without a pass one night, got drunk in a pub and into a fight. Whacked a local construction worker. The military police hauled my ass back to base and I was tested for blood-alcohol level. And that was that, really. Still, I'm happier here. And richer. I was never cut out for a middle-of-the-road life.'

'You had to leave your people?'

'Nah, well . . . the wife had already dumped me. Courtney's back in Carthage, Texas, which was our home town. I've got a boy, Michael; he's the same age as you, give or take. I miss seeing the kid, but not her. So that was the situation: no job, no wife, no chance of an active licence in Europe or the US – I had to come here to get that.'

'When did you come?'

'Mid-1986, just after Museveni and the NRM, whatsit . . . National Resistance Movement, came to power. No cash, no prospects. Couldn't have been bleaker. Still, it wasn't so bad in the end. And I wouldn't have got off my ass if we hadn't gotten divorced. I tell ya, kid, there's no greater spur to putting your life back on track than the contempt of a woman! And here, well, there's just less bullshit. Africa filters out the crap, lets you find peace of mind.'

'What was she like?' Manu asks distractedly, through the vibrations of the plane. He imagines Courtney as somewhat like one of the sun-faded women that caught his eye in the calendars he looked at in the airport; then the processed image gets all mixed up in his head, crossing over with fragments of the ice-cream girl.

'Who?'

'Your wife in Texas.'

'Couldn't tell ya. She's as much a mystery to me now as the day we first got naked in a room together. That went on for years Manu, all through our marriage. Which by the way is an institution I think should be abandoned, even if Aisha has forced me to do it again, mainly because of money. She was a secretary at one of the other air firms, met her over the photocopier! Fucking thing that hardly ever worked and all us freight dogs paid a sub for – we got our own at Normair now – but she bent over real nice, in lycra leggings smooth as syrup. We done fell in love, I do believe, that very day.'

After an hour or so, a sound issues from the panel and a display of red co-ordinates comes on, followed by the letters BUK.

'That's the Bukavu beacon we just went over,' says Cogan. 'I'll take over soon, 'case it gets difficult. Not that difficulty has ever deterred the RPA, Rusyo especially. But first we'll do a checklist scan, see if everything looks OK before you hand over control.'

'We're going to meet Rusyo?'

'Of course.'

Cogan begins to list off things on the checklist – Manu saying yes or OK or no as the case requires, now and then being corrected, but as one or other of them speaks, successive surges of panic rush through him, each one concentrated in glimpses of the archbishop flapping towards him from the fence of SINELAC.

He says at one point, in a half-strangled tone, 'OK,' and Cogan replies, 'Not quite, the HSI is a bit off in fact.'

'That's . . . ?'

'Horizontal situation indicator. I'll fix it. Control mine.'

While Cogan's correcting the plane's attitude, Manu's still barred in by a mental language of verticals, being cast back down into thoughts of what happened in Bukavu, on the ground below – ground already gone, in fact, as they're now well beyond that town of memories.

As the Cargomaster descends towards Kamituga, a line of orange fire sweeps below the plane. Cogan says: 'Uh-oh fuckedy freak show, here we go,' then – speaking into his mike – 'This is Echo Lima, Echo Lima, requesting sitrep Kamituga.'

For a few seconds, as the plane falls through moonlit clouds, all that can be heard is the drone of the turbine and heavy static from the radio. Then comes a faint reply, penetrating the wash of static, 'Echo Lima, this is RPA forward command Kamituga, abort, repeat abort, we're taking heavy fire down here.'

'Balls,' says Cogan, reaching for the mike again. 'Kamituga, this is Echo Lima, unable to comply – we're already on our descent, no fuel to make a change.'

He wipes his forehead before speaking again. 'So fix it down there till it's charlie. Coming in whatever! Get those lumisticks out your ass.'

'Lumisticks are chemical landing lights,' he explains to Manu. 'Green shit that gives you cancer if you break open too many in a lifetime!'

Tracer fire begins creating deadly lines in the sky around the Cargomaster. A rattling noise rises from the ground, and then Cogan's shouting, 'Hold on to your hat, kid,' as he puts the plane into a steep dive, streaking down through the splintered night.

As the plane dives, he adds, as if it were simply nothing, 'That stuff that sounds like a typing pool, it's heavy machine guns.'

A burst of red light, flashing below, pulls Manu's eyes sharply across as Cogan yanks the Cargomaster into a very tight turn.

'RPG,' Cogan says. 'Don't fret kid, just Rusyo's boys doing the business. It means the FAZ are to the left, so we go oppo.'

Deep in the lust of his work, now Cogan's pulling out of the dive, banking round. It's scary all this, taking place as a plume of grey smoke, issuing from the destroyed FAZ position, rises into the moonlight.

'Should be OK now, heh heh, someone got seriously toasted, anyhows.'

Manu still doesn't understand fully what's happening. But it does seem things are calming. The Cargomaster is level again. Breathing heavily, Cogan begins circling over the landing site, waiting for the smoke to clear.

When it does, what's visible is not what Cogan termed 'green shit that gives you cancer' but a double line of faint blue glows.

'Coke and paraffin, my old friends,' he says, 'I've come to talk to you again . . .' then laughs.

'What?'

'Ain't got no lumisticks, the lousy fuckers. Or barrels like we had at Rutshuru. They're laying out the runway with Coke tins filled with paraffin-soaked sand. Still, we're all yappedy doo-dah now.'

He grabs the mike. 'Kamituga, Kamituga, this is Echo Lima. Looks like you have fixed the ell-zee. We good to go?'

'Charlie charlie,' says a voice Manu half recognises on the other side, then pins down as Rusyo's.

Cogan says, 'Kid, case you dunno, double charlie means everything's cool.'

'But what's ell-zee?' asks Manu, feeling like an idiot.

'Landing zone.' Sweat is pouring off Cogan now, soaking his safari jacket.

He increases the airspeed, pointing the plane at the ground, out of which the shapes of hills and trees begin to bulk. Then makes a sweep across the strip, before turning in preparation to land.

The Cargomaster bumps down, braking on the strip, dark apart from the little illuminations either side.

'OK?' Cogan asks.

'Yes.' But he's not really.

'Right, let's go find Major Rusyo. Say, I heard it was a nick-name, that, meaning the grinder, that so?'

'It comes from *urusyo*, the bottom stone for grinding sorghum flour.'

'Sounds like they got it topsy-turvy, 'cos every time I meet him he always wants to be the one on top.'

Manu says nothing, knowing well enough by now about the grinding machine that's not just Rusyo, but the whole security apparatus of the new Rwandan state. What a fool he's been, he realises, to believe he might escape the history that's following him, nose to the ground.

Chapter 7

'Come on, then, with luck Rusyo will have enough fuel for us to return with the generator in the morning,' Cogan says, as the plane rolls to the end of the runway.

Manu can't move, hearing that name again. Frozen in his harness, it's as if his position is not that of a trainee pilot but an experienced one who, having fallen out of the sky and crashed, is unable to move his trapped limbs.

'What's the matter, kid?' Cogan asks.

'Rusyo.'

'Yeah? Well, he won't be taking a stick to anyone on my payroll. Unbuckle your harness. Don't let them fuck with you; if they do, I'll be on them like white on rice. But don't show fear on your own account. These guys are like dogs: if you're gonna shit your pants, they smell it before you're even done.'

Trembling, Manu gets out of his seat.

Once outside the plane, standing by the strip – along which the Coke-can candles are beginning to gutter – he can see that they have landed on the edge of a banana plantation, parts of which have been burned by munitions. An acrid smell remains in the air. Bright clouds are chasing each other across the moonlit sky.

From the blasted vegetation, the lights of two vehicles appear, one a truck pulling a small trailer, the other a pickup. Four Rwandan soldiers get out of the truck and start heaving the heavy generator on the trailer towards the plane. Cogan opens the hatch for them, saying, 'Careful of my rims, last time you guys knocked them out of true – Suraj here?'

One of the soldiers nods, his face lit by the vehicle lamps and moonlight.

Manu follows Cogan over to the pickup, in the cab of which is a man of South Asian origin wearing a leather jacket. He gets out, embraces Cogan, who says, 'How's business, Suraj?'

'Fantastic!' Suraj has got white jeans on; the way they glow in the lights make his legs seem like plastic. 'The clearance of this runway was a risk for the product, though. Always a risk, Cogan. Who's this?'

'Manu, my new trainee.'

Suraj takes him by the hand and shakes, saying with what seems like genuine enthusiasm, 'You're lucky, *Coganbhai* is the best flyer of them all.'

'Evgeny might have a different view,' Cogan says.

'He's a better negotiator,' the trader concedes, 'but not such a good pilot.'

'If you say so, Suraj — let's go.'

The drive takes them along jungle tracks, hidden from the moonlight by the canopy. Now and then, in the swerve of headlights, Manu sees huge gouges in the green, from where mortars have fallen or RPGs exploded.

During the journey, Suraj asks, 'Can you do me a trip next week to Dar to pick up a cargo of electronics? These boys are mad for them.'

'Too busy right now,' Cogan says.

Through the gap between the front seats, Manu notices that Suraj has a pistol in the back belt of his white jeans — almost sitting on it as he drives, which seems dangerous. Must have the safety on. He wishes he could somehow get out of this meeting with Rusyo. But it's impossible to run again.

The pickup arrives at an army camp in a grove in the jungle. Cooking fires and two large arc lamps with steel reflectors, like satellite dishes, add to the fall of moonlight.

Fizzing with anxiety, Manu follows Cogan and Suraj through the encampment, in which Rwandan soldiers and AFDL irregulars are lounging. Some are cooking or washing, but most are just lying about amid the tents, smoking *bangi* or swigging from battered plastic bottles. Women with shaggy hair and long, thin limbs sheathed in colourful material – girls, really – are walking through the camp selling live chickens, sorghum beer, the electronics Suraj mentioned (one has a necklace of headphones beneath her dreadlocks).

Suraj brings them to a bar, a mud hut with a rickety wooden frontage covered with dry banana leaves and plastic sheeting. Next to the bar entrance, as if orienting the very centre of the camp, stand two crossed wooden staves on which the brown-and-white skin of a cow has been stretched out to dry. Manu knows that Major Rusyo must be waiting inside. He's reluctant to follow Cogan and Suraj in, hesitating at the threshold, but knows that he must if he's to keep Cogan's trust.

Rusyo is indeed sitting there, under the yellow light of a Tilley lamp, on a rough wooden bench. Recognition is by his side – somehow Manu didn't expect him to be there too.

They're drinking from dusty clay pots of country beer, with chasers of the same plastic-bottled spirits that the soldiers are quaffing outside. A plump, corkscrew-haired young woman is serving at the bar, her face covered in tribal scars. Behind her, on a shelf, are a range of amulets made of horn and animal fur.

Rusyo is in uniform, the full Sam Browne; Recognition's wearing a second-hand suit and cheap sunglasses.

'Cogan, my favourite American!' Rusyo cries, on seeing him come in. He stands up, shakes the big man's hand, saying, 'Sorry the clearance of the airfield was a bit late – it was more difficult than we expected.'

Manu tries to shrink into the shadows by the doorway, but Recognition is already glowering at him with what seem like hate-filled eyes. He looks drunk, squeezing his small plastic spirit bottle in and out.

Manu expects that what's in the bottle is a moonshine-type liquor – called *lotoko* in Lingala, *pétrole* in local French, and *kanyanga* in Kinyarwanda. Deadly stuff in any language, brewed from maize or cassava.

'Right, sit down, let's do our business,' says Rusyo, rubbing his pale-brown hands. He at least does not seem to have noticed

Manu, who remains by the doorway as Cogan and Suraj take their seats.

As they work out a complex deal involving export of the generator to India, an invoice raised in Dubai and payment made from Rwanda, the barmaid brings over a plateful of fried plantain chips, which Recognition begins munching loudly.

As he eats, his red eyes do not leave Manu's face. Recognition has begun the tobacco habit, he notices, as well as abandoning his uniform. Clouds of smoke rise around him in the hut's dim light.

Manu tries to ignore Recognition's poisonous gaze by studying the amulets above the bar, as if these might protect him.

It's only at the end of the meeting that Cogan, now looking a little green, having consumed at least one of the plastic bottles of home-brew spirit, brings up Manu as a subject.

'Hey Rusyo, you see that young guy standing by the door.'

'Of course, I saw him when you came in. Who is he?'

'One of your AFDL.'

'Not quite,' mutters Recognition.

'Well, he tells me that you beat on him, Major.'

'Did I really?' says Rusyo, looking at Manu over the muttony round of Cogan's shoulder. 'I do have to beat a lot of them. Some of these Banyamulenge boys lack gumption.'

'Well this one doesn't,' counters Cogan. 'Come over, Manu.'

He walks towards them, bending his long body down, as if the person who flew through the sky is resisting being reduced back to an older form: that of one who must identify as Tutsi, or sub-Tutsi, whatever external designation one's forced to acknowledge.

'The famous Manu Kwizera!' says Recognition, blowing out a cloud of cigarette smoke.

'I remember you now,' says Rusyo, silkily. 'The one who shot at the archbishop, without a say-so. Recognition found you at some farm attacked by the FAZ, yes?'

Manu straightens up. Half glimpsing Cogan's kind eyes, he remembers the pilot saying, *Don't let them fuck with you.*

'Yes, I shot at the archbishop. Or near. You made me. I think I missed, and it was your soldiers who killed him.'

Rusyo's face contorts as he looks at Manu. 'And I guess you know *my* name.'

Manu doesn't reply.

'You deserted,' Rusyo says.

'That's all in the past. I'm a trainee pilot with Normair now.'

'That's a fact,' Cogan says. 'And we're all in the same game, aren't we?'

'I hope so,' Rusyo says, giving Manu another horrible look. 'And I suppose he is much more useful to us as a pilot than he ever would have been as a foot soldier. But I don't want any funny business – and that goes for you, too, Cogan. Whatever has happened before, you're working for me right now, not Museveni or Mobutu or anyone else.'

'That's on the cusp of a very serious accusation, Rusyo,' Cogan says. 'If I wanted to get a generator to Mumbai myself, I wouldn't be talking that way. Just sayin' . . .'

'I was only making an observation, Cogan.' As if to emphasise the point, Rusyo brushes the pistol on his thigh.

'Well that's fine and dandy, Major, let's have another drink. I'm hungry, got any more of those fake fries?'

Later that night, lying in his loaned RPA tent and sleeping bag, desperate for morning and the return to Entebbe, Manu fiddles with the threads of his own frayed identity. He considers that he won't find anywhere safe in this complex knot of Congolese, Rwandans and Ugandans; he must simply be a freight dog now, just like Cogan said. That's my group, that's my team, that's the badge I must wear. He's glad he took the American's advice, stood up for himself in Rusyo's company.

But what happens next is that someone else unzips his tent. 'Hey, Manu!'

It's Recognition. Manu clambers out. Although a little dimmed, the moon is still shining and he can see his compatriot's face, looking even more intoxicated than before, a cigarette stuck in his mouth like a twig on the edge of a tree.

'Yes?' He's trying to hold on to his new pilot persona as he comes out of the tent.

'I want to talk to you.'

Manu resists the done-me-wrong sentiment that comes to his lips, some folkloric fragment of Tutsi animus against the Hutu; or maybe the other way round: it's used both ways, that song. Instead he says, simply, 'What is it?'

The reply surprises him, like one of those unusual attitudes when aircraft aren't on the expected straight and level, that Cogan told him about in the training session.

Because what Recognition says is this: 'I am sorry for what happened to you. It has put me in your debt.'

'I don't understand.'

'These RPA, they're fucking us, Manu. They're fucking Kabila, too, even if the fat fool doesn't know it.' He seems different to the intellectual person he was before, even the pattern of his speech having changed, coarsened.

'Us?' Is what Recognition says true – it might be – or is there some kind of deceit going on?

'Don't be stupid deliberately. Us Congolese Tutsis, Banyamulenge, Banyarwanda alike. Since you went, I've realised this.'

'What do you mean, exactly?'

The smoke of Recognition's cigarette whorls upwards. 'Take that generator. It's the property of Congolese people. Property of Bukavu people. Not something to be sold off to fill Major Rusyo's pockets.'

'I thought you were his friend – his protégé.'

'I was. But he, all those top Rwandan echelons, they're just cheating us now.'

'So what're you going to do? Why are you out of uniform, anyhow?'

'They've made me an intelligence officer. But I hate it. It's dirty work. So I don't know what to do now. I just wanted to tell you. Because even though I was rude to you – I was drunk, still am drunk – well, I realised I should say this.'

'OK, but I've been trying to leave all that behind.'

'Can I say something else to you, in confidence?' Crouched on his haunches, Recognition seems to have accepted Manu's new role as a pilot, looking at him in the moonlight with something that might almost be admiration.

'If you like,' Manu shrugs.

'I'm trying to get together a group of us . . .'

'That word "us" again.'

'Banyamulenge, Manu. We need to stick together. Kabila's support, Rusyo's support, it's just a matter of expediency, what's convenient for them. All that bullshit about us being sprung from Rwandan soil that he spoke of—'

'We're not even a tribe, we're just outcasts, like we've always been.'

'That kind of reduction's exactly what I'm trying to overcome. Go beyond tribalism.'

'You're getting into politics, Recognition?'

Manu sees his jaw clench. Have I gone too far, he wonders, straight after he's asked the question. Recognition's still a violent man, despite this apparent new-found wisdom.

'I'm just trying to protect what's truly ours. Safeguard our interests.'

Recognition pulls a white handkerchief out of his jacket pocket, holds it suspended for a second, like he's about to give Manu a final farewell – then blows his nose noisily, waiting for a reply. Far away, too distant to hear, a flare rises into the night sky.

'Look. I told you already – I've left that world behind.'

With that, he turns and climb back into the tent. Only after he's zipped it up does Recognition speak again: 'I know you think you have, but you never will.'

Is he right? Manu wonders, once Recognition has stumbled off.

And a little later, after he has fallen asleep, again the relentless unconscious goes to work on Manu's mind, processing particles of his experience in a haphazard manner, as if they were molecules of air on the trailing edge of an aeroplane's wing, plunging off unpredictably.

During the flight to Entebbe the next morning, after spending an irritating half-hour industriously singing a song called 'Ain't

No More Cane on the Brazos' (belting out its chorus, which is: *they ground it all up in molasses*), meanwhile passing control of the aircraft between the two of them like a relay runner's baton, Cogan finally asks: 'So what was that all about, I mean last night, kid – how'd you and Rusyo end up making a target of a holy man, back in that duckshoot in Bukavu?'

His sweat-lidded eyes slide sideways – as if to say, no need to be coy with me, kid, I'm a guy with secrets of my own. But Manu doesn't want to say much, so he gives Cogan only a rough outline of what happened at Nyamwera market. How could a *muzungu* understand any of this anyhow, how could he even imagine what was involved, flying along under the scented corona of his hair lotion?

At the end, once Manu's partial story has run its course, Cogan says only: 'Quite a tale – but it's all behind you now.'

Chapter 8

Over the next few weeks, lessons continue in the ramshackle Normair office. When Cogan says, 'In meeting a thunderhead, fly along its flank,' Manu doesn't know what he means. Cogan has to explain that 'flank' means 'side', then Manu comprehends: *Oh, like the flank of a cow* – like Joséphine's with its cigarette boxes.

He knows that word only in the French, *flanc*, though it's the same in English, more or less – not being in translation one of those *faux amis* of which Don Javier used to speak: 'false friends' that seem as if they might transfer easily from one language to another, but don't. But the errors are mostly to do with flying rather than language, though flying is, he thinks, maybe another kind of language too.

With each of these failures, Cogan becomes increasingly unforgiving. On 20 December, at the end of this bout of humiliation, he says, offhandedly: 'That's enough for now, you can have five days' vacation, I've got to go back to the US to see my kid Michael – a son should be with his old man at Christmas. You'll have to help Aisha in the bar, though. And Evgeny says he'll increase your hours while I'm away. It's a Christmas Day job though, that Russki don't rest. A flight to Europe, too.'

'Europe! that's OK by me,' Manu says, thinking of his dashed hopes of going to university there.

'I bet. But don't get your hopes up, Europe's not all it's cracked up to be.'

'Where are we going?'

'Best he fills you in on the details. Oh, yeah.' He reaches into his safari-suit pocket, hands over a dark-blue object. 'Congratulations bud, you're now a Ugandan citizen.'

Manu opens the passport, looks in wonderment at the portrait page. His real name, date of birth, everything a fact except the nationality and place of birth: Mbarara, a town in western Uganda. A place where many people of Rwandan heritage have settled. Must be why Cogan chose it. 'Thank you.'

'All part of the service.'

Later that day, Evgeny drops by to tell Manu that he'll pick him up at 10.30 a.m. on the 25th at the bar.

Manu asks if it can be 11.30 because of church.

Evgeny laughs. 'OK, doesn't make much difference, and I'm sure God will keep the sky on hold for us. Oh, and bring shorts and trainers, and a T-shirt. There's a gym where we're staying; it's a good idea to pump some iron between long flights, else your limbs seize up.'

By Christmas Eve, Cogan's in Carthage, Texas. Aisha closes The Passenger at lunchtime, at the end of a heavy week of parties: office parties, family parties, army parties. Some vacation! Manu comes out of the kitchen, carrying the mop, and there she is, sitting at the dimly lit bar, smoking as usual, dull gleams showing on the gloss of her hair, which is more frizzed-out than normal.

The radio is making a wailing noise, interspersed with gusts of static. Aisha looks tired, even a little sad, as she turns over the pages of a ledger in which Cogan keeps accounts for Normair; he has two, a black one for the bar and a red one for Normair. Manu wonders why she's looking at the red book rather than the black one.

'Hello,' she says, brightly enough, belying Manu's impression of her mood. 'Thanks for your work in the past few days, you did well.'

He's flabbergasted at this sudden conversion of the evil stepmother, as he's come to think of her – then, replacing the mop in its metal pot, considers how she ended up with Cogan. Perhaps it was just his kindness, as that can go a long way. He suspects, though, that it was more Aisha's need for financial security – each of her days as an ill-paid secretary a fretful repeat of the next until the one Cogan came up behind her, there at the photocopier, communal and capricious, that Normair shared with the other two-bit air firms based at EBB.

'These accounts are terrible, it's a wonder we get by at all,' she says, slamming shut the ledger. 'What're you up to tomorrow?'

'I guess I will go to church in the morning, then I have a flight with Evgeny in the afternoon.'

She lifts the cigarette to her mouth, that same which used to bite at him in catty remarks when he first arrived. Suddenly, it bites again. 'If you like Evgeny so much, why don't you go and work for him?'

'What?'

'He's the person ruining Cogan's business. You did not realise?'

'No.'

'Well, it's true. Be careful what you say to him about our operations.'

Tick tock, goes the zinc-framed clock on the wall, its minute hand jerking visibly onwards.

'I will.'

After changing into smarter clothes – he has a few more now – Manu walks through Entebbe. Crossing Portal Road in a daze, he nearly gets run over by a Nile Breweries truck. Finally he comes to Kintu Road and then the beach, where the mild break-ers of Lake Victoria are delivering on to the sand traces of water hyacinth. He stops to watch agitating curls of lavender petal and glossy green stalk, over which giant dragonflies are hovering.

High above the lake, clouds are chasing. He's learned that in Luganda, knowing by now a few words of one of Uganda's principal languages, it's called Nalubaale, not Victoria – the latter was introduced by the British to honour their queen.

Looking at the water, he envisages the muddy corpses that during the genocide were said to have rolled down the tributary of the Kagera River that feeds the lake. Bloated bodies of Tutsis mainly, but of Hutu moderates, too. He reconsiders the sickening scenes that he witnessed during the clearance of the camps above Lake Kivu when the Hutus became the victims. It's too easy to judge the second set of events as a direct consequence of the first.

He watches a small brown dog battle with a kite for control of a dead tilapia. Its teeth round the tilapia's tail, the dog's kicking up sand for traction, pulling against the kite that's beating wings about the fish, a claw hooked into one of the fish's gills.

Suddenly the dog and bird separate – did the gill tear? With blood round its mouth, the little brown dog runs off with the fishtail, into the cover of a clump of palm trees. Carrying the remains of the tilapia, the kite flaps up between two brown columns of lake fly, spooling across the sheet of blue-green water.

He walks on – into the still, hot feeling of the hour, the warmth of which, along with the feeling of sand between his toes (he's taken off his trainers) is encouraging him to think no more on horrors, but to consider the simple pleasures of being by a lake, where nothing is more natural than enjoying things just as they are.

Further along, he notices a woman walking ahead of him – her hips swaying *mia hamsini, mia hamsini*, in the 100:50 ratio girls in this part of the world spend hours perfecting. It's the ice-cream girl, he realises: the same one he saw mount the *boda* on his shopping trip, the same one who was swimming at Aero Beach. She's wearing a *kanga* of terracotta fabric with a tree pattern and Swahili proverbs written in black – the one across her bum reading, '*Wa nyuma mbele hafiki*'. This amuses him, because it means 'The one who is behind does not arrive in front.' He watches her make her way to the waterline.

She takes off her flip-flops, pulls up the *kanga*, sits on the sand, letting the surf wash over her feet. Catching up with her, Manu passes another proverb out of the side of his mouth: '*Usiufuate mguu unakokwenda*' – 'Don't follow your foot where it is going!'

She turns her regal head to look at him, her eyes flashing mistrust – no, it's tears in fact. He feels like an idiot.

'I'm sorry, I don't speak much Swahili,' she says in English, swiping a wrist across her eyes. 'Do I know you from somewhere?'

He stutters with embarrassment. 'No, yes, well . . . I saw the proverb on your *kanga*.'

'Oh. I don't know what that means; I just liked the colour.'

She stands up quickly, folding her arms as if to protect herself. Slipping her wet, sandy feet back into her flip-flops, she looks at him hard. 'I'm sure I've seen you somewhere.'

'I was at Aero Beach a few days back. You were swimming. And maybe you saw me before in Entebbe town once. You were eating an ice cream. My name's Manu. Well, Emmanuel.'

'A French name? You're Rwandan?'

'Congolese. I live here now, anyhow.'

'I like swimming,' she says, distractedly. She has a tiny tattoo on her neck, crosses made with lines of dark-green dots, matching the colour of her eyes. 'One of my regrets about coming back here is remembering how many Ugandans don't like swimming.'

'Crocodiles!'

'Probably, but there aren't any round here.' She gives a little laugh. 'Least I don't think so.'

'Where did you come back from?'

'A girl's boarding school in England, where they taught me how to forget to be African. They gave me hell for this.' She touches the tattoo on her neck, then smiles. 'Now I'm relearning.'

'You didn't forget *mia hamsini*, though,' he says, hardly believing the boldness of the words coming out of his mouth.

She frowns, as if she doesn't understand, then gives an embarrassed laugh as if she might have done, finishing by asking: 'Have you been following me?'

'No! I was just walking. I saw you, noticed your *kanga*; I really like those proverbs . . .' His voice tails off; suddenly feeling shy, he doesn't know what to say now.

She sniffs, lifts her head, begins walking off.

'Wait!' he shouts, 'What's your name?' And: 'Happy Christmas!'

But she doesn't turn, just keeps on walking. Manu watches her, keeping his eyeline level with the horizon into which she eventually disappears. Take care; that's what he wants to say, frankly desiring right then (whatever less romantic people might feel) to go to the end of the sky with her, doing the caring himself.

He walks to a stand of palm trees, sits under their green fronds and tall grey trunks. Looking up, he squeezes his eyes closed – as if his future is up in the sky but can only be imagined rather than seen – then opens them, looking down at his present. The sand round the base of the trunks is dirty, thicker than that on the beach proper. More wet chalk than sand, really. He picks up a coconut, hefts it from palm to palm, thinking again about the girl.

He starts weeping. Not for her – why was she crying, anyway; what's a rich girl like that got to cry about? – but for his mother, his father, his sister: for every loss already confirmed.

After a while, when he's expelled the mucus heaved up by his sobs, and it no longer feels quite as if God himself, just Jesus, is sitting on his chest, a bunch of ragtag teenagers run by. They're laughing as they kick a football to one another across the sand, gnawing on sticks of sugar cane like Manu and his friends used to.

The ball rolls over towards him. He gets up, kicks it back.

And now he's playing with them, running along the beach, listening when they call for the ball and calling for it on his own account, each player striving for his next piece of beach, but watchful of its risks . . . pieces of rope and fishing net, splintered fibreglass panels from old boats, empty cans of Mazola oil, Rhodes peaches, plastic bottles that roll underfoot like booby traps.

An hour or so later, once the light has begun to dim rapidly, the outline of the football distorting even as it flies through the air, Manu sits with them under another little clump of palm trees – where he discovers his fellow players to be a heterogenous group of Ugandans, Congolese and Rwandans, part of a troupe of dancers and singers called Ndere. From *endere*, meaning flute, they say. Another new Lugandan word.

One of the footballers, David Kisase, turns out to be Munyam-ulenge like Manu, but a bit younger. The two of them chat for a while. Manu winces as David recounts similar experiences to his own – how he eventually found his way to Uganda, working as a garbage picker until he stumbled on Ndere Troupe. It's an organisation set up to support orphans, he explains, using music, dance and theatre to address what he terms, as if quoting from a brochure, 'trauma and African cultural heritage'.

'Come to our show tonight,' David says, his style of speaking returning more to normal. 'Then you'll understand how to forget all the shit that's happened to us. There's another Munyamulenge in our group by the way. Not here today. Matthias Ngandu is his name. Nine p.m. Ndere's just off the Kisasi Road.'

'Can't tonight, got some business with one of my employers tomorrow.'

'On Christmas Day?'

''Fraid so.'

'What d'you do?' David asks, and Manu tells him.

'Boy, that's really something, better than a gig like ours. Well, if you can make it another night, we're on every Wednesday and Friday, same time. It'll be fun, I promise!'

'One day I will,' Manu says, embracing his kinsman – they're both still really sweaty – and shaking hands with the others. Watching them trek towards town, to get a *matutu* back to Kampala in time for their show, he's embarrassed, almost shamed, that he's been making too much of things that some of them, with no better a history than his own – for there were certainly murdered families there too – are facing down with equanimity, measured cheerfulness, even eagerness.

Once the other guys have gone, he sits a little longer in the darkness, under the palm trees, thinking now about 'Ndere' coming from 'flute' and how maybe there are other options open to him besides flying, despite what David said; also about the tree into which the FAZ guy threw his own flute; and then a third tree, the one he hid in during the camp killings . . .

Manu starts rubbing his head, like he's trying to scrub a shirt on a washing stone, to make the bad thoughts go away.

Once his feelings ease, he walks back through Entebbe, which is coming alive for the night, people gathering and chatting in the lit-up frontages of shops and bars. Smoke fills the air from street-side barbeques, on which skewers of goat meat, beef and chicken are cooking, alongside maize cobs, sweet-smelling bananas, rolexes. Thin, clever dogs slink in the gloom round the stalls, creating a predictable pattern, suddenly disrupted when they pounce for a scrap.

He buys a rolex – a Ugandan speciality – sinks his teeth into its curled confection of omelette, fried vegetables and chapatti, all served in a second roll of newspaper.

Glimpses of hairdresser's, hardware, tailor's shops flit by as he walks in the direction of The Passenger, each doorway illuminated with electric light or kerosene lamps.

Under one of these, batting away insects, Manu reads the grease-stained page of newspaper in which his rolex came. The headline declares: MOBUTU AILING AS ANGOLANS ARRIVE IN BUKAVU FOR RPA TALKS.

MPLA officials Alfonso Mascarenhas and Nuno Gonçalves arrived this week in the Rwandan-held port city to meet with two RPA officers, Colonel Patrick Karageya and Major Gustave Rusyo, along with a number of UPDF strategists. The three parties have agreed an alliance, said a UPDF source, with the twin aim of strangling Angolan rebel outfit UNITA and ousting Mobutu, their long-term host.

'With luck on side,' said the source, 'a triumphing democratic alliance between Uganda, Rwanda and Angola should soon settle matters in the ongoing conflict in eastern Zaire that has brought so many refugees into our country. We're all agreed we want to rid this continent of Mobutu, who has stood in the way of progress for so long.'

However, the Zairean president, arrived back from his villa at Cap Martin on the French Riviera, after recuperating from cancer treatment in Switzerland, was recently given a massive welcome by over a million people on his return to Kinshasa.

Mobutu is said to have secured with French and Serbian assistance the support of a 'White Legion' of mercenaries under Colonel Christian Tavernier. Having been in combat with them just this last week (see MOBUTU'S KEYSTONE KOPS, right), Ugandan People's Defence Force staffer Brigadier Faithful Murumuna characterised these fellows as 'third-rate *abazungu* who spend so much of their time getting drunk and grubbing for money that one almost longs for the days of Mad

Mike Hoare, Jacques Schramme and Bob Denard, when at least we Africans had proper white badasses to contend with!'

Brigadier Faithful's tone makes Manu laugh, as he sits munching the last of the rolex. He tries to square the report with the big-shouldered guy he saw coming off Cogan's plane that first day, then met with Gerry at the bar.

And overall, this day, this Christmas Eve, seems to him to have been a good one, as it comes to its close, better than many days in the horrible months that have led up to it. He heads back to his little room at The Passenger, thinking later as he lies in bed of the *mia hamsini* hip-swing of the green-eyed girl, the skitter of the ball on the sand, and the taste of the rolex. All these seem to him now like things that could help dilute the cocktail of feelings – grief, disconnectedness, guilt at being a fugitive – that's been poisoning him since he walked out of Bukavu, slinking like one of those thin, clever dogs up the volcanic spine of the continent.

Chapter 9

For a Christmas breakfast, Manu has coffee with milk, dipping into it some stale bread he finds in the kitchen of The Passenger. Surprisingly good but too sweet: Ugandan bread's like cake, he reckons, compared to Congolese bread.

On the way to church, he joins beaded-haired girls in frilly frocks: little angels they seem like, better even than the real ones he used to believe in. Joining solemn little chaps in suits and bow ties. Joining mothers in their smartest, shiniest *busutis* and braided weaves. Joining fathers in spotless white *kanzus* and dark jackets – as they all promenade to the Christmas Mass.

As he walks among these people he remembers other Christmas times back home, when his conscience was clean, and his family still alive.

He enters this other church, the Sacred Heart in Entebbe, sits behind some blue-costumed nuns, stowing his long legs under the pew. In the sermon, the priest speaks of being grounded in grace, which he characterises with words like timeless, words like golden, saying grace is the effect of God's understanding in the face of human failure.

Manu feels impatient, listening to all this, reckoning he's floundering too deep in the filth of a fallen, time-ridden world ever to access anything like grace again. Is it simply habit that's brought me here? he wonders. He does not take Communion, telling himself that the bread of life, like Ugandan bread, is too sweet for someone who's been soured like him, someone whose core entity has been so changed, the cross torn out of his heart.

As he steps outside, however, into the bonhomie of greetings between friends and relatives in the porch, a curious after-glimmer of the sermon glows in his mind – not the words themselves but something behind them, unsounded but sensuous, still trying to hook him back into the sky. It's almost like the feeling he had after his initiation ceremony, of something artificial – ritualistic – but imaginatively authentic at the same time.

At The Passenger he finds Evgeny waiting for him. Sitting smoking on the bonnet of his vehicle, feet on the bumper, leather flat cap on his head, the Russian strikes a worldly pose that refutes any spiritual thoughts.

Evgeny jumps down. With his Thuraya satphone holstered in a thick, light-brown belt on his jeans, and wearing a T-shirt, he looks more like a workman than a pilot as he shakes Manu by the shoulders. 'Happy Christmas!'

Manu fetches from his room a flight bag containing a change of clothes and the gym kit Evgeny demanded he bring, and they get into the 4×4. Evgeny's white Isuzu is less boxy than Cogan's Cherokee, and less battered, too. 'Hope you're feeling holy,' he quips on the way to the airport. 'Got your passport?'

Manu taps his shirt pocket. 'Yes.'

'And a visa for the Czech Republic?'

A wave of panic: something he was meant to do and hadn't? 'No, I didn't know . . .'

Evgeny laughs harshly. 'Just teasing! I have one for you – Cogan gave me the details.'

On arrival at EBB, Evgeny asks for the passport. Taking a small piece of paper and a bottle of Cow Gum out of his own flight bag, he pastes in the visa.

'It's not real, Manu,' he explains, patting the bag into which he's returned the plastic pot of Cow Gum. 'None of the documents in this are. But they will get our *biznes* done. Got another present for you too, on the plane – one of my old flight jackets. Cogan said you'd never been to Europe before . . . cold compared to here! Come on, let's go.'

Manu follows Evgeny across the tarmac to his Antonov AN-12, a big beast of a plane covered in scars and oil stains.

Their destination, Evgeny tells him after take-off, is Brno in the Czech Republic, where they're picking up weapons for the RPA, making five stops on the 3500-mile journey to refuel. Manu immediately squashes down his feelings about the client being the RPA. Specifically, the job involves collecting munitions with false end-user certificates and delivering them to Kigali, the Rwandan capital. During the flight Evgeny explains how to create the false documents.

'I just get a printer in Kampala to do mine. You have to be a bit clever with the serial numbers, in case the authorities check, but they rarely do. Like magic, cargo is released! The key is the countersignature for a clean end-user country. Ours are counter-signed by a guy who used to be in the defence ministry of the Ivory Coast. The Ivory Ghost, I call him, because he's been out of office for years. That's why our flight plan back is for Abidjan, but we'll just skirt it, wiggle in through Equatorial Guinea and across Zaire to Rwanda – western part of the Gauntlet.'

'What's that?'

'I'll explain when we're in it. And hey, en route we'll be able to get you type rating for the Antonov.'

Just as Evgeny predicted, the pick-up of the arms goes off fine, and just as Cogan predicted, Manu's underwhelmed by his first experience of Europe. Brno's ancient and full of grand buildings, but its pastry shops and cafés are peopled with unfriendly faces, it seems to him.

'Maybe it's because I am Russian and you are black,' jokes Evgeny, after two women they chat to in the hotel bar leave without explanation. Both were plump and wore roll-neck sweaters, jackets with shoulder pads; one had a very large grey handbag which sat on her knees like a lump of concrete during the whole conversation, which proceeded in a halting mixture of Russian, French and broken English.

Listening to the blues playing on the hotel speakers, Manu finishes the herby spirit Evgeny said he should try. 'This stuff's as sweet as a love story,' Evgeny says, his tongue flickering over his moustache. 'Never forget, Manu – what we're in, isn't that!'

The morning of their departure, after the weights session with Evgeny in the dusty gym of the hotel, he goes for a walk in the streets. Children on a school bus make monkey gestures. Toiling back to the hotel in Evgeny's old flying jacket — trudging through slushy streets, under painted eaves stacked with snow — he wonders if he could ever live among white Europeans.

During the last leg of the flight back, over Equatorial Guinea, which Evgeny terms 'the sphincter of West Africa', the Russian climbs to about 12,000 feet, turns off all radio emissions and enters the Gauntlet, the term he said he'd explain later and now does. It covers most of Zaire, southern Sudan and the CAR, parts of Uganda, Zambia, Tanzania and Malawi — 'a radar-free zone full of unreported aircraft', he says. Then he gives over control to Manu, because — as he pithily puts it — 'in the Gauntlet no one gives a flying fuck who's fucking flying.'

Manu's shoes are still wet from snow, and his thighs and biceps ache from the weights Evgeny made him lift, but he manages the big plane OK. As they reappear on Kigali radar, Evgeny takes back control. 'Hey, want to come for supper tonight?' he asks. 'My wife's just back from the Emirates, where she's been setting up a new house. Two of my kids are already in school there.'

'That would be good,' Manu says. The excitement of having had the chance to helm such a big ship has made him hungry.

Evgeny has to make a tight move between two mountains on the way into Kigali; as they pass between sheer rock faces, without much clearance, Manu wonders if he, were he still flying, could have pulled it off so finely. The drop-off of the arms goes fine too, though as they refuel he's constantly expecting Rusyo to appear and haul him off for punishment. But now, having faced down the Rwandan officer once, it's more a case of disquiet than outright fear. And it doesn't happen anyway, reminding of him of a wise lesson he'll keep for later in his life, which that so much of human stress involves bad outcomes we imagine in error, foolishly seeding the future with their possibility, when another option, that of hope, is still always in play.

Chapter 10

Evgeny's apartment block in Entebbe has two giant, ivory-like tusks over its portico. The Russian rings the buzzer – 'never have keys, always lose them' – waits till a sleepy, one-armed *askari* appears from behind one of the tusks and lets them both in. The empty sleeve of the watchman's greatcoat flaps in the breeze that's developing from the lake.

They ascend in the lift, Manu feeling as exhausted as the lift seems to be, juddering from floor to floor. It's already 9.30 p.m. Evgeny bangs on the door, which opens to reveal the face of a small white woman with dark hair drawn tightly over her skull, like a helmet.

'My wife,' Evgeny says, in a proud, deep growl. 'Maria, this is Manu, the young man I told you about.'

'Happy Christmas!' she says in greeting, in a strong Russian accent. 'I hope you are not vegetarian. Or Muslim. We're having pork stew. Not quite the proper Christmas meal, but the best I can do.'

'It would be stuffed pig's head back home!' laughs Evgeny. 'Or goose with apples! Or sour cream hare!'

His wife rolls her eyes. Manu frowns, trying to keep up. But before he can answer that it's OK for him to eat pork Maria disappears into the kitchen, from where a rich smell of cooking is emanating.

'Let's have a drink first,' says Evgeny. He follows his wife into the kitchen.

Manu looks around. It's a smart place, but a bit bare, despite pots containing tropical plants with thick green leaves. There are a few pictures – stock scenes of Red Square and the Russian steppes. On a brown leather sofa, a glossy magazine lies at an angle between two pink satin cushions. He sits down on one of the polished-steel chairs that surround a table laid for dinner as Evgeny re-emerges with a frosted bottle of vodka and two glasses.

He joins Manu, pours the vodka under the yellow lamp which hangs from a chain over the plates and cutlery, knocks back his whole glass, all even before Manu has taken his first sip.

'Drink.'

Manu picks up the glass: heavy, a kind of crystal-cut vessel that he's never held before.

'Drink! It's good stuff.'

He drinks, coughs at once, because of the strength, because of the cold.

'You flew well today,' Evgeny says.

'You are very kind.'

'That's not what most people say about me.'

'They say you are a good negotiator.'

'Maybe. Who said that, anyhow?'

'Suraj, an Asian trader I met with Cogan.'

'Well, he'd know. There's something I want to negotiate with you, actually.'

'What?'

'We'll talk after supper. And Manu?'

'Yes?'

'You really did impress me when you took the controls. You're a natural.'

'Thank you,' he says, perplexed that Evgeny is more or less repeating a compliment he gave a few seconds ago.

With a polite smile on her face, Maria brings forth a dish. The stew is thick and glutinous, round white potatoes showing in it, along with the lumps of dark meat.

They eat, Evgeny doing so with speed. A Kivu farmer, Manu thinks: *my dad*, over his bowl of beans. The wife, she's much more delicate. He wonders how they ended up together, as he did about Aisha and Cogan a few days ago. These two seem another affectionate, if ill-suited couple: the one an adventurer and rule-breaker, the other clearly a diligent housewife and kind mother, even if she must have had a wild side once, he reckons, to have chosen Evgeny in the first place.

Near the end of the meal, as Maria offers Manu foil-wrapped chocolates, Evgeny says: 'Hey, that was some trip we made to Brno, wasn't it? Did you enjoy the Gauntlet?'

'It was special.'

'My favourite, too. Flying above the clouds, above places where there is no radar, deep in quietness. As if you are a god. No controls, no limitations, nothing preying on you. Perfect freedom.'

'I understand that,' Manu replies, self-doubt running its fingers over his feelings even as the words come out.

'No compliance necessary,' Evgeny says – in the same, almost hypnotic voice. 'Good how we got those fake certs through, wasn't it?'

'Yes, it worked well.' Manu considers the cursory way the customs men in Brno checked over the outward manifest, asking him as well as Evgeny to countersign the end-user form. He sees again his own, trembling hand holding the biro.

A drawn-out wail sounds from one of the other rooms. Maria gets up at once. Evgeny lights a cigarette.

'That's my son, Yuri,' he says, doing his thing of seeming to exhale without any smoke coming out.

Manu's puzzled. 'I thought your children were in the Emirates?'

'I have three. Besides Yuri, twin daughters, both at a boarding school in Dubai. Beautiful girls, with the long, dark hair their mother used to have before she cut it off. Women do strange things when they start the menopause, Manu. That's what she's been reading about there.'

He uses the cigarette to point at the glossy, Cyrillic-scripted mag on the sofa. 'The "magic of the menopause", it says on the cover. I hope she'll be happier in Dubai. That's what I wanted to talk to you about.'

Something to do with women's things, this impending conversation? But then Evgeny says, 'I'm in the process of moving my whole business from Entebbe to Dubai.'

'Why?'

'Good place for people looking for quick *biznes*. I have a man there who runs the whole cargo hub and he's constantly offering work. Pleasant enough place to live, too. Only, schools are expensive!'

He pauses, studying the big, blunt nails on his hands; they're much cleaner than Cogan's. 'There's one more thing, Manu: I'm getting heat from authorities. An investigation by the US government. I'd be a bit more protected there.'

'What do you mean?'

'In the Emirates there's a tight system for such things; those sheikhs don't like outsiders interfering. Fair enough, I say. Anyway, being much more there, Manu . . . I may need some assistance here to take care of the African side, assuming you qualify?'

Startled, he says, falteringly, 'Me?' What have I done, Manu wonders, to inspire such trust, from Evgeny now as well as Cogan? Is it just that he's biddable, like a dog? It's not good, this feeling that he's somebody's dog. It hangs about for too long, like the smell of dog shit itself, now interpenetrating from his mind with the smell of leftovers from the stewpot.

'Yes, I need someone I can rely on and none of the others . . .'

'What about Papa?'

'Too virtuous, that priest, and too tired. He often speaks of retiring, something I don't expect I'll ever do.'

'Cogan?' The vodka is making Manu's gums feel raw.

'Cogan is Cogan. If I didn't have to, I wouldn't let him flush my toilet. We work together sometimes, as you know. But essentially, we're still competitors. The same goes for the others too, really.'

'I can't,' Manu says. 'I owe Cogan.'

'In our game, as you'll learn, the only debts are in US dollars. And the only income, too – well let's say, I'd pay you much better than Cogan ever will.'

Maria comes through from the bedroom, carrying a tousled blond boy on her hip. Wearing *Star Wars* pyjamas, the boy looks at Manu with grave, wet eyes.

'I'm sorry,' she says. 'I'll have to take him into our bed.'

'Again!' cries Evgeny, in mock outrage.

'Good night, Manu.' She lays a snow-white hand on his arm. 'My husband says you're very dependable.'

'Thank you for the meal.'

Once she's gone, Evgeny asks, 'So what do you say?'

'It's my duty to stay with Cogan.'

'I thought you might put it like that,' he sighs. 'You really do have a lot to learn. And you need to get your licence first whatever. Once you have, let me know if you change your mind.'

The next thing he says has more of the nature of a threat. 'Oh, and Manu, it would be better if you don't mention my move to the others just yet. They'll find out in time.'

He rubs his shovel-like face with his hands, now seeming troubled, or like he just wants Manu to leave.

On the way back to The Passenger, gusts of cold lake wind sway the street lights, dust and rubbish swirling round. It's two in the morning, and Entebbe's deserted, desolate-seeming almost, tattered Christmas decorations draped over the doorways of shut-up bars and shops. He wonders if he's done the right thing in refusing Evgeny. There's no moon tonight – nor, unusually, many stars above the lake. Even the Southern Cross seems faint, as if it has been sucked into the black void next to it. He recalls Don Javier's speaking of stars falling from the universe like green figs in Revelation, in the course of what was meant to be a science lesson about astronomy.

He shakes himself, trying again to forget what has departed. Focus on the present: this, now, this always about-to-be exceeded quantity which he can never grasp.

Chapter 11

On Cogan's return from Texas, he doesn't at first say much about his trip. When there is a chance to chat, one night in The Passenger, Manu in turn doesn't say anything about Evgeny's move to Dubai, just enthuses about flying the big Russian plane.

'He let you fly the Antonov, eh? Well isn't that cool as a dog's nose in a wire muzzle?' Cogan lights a cigar, tipping back his chair. 'Evgeny say anything else?'

'Well, we had a meal – he seemed worried about some investigation.'

With the speed of a cash register, Cogan's eyes flicker shut, then open again. 'We all get that; first governments use us, then they shaft us.'

Manu wonders what this reaction amounts to, but Cogan doesn't quiz him more, instead confessing, 'Wanted to bring my son back with me this time, show him a bit of Africa, but Courtney wouldn't let me. Not sure he would have come anyway . . .'

He takes a sip of his Scotch. 'So I guess you'll have to do, Manu, not that I need to show you anything about this place. Still thrills me, being here. Don't lose the excitement yourself! Well, you probably won't anytime soon 'cos we've got a job on New Year's Day. Hope it's a good omen for the rest of '97, working on a day we'd normally be hungover on.'

Not in my family, thinks Manu, remembering New Year's Day last year, when he was guarding cattle as normal in the hills, thinking about the impending bus journey down to Bukavu, his final term at school beginning two weeks later. He suddenly feels old, much older than he is.

'Oh yeah, bring a sheet sleeping bag. Get a tailor in town to run one up for you. And bring a flashlight, too. Dark as fuck, where we're going.'

Manu's eyes narrow as he eases the Cargomaster off the runway at Entebbe. He rolls the trim wheel forwards. The plane climbs into the sky, following a course to north-east Zaire: a mining region called Kilo Moto.

'Where we're going, will Rusyo be there?' Manu asks.

'No, just a Ugandan outfit. Get that guy outta your head.'

'OK.'

'And Manu, one thing – best not mention this trip to Gerry. Faithful, the UPDF honcho we're meeting, usually gives his jobs to Gerry, but he's asked me because Gerry's got other work in Kenya right now. Flying for some big cheese there, between Malindi and Athi River. Must be lucrative, whatever he's doing, to beat war work.'

'I've met Brigadier Faithful. With Gerry, at the bar. And he was there when you first picked me up, meeting Rusyo.'

'So he was!' says Cogan. 'I'd forgotten. Well Faithful and Rusyo might have seemed friendly then, but that's just tactical. Faithful actually hates Rusyo. And all those top Rwandans who used to fight for Ugandan freedom under Museveni and the NRM in the bush wars against Amin and Obote and the others, and who now play hooky. Guess the NRM thought the Rwandans would just keep doing what they were told!'

Three hours later they approach the long runway at Kilo, passing over gouged hills, immense iron-strutted wheels for winding cables and yellow excavators carrying ore. The smoking chimneys of a refinery compete for height with the trees of the surrounding forest.

A unit of UPDF is waiting by the runway. Next to a helicopter stands Brigadier Faithful, looking a little downcast: not the jovial man whom Manu last saw at The Passenger, or read of in the paper, joking about incompetent white mercenaries.

He embraces Cogan, who says: 'Hey Faithful, why the long face?'

'We lost a few men on the way.'

'FAZ get you?'

'No, UNITA, but we saw them off in the end. Serious fighters, those guys, but getting quite old.' A soft laugh. 'Some won't be getting any older. Still, if they weren't supporting Mobutu, I guess the Angolans wouldn't have come on side, which has got to be a good thing.'

Cogan smiles grimly. 'Maybe. Right, where's the merchandise?'

'*Twende!*' orders Faithful, his hands on his hips. At once, the company of UPDF around him get to their feet and begin loading the luggage area of the Cargomaster with what Manu works out must be crates of gold . . . they're long, these crates, about three-quarters the lengths of a coffin.

By the time the job's done, night has fallen. After setting a guard round the plane Brigadier Faithful drives them to a village, where one of his soldiers shows Manu and Cogan to separate huts. After turning on his flashlight, Manu goes inside. Containing some rudimentary furniture, the hut smells of mud, insects, woodsmoke. He unzips his flight bag, lays out the new sheet sleeping bag on the straw mat that's there, comes back outside to look round.

Lit by campfires, by torches made from bundles of papyrus soaked in kerosene and by Tilley lamps powered with the same fuel, the location's loud with Congolese music, playing from a boombox. It's filled, this village on the mine's edge, with soldiers and militia wearing a bewildering array of uniforms.

Some women in colourful robes are there too, dancing in what seems like a semi-formal manner, stamping their feet and chanting. They look like foreigners, but there are also many people whom Manu takes to be the original villagers, rushing about with drinks and food.

He walks about. It's a strange, uneasy place, dominated by a large TV screen hoisted into the branches of an enormous mango tree, its power cable dangling down to a series of extension leads connected to a generator, the continual thump of which adds to the cacophony of the boombox that it's also powering. At the top of the tree, in a spot clear of leaves and fruits, a satellite dish is affixed.

But there's nothing on the TV screen at present, just white-furred static. More Tilley lamps are hanging from the boughs of other trees, cluttering the darkness with shafts of yellow light.

Faithful and Cogan cram their huge bodies into collapsible camp chairs, next to a fire. The brigadier begins drinking from a bottle of Johnnie Walker that Cogan has offered to share with him. Manu sits cross-legged next to them, not sure how to conduct himself as they discuss the war. Raising his arm, Cogan offers him a slug from the bottle, which he takes.

The group of dancers — are they nomads, he wonders? — gyrate nearby. Mostly plump, square-faced, middle-aged women, they have earrings and bangles and anklets that gleam in the light of the lanterns. He takes another slug from the offered bottle.

Faithful orders food. Strips of beef arrive in small tin dishes, together with a slew of boiled peanuts and greens, plus the inevitable mass of *ugali*, which Manu scoops up in his fingers. As he eats, the meal fortunately taking an edge off the booze, he's aware of the movement of the dancers nearby, giving off an odour of sweat and sandalwood. No men are dancing with them, most not even watching. Because by now the TV in the mango tree is on.

A Manchester United game is showing. Most of the soldiers are supporting the Reds against Aston Villa. At the end of the match, a draw, the dancers pick up pace. Among them at this point, three younger women in Western clothing appear. Two look poor, like they're from the village, but the third seems more sophisticated and urban. She's wearing white Converse high-tops and a shortish, black linen dress with pockets, fastened with a cowrie-shell belt. She has a little brown bag over her shoulder, the strap bisecting her breasts.

This young woman, the one with the little bag and the cowrie belt — it's the ice-cream girl, Manu's shocked to realise. Her green eyes, glossy hair, the tattoo on her neck consume his attention, even as he wonders: what on earth is she doing here? He watches her dance, noticing the definition of her calves, the gleam of her teeth.

He gets up, buys a Nile from one of the sellers wandering about with baskets of beer, keeps watching the girl, wondering if he might pluck up the courage to join her. The dancers around her begin to wail. Smoke drifts across the village.

He moves a touch closer – she's noticed him now, he presumes, at least is casting her green eyes in his direction – but at once there comes a pause in the music, someone changing the tape. Two soldiers start to fight, wrestling on the rubbish-strewn ground, until others separate them.

The girl takes advantage of the noise and confusion caused by the fight to come near him, surreptitiously touching his forearm with her own. 'Hello Manu, I thought you said you weren't following me?'

'I'm not,' he says, astounded she's remembered his name. 'I'm here for work.'

'What do you do?'

'Trainee pilot.' He gestures at Cogan. 'With that white guy, doing something for the UPDF high-up.'

'You mean Brigadier Faithful?'

'Yes.'

'He's my dad.'

Manu's amazed by this, but before he can say anything she touches his arm with hers again. 'Where are you staying tonight?'

'In a hut.'

'We could go there.'

'What?'

'You know your shyness makes me quite horny? It did on the beach, but I was too upset then.'

Manu's throat goes dry; he's stunned.

He looks back at her, straight into her eyes, and says: 'Now? What about your dad?'

'He's drunk. Gone to bed just now.'

Manu looks over, sees that Brigadier Faithful is indeed no longer in the camp chair he was in a few seconds ago. Cogan's still there though, lighting his cigar – sitting back – exhaling.

She gives a nod of confirmation. Without hesitating further, Manu begins walking towards his hut, hoping she's following, turning on his torch so she can see where he's going.

Inside the hut there's a table and chair made of old wood, mine beams it seems like. Despite the torch, which he props up in a corner, it's almost too dark to see. He turns, aware that she has silently followed him in, which he wasn't at all sure she would, despite what she said.

The music outside has switched tempo, and the women are ululating in ever-shriller tones. But none of that matters because she's kissing him, her tongue pushing inside his mouth. Items – groundnut shells? a plastic bottle? dead beetles? – crunch underfoot as their bodies press against each other. She tastes sweet. Suddenly she stops kissing him, wanting to tell him her name: Edith.

'Why were you sad, on the beach?' Manu asks.

She places her soft, cool palms on either side of his face.

'That guy you saw me with in Entebbe, eating ice cream? We were going to get married, but he dumped me.'

'I'm sorry.'

'Don't be,' she says, 'he was an arsehole.' She kisses him again, then disengages, lifting the strap of the handbag over her head, dropping it on the floor.

'Is the brigadier really your father?'

'Yes, why?'

'Just can't see why he'd put you in danger by bringing you here. I heard there was a battle on the way.'

'It's what he's used to. Me too, in a way. I was born in the bush war against Obote; and Dad's wife isn't my mother. She was in the NRM herself, an active combatant under Museveni like my father.'

'There were women soldiers, in all that?'

'Many. And so all my early childhood was in militarised villages like this one, moving from one to another. I learned to shoot myself, all the rest of it too – so I wasn't scared when UNITA attacked us. After Museveni won, my father got promoted so high and we were in Kampala . . . he went back to his real wife, had other children. But I've always been his favourite. That's why he sent me to an expensive school abroad. Also to get me away from my stepmother, who treats me like shit.'

'What happened to your own mother?'

'Died of malaria.'

'I'm sorry.' Manu touches her hip, and she puts her arms round his neck. Again they kiss.

'So where did you do your schooling?'

'Malvern Girls' College. A place in England . . . I got A-levels, learned how to play lacrosse.' She laughs, undoing the buttons of his shirt. 'Other useful things like that. But Dad now says I need toughening up again, reminding of how things really are, so I'm getting all these trips in his helicopter. He figures I'm going to be a politician. Uganda's first female president!'

'Are you?'

'No way. But what about your own family?'

'Lost in this war.'

'Dead?'

'Yes.'

'I'm sorry.'

There's a pause. Manu wonders whether to tell her anything more of his own story. But he wants to touch her more than talk, and anyway it's immaterial now, this decision – she's already stroking his stiff cock through the fabric of his trousers. He pulls her towards him, but she pushes him away slightly, shrugs herself out of her dress, the cowrie-shell belt clicking to the floor.

He steps out of his trousers and underwear, and as he straightens up she puts her arms round him again, pressing his back, swaying her hips against him.

'Do you have a condom?'

Manu shakes his head.

'Well it's lucky I've got one.'

'OK.'

'You promise you'll wear it?'

He nods, and she kneels down, finds what she's looking for in her little brown bag, unwraps it.

She rolls it on to him, then leads him to the rough-hewn table, turns, leans back against it, lifting her mouth to his. He touches the divot of flesh between her parted legs, puts another hand on one of her breasts, feeling the excitement of its nipple under his palm. She gives a choked intake of breath, which he takes as a signal to move his lower hand to her thigh, grip her hip, and enter her slickness in a single movement.

Driving her body against him, she meets his thrusts with such force that he quickly senses he's about to come, and very soon, too soon. When he does, it's like life itself is trying to wrench understanding out of his head – replacing, if only for a few seconds, the tyranny of thought with a divine forgetfulness.

As he's pulling off the condom, she sits up on the table, swinging her legs. Hands either side of her, palms down, she tells him: 'That was a bit quick. You've left me panting, Manu.'

He doesn't say anything, just takes her wrists, draws her to the mat and sleeping bag in the corner of the hut . . . till they're lying down together, her neck in the crook of his arm. He traces the outline of her collarbone, strokes her breasts, strokes her belly. She gives a sigh, impatient-sounding, pushes his hand down to her crotch.

And so he begins rubbing her with his fingers, slowly, and she opens her thighs slightly more.

After a time, she says: 'Do it harder.'

He tries to keep his fingers in the rhythm she seems to want, even though he's not sure, but it seems like it's OK because after a few minutes she's getting much wetter. But after a further lapse of time she says, again with a hint of frustration: 'Just suck my tits.' He does. Cocking a finger, she begins to masturbate with impressive efficiency. He's amazed by the sticky noise. After a while, her legs begin shaking, and she urges him to put his fingers inside her.

'This was all a surprise,' Manu says, a little later. He's quite shocked, but also excited, by how she took control of the whole encounter. Already desire, with all the banality of water filling a basin, has begun to rise again in his balls.

'Yes,' she says. 'For me also. But I was very happy to see you.'

'Will I see you again?'

'Who knows? I've applied to a few universities in the States, but Dad wants me to stay at home. Look, do we have to think about all that? Where's your home anyway, Manu?'

'Entebbe's where I live now, at a bar called The Passenger.'

'I've heard of that. Bit of a roughhouse, isn't it? Our place is further out, on the Garuga peninsula – quite a big spread on the lakeshore. Do you like Entebbe?'

'Yes, very much. My homestead was Pendele, though, which is a village on the west side of the volcano near Goma. A long way from here, and all burnt now.'

'By the volcano?'

'By Mobutu's soldiers.'

She strokes the flat of his stomach with her palm.

Manu's woken in the early morning by Cogan giving him a pinch. 'Come on, Sweetback, we've gotta go,' he says, glancing at Edith's barely concealed form as he leaves. As Manu gets to his feet, feeling groggy, Edith wakes. Sitting up, holding her knees, yawning languorously, she gives him what might be a fond, and is certainly a sleepy, look.

Not sure what to do, he bends down, kisses the tattoo on her neck, says nothing. Because he knows, already, that she's one of those young women who don't want to talk about tomorrow till it pitches up.

Outside, some fires are still burning, and there's a couple of *bodas* waiting, which Cogan must have booked the previous night. As they ride to the airstrip on the motorbikes, the sun rises, the moon going down opposite: it's as if the two celestial bodies, like everything else round here, are connected by a cable being pulled down – through the treetops of the forest, through the fire-smoke of the village, through the waste and futility of war – by the vast wheels of the mine, which are already turning, despite the early hour.

Chapter 12

Once the plane has reached altitude, Cogan says, 'Look, Manu, in our business, there's not time for too many human contacts. No man of feeling ever does jack shit in the real world. Understand?'

'I think so,' he says, though he isn't sure in fact what Cogan means. What he does know is that the experience with Edith – the primal human touch of it – has given him a little hope.

'You had a moment like that last night, I reckon?' Cogan asks, with more than usual delicacy. Which he then undermines by adding, 'Hot diggety, she looked good!'

Embarrassed, Manu doesn't reply, watching the landscape rolling past beneath.

Cogan says nothing for a while, after a few minutes turning on the radio, tuning it to the BBC Africa service, on which Mobutu is ranting away, assuring the world that he's still in charge.

'You're aware all this he's saying is complete hogwash, every damn word?' Cogan says. He taps his cigar into the overflowing ashtray in the side of the cockpit door.

'Yes,' Manu says.

'Don't be under any illusion, the two people in charge over there now, they are the very ones you've met: Rusyo on the Rwandan side, Faithful on the Ugandan. Faithful's an absolute lion, been in battle since he was fourteen – afraid of nothing, whereas Rusyo's just a psychopath.'

'What about Kabila?' Manu asks, wondering if Cogan realised Edith is Faithful's daughter. Probably not, he reckons.

'Not half as powerful as he supposes. Still, apparently he's actually gonna meet Mobutu with Mandela on a South African naval vessel off Pointe Noire on the Congolese coast; old Madiba has plans to broker a peace deal.'

Cogan eases up the flaps, breaking momentarily into a ditty – 'Did you ever go to meetin', Uncle Joe, Uncle Joe, did you ever go to meetin', Uncle Joe, Uncle Joe?' – before continuing: 'Whatever happens on that ship, the ordinary Congolese, well they're basically fucked by the geopolitics of it all. The likes of us can't fix that. You know the main thing, Manu, is to be in charge of and look after number one. Re last night, that includes rubbers. Hope to Christ you used one?'

'I don't think I've got anything to worry about.'

'Good. Don't go Mungo Park.'

'What?'

'Mungo Park was an explorer who didn't like to wear socks. It's an ad you see in Ghana, to promote condom use.'

'OK.'

'So you know what I was saying, about looking after number one?'

'You just told me.'

'This is different . . . in a while we're going to put down, OK?' He flexes his shoulders, as if what's going on is more stressful than his casual attitude suggests.

'OK,' Manu says, still wondering what Cogan means; but the big, bleary-eyed figure next to him doesn't say anything else – instead restarting the song about Uncle Joe that he began a few moments before.

After about two hours' flying, Cogan points at a town below and says, 'So that's Fort Portal, there's an old British airstrip near here, at Kikorba, that no one uses, we're gonna land there, right?'

'OK,' Manu says again, still unsure what he's up to.

It all becomes clear another thirty minutes later, by which time he's helping Cogan heft one of the crates of gold to the edge of the airstrip. This one has been marked with a spray of red paint, Manu sees.

Cogan picks a big *mvuli* tree, on which a collection of sleeping bats are hanging, then says: 'Right, you go back to the aircraft and behind each of our seats you'll find two little spades, get them both and come back here.'

Once he has done this, Cogan instructs (chuckling with what seems like a hint of bitterness), 'OK Manu, so now we dig a hole.'

Manu does as he says, helping him. After the pair of them have dug a hole about a metre deep, Cogan gestures to Manu to help him heave the marked crate into the cavity – then fill it up again. As the dry soil rattles on the wood of the crate, Manu dwells upon the rushed burials by which his family was committed to the earth.

When it's done, Cogan puts his foot on the lug of the spade, saying, 'Well obviously, what just happened is something you can't ever tell anyone, yes?'

'I understand,' Manu says; but inside he's trembling. He's realised how much he needs to watch out: these freight dogs are as faithless as water, no more reliable than those nets of kinship that were supposed to have protected him back home. Somehow, he knows, he must become more deeply his own person, find solidarity in himself, not rely on it coming from someone else, perhaps especially a white person whom he has imagined as his saviour.

'But do you understand, really?' says Cogan. He drops the spade, comes up close to Manu, holding him by the shoulders and looking directly into his eyes. 'Can I trust you?'

'Yes,' Manu says, steadily. 'I won't tell anyone.'

'Good,' he says. 'Main thing now is, both you and I remember where this fucking tree is, just in case I get done in, or lose my memory. Which is happening more and more. So how're we going to do that?'

Manu looks at the *mvuli* tree. Part of what seems like an avenue on either side of the old airstrip, it's more or less indistinguishable from its neighbours, apart from having slightly more bats hanging from its branches.

'We could mark it,' he suggests, picking up the spade.

Cogan shakes his head. 'Too damn obvious. Tell you what, if I use this, we can get the exact GPS.'

He pulls a little yellow Garmin GPS receiver from his safari-suit pocket and punches a few buttons.

'OK, we got it: 0.66175 30.2747. But how I am going to get you to remember this?'

'Write it down?'

'Very old-fashioned! But you're probably right. There's a permanent marker in the map pocket next to my seat – can you go and get it?'

Manu jogs to the plane again, and after digging around in the dusty pocket, finds the marker. When he gets back to the *mvuli*, Cogan takes the pen, pulls up his sleeve and writes the co-ordinates on his arm, next to the lower part of his tattoo. Then, as he holds out the grey-lit display on the Garmin, Manu does the same.

'Write those down on a bit of paper when we're home, and put it somewhere safe,' Cogan says.

On the way back to Entebbe, Manu finally asks Cogan what's been on his mind the whole time: 'Aren't you worried what Brigadier Faithful might do if he finds out a crate is missing?'

Cogan laughs. 'Believe me, you don't need to sweat that. I know exactly what I'm doing, and so does Faithful. It's his idea. I'm not going to explain now, but you just need to trust me, Manu, OK? And don't go blabbing.'

'OK,' he says, but with some uncertainty.

So now he has two secrets: Evgeny's impending departure to Dubai and Cogan's crate beneath the *mvuli* tree. The plane gives a little shudder under his hands. He doesn't know why, but he worries that both these confidences he's been asked to keep could get in the way of what he wants: to qualify as a pilot.

There's something else deeper, though: a longing for security, maybe in the arms of a woman, but not just that. His feelings skim back to Edith all the same, her fingers still somehow present on the atlas of his body: his lips, the skin of his stomach, the tip of his cock.

The map reference that Cogan has given him feels like a risk. He decides he will write it down not on paper but on the bottom of one of the drawers in the chest with brass handles in his room in The Passenger.

He does so as soon as they get back there, going into his room as Cogan pours them a couple of beers. By the time he has come out, Cogan has constructed a little aeroplane by folding a dollar bill, origami-style. 'Pretty neat, hey? But damn thing won't fly.'

There are no more real flights for a while. Cogan's run out of more serious cash, is waiting to be paid, so he can buy fuel. Manu's mentor spends the expanding time doing more of these sculptures out of dollar bills: birds, butterflies, a winged man . . . And yes, dogs, he makes those, too; it seems to be some kind of stress reaction, all this anxious fiddling with dirty fingers as Cogan sits on the veranda of The Passenger, his face appearing to exude wax from its pores when the sun reaches the right angle to ray on it.

Manu, meanwhile, works in the bar, studies the training manuals, fretting he'll never pass the upcoming exams on all this. During breaks from study, he makes several attempts to co-ordinate with Edith, pleading with the *askaris* at the gates of Brigadier Faithful's mansion by the lakeshore to pass her notes, requesting she contact him at The Passenger. But he hears nothing back, and reckons she knows where to find him, anyhow.

On the last of these occasions, one of the guards tells him that Edith has gone to study at Ohio State University in the US. So she won that battle with her father at least. He tries to put her out of his mind. But she keeps coming back, bubbles of physical sensation returning incessantly – little touches of justice and mercy, floating on the brew of his consciousness.

Chapter 13

After landing in broken cloud one evening at Bunia, Manu eats with Cogan in a Lebanese restaurant – a meal of tartly flavoured rice and diced chicken skewered on metal rods, which the Texan garnishes with the acidulous comment: 'Only one thing that you shouldn't expect less of in Africa than maize, and that's the Lebanese.'

The reason they're here, in this depressing town in eastern Zaire, where the atmosphere of ethnic conflict is as obvious as the windowed sky, is to pick up some leading members of the Hema tribe. The job is to take them to the ranch of the Ugandan president, Yoweri Museveni, in central Uganda for a high-level meeting the next morning.

Later that night, after the meal, Manu's shaving in the bathroom of his room in their cheap hotel when there's a knock at the door. He rubs foam off his face, goes to answer it bare-chested.

The man at the door is Recognition.

'Quick, let me in,' he says, pushing past and closing the door.

Recognition sits on the bed, and Manu's shocked by how different he looks. The second-hand suit and sunglasses are gone, replaced by a simple pair of black trousers and a white shirt; his hair is much longer, too, and his face looks drawn.

'What do you want?' Recognition is the last person he wants to see.

'Your help. I've deserted like you did. I'm going to the bush Manu, setting up a militia to protect Banyamulenge from all those who pretend to be our allies but aren't. Also from the

Mai-mai, who are at least frank in professing themselves enemies. Rusyo and Kabila are just counterfeit colleagues, like those famous British colonialists of the past, who tramped all over Africa laughing with us blacks tribe by tribe, then stabbed us in the back the moment we turned.'

'And?'

'We need our own pilot.'

'Yeah right. Other requests being?'

'Nearly all the forces in the east are aligned against genuine Banyamulenge interests now, either secretly like Rusyo and Kabila, or *en clair* like the various *Mai-Mai*. Last week, down in the south, the *Mai-Mai* there climbed the Massif d'Itombwe and gunned down a whole Tutsi village on the plateau. They all still seem to think we're part of a Rwandan invasion!'

Manu swallows his fury about having been tracked down. 'Many of us were part of that, as you well know,' he counters. 'Anyway, I've told you already how I feel about all this: we need to move away from kicking the shit out of each other!' He tries to keep his voice down, even though he wants to tear into this unwanted visitor. 'Who the hell do you think you are anyway, coming in here, endangering me as well as yourself?'

Recognition sits up, and his voice takes on a fearful tone. 'I haven't got long, Rusyo's men are after me, Manu.'

'So? You wouldn't be the first, if I remember rightly. How did you find me?'

'You know how I work.'

'Yes, and I don't like it: that's why I left the AFDL.'

'I understand. But it doesn't matter, this is about your duty.'

'You're out of your mind if you think I'm going to help you, after what you made me go through.'

'Whether I made you do anything or not is a matter of opinion.'

'How did you find me?' Manu asks again.

'It wasn't hard. One of the Hema officials you're taking tomorrow is trying to get my group on his side, joining in resistance to Lendu incursions. Together, if he's in good faith, we might just truly liberate the occupied east, with solid self-defence for all communities. Those Hema, they're unhappy because some Ugandan commanders – same guys who want a piece of the gold and diamond trade round here – have been siding with Lendu and Hema militias alike, as it suits them. My guess is that's why your American was hired to fly the Hema leaders to Museveni's spread at Kisozi, so it can all be thrashed out with the big man. In the time before, as I am sure you know, the Lendu not the Hema were the enemy of the UPDF and the RPA, but everything's changing day by day. And in a way it's good, this not sticking by your ethnic group, as you realise those in the same category will not stick by you. Don't you think?'

'I don't know what you mean by "you", and perhaps you know more about all this than I do. Why do we need another group anyway? There are already far too many of these militias and parties and tribes covering over crimes with a set of initials. All this talk of resistance and liberation just makes for more war. What you call self-defence simply involves cutting the balls off another group.'

'And you think you're clean, do you? Flying guns to all and sundry from what I hear, or otherwise taking out valuables to Uganda, or Rwanda. Like that generator at Kamituga.'

'You were part of that too.'

'We need to defend our interests without others pulling the strings.'

'Be realistic. Why do you think these officials are going to see the Ugandans if not to prefer their own interests against the Lendu?'

This was the other ethnic group round Bunia, historically in violent conflict with the Hema over land usage. Now the two groups, Manu knows (he and Cogan ploughed this very sea of grief during their conversation at the Lebanese restaurant), are copying the Hutu-Tutsi categories that figured in the Rwandan genocide: Lendu people thinking of themselves as kin to Hutu, and Hema people identifying as Tutsi – a sequence of connections inflaming ancient disputes over whose field is whose into something much more dangerous.

Listening to Recognition talk, Manu shudders . . . feeling as if these local events, unrelated to him save as a pilot, are about to crammed into his personal bucket of memory, bruising more the already-bruised fruit that is there. 'What's your group called anyhow?'

'We're still thinking, we can't agree.'

'Ha!'

Recognition looks pathetically downhearted – staring at the brown carpet of the hotel room as if it's a calamity, his inability to string a few simple words together and make yet another acronym. His eyes sink further into their sockets, his face seeming as inflexible as the wood of a sculpture.

'You really need to help us, Manu.'

'How?'

'Fly a bunch of us out of Kinshasa back to the Kivus.'

'That's all? No chance. I haven't quite got my licence, anyhow.'

'When the time comes?'

'Will you ever leave me alone?'

Recognition stands up. As he does so, the hardness Manu remembers from the days of camp-clearance comes back into his voice.

'You remember the archbishop?'

'Of course.' Manu remembers all right.

'His tribe was Shi, right?'

'Yes?' What's he driving at?

'Members of the Ngweshe clan of the Bashi have developed into one of the biggest *Mai-Mai* groups round Bukavu; they're very keen to find out who killed their most senior cleric.'

'And you'd tell them?'

'I might.'

'Fuck off, Recognition.'

'Can you imagine what they'd do to you? I'd probably have to tell them through another person, as they are angry enough just to kill me too for having been in the vicinity myself.'

'Get out.'

Once Recognition has gone, Manu gets into bed feeling chilled. He remembers something Recognition said when they first met. The Rwandan column was making its way up to join the camp in the mountains, when Recognition broke into French saying, in a voice of low bitterness, '*misérables vengeurs d'une juste querelle*'.

Some line from a play, Manu recalls him saying. Wretched avengers of a righteous quarrel. But he didn't see, back then, that in this passing observation lay the source of Recognition's future antipathy, now revealed, to the RPA, to whom he was inured for so long.

He doesn't say anything about any of this to Cogan, not least because shortly after take-off from Bunia the next morning, a round bursts near the tail of the Cargomaster, causing the Hema officials in the passenger seats behind to shout in terror.

'*Mai-Mai*,' Cogan says casually, referring to the guerrilla units that have formed to protect local villages from the RPA and Ugandans and FAZ alike. 'Though where the fuck did they get heavy ordnance? FAZ leftovers, probably.'

A few minutes later, there are more explosions around the aircraft. Cogan at once banks to the right at high speed. During this manoeuvre he remarks, still speaking calmly: 'Most people live in a 1-g world. Up here when the g-force is higher, you got to watch out for false impressions, sensory illusions. And the moves sure can get fiddly. For instance, if I do this one, which South African pilots call the *pantsula*, after some crazy dance they do down there. . .'

He decelerates while making a sharp turn to the left, then right, left again – then dives fast directly towards where the flash of the artillery came from, before turning sharply in a direction that takes the plane behind a hill of green.

Some jiggery-pokery's at work, but Manu's not sure what, and asks.

'The rapidly changing position of the aircraft make it seem on the ground as if we were turning right the whole time,' explains Cogan. 'But we weren't! That's why this *pantsula* foxes the gunners. But it's easy to lose your own head too. As you come out of cover, make a visual reference to the natural horizon or any other landmark to get your bearings. Got it?'

'Yes.' But Manu can't see any landmark, just a churning wall of clouded air. The green hill has gone.

'OK, we're clear, your control.'

They're now out of range of the artillery, but Manu takes the column with trepidation all the same.

'If this ever happens to you, just relax your way through it, doing that move,' Cogan says, still speaking calmly as he routes for Kisozi, in order to deliver the Hema officials for their meeting. 'Especially good for MANPADS, portable surface-to-air missiles.'

On the way out of Kisozi, Cogan does a banking turn after take-off, sweeping over the presidential herds, when Manu spots, among the cattle at grass by the runway, a longhorn beast whose brinded markings remind him of Joséphine's: that line of boxes like cigarette packets, running across both flanks. He pursues an internal fantasy that Joséphine somehow escaped the FAZ cull of the Kwizera cattle and wandered over the border, joining Museveni's much larger herd.

He wants to say something: stop, return, check. But it's too late, too late to check, too late for anything really.

'You're doing pretty well, kid,' Cogan comments a little further on, en route to Entebbe from Bunia. 'You've done what, four missions already?'

'I think that's right.'

'Way things are going, probs you'll make your licence within seven months rather than the eight Gerry and I bet on. And it looks like this war will be over soon, too. Kisangani's fallen, and that's a big one. Ladies and gentlemen, the movie's ending sooner than we thought! With luck we'll pick up loads of work from Kabila's new administration, once the guy's got his trotters under the desk. *Paaardy!*'

He's right, about the war looking like it will end soon. As Cogan predicted back at Aero Park, all the Congolese cities are tumbling . . . Even the mining capital Lubumbashi has folded. With only really Mbandaka and Kinshasa to take, Kabila has already declared himself president, renamed the country Congo, and started doing deals with mining companies.

In early May, after Mbandaka has been captured, Manu's over forest country, flying again with Cogan, but this time in heavy weather – pushing through a river of rain, bolts of lightning, claps of thunder. They're trying to find a strung-out column of RPA on the road from Mbandaka to Kisangani. At Mbandaka itself, site of their first drop that morning, the sight of hundreds of Hutu bodies piled up like sacks of sand next to the river filled Manu with dread. Refugees from the earlier exterminations in the east, they'd been waiting, after their very long journey of escape, to board boats to Congo-Brazzaville when the RPA and AFDL opened fire on them.

Cogan saw Manu shaking when he spotted the bodies. 'Pretend it's night and you can't see shit,' the Texan advised. 'And just remember what some of those hound dogs did with their hatchets in Rwanda. That's what started all this.'

Another clap of thunder judders the plane. 'Work out where it whacked us, go to the edge of the formation, fly along its flank, just like I once said. You gotta exercise your will in storms. If you let them take a ride, they'll break a plane like French fries too long in ketchup.'

'I'm trying!'

'Yeah yeah,' says Cogan. But then he gestures at the instrument panel. 'Mind you, look at that, this one's a biggee.' The instrument he's pointing at, the magnetic compass, is shaking like Manu was, back in Mbandaka that morning.

'Thing is, Jonathan Livingston fucking Seagull, you can't assume the compass is working properly, as storms can affect its operation,' Cogan says next. 'Volcanoes, too. Don't trust anything, specially not in this kind of weather. Always calibrate against the heading indicator.'

He grabs a bottle of water, downs a couple of pills. 'Amphetamines,' he explains. 'Gotta keep focused. Let me know if you ever need some.'

'Why did you call me . . . seagull?'

'It's a book, about a bird learning to fly. Now where are those troops? Take the bus down a touch, we don't want to miss them . . .'

'Well done, Manu,' says Cogan, scrabbling to find his lighter in one of the cubbyholes between the two seats as Manu lands at Entebbe later. The storm has followed them home, along with the memory of the poncho-wearing RPA straightaway breaking open the dripping crates he and Cogan brought, clipping the magazines into their rifles. 'Thought we'd sunk back there!'

The Cargomaster taxies towards its hangar, bringing Manu's fifth mission to a close. Only two more to go. As the plane comes to a rest, Cogan lights his cigar; at once, as Manu recalls him doing the same as they went into the hut at Kilo, Edith flares into mind. He imagines her – so far as he's able, for the imagination is a faithless forge – in a university room in Columbus, Ohio.

Looking at the rain still lashing the Perspex of the windshield, then suddenly stopping when they roll into the hangar, he undergoes a lashing of his own, an overwhelming flood of emotion at all the love that's been washed away from his life.

Chapter 14

A few days after the trip to Mbandaka, Manu and Cogan fly to Gbadolite. His sixth training flight is the most dangerous job of all so far, its purpose being to pick up Evgeny from Mobutu's palace, a mission provoked by a call from the Russian to Cogan at The Passenger, saying, more or less: 'Come get me tomorrow.'

The tomorrow in question happens also to be Manu's twentieth birthday, but he doesn't say anything about that to Cogan during the journey.

The palace lies seven kilometres south of the Ubangi River, near Congo's border with the Central African Republic. It's filled, so Cogan tells Manu on the way, with Italian malachite, Venetian goblets, gilded taps . . . 'And all the other crap these dictators like! Even a private menagerie. A contingent of elite presidential guard is stationed there, too.'

Inhaling his cigar, shirt half undone, he coughs like a white-breasted cormorant. 'DSP they're called, *Division Spéciale Présidentielle*. Once super-loyal to Mobutu but now – not so much.'

'Why?'

'Because when one regime's dying and its replacement is waiting to come outta the swamp, the only thing you can be sure of is not getting paid. Which is why Evgeny asked for cash up front. Me too, in terms of my cut.'

They land just as Mobutu's flying off in the UNITA-loaned Ilyushin that Evgeny has brought to convey the dictator, bullion and entourage to Togo – then on to Morocco, which has offered him refuge now he's finally fleeing, after hanging on till the very last minute, hiring more mercenaries and mustering special forces from wherever he could.

The angry, unpaid DSP open fire on Mobutu's ticket out (another pilot taking over from Evgeny), almost bringing the plane down. Having lost the chance to kill Mobutu, these pissed-off presidential guards then go on the rampage, looting and looking for some '*mercenaires blancs*', who've earlier been brought to the airport to help repair and fly the dying regime's broken Mi-24 helicopter gunships.

At first, the DSP are under the impression that Evgeny and Cogan, who've rendezvoused by now next to one of the hangars, are part of this helicopter team.

They get threatened with guns, there's lots of shouting, begging, pleading . . . all eventually resolved by payment of a bribe and Manu speaking rapidly to the DSP colonel. He happens to be Tutsi like Manu, rather than Ngbandi, like most of these guards from Equateur province who are hassling them.

As the Cargomaster lifts off, a volley of shots rings out about it nonetheless, one cracking into the co-pilot door, near where Manu's sitting, but not making it through. On today of all days . . . though he still hasn't told anyone about his birthday.

'MANPAD launching,' snaps Evgeny soon after, and Manu sees the flash of the surface-to-air missile.

'Oh my grandma's jugs,' shouts Cogan, 'it's *pantsula* time, kid.' He makes the plane do the rapid series of left-right jinks, followed by dive, cover and climb – same as he taught Manu on the way out of Bunia. By the end of all this handwork, footwork, flapwork, Cogan's Stetson is perched on his head at a precarious angle, and runnels of sweat are pouring down his face.

'Good stuff,' the Russian says approvingly, as the missile falls into a maize plot by the edge of the runway, setting a spilth of fire into somebody's crop. 'Thought it was all over for your apprentice here. Us too.'

'Horsecrap. Those guys couldn't hit that big ship you brought for Mobutu, how they gonna hit this little thing? Still, I'm glad we got out.'

'You know it was Kiley, Cogan, that the DSP were looking for?' Evgeny remarks a little later. 'The *mercenaires blancs*?'

Evgeny explains that this is Neil Kiley, a near-legendary helicopter pilot who, Cogan drops in, is a 'notorious hellraiser' (as if he himself were heaven personified), and Evgeny dubs 'maybe the only person in Africa who's pulled more Gs than us two'.

The Russian adds that Kiley was with a man called Dan McLintock, and another called Brett Zuckerman.

'KMZ, helicopter firm running out of Joburg,' Cogan glosses for Manu's benefit. 'An Irish American, a Scotsman and a South African Jew—'

'Walk into a bar . . .' interjects Evgeny.

As the plane crosses the Ugandan border, switching radio stations, rain cascades around them: yet another green curtain partitioned by jags of lightning and thunderous explosions, though not so heavy as they went through last time, reckons Manu, on the arms drop on the Mbandaka–Kisangani road.

Cogan must be thinking the same thing. 'Now you're the storm expert, Manu, you can take over.' As he does so, Cogan starts to sing his favourite song again, the one about cane plantations on the Brazos River in Texas . . . something about the workers there, women and men, back in 1910. Clearly having heard it many times before, Evgeny joins in, his accent as thick as his moustache as he grinds out the word *molasses* in the chorus.

There's a pause as Cogan checks in with EBB tower. Once he's done, Evgeny says: 'Shit, we shouldn't be singing this, we should be singing the hat song of Meester Bob Dylan. In honour of Mobutu!'

'He wasn't wearing it when he got on the plane,' Cogan observes.

'Left it behind!' says the Russian.

'Why would he do that?' muses Cogan.

Evgeny reaches into the pocket of his flying jacket and pulls out two iterations of the dictator's famous leopard-skin hat.

'You're some devil,' say Cogan, chuckling.

'I took a wander in the empty palace while I was waiting for you fuckers. These were hanging on a rack of ebony pegs.'

'One for me, I hope?' Cogan says, flipping his Stetson into Manu's lap.

'Naturally, who would it fit better?' Evgeny says to Cogan, putting one of the leopard-skin hats on his own head and clapping the other on Cogan's, who laughs and starts singing the Dylan song instead.

That night, back at The Passenger, they all get drunk to celebrate the escape from Gbadolite. 'What the shit you think you were doing?' Gerry asks, rolling a long joint, as Evgeny disappears to take a call on his Thuraya, the leopard-skin hat now tipped like a beret down one side of his head. 'You better be careful, the Rwandans will scratch you if they hear about you helping Mobutu.'

Cogan replies: 'Rusyo's got enough to worry about.'

'Still, you wouldn't want him holding a pipe to your melon,' counters Gerry. 'He's a wild one, that guy, but what actually went down, Norm?'

'We got out by the skin of our teeth, took a round on the way up. Manu helped.'

'Good for you, Manu,' says Papa, who's also there – up till now chatting to Manu about his plans to go back to Belgium, escaping this 'big fat knot of *morbidité postcoloniale*', as he put it, breaking into French.

'Too right,' says Cogan. 'And good for me too. It's quite a responsibility having Manu on board, Gerry, but I think you're gonna to have to put some cash aside for that bet.'

'We'll see. Just how many hot landings has he done?'

'Well, this was one hot take-off,' Cogan replies. 'Like I was saying, the DSP took potshots at us as we left, just as they did at Mobutu. I was flying with my usual genius, so we dodged those. But we might not have dodged what went on down on the ground, without this guy talking the talk.' He claps Manu on the back. 'Not bad for a nineteen-year-old kid.'

'Twenty, actually!' Manu says.

'What?' says Cogan.

'It's my birthday today . . . or yesterday now, I guess.' For it's now well into the early hours of the following morning.

'Well why didn't you say so?'

He shrugs, and Cogan shouts, 'Aisha! Drinks for the birthday boy!'

On his return to the table, carrying a bottle of vodka and a glass full of ice, Evgeny relates the fate of Kiley and his helicopter crew. The *mercenaires blancs* did not have an easy a time of it after Gbadolite, having to run through the bush and take a leaky boat across the Ubangi River.

'That was Kiley on the phone. Asking if I'd pick him up from Bangui.' He sits down in one of the wicker chairs, opens the bottle of vodka, pours some into the glass. 'Grimmelshausen was meant to come up from Windhoek in his Learjet if there was trouble, but the idiots didn't make their deposit, so he bailed. Myself too – I told them no money, no honey. Zuckerman was with Kiley, and the Scottish man too: the DSP first made McLintock take his trousers off because they thought he had a hidden money belt, then the others also. Found a .32 on Kiley but no cash.'

'That's just a popgun to those DSP goons,' comments Gerry.

'They all got out, though?' Papa asks.

'Pushing on through to Bangui as I speak,' Evgeny says. His seat creaks as he leans back, tossing the contents of the glass into his mouth.

'Kiley always survives, he'd have dollars up his arse in a charger for sure,' says Cogan. 'We don't need to go, he's a helicopter pilot after all, not one of us.'

'What if it was you though, Cogan?' says Papa.

'Hey, didn't I just go fetch brother Evgeny here?' Cogan affects a Russian accent. 'Pull the son of maather Russia from Mobutu's tit?'

'Don't worry, Cogan, I'll pay you,' says Evgeny, vodka gleaming coldly on his moustache.

'Too bushed to go anywhere now, anyhow,' Cogan says.

Manu watches him tap his ash. Poor Cogan, this man who

has lifted him up, but who seems so subject to the G-forces in his own life – Aisha, for instance, approaching now to jab his chubby shoulder with the painted nail of her forefinger, saying, 'Hey you, come help me cash up – I don't see why I have to do all this on my own.'

And as she speaks, Manu notices that Gerry has a smile on his thin, purplish lips, between which he now introduces the brown end of the joint, the length of which has been much reduced during the tale of Kiley and colleagues, roaches doing the rounds, same as stories.

Seated there, looking at them all, Manu wonders: what if it was me who found himself translated to the other bank of the Ubangi? For all the talk of brothers, would any of these men come and get me, birthday or no? Are they *faux amis*, like those of which Don Javier used to speak in another context of translation, false friends or true?

Chapter 15

His seventh and final training mission is with Papa – non-military, thank God, picking up bales of tobacco and flying them back to Entebbe. The destination is Mzuzu, a town in northern Malawi.

'You do know,' Papa says as they fly, 'that load factor increases significantly in a steep turn, two consequences being a greater G-loading and a higher stalling speed.'

'Yes,' Manu replies, puzzled. 'But we're not in a steep turn.'

Papa's drinking milk as he flies, and also playing a Beatles tape. The familiar tunes edge one into the other as the landscape unfolds beneath – rolling like the tape inside the quaint, old-fashioned cassettes he has, their cases all scratched and the labels half gone to goo in the heat.

A few bars of 'The Fool on the Hill' pass before Papa explains.

'I'm not talking about our current flying conditions, Manu, I'm talking about you! You're going too fast – you don't need to do all the things the rest of them do.'

'What do you mean?'

'I mean the drinking, I mean the drugs, I mean the crazy talk . . .'

'I don't understand. I drink some beer, sure, but I don't really participate in the rest of it.'

'Well OK, that's good. But I'd noticed you'd started smoking, which you didn't used to do. All I'm saying is, don't start popping the tablets that *gros tas de graisse* absorbs daily.' Fat lump, meaning Cogan. 'Or smoking Gerry's super-strong weed, or downing vodka like it's water, like Evgeny does. That's partly what makes them all so crazy. It causes unnecessary risk, and there is plenty enough risk in this job as it is.'

'I won't.'

'Good. Because I've had enough of it all myself, like I was telling you.'

'You really are retiring?'

'Soon. I have a little potato farm back in Belgium, on the Messines Ridge in Flanders. There's an old Dakota in a barn back there which I want to do up. Been looking forward to it for years. Old thing has done everything. Military transport, crop-spraying, skydiver-shuttling, sightseeing . . . Right now it's more a collection of parts.' He laughs. 'Actually DC-3s are always a collection of parts, flying in loose formation! Very rugged, though. Oh fuck. Control with you.'

Papa has spilled his milk while trying to pour it from its bag into the chipped china mug he carries with him. Manu watches aghast as the wizened old Belgian mops it up with tissues.

They pass over a lakeside town called Karonga, which Papa tells him was a big deal in the slave trade, in the time when Malawi was called Nyasaland. 'Stronghold of Mlozi, a notorious Swahili-Arab slaver in the early 1890s. The British hung him, mostly stopped the slave trade – fair enough – but then their African Lakes Company promptly claimed millions of acres of land. It was Scottish mainly, that company, but the money to grab Nyasaland mostly came from Cecil Rhodes, down in South Africa. But then he fell out with the Lakes Company and the British government took over. They always fall out, these people, like everyone will with Kabila, because of all those mining contracts he's been issuing. Just you wait.'

'But you're talking about over a century ago!'

'Doesn't seem that different. Greed doesn't age, it just gets fresher. Anyway, that African Lakes Company is still going even now.'

Once they have landed and the tobacco bales are on board, they check into a hotel, the Mzuzu Inn. There's not much to do in Mzuzu, but Papa seems keen to go out. They head to a bar he knows, Mama K's.

There Manu drinks a Green, as Carlsbergs are called in Malawi, and Papa sends out for milk. He says nothing when Manu lights up a Sportsman, the beer glowing in his stomach in accord. After a few minutes, Papa starts telling Manu stories about his time in Malawi, when Hastings Banda was president.

'Hey, you know why this place is called Mama K's?' he asks, after a few of these tales.

'No.'

'It's a joke. Banda's official hostess was a woman called Cecilia Kadzamira, thus Mama K's. Once, when they were having relationship problems, he banned the Simon and Garfunkel song "Cecilia" . . . you know the one: "breaking my heart". Banda's a really common name in this country but it was certainly the right one for him, as he really liked to ban things, that guy, including gays. Shall we eat?'

Outside Mama K's, once they've put in their order, an advertising vehicle passes, blurting out jingles for Omo soap powder, reminding Manu of Beatrice. Inclining his head, Papa asks, 'Tell me, have you ever been in love?'

He doesn't know what to say. He looks into the blue eyes behind Papa's old-fashioned spectacles, hoping that something will rescue him from the question.

'I mean really in love, like in the movies?'

'Is that the same?'

'No, I guess not. What I mean is when you can't think of anything else, and all your actions, even if you try to disguise them as otherwise, are concerned with being in touch with the absent person for just one second longer, however it may turn out? And if they do contact you, by letter or phone say, or if you are very lucky, actually meeting physically, your hope springs like a lamb, even if you may know, deep down, that they are merely being practical, remaining hard-hearted underneath?'

'No, not like that,' he says, taking a sip of his second Green. 'But I'm hoping that one day I will find someone.'

'Find someone?' Papa says, almost sneering, as the Omo ad ting-a-lings outside again, now reminding Manu of the chimes of the ice-cream seller in Entebbe, when he first saw Edith; it's a welcome substitution, at least banishing the image of Beatrice's sprawled body from his mind. 'Be careful what you wish for. There's such a big difference between fantasy and reality. Same-same with the flying, when you start thinking you own the sky, like Evgeny does when he bores on about the Gauntlet. The someone! The one! That's just unreal — unfair too, because it means you idealise the actual person you might be with, making them magical, with the result that they inevitably fail the tests of reality.'

'I understand that,' Manu replies, thinking of being with Edith physically, but also of himself professionally, well on his way to becoming a pilot.

Papa takes his hand across the table. It doesn't seem creepy, at least not at first. 'This very illusion happened to me here in Malawi, Manu. I was living a double life, doing priest work in the day, seeking young men at night, in a place where being one such as myself is criminalised.'

He unclasps his hand from Papa's, making to drink his beer. Papa says: 'Don't worry! I've given up sex, not interested in that any more. Just wanted to tell you.'

'OK.' But he still has an uncomfortable vibe.

The old Belgian takes a sip of his milk, for which the bartender at Mama K's has brought a glass, lets out his breath in what might be satisfaction, and embarks on a long story about a former lover whom he thought was 'the one', a guy called Chisisi who lived on a hill near Papa's church and was one of his flock. 'It was at this time, Manu, that I faced my greatest temptations as a priest, even though Chisisi was much the forwarder of the two of us . . .'

By the end (it didn't end well), Manu doesn't know what to say, or why Papa's offloading on him like this. Why in fact do any of these whites tell him the things they tell him, as if he's some kind of carrier, like those who used to carry munitions, or tote firewood, for men with moustaches in colonial wars?

Papa carries on, seeming to sense the need for explanation. 'I'll tell you why I'm saying all this, Manu, because I can see that you're wondering: it's because you need to follow your own track always, and not get drawn too much into the dramas of others, which is a fatal trap. I'm not a good man, and neither are the rest of us who gather like flies in The Passenger, but you still have time to be one. My best advice is, follow your heart, but don't pledge yourself to other people too much.'

That night, sweating in the itchy, over-detergented sheets of his room at the Mzuzu Inn, Manu gets up, opens the window. The light of the moon is beaming strongly, as if trying to dispel its own shifting orb on the surrounding clouds.

Lying back down, he remembers walking across the meadows with his mother, going to pick mushrooms on a similar moonlit night. He must have been about eleven or twelve. This was one of the occasions on which his mother told him tales of the Empire of Light, the medieval African empire briefly alluded to in Don Javier's history lessons, that covered so much of Central Africa, even Malawi, the very country he's now in. Part of it was run for a time, so she said, by that dynasty called the Chwezi, from whom Tutsis and other regional tribes sometimes claim their lineage.

Was it true, this story of Tutsis invading from the north and taking hold, in about 1300, of what was now Rwanda, western Uganda and eastern Congo? Or yet another of those mythic stories of origin that sprout up across the Great Lakes – often put, he remembers her saying, to divisive political use by the whites who once ruled us? When Don Javier mentioned it in class – was that what he too was doing? But it wasn't just *wazungu* who deployed history politically: the Chwezi inheritance was also what Rusyo referred to when, up in the mountain camp, he spoke of Greater Rwanda. In any case, Manu falls asleep remembering his mother's care-lined hands touching his as they put mushrooms into the basket. That at least was true.

After breakfast, Papa buys a packet of straws and a plastic jug in the market on the way to the airport. The in-flight milk-drinking goes easier after that, because he puts the bag in the jug and the straw in the bag. Lennon's singing about feeling fine, and the air in the plane is suffused with the sweet smell of the tobacco bales in the hold. Edith might be in America and good luck to her there, but Manu realises that, for the first time in ages, he feels fine too.

On the radio back at The Passenger, after they've landed, Manu hears that the Rwandans and AFDL have taken Kinshasa, the Congolese capital, slipping in quietly without much opposition. Angola's intervention has been crucial, the reporter says, and the war is more or less over. He doesn't say the first Congo war is over, because he doesn't know it's the first yet, but that's what it is – something in a series, like Manu's seven missions. The old, post-independence, pre-Mobutu flag, featuring a single large star and six smaller stars on a blue background, has been raised over the capital. Kabila's presidency of the Democratic Republic of Congo is finally confirmed, quickly being recognised internationally.

Some democracy, Manu sniffs, listening to subsequent broadcasts out of Kinshasa over the next few weeks. As Kabila establishes a new government and army and does more deals with mining companies, the Rwandans and AFDL busy themselves with seeking out potential opposition in the city. In their keenness to elicit information, according to UN observers, the AFDL – made up principally of Manu's Banyamulenge kin, at least those who haven't fled east to join Recognition and other renegade bands – develop a strong predilection for the *chicotte*, a leather-tongued whip introduced by the Belgians.

It makes Manu sick to hear this; and the sense of feeling fine that he briefly experienced on the way back from Mzuzu is further licked away by other items of bad news coming out of Kinshasa. The idealism, if it ever was that, of toppling Mobutu has clearly already degenerated into the usual run of grab and graft. All Manu wants to do is erase what's happened to him, erase what has happened to his country, erase time itself.

Tick tock, says the zinc-framed clock in The Passenger, blinking its lashes in reprimand whenever he glances at it. *Your exam's coming up*, it seems to say, *the examination on your work in progress, Manu Kwizera, you who have been through absolute horror but have moved into your new life too seamlessly.*

153

III

The Interbellum

June 1997–August 1998

Chapter 1

To his great surprise, the exam goes well. Exams, in fact, as he's built up such prodigious hours over the course of his seven missions – with all their zigzag, in-and-out, to-and-fro – that he's able to do the private and commercial exams back to back, and much more rapidly than normal. As soon as the results come through, Cogan takes him to the aviation authority offices in Entebbe. Once the paperwork is done and his commercial licence issued, they career in the Cherokee from Entebbe to Kampala, where Cogan's organised a party that evening. Or two parties, as the celebration for Manu coincides with Evgeny's farewell, his departure to Dubai now being common knowledge.

It's an exciting moment all right, holding the licence card in his hand. As well as feeling that the effort to get it was worth it, he also has a sense that he has learned something significant from each freight dog.

From Cogan he's learned, as well as the basics, how to land and take off under fire, also that clever *pantsula* move, said to fox surface-to-air missiles (though he's not sure he'd ever be able to do it himself); from Evgeny he's learned how to forge end-user certificates (though he hopes he will never be in a position when he has to do that); and from Papa he's learned – what, exactly? Grace, understanding, self-care? Something, anyway, quite different from the lessons of those other apprenticeships.

He's oddly troubled, all the same. He might have done the seven missions, but it doesn't feel like heaven. More that all this while he's been visiting an asylum and just realised that he too is one of the patients.

As the Cherokee speeds along tree-lined residential avenues, then crosses through an industrial area, leading to a junction thronged with *boda* bikes, part of him desperately wants to voice his real feelings to Cogan: that yes, he owes him so much and knows he's lucky to have this chance of a livelihood, but also that he can't keep going on in the same way.

He doesn't express this, of course. Not least because, having dodged through the *boda* pack and butted between two *matatus* at the next junction, Cogan's already slugging from a half-bottle of his favourite even as he drives, lifting that same, thick-veined, tattooed forearm that Manu first saw emerge from the Cargo-master at Rutshuru.

The party's at the Sheraton on Ternan Avenue, in the middle of Kampala. On the way into the hotel, Cogan stops to do up a shoelace on a step, grunting – almost falling over – with the effort of it. Inside, Michelle Tikoto, Gerry's favourite singer, is dancing on stage to the rhythms of the house band.

Cogan plucks the licence from Manu's hand as the two of them approach the table where the others are waiting, waves it in front of their faces.

Gerry at once grabs the licence. As nattily dressed as ever – in white suit, silk shirt and crocodile-skin shoes – the Kenyan inspects the laminated document, feigning a ceremony of due diligence.

'Definitely a fake,' he announces, before it's passed round. But eventually, passing a hand over his straight-cut, pillar-like half-Afro as if to absolve himself of failure, he pays over his wager to Cogan, who gives a snort of triumph.

'Told ya!'

Gerry says blandly, 'Yes, you did, Cogan.' He pulls down the cuffs of his suit, as if trying to regain his self-respect.

Manu's congratulated by Papa, who hugs him, and in a manner by Evgeny, who just nods his big head. The Russian seems anxious. Manu has his first drink, watches the reeling circumvolutions of Michelle Tikoto and her sisters, if the other women on stage really are her sisters.

Studying them, as the music rings in his ears, he recollects Edith. Her cool, lithe fingers on the back of his neck. Is he missing her? He's missing something. To turn off the chatter in his head, encouraged by the others except Papa, he drinks: drinks as if this is the real and only sign of becoming a fully paid-up member of the company of freight dogs. He drinks so much, in fact, that he loses track of the liquid courage for his future – foamy, troubled with mixers, spiritually confused – that they're pouring down him, there at the Sheraton bar – beginning with Nile Specials and Clubs, followed by a whisky courtesy of Cogan – that same Johnnie Walker Red Label, just as the Texan prefers – plus a gin and tonic from Gerry, and then a rum and Coke from someone else, and a few ice-cold lagers to 'cleanse the system', as the Texan puts it. 'Hair of the dog before it's bit ya,' he adds.

Later, Cogan stands up and says: 'Guys, we're not just sayin' hello to Manu as a newly qualified fly boy, we're also sayin' goodbye to Evgeny, who's going to live in Dubai.' He points his cigar at Evgeny, who's scowling like a thunderhead. 'What none of us understands is why you're going, who the fuck wants to be stuck in the desert? If it's the investigation, brother, don't be anxious, we'll all cover for you.'

The Russian stands up, glaring at Cogan. It looks like he's going to hit him. 'You're a *peez* of shit, Cogan,' he fires back. 'I don't know where you got your information from about any investigation . . .' He pauses, gives Manu a glance as cold as the lager he's been sipping, then raises his voice. 'But I know something doesn't have to be true to be sold.' He turns and looks at the rest of them. 'You know, until I came here, I really didn't think this was such a filthy *biznes*. Now I do know.'

He leaves, slouching down his big shoulders as he walks off.

Manu struggles to process this, because if anyone's up to his eyes in the filthiness of what the freight dogs do, it's Evgeny. But what Manu suspects is that he's worked out it was he who told Cogan about the investigation. And it's true, Manu did tell Cogan when he came back from the US, but . . .

'Who's he reckon he is, anyhow, hollering at me like that?' Cogan grunts.

Stung by Evgeny's look, Manu tells the others he needs the toilet and heads in that direction, before doubling back out of sight and going into the car park.

It's almost dark by now. Evgeny's Isuzu is already pulling away; it stops for a second, as if he's seen him in the rear-view mirror, then roars off, Manu running after it like a dog on a lead. What he wanted to say is, you asked me not to say anything about going to Dubai, which everyone knows now – not about the investigation; that wasn't the secret I was asked to keep!

But what he realises, standing there on the asphalt as the Isuzu's red tail lights speed down on to Ternan Avenue, is that regardless of the facts, he might still have betrayed the Russian. Are you just a fool, he asks himself, someone who can't keep his mouth shut?

He comes back in to find Gerry and Papa quizzing a now very drunk Cogan about the investigation.

'Yeah, Uncle Sam doing the honours,' slurs Cogan. 'I heard it way back from a guy in Kigali, a pilot I used to work with in the air force.'

Manu's relieved that he wasn't the original source of Cogan's information after all; and, at the same time, regrets that he isn't able to tell Evgeny so.

'But relax, *hombres*, we should be all right,' Cogan continues. 'They won't mess with our clients. Even if Rusyo and co. are getting a bit antsy, there's just too much at stake for Washington to lose in terms of resource, strategic control, all the other stupid terms in which they and the Europeans conceive Africa. Just gotta keep on trucking!'

'It's a pity he went like that, though,' says Papa. 'It shouldn't be this way, we have all shared so much.'

'Boo hoo,' says Cogan.

After all of which, at the end of their set, the Tikoto sisters join the freight-dog table, stomping over in matching leather skirts and wax-printed blouses. Glistening with sweat, they're hungry and order curry from the waiter.

They are, Manu decides, clearly not sisters, not least coming from different countries in West Africa. As they eat, complaining about the quality of the rice accompanying the curry, a conversation ensues about which West African country makes the best jollof rice, who invented it in the first place, and why East African rice is such a poor relation.

This talk of food, about which Papa is surprisingly knowledgeable, makes Manu think of his mother. She was a fish person. Full fish, made with okra. Fish with bones preferred, rather than as fillet, like white people serve it.

Considering how much more than normal he has drunk – they're good reservoirs, those long legs of his – Manu's OK, but Cogan can hardly stand by the end of the evening, by which time Papa has already made his excuses. Gerry and Michelle Tikoto disappear to the lift, followed by the two other singers, their platform heels clacking on the tiled floor.

'Hop up, my ladies,' Cogan murmurs, giving a wolfish grin.

'What?'

'Mebbe he's got plans for all three,' he explains, and Manu doesn't know whether he's jealous or admiring. 'Let's have another Scotch.'

So they do. The Tikoto band having packed up, the speakers in the hotel bar are playing a Rolling Stones song, 'Sympathy for the Devil'. As this and the next song, whatever it is, run their course, Cogan tries to do one of his origami sculptures out of a dollar bill.

The winged man, it seems to be.

But his hands are shaking too much and eventually he just scrumples it up, flicks it across the table to Manu. 'Well you know what some guy once said, kid: forget the wax and feathers, do a better job on the wings.'

Unable to drive, Cogan lurches to the Sheraton's front desk and books the two of them a room. It's meant to have twin beds, but on arrival they find it's a double. Manu watches in disgusted wonder as Cogan kicks off his shoes, throws off his safari-suit jacket and then stumbles about the room, trying to take off his trousers.

He falls on to the bed, saying, 'Sorry, kid, no one needs to see this. I've got this history with drinking, but, fuck it, history's . . .'

He stops speaking, stops breathing, it seems like, before croaking out: 'History's an idiot anyhow, else none of this stuff would've happened.' His voice falters again, gets fainter, like the signal on the radio in The Passenger sometimes. 'Maybe two idiots, one writing a flight plan, the other fucking with it as soon as the ink's dry.' He starts to snore then – head snapping back, Adam's apple quavering like a marula fruit in the wind.

He stays like this for a while, Manu sitting on the end of the bed, still gawking.

The snores get louder, their rising drone becoming a series of alarmingly short nasal explosions, at the apparent end of which Cogan abruptly sits up. Fistfuls of fat bubble over the waistband of his half-undone trousers. But the nap seems to have somehow poked Cogan's thoughts back into something like coherence. 'Kid, 'pect wonderin' about that bust-up with Evgeny. Not my fault, what happened . . .'

'What did happen?' Manu asks, exhausted but interested to know the origin of the row.

'Rusyo cancelled all Evgeny's contracts. He heard about the investigation, didn't want the US crawling all over the RPA.'

'But I thought the US was supporting the RPA?'

'They are – and the Brits, too, the sneaky fuckers. Only the French have a genuine beef with Kigali, if you don't count all the African governments who wanna stick their pinkies in Congo pie. But even if one bit of the US government's breaking the frigging law, don't mean another part's not gonna try play policeman.' He gives a long, hoarse sigh, while managing to free himself fully of his trousers, revealing a pair of surprisingly white boxer shorts.

Dirty mouth, clean pants.

'Don't worry about Evgeny, he was always a scumbag. But we're all scumbags!' With which wisdom, Cogan slumps backwards, hitting his head on the headboard.

He groans, turns over on his side – his enormous midriff following his shoulders, rolling down. A plum-coloured ball slips out from the side of his boxer shorts. He rubs the back of his head, flails his tattooed arm in search of the sheet, finds it finally, gives it a tug and Manu a glazed look, promptly falls back to sleep.

Manu despondently gets undressed and lies down on the bed next to Cogan, ramrod-straight. Sweating like an overripe pineapple, half covered by the sheet, the Texan's maggoty-white body seems more prodigious than ever. Cogan groans again, turns on to his back; is he ever going to settle? Not yet, at any rate, because next he throws out a hand that catches Manu hard on the cheek.

Chapter 2

Manu's first couple of months of solo flying mainly involve the tobacco run to Malawi that he first did with Papa. He gets to know the route well, beginning with the crossing over the silver surface of Lake Victoria, then on into the vast grassy plains of Tanzania, before entering Malawi near Karonga, the lakeside town which Papa told him was formerly a centre for slavery.

On the Tanzanian leg, he passes over a number of game parks and takes the opportunity to fly low, looking at elephant or wildebeest, the little shadow of the plane dwarfed by the size of the herds. Then on, over the Nyika escarpment and landing on to the runway at Mzuzu, trundling to the end and tying down the plane.

He spends night after night in this drowsy town – staying at the Mzuzu Inn, drinking Greens at Mama K's bar, listening to that same jingle van going up and down, selling Omo and traumatic memory, consolidated in the brain; then out again next morning. He realises that he misses flying with Cogan and Papa. But Cogan's in Kinshasa, and Papa's flying less and less as he winds down for his retirement.

Having taken a contract flying Kabila about on official duties, Cogan reported on his last visit to The Passenger that the new president often keeps ambassadors or even heads of state waiting, sometimes doesn't even turn up at all to red-carpet events. Among the folk kept waiting, Cogan added, are a bunch of UN investigators who've been drafted in to look at the massacres perpetrated during the invasion, their permits to go into the interior being constantly delayed.

'They're not gonna find much holed up at the Intercontinental,' Cogan told Manu on the same occasion; when not dropping back into Entebbe, he's staying at this well-known Kinshasa hotel himself, now that he's in funds again. 'Funny thing is, they don't seem to care so much, lying by the pool on expenses. You know how the old song goes, "Don't mind the weather when the wind don't blow"!'

On Friday nights, back from Mzuzu, Manu goes to see the Ndere show in Kampala rather than hang about in The Passenger. David Kisase, the Banyamulenge guy he played football with on the beach, becomes a friend. It's a great show that he and his colleagues put on: amazing drummers, and dancers balancing two, three, in some cases up to ten clay pots on their heads, swaying in time to the music. After one show, David introduces him to Matthias, the other Banyamulenge refugee he mentioned, and the three of them go for a drink in a bar near the outdoor theatre where the shows take place.

'You know you're famous?' Matthias tells Manu as they sit down.

'What?'

'I'm in touch with some of our folk over the border, ex-AFDL trying to set up their own shop. They talk about you as the one who got away and stood up to Rusyo, which is what they all want to do now.'

'That's hogwash,' Manu says authoritatively, sipping his Nile, realising only after the words have left his lips that he first heard that expression from Cogan. 'I might be partly free of that world, but I haven't got away from anything. You two have escaped more, doing your theatre. I feel like I'm still in the conflict.'

'What do you mean?' David says.

'Well, put it this way, every time a cargo plane goes into Congo from here, it's not carrying sacks of millet or dried fish.'

'Guns?'

'That's not what I'm doing right now, I'm just flying tobacco up from Malawi, but . . . yes.'

''The theatre of war pays better than the theatre of theatre,' announces Matthias, in a pleased-with-himself way. And then they both give Manu a look across the table that makes him feel uncomfortable; it's the same look, Manu knows now, that he used to give Cogan and the other whites: a kind of cringe, based on nothing but money and power, the same forces driving events in the world beyond the bar.

'What do you mean, ex-AFDL guys setting up their own shop, anyway?' he asks.

'Oh,' David says. 'You didn't know? A lot have deserted and joined a militia under the command of a guy called Recognition Gahiji. But there's loads of others still stuck in the new Congolese Army in Kinshasa, all pissed off about being integrated with units of mixed ethnicity. They're calling it *brassage*, but from what I'm hearing it doesn't work.'

Manu doesn't say anything, seeing again Recognition's face as he pleaded for help in Bunia.

Later that night, which he spends at a cheap hotel in central Kampala rather than returning to Entebbe, his memories of the past are sharpened further by a CNN documentary showing on the TV in the hotel room. It's about Bukavu's recovery from the war. Well, 'recovery' or something like that was in the title, but what the programme revealed was that his old school, and other familiar places in the town, were burnt down during the war.

A few weeks later, when he's back in Entebbe, the telephone rings at The Passenger. It's Cogan, calling from his room at the Intercontinental in Kinshasa. 'Kid, we got a new contract, a scientific outfit in Belgium concerned about the Virunga volcanoes. So you can drop the cob runs to Malawi, I'll find someone else for them, and get on this.'

'What do you mean, cob runs?' Manu says over the crackly line.

'Oh yeah, sorry kid. Ask Papa, he'll explain. Anyhow, this new job, it'll last about a month, there'll be a bit of ground operation, too. Area of coverage is from Goma for that big live one there, forget what it's called . . .'

'Nyiragongo', he tells him, feeling dread about the prospect of going near his old home and its volcano.

'And then into Rwanda to see the ones there . . . Anyhow, get yourself to Arusha in Tanzania on August first for the pick-up. I've sorted out the fuel, and some exes for you. Expect a lot of kit, kid, 'cos those science folk always have that. Client's name is Anke Desseaux – you'll have to get Papa to tell you how to pronounce that properly.'

A couple of nights before Manu's due in Arusha, he meets the old Belgian, who's sitting alone on the veranda of The Passenger, looking gaunt. He tells him about the job and asks about the Belgian name.

'Anke as in "blanket", Desseaux as in "sew". She must have a Flemish mother and French-speaking father, with that name.'

Manu wasn't quite sure whether Cogan, in saying the name, spoke of a man or a woman. But Papa has other news for him. 'Manu, I've decided to finally cash in my chips. All this is getting too much for me! Just want to go back to my farm in Flanders, plant potatoes, do up that old bird that's been waiting there for me. And do some cooking; I'm sick of having my food cooked by a houseboy all these years, though I guess that was my choice. And I'm quite ill, too, anyway. I need to see a specialist.'

'What's wrong?'

'Christ knows, just feel exhausted all the time.'

He senses that Papa's not telling the truth, but he's also desperately sad that the old guy's leaving. 'When are you going?'

'Next week. I'll be gone by the time you get back from your trip.'

'I'll miss you.'

'You'll get over it.'

'There's something I need to tell you.'

'Oh yes?'

'Evgeny spoke to me about the investigation Cogan mentioned at his send-off . . . and I told Cogan.'

It's a relief to unburden himself.

'So? It didn't surprise me that there was an investigation, when it came up at the Sheraton. In fact, I can think of this coming up at least three times before, since I've been here.'

'How can we know we won't get drawn into it?' Manu asks.

'We can't. You're still a bit of a worrier, aren't you?'

'Should I say something to Cogan about why Evgeny was angry?'

Papa takes a suck of milk from his glass. He has a small, black mark on one of his cheeks, like a beauty spot. 'That's up to you. You need to start making these decisions on your own. No one will look after you but yourself.'

'I know. I've been happier not flying weapons.'

'Well, don't think just not transporting guns will keep you clean. Everyone knows the trouble that comes with diamonds and coltan and gold. Even something as apparently innocent as palm oil can make a prisoner of a person, causing them to lose their self-respect. That trade has hardly changed in three hundred years. Ditto sugar, double ditto minerals. We might seem as if we're in a postcolonial world, Manu, but we're not, not really. Don't become anybody's slave.'

'I won't,' he says, wondering if it's already happened, and then remembers something. 'Oh yeah . . . Cogan called the Malawi flights "cob runs" – he said you'd explain.'

Papa wipes milk off his lips, looking embarrassed. 'Yes, we should have told you about that.'

'About what?'

'Those tobacco bales?'

'Yes?'

'Well after a couple of kosher layers of tobacco, most of them are hollowed out and packed with empty maize cobs filled with Malawi Gold, which are then sent by truck to South Africa or Kenya, and then by ship to Europe. Know what I mean?'

Manu nods. He does know, because all through central and southern Africa – even back home in the Kivus, which grows plenty enough *bangi* of its own – Malawi Gold, wrapped in leaves from maize cobs, is famous as one of the finest strains of cannabis.

'Sorry, my fault really, I should've told you when we were first flying it.'

When they say goodbye, Manu gives Papa a big hug, causing the old man to groan in what seems like genuine pain. He's conscious of how thin the Belgian has become, being able to feel his ribs under his shirt.

Chapter 3

He lands at Arusha, a domestic airport in northern Tanzania, mainly serving visitors to game parks. Entering the modest, green-roofed terminal he spots a figure who might be his passenger, sitting with her back to him on a banquette. The building has a few vintage posters, linocuts showing exotic images of lions, giraffe, kudu . . . relics of safaris past.

No other passengers are waiting. Bulky equipment bags of brightly coloured plastic, surrounding her, are further evidence that this is indeed Anke Desseaux; Cogan said there'd be a lot of kit. He takes in the curve of her back, her strong shoulders, white T-shirt, black knee-length shorts, strappy fawn sandals. Her hair – thick, blond and long – is bisected by a significant parting that draws attention to the almost perfect roundness of her head.

She's writing something on a laptop, resting it on her knees. He taps her on the shoulder. She jumps, swivels round in panic.

Manu smiles. 'Sorry, I didn't mean to startle you, are you . . . Anke Desseaux?'

She nods, but retains an anxious expression as he continues, 'I'm the pilot you booked through Normair. Manu Kwizera. Pleased to meet you.'

'Likewise,' she replies. Her face looks work-tired, and she has a large mosquito bite on her forehead, but she's still disconcertingly attractive. He's suddenly over-conscious of his cheap pilot's uniform and the cracked shoes he's been meaning to replace ever since Brno. She smiles, all the same.

'The plane is ready whenever you are,' he offers, looking at the bags piled up round her. 'It'll take a bit of time to load all this, though.'

'I'm sorry, it's rather heavy, too.'

'What is it?'

'Equipment for monitoring volcanoes. Batteries, mainly. You do know what we're doing, don't you?'

He pulls the job sheet out of his back pocket. 'I've got Goma and neighbouring districts, then Fort Portal. Then back down into Rwanda. But routing to Entebbe right now.'

'I'll explain on the way.'

'OK, I'll get a porter for all this stuff.'

It takes a while, everything moving slowly in Arusha.

Manu waits at the top of the plane's steps for Anke to follow him up, the equipment finally having been loaded – then turns away, having glimpsed a sprig of bra strap, green and slightly laced, showing beyond the neck of her T-shirt. What's happening to me – am I becoming a womaniser like Gerry? Hardly, yet there he was, staring.

Anke's a little older than him, maybe five years. 'So who do you work for?' he asks, guiding her to the co-pilot's seat.

'I'm employed as a research fellow at the Benelux Volcanological Consortium. It's attached to a museum.'

'What's a museum got to do with volcanoes?'

'It goes back to colonial collections of rocks, but basically I'm part of a group of scientific organisations that includes universities and my museum. The BVC's focused on the Virunga volcanoes, but we also cover African volcanology more generally.'

'Where's your museum?'

'Just outside Brussels. The Royal Museum of Central Africa, in Tervuren.'

'Is that a good place to live, Tervuren?' Manu worries he might be saying the name wrong.

'It's a nice place, yes, but I don't live there. I live in another town nearby: Leuven. Also a nice place.'

He passes a set of headphones to her, noticing as he does so that the cockpit window is steamed over. He picks up a sponge, wipes it.

'Oh!' Anke says, as if this seems far too low-tech a thing to do on an aircraft, even one as basic as the Cargomaster.

A speck of male boasting creeps into his speech. 'These are very simple machines, but I have also flown others – even an Antonov, one of the biggest aircraft!'

'I'm happy to hear it,' she says, turning her round head to look at him.

'How long will it take to Entebbe?' she asks, as he goes through the pre-flight checks.

'About two hours,' he replies, beginning the take-off roll. 'So, what have you been doing here in Tanzania?'

'Gathering rock samples from Lengai, the volcano nearby, and checking the equipment there. This trip's mainly about servicing the seismographic and other equipment that monitors most of the volcanoes in the region. What we're going to need to do in the next month—'

'Uh, let's talk in a minute or two, once we're airborne.'

'Sorry,' she says.

On reaching altitude, he says: 'OK, tell me.'

'We've got a number of small monitoring stations across the Virunga range in Congo, Rwanda and Uganda, plus Lengai here in Tanzania, that send data back home by radio signal. These stations mainly measure tremors, earthquakes basically; the movement of magma in the depths of volcanoes is triggered by shifts in *plaques tectoniques* . . . tectonic plates.'

All this time they have been speaking in English, so he says: 'We can speak in French if you like.'

'*D'accord*,' she replies, flashing him a heart-stopping smile. 'But it's all the same to me, I did my PhD in Edinburgh, so I had to sharpen up my English. Or Scottish at least! But how come you speak French – I thought you were Ugandan?'

'Originally from Congo,' he explains, still speaking English, as she seems to prefer. 'But you were saying, about the measurements?'

'Yes, we also measure deformation, shifts in the surface

ground. The instruments are powered by solar panels feeding batteries . . . but these batteries sometimes lose charge, all the same. They have to be checked every four years, roughly. They were last checked in 1992, but we think a number of the stations have been vandalised during the war because our data flow has dried up completely at some sites. I'm basically here to go and look.'

'On your own?'

'Yes, I was here on the '92 trip as a post-doc, so I know what to do. Also, we're a bit short-staffed. They chose me partly because I grew up here – in Bukavu, anyway.'

'You grew up in Bukavu?' Now he's amazed.

'My father was a scientist; he measured carbon dioxide levels in the lake. My mother was a sculptor; she ran a cultural centre.'

'I remember that place,' he says. 'I went to school in Bukavu, you see.'

'Did you? My parents left in 1989. I'm hoping we can visit my mother's centre on this trip, even though it's not quite on the itinerary.'

He sighs. 'I think that place got burnt down in the fighting. I'm sorry. A lot of things have changed.'

She sits in silence, absorbing this news.

'My own school was destroyed, too,' he adds, as if it might make things better. 'So – tell me what you've got planned for this trip.'

'We go to four of the volcanoes in the Virunga range, so Nyiragongo, Nyamuragira, Karisimbi and Gahinga, landing locally and hiring a vehicle and porters to help us climb. Then back into Uganda, up to Fort Portal to look at the extinct volcanoes round there.'

Manu laughs. Cogan hadn't told him much of this detail. He thought what Cogan had described as 'ground operations' meant just calling a few hotels and taxi firms for her.

'What's amusing, please?'

'Nothing. Just thinking we'll be lucky to get all this done in a month. Have you booked vehicles in all these places, and porters?'

'Your manager, Mr Cogan, said you would organise all that.'

'*Did* he?' Despite laughing just now, Manu's starting to feel quite angry. 'I wasn't informed. You know, you'd have been better off using a helicopter for some parts of this job.'

'We looked into it, but the only people who would quote was a firm in Johannesburg. It's very expensive getting insurance for this sort of expedition; your Mr Cogan offered us a cheap rate, so we could also afford the cover on top.'

She turns her eyes towards him, asking, 'You will be able to help, though, won't you?'

'Yes, but it's not going to be easy. You have dollars?'

'Of course. I thought we'd start with Nyiragongo – get the most difficult one over first. It's safe there now, right?'

'Well, the war is over, thank God, but—'

Before he can say anything else she calls out, rather excitedly, 'Look, there's Lengai, where I was just now, can we fly over the crater, please?'

'What's the deal with planes and volcanoes?' he asks, vaguely remembering something from the flying manuals as Mount Lengai's white-capped cone rises out of the savannah.

'Ash,' she replies, causing a memory of burying his mother to drift into his mind. 'If there's an ash plume, or cloud, you need to keep away from it, but just flying in the vicinity of lava is fine.'

'Really?'

'Really. I've done it myself in South America and also other places in Africa – like Ethiopia. Of the peaks we're going to, only Nyiragongo and Nyamuragira are active anyway; all the rest are dormant or extinct.'

'What's the definition of "extinct"?' he asks, starting a circuit of Mount Lengai.

'Hasn't erupted in ten thousand years.'

'And dormant?'

'Not expected to erupt soon, according to current measurements.'

'But what does "soon" mean?'

'That's harder to answer – you're dealing with time spans in which next Tuesday, next year and three hundred years in the future are almost the same, at least from the volcano's point of view.'

'But Lengai's extinct, right?' He feels a need to get the right perspective on all this.

'No, it's active, but its last eruption was 1966, so it's maybe coming up for "inactive", another term we use.'

'Well 1966 is good enough for me,' he says, making a turn.

'I want to take pictures.' She gets a camera out of her bag. 'Can I open the window?'

'Sure.'

He comes in low over the crater, does a go-around. Then banks again and – really testing his skills, it's a hard manoeuvre – dips quickly down and up into the crater on a pass, narrowly skirting its rocky lip.

All the while the shutter from her camera is clicking like crazy. If she's impressed by his flying, she doesn't say so.

Further on in the flight, he confesses to her: 'I lived near one of your volcanoes once.'

'Which?'

'Nyiragongo.'

She looks across at him, surprised. 'We really do have quite a lot in common. Have you been in the crater?'

'We didn't go up much. Not something my people would normally do. It was almost as if we didn't notice it, or it was just part of the sky.' This is true: however near, the volcano was something upwards rather than proximate, or even present to mind, something to be occasionally noted as you gazed up and saw the cotton-white thread plying from its crater into the clouds. 'I myself only went one time, with my father, when I was about ten. We tended to stay near our village.'

'Which was. . . ?' she asks. 'I've been studying maps.'

'Pendele was the village, but we lived a bit away, in our own complex. Both were destroyed in the war.'

Now it's her turn to say 'I'm sorry'.

He tries not to let images of his family wisp into his head again, but they do all the same, sneaking in through mental crevices. 'Do you think Nyiragongo will erupt again? My father used to speak of an eruption in 1977, the year I was born.'

'We don't know. Each volcano has a different personality, different behaviour.'

'You speak of them as if they're people.'

'They are in a way. Just as unpredictable. An eruption can change its intensity and its period, rumbling on for decades with little bursts every ten minutes before unexpectedly going cataclysmic.'

'But can you actually predict it, like the weather? As pilots we have to think about the weather a lot.'

'To an extent we can, looking at tremors and deformations like I said, sometimes gas emissions – though that's a new field. We can also look at rocks from previous eruptions, try to work out what's happening in the subsurface.'

They pass through some turbulence; the plane rocks on the cushion of its own speed. Not worrying for him, but it seems to make Anke nervous, causing her to grip the edge of her seat with sharp, pale-painted fingernails.

'Don't worry,' he says. 'This is not something to be frightened of.'

'I'm not frightened!'

As they approach Entebbe he has a sense of homecoming, cheering up about the impending trip back into Congo. *This* is his home now, not there. What happened before can be kept in the past, something tragic but over now. Period, as Cogan sometimes said. After landing, he makes arrangements for storing her equipment, and they share a taxi to the guesthouse she's staying in. They have dinner together, make plans for the trip to Goma and the ascent of Nyiragongo.

That night, back at The Passenger, he's shocked to find Anke's hair entwining the propellors of his mind as he tries to sleep. He dreams of burying his face in it.

For so long, he's just wanted someone to hold him at night. It's not the physical or even the emotional lack, it's talking, just plain talking. Forgetting the bar girls in The Passenger, who hardly speak except to petition for sodas, putting aside (as he's had to) the tale of early life in military camps that Edith told him in Kilo Moto, he realises that Anke is the first woman he's properly talked to in ages.

Even if she did mostly talk about volcanoes.

Chapter 4

He grimaces at Anke; she smiles back, assuming no doubt it's the effort of walking at altitude or whiffs of sulphur that's making him pull this face. What else could it be? Not his irrational fear that he'll see the charred remains of his family compound, even though it would all in any case have been covered over by vegetation now, and they're on the other side of the mountain. The idea of crossing over and trying to find his old home is not something he can countenance.

Manu almost feels like the alien here, as he watches Anke walking; she's pulled further away up the slope, hair in a ponytail swinging behind her. Next to her is the green-uniformed figure of Monsieur Georges, as he insists on being called.

Georges Bamwisho, their guide and driver, rifle over his shoulder. An experienced man, into whose trust Manu's happy to put what Cogan called the ground operations. Short and barrel-like with a very deep voice, he was part of the old, government-run ranger team that did tours of the volcano before the war. Now he's set up as *patron* of his own business, perhaps the reason for the insistence on *monsieur*.

Manu has not told him anything about his own connection to the area; what he noticed, the two days he and Anke were in Goma, is that nobody dares ask questions about personal ethnicity any more. It took a long time to find someone trustworthy like Monsieur Georges, who also possessed a vehicle; Manu and Anke went about the bars and hotels in the city, asking all and sundry, the old systems of excursion tours and so on having largely broken down in the war.

In the hotel they stayed in while searching out this assistance, mangy stuffed wildlife adorned the lobby and there were gorilla dolls for sale, hanging from a revolving display. There was also a wood-framed panel behind glass, outlining local beliefs about Mount Nyiragongo:

> The memory of former eruptions is preserved in accounts of battles between Ryang'ombe and his enemy, Nyiragongo, who then lived in Mount Mikeno. Ryang'ombe, with his fiery sword, cleft this mountain from top to bottom, and drove Nyiragongo westwards to the mountain which now bears his name. He then cut off the top of this peak with his sword, threw Nyiragongo into it, and piled hot stones on him to keep him down. One is reminded of Enceladus and of Typhon, Giant and Titan respectively. Sons of Gaia by different fathers, both were sealed under Etna by Zeus. Note that the type cult of Ryang'ombe, or variant names, 'the man who eats a whole ox', is fairly widespread in southern Africa, where he appears as an over-reacher, at first defeating other monsters, such as resident volcanic spirits, as in the Nyiragongo version, but then meeting his match in a giant ox: typically, this figure is one who sets out to fight ogres, but dies when he swallows an ogre so fierce that it bursts from his stomach.
>
> WERNER, *MYTHS AND LEGENDS OF THE BANTU* 1933

This text made Anke laugh.

On the mountainside where they are now, if Manu turns he can see the two porters that Monsieur Georges hired for them, lugging Anke's equipment bags on their shoulders: Deogratias and Virgil, they're called.

He catches up with her. The ascent takes them over cracked, razor-sharp ridges of long-cooled lava interspersed with plants: purple-flowered lobelias, vines, stunted thorn trees. Some of the lava fragments are round rather than sharp; it's like walking over stone tennis balls. All up this way of loose rock, hot underfoot, Monsieur Georges keeps calling out, in French, '*Courage, courage!*'

As they get nearer to the crater it sounds thunderously, now a vast drum, now the bell of a great cathedral. Clouds of noxious vapours roll down towards them – the result of eruptive gases exploding far below the surface, Anke explains.

The monitoring station is about a quarter of a mile down from the summit. Anke tells them to look for a solar panel and radio aerial mounted on a concrete column, at the foot of which, she says, are boxes containing the battery and seismometer. Plus, nearby, something called a 'tiltmeter', which she explains as a sort of spirit level on a gimble, able to rotate as well as tip from side to side.

All this she tells Manu about as they make their way up to the slope, naming each part as they climb and explaining its function.

On finding the spot, however, they can see that the box that contains the battery is shattered and covered in scorch marks. The solar panel has been smashed and the concrete column is covered in soot. The tiltmeter, too, has been knocked off its gimble and the probes of the seismometer pulled out of both its box and the ground.

'Ruined,' Anke says, looking downcast.

'Somebody's shot at it,' Manu says, seeing there are bullet holes in the concrete and that the battery itself has also been pierced in several places.

'Yes,' she replies. 'I was warned there might be cases like this. It looks as if the battery has caught fire also.'

She pulls on a pair of gloves and starts removing the battery, which is leaking chemicals.

He's impressed by her brisk, professional manner, and it doesn't take long for a new battery to be unpacked from the equipment bags and connected to the installation. She manages to reconnect the wires linking the probes to the seismometer. She asks him to dig the probes into the ground with a little spade that's part of the kit she's brought.

'What about this?' he asks afterwards, holding up the pole of the smashed solar panel, the plastic parts of which are slightly melted, congealed like candle wax.

'Nothing we can do, at least on this trip; it will need a new one and I didn't bring any. This battery will hold its charge for a while. But I won't know if it's actually transmitting till I check with my colleagues.'

'I'm sorry.'

She shrugs, still fiddling with the seismometer. 'It's why I'm here. Now let's see if this thing can be made to work again.'

Having made such repairs as she can, Anke suggests that the party climbs closer to the crater. The porters refuse to do so, partly because their flip-flops – they're both wearing these – are melting, partly because they subscribe to the view that the caldera of Nyiragongo is where their ancestor spirits dwell. Monsieur Georges doesn't want to come either, having, he says, seen it many times before.

'In the old days,' he discloses, 'we had hundreds of tourists coming up here – it brought in lots of money; it just makes me sad to go there now.'

Monsieur Georges squats down next to the porters, by now smoking leaf-cones of rough tobacco, holding them in their fists and sucking through the tube of their hands. Though now a smoker himself, Manu can't imagine how anyone can do so up here, the air being so caustic. As he and Anke begin the final ascent, one of the porters calls out something in Swahili.

Anke asks what it means, and Manu explains: 'He said, "If you see my father down there, say hello to him from Virgil!"'

She laughs: 'I'd heard of this belief, it's the same with volcanoes in other parts of the world. There are also many myths in which one volcano is the argumentative sibling of its neighbour. Or they're squabbling spouses.'

After a pause, she asks, 'Are you married, Manu?'

'No!' he replies, with perhaps too much force. 'But I've heard people say that thing about Nyiragongo and Nyamuragira being brother and sister.' It's quite funny, this *muzungu* woman telling him myths he has heard since he was a small boy; but he doesn't say anything, letting her rattle on.

They reach the edge of the caldera, get down on their bellies, feeling the heat on their faces increase as they creep closer. Neither of them says anything at first, as they stare at the lake of molten lava. The huge waves below switch between black and red, and secondary shades of grey and orange. The lava appears to promise organisation; predictability; a sequence: then summarily undermines what's been promised. Their clothes begin to soak with condensation.

The pool of bubbling magma is almost a kilometre wide, and its waves are constantly changing shape, as well as colour. As all this is happening, a bass grinding sound can be heard, coming from deep in the crater, which acts like a loudspeaker.

The lava skin suddenly turns grey across its totality. Manu remembers it was like that the whole time when he saw it with his father a decade or so ago. 'Is that normal, the changing of colour?' he asks Anke.

'There's never a norm with volcanoes. Best think only in terms of probabilities.' Even as she speaks, the grey mass breaks up, orange fragments piercing through, the whole picture making Manu think of a particular type of giant toad, sometimes found in the forest, which has similar cryptic covering, making it difficult to discern.

'But there must be patterns, different types of behaviour that you categorise?'

'Yes, we do that frequently. But you have to really careful, keeping on observing, keeping on measuring, because quite often what you believe to be a pattern doesn't sustain itself; that happens even in eruptive phases. You think it's going to be a big one, all the measurements suggest so; and then it just . . . peters out. Normal people, farming down on the slopes, or in a nearby city, think the hazard from above is over but the truth is, science doesn't know whether the burp of gas or subsurface tremor which we wrongly thought signalled a major eruption yesterday is actually part of a longer-term pattern that will, tomorrow or tomorrow or tomorrow, produce that big eruption. In other words you're never quite sure if the horse has bolted or is still in the stable – if you see what I mean?'

'Sort of.'

'It's like what I was trying to explain to you when we flew over Lengai.'

The way that she pronounces the syllables of 'trying' makes him wonder if she thinks he is too stupid to understand; but there's no time to consider further this self-abasing hypothesis as a spatter of lava shoots out across the pit – hitting the other side, it makes him jump.

She laughs again. 'That's just one hazard. The most dangerous are pyroclastic flows: currents of gas, ash and hot rocks that stream down the mountain, really fast.'

Her thigh is right next to his as she tells him this. A gust of sulphurous wind blows a few strands of her hair into his face.

'Sorry!' she says, brushing it back down.

But he knows she's just a woman scientist regaling him with facts, not trying to seduce him, however much his ego – the ego of any man, perhaps – might flirt with that prestige.

They hear Monsieur Georges' voice calling from below, telling them that it's time to get moving.

Fog develops as they descend, fog mixed with tendrils of gas. Monsieur Georges says, 'We'd better take a different path back to the vehicle; this one's too dangerous.'

So, following him, they change direction. The path alters from cinder blocks to lava dust, then desiccated earth, finally the black soil Manu knows from his own district – asking all along, like all paths do, *what next, what next?*, half giving an answer with each step forwards, as the landscape of volcanic destruction becomes that of volcanic fertility: a thick, humid forest that eventually presents, as they round a corner, an enormous baobab tree, its twisted roots straddling the path. A column of *siafu*, army ants, is climbing up it, and Anke stops to look.

As Monsieur Georges talks about this upward phalanx of safari ants, many thousands of them, Manu realises with a jolt that he *knows* this tree. It marks the entrance to the grove where his initiation ceremony took place. Sure enough, there's another smaller path – branching off the main one, and arched by bushes. He tells the others he needs the toilet. Monsieur Georges extracts a roll of toilet paper from his rucksack and hands it to him.

It's further than he recalls, but eventually the tributary path – parts of which are very overgrown – gives out into the grove of memory. There has, as at his homestead, been a fire here, too, its effects masked by new growth, but there's no mistaking the flanks of the *omuku* trees, and the scorched remains of the ceremonial hut. Tears filling his eyes, he pulls back the bushes now choking the place, half expecting to find a body, evidence of another moment when God looked the other way.

He squats down, as if really having the shit he's pretending to, heaving deep breaths until he hears Anke and Monsieur Georges calling him.

On his return to the main path, Anke says, 'Thought we'd lost you,' but Manu doesn't reply, handing back to Monsieur Georges the unused roll of toilet paper, memories continuing to swab at him as they carry on walking under the green canopy of the trees.

After a couple more kilometres, they suddenly enter a zone of waste ground: a mixture of burnt tree stumps and basalt flats.

'This was a firebreak,' Monsieur Georges says, pointing at the trees. 'After Nyiragongo erupted in 1977, our forefathers tried to prevent fires spreading in the forest by making these, but it didn't work. Many of the animals fled from that time, shifting elsewhere or dying. There was once a herd of forest elephants here and they stampeded during the eruption; some became locked in lava. It is said that the remainder of the herd used to come back on to the lava field and stand in a circle around the mummified bodies.'

'Really?' Anke asks.

'For sure. My father actually saw this. He also was a ranger here too, but against poaching – not for the volcano. The elephants are long gone, and the gorillas nearly so, but there once used to be a lot of animals up here.'

After another tract of forest, they come into the village where Monsieur Georges parked his jeep. The place is on a sharp mountain edge, the land below dropping away fast, but still cultivated. A young woman balancing a yellow jerrycan of water on her head checks Manu out as she passes, and he experiences a flutter of anxiety that someone might recognise him here. But he's fairly sure he hasn't been to this village before, which is still quite far from Pendele.

At a kiosk with a sign painted on flattened tins, RESTAURATION ROYALE, everyone orders sodas. A generator is rumbling at the back of the store to keep the fridge going. Manu says goodbye to Deogratias and Virgil, and Anke pays them off. He notices while she's doing so that there's a viewing point from which one can see the cobalt-blue surface of Lake Kivu, far below.

He goes out to it, standing behind a roughly nailed barrier. A little later, Anke appears next to him and, seeing he's gazing down at the lake, says: 'It looks beautiful, but it's full of methane and carbon dioxide and if Nyiragongo ever had a big eruption, it could spark an explosion of methane and deadly release of carbon dioxide. That was what my father researched. Another hazard of these parts.'

'War's the biggest hazard,' Manu says, sipping from his bottle of Coke.

'Well at least that's over now,' she replies, surprising him by placing, very lightly and briefly, a hand in the small of his back.

But the attraction he felt on first meeting her has gone now, fizzing out like the bubbles of Coke in his mouth. Perhaps sensing his remoteness, Anke says, 'I think we are going soon,' and turns back towards the kiosk.

Staying for a second, he looks at the terraces below: rounded humps of hard-won tillage, blue-green and brown, riding like waves down to the water in the distance. Despite the beauty of the landscape, and the familiar rhythmic thump of a pounding stick from a spur of huts further below, the feeling he has is that something is burrowing its way under each terrace, under the whole land, and the lake, too, disregarding all borders, all social divisions, disregarding all human domains because it, whatever this thing is – he conceives of it as a great worm of time – is from another place than the human.

Chapter 5

Manu sits in the front of Monsieur Georges' jeep, the ranger's gun sticking up next to his knees. Anke's in the back. Removing a bottle of hand sanitiser from her rucksack, she sprays it on her palms. Monsieur Georges extracts a packet of biscuits from the glove compartment and, after taking one himself, hands them to Manu to pass round. Declining one, Anke next produces her laptop from her rucksack. Her ponytail's draped over the front of her T-shirt, its end almost touching the keyboard.

As they descend through dense green, amid which the dirt road winds like a slalom course, air with more oxygen reaches into the open windows of the jeep, the last tendrils of fog and gas, which have been whipping by the wing mirrors, dissipating with each successive turn.

'I've just been looking at maps,' Anke says from the back after a while. Manu remembers she said something similar on the plane. 'I was wondering, on the way down, whether people round here ever feel a sense of kinship with people in other parts of the Great Rift?'

There's a pause and maybe, during it, Anke senses the need to rephrase her question. 'I suppose what I'm asking is whether cultural identity goes beyond natural boundaries – do people in this part of the Rift, west of Lake Victoria and Lake Kivu, feel any sense of kinship with people of the East Rift?'

'I've never thought of it like that,' Manu says, wanting to reply: *Mostly we feel a connection to our tribe or clan, sometimes our country if we're lucky.* But he doesn't because he fears it would sound churlish or backward to appear so ethnically rooted; and in his case, anyway, he's no longer sure of any of these communities, which seem now to offer only more conflict rather than security.

Monsieur Georges is more relaxed about giving an answer. Putting the jeep into a sharp, sliding turn, he just laughs, before saying: 'Oh yes, here we all are, inside or on the edge of the Rift, it doesn't matter which one, it's still a rift. Always, my friends.'

He speaks in a philosophical tone, as if the Rift were not a geological fault line but a gap in knowledge, a rip in the historical or social fabric.

'And you know what?' he continues. 'Though I understand the great majority of the moving-apart of the Rift occurred in ancient times, before mankind, I've been told by other scientists who've come to the volcano that some of the movement happened just in the time of human memory. The Rift is certainly mentioned in one of the myths of my tribe – the tale of Mwindo, who follows his evil father to the edge of the Rift, where he must climb into the clouds on a stack of wooden bowls, then gamble with the Sky God until his father is given up for his punishment, which is to watch Mwindo ruling better than he did. But about the splitting, well I don't know . . .'

Closing her laptop and putting it back in her rucksack, Anke says: 'That sounds like a great story, I'm going to look it up; but it might be yet to come, the biggest split. Over the very, very long term – I mean by which time humans might not even exist as a species – this whole region could separate from the African land mass. If the East Rift went, there'd be another vast island off the coast, like Madagascar. Bigger if the West Rift went too. Imagine all those freshwater lakes, the source of the Nile itself, thrown with the land into the ocean!'

To these remarks, so far from present concerns, Monsieur Georges doesn't reply, instead suddenly turning his head sideways to look, puzzled, into the vegetation at the side of the road, the jeep slowing slightly. They've just passed the SORTIE PARC NATIONAL VIRUNGA sign.

The ranger gives a stifled groan as a long-limbed young man in camouflage steps smartly out of the bushes, on to the mohican of grass that runs down the middle of the track. Very slowly, very deliberately, the young man raises a rifle.

The bullet hits one of the front headlights, not a tyre, which is probably what he was aiming at. Manu expects Monsieur Georges to increase speed and drive at the man, which is what he reckons he would have done, but the jeep stalls, comes to a juddering stop.

'Lie down!' Monsieur Georges shouts. He reaches into the footwell next to Manu to get his gun, half opens the door on his side and, resting the rifle on the hinge of the door, starts firing. But almost at once, he's hit in the chest – not by the original young man but another shooter.

Anke screams, as if she has only just realised what is happening. Manu crouches down in the footwell, looking up for a second at the blood surging from Monsieur Georges' wound. Then he grabs Monsieur Georges' rifle and starts firing, taking out two of the attackers very quickly. Sensing a splash of camouflage to his side, he's aware too late of something clouting him on the head.

When he comes round he's lying next to Anke outside the jeep, with two young men standing over him. He's on his back, she's face down. He squints up, blood flowing into his eyes. One of the men is in an old Adidas T-shirt, almost reduced to rags, the other is bare-chested, with dreadlocks, and a bandolier round his neck. Both have *pangas* sheathed in their belts. Manu is dragged in front of a figure in the finest RPA battledress, whom for a second he assumes is Major Rusyo. But it's not, he realises, wiping his bloodied eyes on his arm: it's Recognition, holding a sub-machine gun.

'Hello, Manu, how are you?'

'How do you think?'

'Leave her!' Recognition shouts at one of the men, who's lifting Anke by her ponytail like she's a doll. She seems to be unconscious; her body is limp, at any rate; the man drops her. 'Don't touch her! I, General Racine, have given you an order!'

Ignoring him, and the other men, Manu gets on to his knees, turns Anke over. There's blood under her nose but she's still

189

breathing. He untucks his shirt and uses it to wipe her face – her eyes open, then close. At least she's alive.

'Why are you doing this?' he asks, standing up.

'Well,' Recognition says, smiling thinly, 'when our guys in Goma heard that a pilot called Manu was asking around for a guide, I knew it must be you. And we have unfinished business, don't we?'

'That's really been wrecking my life, Recognition,' Manu says, cursing himself for not having been more circumspect.

'Recognition is not my name now.'

Manu looks down at Anke, who's stirring. He makes another move towards her, but Recognition prods him with the submachine gun. 'I am now called General Racine.'

'So I gather. Congratulations. But the war's over, by the way.'

'Perhaps so, but not our war – we're fighting to reclaim this part of Congo from Kabila, from Rusyo, from all of them. We're going to protect the very heart of Congolese Tutsi culture; we're setting up an independent republic.'

Manu laughs bitterly, surprised he's not feeling frightened. Instead, he's just flat. 'With this lot, you won't do much reclaiming of anything. The way I heard it, you were building a big militia? What happened?'

For a second, Recognition seems bewildered, staring at him blankly. Then his eyes flash. 'We are many, you will see, they are busy with other operations. Listen, you will die today unless you obey.'

'Obey in doing what?'

'As I said in Bunia, I need your assistance. I want you to make a series of flights into western Congo and pick up the Banyamulenge there who have pledged allegiance to me.'

'Why would I do anything for you?' Manu glances again at Anke, who's moaning. Seeing him look, Recognition says: 'She your girlfriend, is she? I'm sure my men would like her to be their girlfriend too, or we could simply dispose of both of you. You did shoot two of us, after all.'

Manu makes a calculation, saying nothing at first, glancing at Recognition's two remaining men, now in the process of removing everything of value from the jeep: water bottles, Monsieur Georges' rifle, the packet of biscuits he brought, now sprayed with blood flecks, Anke's rucksack, binoculars, the equipment bags with the remaining batteries and other kit, even the jack and tyre-iron from the boot.

The bare-chested man with the bandolier grabs Anke's plastic bottle of hand sanitiser out of her rucksack and inexplicably begins squirting it on to his torso and arms, rubbing it in till it's all used up and he's glistening. Then he rummages again in the rucksack, eventually empties out the whole bag, passport and money and ticket, clothes and computer all tumbling on to the track.

The other man starts eating the biscuits, chewing as he goes to drag Monsieur Georges' body from the jeep. He pulls it to the front of the vehicle, so it lies parallel with the front bumper.

'Well?' says Recognition, watching this process like Manu is. 'Both she and you could be lying next to him in a second.'

'She's just a client.' He shrugs, looking again at Anke's body, desiring desperately to kneel down and help her properly, at the same time not wanting Recognition to take her as a hostage, the obvious course of action.

As a diversion, Manu continues to adopt a nonchalant air. 'She means nothing to me. And neither do you. I've left all that behind. What's happened has eaten me all up. You, too, by the look of it. Why are you dressed up like Rusyo, anyway?'

'The RPA have been encircling us. We attacked a unit of them and I took this uniform from the officer. We've been walking backwards to disguise our tracks.'

Hearing laughter, Manu looks over at the two men. They're busy pulling out Anke's batteries and other kit from the equipment sacks, giggling like kids at Christmas as they drape themselves with wires, playing at being engineers maybe.

'Whatever you're wearing, I've no interest in your proposition,' he tells Recognition, realising even as he speaks that he needs to go further and suggest Recognition's own options back to him. 'The way I see it, you either kill me now, in which case you have no pilot. Or you take her hostage, in which case I ignore your demands and you still have no pilot. Or you just let us both go, and then I might be in a better position to listen to you.'

'You want to go? Then you must do what I say! Are you not afraid of what I might do to you?' He gives Anke a petulant little kick. 'Or her?'

Manu senses his anger accelerate, but he pops out another shrug, still pretending nonchalance. 'If I die, I'm ready. It makes no difference to me, like God's been waiting for me for a long time!'

'You still believe all that?' Recognition waves the gun in the air.

He knows he must keep it up, this pretence that Anke's fate is of no interest to him. 'Either way, you don't get a pilot. If you wish to kill me, or her, it doesn't matter, you still have no pilot. That's just the way it is.'

Recognition looks furious, and Manu believes for a second that his ploy has worked.

It hasn't, of course. Recognition sticks the muzzle of the gun against his chest, pushing him to his knees, next to Anke. 'You think I'm playing hide and seek?' he says, his voice loud and swaggering.

Suddenly, from near the pile of goods purloined from the jeep comes a noise like frying. One of the men shouts. Recognition looks over, moving his sub-machine gun slightly in that direction.

A strange, gimcrack theatre develops. The pair of idiots have shorted two of the batteries for the monitoring stations and one man has fallen over, obviously having received an electric shock; the other, still draped in wires, is helping pull him up.

Manu knows that this is his moment, while there's a distraction and the gun's pointed away from him. He reaches out very quickly and pulls the trigger, making the gun go off. The recoil makes Recognition reel backwards. Jumping to his feet, his ears ringing from the report, Manu yanks the gun out of Recognition's hands, kicks him on to the ground then turns and fires at the two men, hitting both.

Recognition sits up, shaking his head from the ear-numbing clatter of the sub-machine gun. Sunlight, coming down through the trees, is patching his face; all around him, too, are dapples on the ground that reflect the passage of light through gaps in the canopy above.

'Am I hit?' he says, patting over his body, like someone looking for keys.

Manu shoots him in the shin.

'You are now.'

He stands above Recognition for a second, watching the blood flow out of the wound from the hole in his camouflage trouser leg, him jittery and shaking, wriggling backwards.

There's a moan and some movement from one of the men draped on the batteries; hardly looking, Manu sends another short, one-handed squirt of slugs in their direction, unfazed now by them or by Recognition's pleading.

'You're going to kill me too?' he whines, his bowels voiding, creating a harsh and sudden stink, as Manu turns the gun back towards him.

'Just wish I'd told you earlier what a silly name Recognition is, even sillier than General Racine.'

Recognition is biting his lip repeatedly, champing like a dog, one whose bark then takes on a jeering tone. 'Kill me, then, if you're going to, but you're not strong enough, are you?'

'Believe me, you dragging me away from where I lived, making me see what I saw in the camps, then making me attend the assassination of the archbishop – these are exactly the things which have made me strong enough to kill you.'

'I *saved* you! It was because of me that Rusyo granted your reprieve!'

Manu laughs drily. 'If that is how you want to see it.'

With which words, he moves forwards, intent on doing what the gun and personal history – two histories, his and Recognition's, diabolically entwined – are calling him to do. But then out of the corner of his eye he sees Anke roll and sit up. He doesn't want her to witness him execute someone. She collapses again at once, and it suddenly doesn't seem to matter any more what Recognition has or hasn't done.

He steps forwards quickly and, upending the gun in the

self-same movement, clubs Recognition on the head, wanting in this last, swift lunge to be free of the hot burst of hate that has enabled him to do it.

Then in that roadside patch of tree and scrub, which has taken on the air of a grove of sacrifice, its boughs dressed with fumes of cordite, he rushes over to Anke's silent form. He lifts her in his arms and carries her over to the jeep, feeling horror at the slackness of her body as he lays her on the back seat. She's still breathing, though, and begins mumbling a little, her face a bruised, wan oval, flecked with dried blood and dirt.

He gets out of the jeep, quickly studies his persecutors, none of whom are moving – neither is Monsieur Georges, clearly dead – then, suddenly snapping to, starts to collect a few essential objects: a water bottle, Monsieur Georges' rifle, Anke's computer and passport, money and ticket.

Chapter 6

Down, down, down Manu drives, the sun's slanting shafts coming in through the window. He stops whenever Anke wakes and calls for water. 'I've got pain,' she said hoarsely the first time he stopped, and touched her side. He gently lifted the white fabric of her shirt where she was pressing a palm, but his trembling fingers found nothing but red marks.

They pass through villages. At one he knows, called Kibati, he buys Anke a Coke and a rolex, but she won't eat. 'I feel weak,' she says, sipping the Coke. 'But I can't eat yet. You need to tell me what happened – that man, he seemed to know you . . .'

As Manu continues driving, he makes an inexplicit account of his previous history with Recognition, and also of the violent actions that enabled him and Anke to get away; how much of this she heard or saw, he's not sure, and she does not reveal.

While talking, he keeps turning back to Anke, almost coming off the road at one point. Bruises and cuts are what he sees, together with a physical enough look of shock, which has chased away the all-knowing scientist of before. Her oval face, even the matted ponytail, now separated and dishevelled – all these seem to have become the features of someone he might love; but at the end of Manu's account, all she says is: 'Thank you for what you did . . . I never, ever, want to come back here again.'

Not long later, reckoning that they are safe now, but not wanting to have to explain anything to troops or police on the outskirts of Goma, he halts the jeep and, taking Monsieur Georges' rifle out of the cab, throws it into some bushes – two memories coming to mind as he does so, the first of the FAZ man throwing away his flute, the second of himself throwing away the rifle he had in Bukavu.

At a hospital in Goma, a doctor pronounces Anke's injuries to be nothing other than two cracked ribs, along with superficial lacerations. Manu's plan was to fly her back to Entebbe once she was discharged, but, not surprisingly, she's determined to get back to Europe as soon as possible, using the cash that Manu rescued to buy a ticket at the Ethiopian Airlines office in Goma. The pair of them then book into the same hotel they stayed in on arrival in the city, the face of the receptionist expressing surprise at their changed appearance.

In the morning, as their existing ones are both filthy, they buy some new clothes together. It makes him feel oddly sentimental, this couple-like act of purchase – culottes and a yellow T-shirt in her case, along with a zip-up hoodie; and for him, the usual black trousers and white shirt – as usual for him now as Cogan's Johnnie Walker, because what he's learned, despite becoming a captain and deserving of the same epaulettes as Cogan sometimes wore, is that it's better not to stand out, staying secret like the priests of Luxor of whom Don Javier used to speak comparing them with the more open Athenians.

During the course of this shopping trip, he sees on a billboard an advertisement for powdered milk. It shows a mother and child and the logo '*Lait entier en poudre instantané*'. Full-fat milk turned into instant powder. Would she, Anke, make a good mother? he wonders.

They return to the hotel, change into the newly bought garments in their separate rooms, then try to find some way of contacting Monsieur Georges' family, name of Bamwisho, to tell them what has happened. But no one at the hotel seems to know how to contact them.

In the end, Manu decides the best thing is to leave the jeep in the hotel car park, along with a note at reception, telling any relatives or associates to contact him at The Passenger in Entebbe. It's an inadequate solution, hardly proper – there's no way of pasteurising the facts of what happened – but he doesn't know what else to do.

After this, Anke makes him take her straight to the airport, in order to catch a flight from Goma to Addis, and thence to Brussels. It upsets him, this, the speed with which she wants to get out of Congo, as somehow – perversely, probably – he's begun hoping again that she might be the person to whom he could reveal the parts of himself that he has hidden from others; but it isn't at all surprising, her wish to leave.

At the terminal, Anke winces as she lifts her rucksack. 'You're still sore?' he says, concern in his voice.

'I'm OK, Manu,' she says, looking him in the eye. 'My ribs are hurting but . . . well, I need to say that I know you saved my life. I'll never forget that. Let me give you my contact details.'

She takes off her rucksack again, looks in it for pen and paper, realises she does not have any; so she goes back to the ticket-sales counter, interrupting the customer there, a bespectacled *blanc* in a suit who remonstrates with both her and the woman at the counter.

On coming back, Anke says, 'They're very grumpy, some of these people.' She bends down, groaning again, to write her phone number on the back of a redundant form. 'This is the address of the museum in Tervuren. Look me up if you are ever in Brussels.'

'I will.'

'Do!' She now seems oddly upbeat, as if like a wrestler she has thrown down the challenges, physical and emotional, of her journey to Congo and won.

He follows her to the departure gates. She's moving at quite a pace now, desperate to go, but as she reaches the gates she turns and says, 'You're an amazing guy, Manu – thank you.'

'You've nothing to thank me for, I'm sorry it was such a disaster.'

Almost in passing, moving as briskly as a little bird, she gives him a hug; he holds her for a second, patting her on the back.

'Don't pat!' she cries out, half laughing, 'I had a boyfriend who used to do that and it always made me feel like a Labrador!'

She kisses him lightly on the forehead, then disappears into the crowd of departing passengers; and very suddenly, there's no more Anke Desseaux for his hopes to latch on to. He looks for her slim calves among the other legs, feeling a wave of something – disappointment maybe, he's not sure – then makes his way miserably over to the cargo department to get a pass for the apron, in order to check on the Cargomaster.

Chapter 7

As soon as he gets back to Entebbe, Manu calls Cogan, who's still in Kinshasa, but he doesn't seem much interested in what happened on Nyiragongo. Of Recognition, he says: 'Should'a given him a gut shot; thing about stiffs, they don't bother you no more.' He frets mainly about the likely cessation of the volcano contract, as though individual people weren't involved at all in what happened on the mountain, as though Monsieur Georges wasn't killed, and Anke and Manu weren't in genuine danger.

When Manu, very upset indeed by this disregard, tries to return to the details, Cogan just grunts down the phone line – saying, as if the politics could stand in for the real human factors: 'What I'm hearing is that rebel movements of every stripe are gathering in the east, not just your guy Recognition. Meanwhile Kabila's arguing with both the Ugandans and the Rwandans, mining companies, embassies, everyone he comes into contact with, pretty much.'

It's just like Papa predicted, Manu thinks, remembering what the old priest, much missed, said when they were above Karonga on his final training mission.

'When I'm flying Kabila,' Cogan continues blithely on, 'he's as moody as a bull elephant. Anyhow, probably best you carry on with commercial jobs for the foreseeable. Get in touch with Suraj – he'll sort you out, mostly with Mombasa gigs, I expect. I'll keep a line of credit open for you for fuel, but keep me posted on all the jobs, yeah? Mind he doesn't stiff you on the fees. Oh, and Manu, flying into Kenya, watch out for Tororo Rock;

fuckload of pilots have crashed into that thing. There's meant to be a warning light on top but it's often not on.'

As instructed, swallowing his rage at Cogan for the way that he's dealt with all this, Manu contacts Suraj. Once he's found Suraj's premises, the Asian businessman greets him like an old friend, even though they've only met once before, at the RPA camp in Kamituga in November 1996, just after Manu started working for Cogan. They sit down in Suraj's office and he asks Manu a little about himself, congratulates him on getting his licence, which Cogan has told him about, then without invitation launches into the story of his own life.

Having lost and made several fortunes in the course of successive regimes, Suraj eventually built up, under the peace dividend that came with Museveni, his grandfather's original corner store into a million-dollar trading enterprise. The old store sold soap and razor blades and salt and foodstuffs; now he's into everything, but his main line is the Ugandan agencies for various multinational soft-drinks and electronics companies.

The soda crates come in by truck from Kenya, but Suraj now prefers to have the electronic goods flown from Mombasa because the trucks keep getting robbed, usually at the customs post at Malaba, a town straddling the Kenya–Uganda border.

'Avoiding this is where you come in, Manu,' says Suraj, grinning at him across his large, leather-inlaid desk, which is dominated by an executive toy – a mechanical device constructed from silver ball bearings that hit and swing on a row of metal strings, progressing and reversing until they run out of momentum.

For the next six months, Manu will flog the Cargomaster between Entebbe and Mombasa, taking out high-value agricultural goods, such as vanilla and stevia, and flying back TVs and hi-fis. He makes sure on the way to skirt Tororo Rock, an elevation of nearly 1000 kilometres above the town.

His evenings off he spends either with David and Matthias at Ndere Troupe on Kisasi Road, or helping Aisha at The Passenger back in Entebbe. He doesn't tell the Banyamulenge guys anything about what happened with Recognition.

There are often pretty girls in the audience at Ndere. Many of David and Matthias's female co-performers are attractive too, especially the slender young women that do the balancing pot dance, who remind him of Edith.

But he makes no effort to chat to any of them. It's as if his very different experiences with Edith and Anke, one consummated (after a fashion), the other not, have knocked all desire out of him: the ice-cream girl is in America and the volcanologist with the golden hair has gone into the ether, burned off into the sky like her Addis-bound jet, both sucking a little more out from his already half-drained reservoir of hopes of happiness.

He put the piece of paper with Anke's contact details in the drawer of the chest in his room, the same one on the underside of which he wrote the co-ordinates of the crate that he and Cogan buried at Kikorba – a subject that neither has mentioned since.

When not on jobs for Suraj, he works in the bar with Aisha, not seeing much of Cogan, or Gerry, who's currently flying tourists round game parks. Of Papa and Evgeny, respectively in Belgium and Dubai, there's no news whatsoever.

As for Aisha, she's started being more pleasant to him, as if she actually values his contribution, not just to The Passenger in his off hours, but also to Normair in recent months. She confesses to him that not much of the income from Cogan's Kinshasa contract is staying in the company bank account, and that it's really important he carries on with the runs for Suraj.

After closing time one night, they're both sitting on the stools on the veranda of The Passenger, drinking successive *waragi* cocktails, when she suddenly says: 'I don't know if I'm made for marriage, Manu – all this business of staying with one person for the rest of your life, it doesn't make sense! What do you think?'

Manu smokes his cigarette, wondering if this is, tacitly, some kind of offer. There is no denying her fierce beauty, and the appeal of an older woman.

A late-night *matatu* rattles along the street as he replies, 'Never given it much thought.'

Aisha yawns, itches the scar of her *boda* burn. Manu hauls himself off to bed in his room at the back of the bar – eyes sagging, tongue swollen with too much Ugandan gin.

Sometimes he considers how she must feel, deep in her heart, how unhappy she must be with Cogan, if what Papa once said is true; being an unhappy wife can't, at least he reckons, be so different from being an unhappy apprentice. But surely I'm not that any more, he thinks, now I'm a pilot in my own right?

On the radio in The Passenger, he listens to ominous reports about arguments between Kabila and his presidential counterparts in Rwanda and Uganda. One night, after one of the flights for Suraj, he gets back there much later than he intended. Arriving at the bar, he goes up the veranda to the door, but it's locked. He reaches into the pocket of his uniform, then realises that he doesn't have his key. Must have left it in his casual clothes.

Maybe get in by the small window of his room? He goes through the littered alley, stumbling over the same rubbish, or recycled versions of it, that was there when he first came. Using a piece of flattened lead pipe and standing on a beer crate, he's able to lever open the window. He wriggles up, gets himself through (gouging his hip a little on his way over the latch), drops in a heap on the floor.

He begins getting ready for bed, when he hears faint voices from the bar. Inching open the door, he sees a muted light: the one above the spirits optics that always has a carapace of dead insects. Two people are talking.

One of the voices is Aisha's – saying, if he hears it right, 'It's necessary.'

Feeling nervous, he silently pushes the door open a little further, in order to see the other person. It's Gerry, perched on a bar stool, sipping a gin and tonic. His tall, bushy haircut and the fall of his linen suit are cut out of the scant surrounding light almost to make him seem like a silhouette. Aisha sits very near him, her face almost indistinguishable from the curls surrounding it.

'But not yet,' Gerry says.

'We can't wait too long. He spends thousands of dollars a month. And I've heard from a girlfriend in Kinshasa that he's going with other women . . . so much, Gerry! I'm amazed he can still get it up, but they say he can. He can't with me. I'm so sick of him. With luck he will die from a heart attack while fucking, or from drink or drugs, and then I'll finally own this place.'

Trembling as he listens, Manu realises they are discussing Cogan.

'He needs you much more than you need him.' Gerry reaches out to touch Aisha's hand. 'Don't worry, I'll find a way to help you. Since that one time, I've thought about you a lot.'

'I'm not the only one you think about,' she grumps. 'I need a solution.'

Aisha's bangles ring as she reaches out to stub her cigarette. Her sharply browed eyes are suddenly visible across the murky taproom; for a second, he believes she's seen him.

'And it needs to come soon,' she says.

'It or you?' Gerry says, slyly.

'Both,' she replies, and with these words leans over and kisses him full on the mouth.

They slide off their bar stools, quickly fold into one another, continue kissing for some time. Manu watches in transfixed horror. After a few minutes, Aisha gives a groan, Gerry shrugs off his jacket . . . removes his patterned shirt, his trousers, too, produces a condom from his wallet.

Manu experiences a weird translation, like he did when the RPA were killing the refugees in the forest and he hid in his tree: a feeling that simply by observing he has been drawn into what's happening.

It seems, anyway, that they are going to go what Cogan would call 'the whole nine yards'. Simultaneously disgusted and aroused as they fall to the floor, Manu continues watching it all in the tarnished light. Gerry thrusts into Aisha, she rises to meet him – just two ordinary beings having sex.

Except that what was said earlier about a 'solution' didn't sound at all ordinary. He wonders what it entails; not just the show in front of me, he reasons, glumly watching Gerry's buttocks move to and fro between Aisha's thighs.

He has the distinct impression of a mechanical arrangement – like the executive toy on Suraj's desk – though he knows well enough that what he's witnessing could bring about serious changes for all involved. Will she finally leave Cogan? What will that mean for the bar, for me? Most of all, how can he tell Cogan what he has seen?

Afterwards, the two of them lie together for a while, until Gerry stands up. In its swatch of wet latex, glistening under the light above the optics, his slackened cock has the appearance of an eel wrapped in a leaf, ready for cooking by a Kivu fireside.

Gerry removes the condom and, taking a tissue from a box on the bar, wipes himself. He scrumples the condom into the tissue, drops the package into a bin. It's so sordid it makes Manu want to weep to high heaven, but for all that he can't stop watching.

'Hey,' Aisha says from the floor, head propped on an elbow, 'I'll have to clean that up.'

'Where else am I meant to put it?'

'Take it outside, throw it on the way home.'

She gets up and they both pull on their clothes.

'We could start meeting somewhere else,' Gerry says. 'I'll find somewhere in the city.'

'Like you do with Michelle Tikoto?'

He embraces her, looks into her eyes. 'You really didn't think that was true, did you?'

'I wondered.'

'Never touched her.'

They leave, going out of the front, unlocking and then relocking the door. Manu goes back to his room and lies down. But he cannot sleep, of course.

Should he tell Cogan? How would he put it? He doesn't know.

He decides that the best thing to do for now is simply nothing. He knows what Don Javier would have said: act as soon as possible, save people from harm, tell the truth. However, the priest was a man that I maybe killed – this is the run of his thoughts . . . And what Manu senses, right now, in that squalid back room, as mosquitoes whine about his ears, is that time is becoming foreshortened: that all routes to any definitive, life-changing act are decreasing by the second.

But definitive acts are reserved for the heroes of the folk tales that his mother used to recount, not ordinary people in everyday life. She herself was typical of the wise women who can be found in the more rural regions of the Great Lakes: a devout Christian, clicking her wood-corded rosary beads, yet also someone still attached to the old African spirituality. He wonders, as he tries to sleep, if there's a way he can similarly be both, can stay among freight dogs but be clean of their sins? It doesn't seem possible any more, just as it doesn't that Congo or its neighbours can hover in the middle region of the interbellum.

Chapter 8

Stetson!

Manu's eating breakfast in The Passenger, listening to the radio as usual, when a hat spins through the air and lands on one of the beer-pump levers – a manoeuvre Cogan's been trying to perfect for the past two weeks, since his return from Kinshasa at the end of February 1998. As he was piloting one of Kabila's own planes for that contract, Manu had to go get him, flying him back to Entebbe in the Cargomaster.

During the single evening Manu was in Kinshasa, the capital city which loomed so large in his early hopes of university, Cogan took him out on what he called a pub crawl, a term he learned when stationed in 'Great Britain', as he sarcastically put it.

This night in Kinshasa ended farcically, Cogan falling over and banging his head on the concrete edge of a ditch full of faeces. Manu put him to bed in the Intercontinental – separate rooms for each of them this time, thank God – but the Texan must have woken in the night and gone out. In the morning, Cogan having lost his wallet, Manu had to pay off a girl he'd picked up, knowledge of whom the Texan denied utterly.

This despite the girl's clothes being dispersed across the room when she let Manu in, dripping-wet from the shower and completely naked except for a fluffy white towel wrapped round her head like a turban. He told her to get dressed and went to get Cogan some coffee . . .

Now, Manu looks at the hat, wobbling on the beer lever. The fortnight Cogan's been back, he's been weighing up whether to tell him about Aisha and Gerry, not that he even knows whether their liaison is continuing; even in the few moments he's seen them in the bar together, there's been no evidence of it. It's almost as if he imagined the whole thing.

'But:

Do you know what's happening, Cogan? That's what he still wants to say, or, more forcefully – *Don't you realise what the fuck's going on? And who can blame her, given what you're up to?*

'Happy birthday, by the way.'

'My birthday's the sixteenth of May, not sixteenth of March!'

'Oh. Well I might be early, bucko, but that just shows how much I haven't forgotten. I've got a present for you.'

It seems impossible to find the right moment or words to tell him. Must do something; but what?

'Close your eyes and open your hand.'

He does as Cogan says and something jinks into his palm. He opens his eyes.

It's a set of car keys.

'Come outside, kid. I've made a bundle of dosh out of Kabila and I thought you deserved some of it.'

On the street there's an unfamiliar car, a metallic-blue Datsun, quite old and battered.

'It's yours,' he says.

Manu looks at the vehicle in amazement. 'But I can't drive!'

'Easily sorted, and that's not all, kid. I've decided you're too much of a big boy now to be sleeping in that little bed at the back of the bar, so I've rented you an apartment of your own. All on Normair. It's between the zoo and the marina, in a block adjacent to a stand of mango trees and a small stream, running down to the lake.'

'I'm . . . so grateful, Cogan, thank you,' he stutters. How can he tell him about Aisha and Gerry now? Everything in the world depends on correct timing, and this is most definitely the wrong time, isn't it?

'Get your stuff.'

Manu goes to the little room where he's spent so many nights. He gathers up his few clothes and belongings, making a pile on the bed, before going back out to the kitchen and finding a bag in which to put them. Checking through the drawers of the brass-handled chest, he sees the little piece of paper with Anke's contact details on it. He visualises her golden hair and slim legs for a second, then slams the drawer shut, leaving the paper inside. Time to forget romantic rot.

As for the co-ordinates written on the underside of the same drawer – thrown by Cogan's sudden largesse, Manu doesn't think about them at all at that moment, nor of the crate of gold buried at Kikorba to which they refer.

Returning to the car outside, he finds Cogan waiting with the boot open. 'Let's go take a look at your new lodgings!'

He gets into the Datsun, the seats of which are trimmed with fake fur – inappropriate for the climate and, already off-white, slightly dirty. Cogan starts driving, then it strikes Manu like a leopard's paw: the reason he, Evgeny, Papa, all of them, are or were so generous to him, so giving of their time and their knowledge and in Cogan's case wealth, is simply guilt. They have come to Africa and simply taken things; well, not quite simply, as their actions have caused more complex ripples of harm directly and indirectly through the war. And in me – Manu figures, as Cogan drives the Datsun – they see a way to make amends, redeem themselves. But their fragile gifts come with reciprocities fierce as ripping teeth, he's beginning to reckon . . . ones that keep him in a subsidiary position, ones that keep him battened down.

Is that how it is? Having received this gale of thoughts and emotions, he's now not sure at all. Still, he can't help wondering what's in him that's so attractive to this group of men, as he can find very little of that nature in himself.

For all that, arriving at the apartment, he wants to hug Cogan, but hesitates at the last minute, instead feeling that the thing he should really do, and now, is tell him what he needs to tell him. It's an odd cocktail of feelings all right – genuine thanks and affection, obligation and guilt, all mixed up together.

Inside the barely furnished flat, the two men hover round each other, the one vast and sweating, the other tall and thin. Manu's delighted; this is a place of his own, and about time, as sleeping in that mean little room at the back of The Passenger was like sleeping in a coffin.

After regaling him with boastful tales of his own first vehicle, a Ford Mustang, Cogan says, 'You'll have to get lessons for the car – can't be too many people who've learned to fly before they've learned to drive! I'll leave it here, get a *boda* back.'

Driving a car, Manu finds, is easy by comparison to flying. Within another month, having taken intensive driving lessons – with the Divine Brother Defensive Driving School, no less – and passed his test, he's driving to and from the airport. He's living on his own too, feeling free as a hawk, despite the troubling issue that's still stuck in the beak of his conscience.

'How's the car?' Cogan asks him, one night at The Passenger.

'Fun.'

'You need a chick to ride with for it to be really fun.'

'There's no one I'm in love with.'

'You youngsters are in such a hurry for the big romance. My advice is to fuck as often as you can, 'cos youth flies away from you till it's only a speck on the horizon. Don't trust the heart, the heart's a bitch.'

When Cogan gives out these absurd nuggets of life advice, which seem to be getting more and more cynical, Manu likes him less and less, despite all the kindness he has shown; the cynicism makes him wonder, too, whether Cogan already knows about Aisha and Gerry. Perhaps he's off the hook, his conscience cured.

But it's true the car is fun, as during this interval he gets a good deal of pleasure from gunning the Datsun round Entebbe, diving down its lanes and avenues as speedily and shinily as the kingfisher with spectacular blue feathers that nests in the bank of the stream at the bottom of the garden of his flat.

The only thing missing, like Cogan said (that at least was true), is someone to sit beside him in the passenger seat. It's not as if he hasn't had chances – they just never seem right, those girls he talks to on the Ndere nights, or in The Passenger. The clever ones are too solemn, and the ones who seem like they'd let him kiss them are as annoying as the trilling of the kingfisher. Edith was a good balance of seriousness and physicality, he reckons, even if he hardly got the chance to assess what a relationship with someone like her would really be. He tries to imagine her in the States, but he can't really picture how she lives now.

Driving into Kampala one afternoon, the day of his actual birthday in fact, Manu spots Brigadier Faithful standing at the edge of a *matatu* park. The sight of him immediately makes him think of Edith again, and then of the co-ordinates under the drawer back at The Passenger, and the buried crate at Kikorba. Faithful's looking at the minibuses and their drivers, at the screeching touts and the roast-maize sellers, and the passengers with baskets and bundles or struggling with children: a khaki colossus on the kerb, rapping his swagger stick against his boot, smiling paternally at the assembled incoherence, smiling at all the ordinary people, laughing, arguing, complaining, making do in the city.

Life at the moment seems a curious mixture of renunciation on the one hand and action on the other. Manu can feel he's almost bodily pulling back from the excesses of the freight dogs; but knows how much he still needs to work, keeping up their frantic pace. Like now, the evening of the day he saw Faithful, as he's sitting at the Formica-topped table in the kitchen of his flat, preparing a flight plan for tomorrow's flight to Lubumbashi in Congo. He has to deliver a new set of control dials for a trommel screen at one of the diamond mines near there. Hearing its call, he turns to the window, hoping to spot the kingfisher flit from a tree to its burrow in the bank of the stream at the bottom of the garden. But it's too dark to see.

Chapter 9

Darkness falls again as Manu's driving the Datsun back from EBB to his flat, having dropped off the trommel screen in Lubumbashi. Congo's second-largest city was humid, busy and as full of cash as it was of poverty. The business district there was something else, packed with the offices of mining companies from which executives, by no means all *blancs*, constantly emerged, delivering themselves into waiting Mercedes. War didn't seem to have changed any of that.

He passes an illuminated sign advertising Niceboy Milk – DIRECT FROM NTUNGAMO TO YOUR HOME, it says below. And home's right where he's going now, desperate for a shower.

The milk ad makes him think of Papa, and then of Anke. What is it about Belgium that, once someone goes there, they never get in contact again, as if Belgium's the Bermuda Triangle or something? The flute part in 'The Fool on the Hill' creeps back into his head.

He's whistling it when he spots a shape that doesn't make sense. A vehicle has gone over into the concrete ditch next to the road. It's tipped up. The tail lights are still on, so the incident must be recent.

He pulls over and gets out; and it's only then he realises that the crashed car is Cogan's red Cherokee. Cogan is slumped in the front seat, head on the steering wheel. His Stetson is stuck between its struts and some kind of music – swinging, swaying, blue – is playing from the speakers.

There is no time for registering shock, even though recognition of his mentor's body shocks him like the vibration of a bell in his very own heart.

With difficulty, as the 4×4 is on its side and Manu has to keep the door open with his back, he manages to pull Cogan's body out. He's wearing a Hawaiian shirt, several buttons open, showing a bullet hole in his chest and blood spattered down his belly. But he seems still to be breathing, just about. Without hesitating, Manu begins dragging him – he's very heavy – to the Datsun, somehow jamming him into the back seat, making a big red mess of its fur trim.

He drives like a demon to St Mary's Clinic in town. Stopping at the gate, which is shut, he sounds the horn.

A couple of *askaris* come out, shining torches.

He jumps out of the car. 'Let me through, let me through! This man's been shot.'

They shine the torches in Manu's face. 'No way, we don't let criminals in here.'

'What?' He takes hold of the bars of the gate and rattles them. 'He's dying!'

They shake their heads, these two fuckers in old army coats, and return to their hut.

He goes back to the Datsun, checks Cogan on the back seat. Still breathing, but unconscious. He rushes back to the front of the vehicle, continues hooting, but no one comes to his aid. It's as if the streets of all Entebbe have been struck down by an epidemic. Ages seem to pass, during which a large passenger jet takes off from the airport, traversing the sky above the town like the Passover angel.

He returns to the gate, shouting for a second time. 'Hey, come out, this is an emergency.'

One of the guards shambles out again. 'Yes?'

'Let me in.'

'We're on strict orders not to let in any gunshot wounds. Too many gangsters in this town.'

'That's bullshit. Let me in!'

But the man won't relent, slinking back to his pillbox, mumbling about ringing the police.

Manu rushes to the car again, gets in the back seat. With Cogan's balding, grey, enormous-seeming head in his lap, he tries to staunch the bleeding by pressing his palm against the chest wound.

Something, likely the pressure on the wound, brings Cogan back to consciousness. There is so much blood on his shirt that its pattern has almost disappeared. He regards Manu with one half-open eye.

'I'm sorry,' Manu says, 'they won't let me in.'

Cogan gives something halfway between a cough and a laugh, spattering more blood down his shirt. 'St Peter, he say no? Well, I'm not surprised, kid.'

'I mean the hospital!' Manu presses down harder on the soft island of the wound, from which blood continues pumping, and Cogan gives a groan.

'I'm sorry,' Manu says again, covered in blood himself now. 'There is something I should have told you. Gerry and Aisha . . .'

'It's all right, kid,' he gasps. 'Know all about that. He's been on her tail for ages. All that time I was sayin', Baby, please don't go. But she done it, and now it looks like – worse than that. Dunno who shot me but I bet . . . those two ordered it, sure as cowboy . . .'

Manu tumbles into mental torture. *Why didn't I say something earlier? What's the matter with me?*

'Cheerleaders wear short shorts!' Cogan says finally, his mouth ejaculating a coral-coloured mixture of blood and saliva.

The pattern of Cogan's breathing changes with the effort of spitting this statement out – becoming shorter, then getting faster each time he tries to speak. 'Changed my will soon as I got wind she was runnin' wild. The bar's going to you, and the firm – no point in leaving it to my son, if he won't even come here. But look out, kid, 'cos Aisha'll try to hide the new will if she finds it.' He gives another groan: 'But there's a copy at my solicitor's, Atul Khan . . . *molasses!*'

And that's Cogan's last comprehensible word, *molasses*. And as he speaks it, Manu is conscious of a peculiar feeling that whenever there is a copy, there must indeed be a sacrifice, just at the elder said at his initiation ceremony. Memory of the ritual comes to Manu in a horrible flash, horrible because it's mixed in with the present sight of Cogan's face, bespattered with a spider-tattoo of blood, and vengeful thoughts on Aisha – *did she really do this?* – and then ones disbelieving that possibility, involving her turning to look at Cogan at the photocopier where they first met, and truly fell in love, before this all went so wrong.

Cogan stays conscious for a while, though, his fat hand patting against Manu's shin. There seems to be a rhythm to it, this movement of Cogan's hand and arm, on which the tattooed image of the woman, glass, dice and dollars is now sticky with blood.

Is it Morse – being unable to speak, is Cogan trying to communicate with him another way? After a few minutes, during which Cogan starts moaning half melodically, Manu realises that it's that Texan song that he liked to sing, 'Ain't No More Cane on the Brazos'.

As best as he can remember, Manu begins to sing it to him – and then, when he forgets the strange words about being ground down to molasses, which is what he must have been thinking of in his last utterance, to hum it. A tear runs from Cogan's half-open eye, the other being completely closed. Manu wipes the tear away with a forefinger.

Again Cogan's breathing changes, the gasps becoming rasps. The hand stops its patting. His one functioning eye keeps regarding Manu as this happens, latching on like the eye of a lizard, but in its depths all sorts of feelings are stirring – Manu seems to perceive this – as from its corner, tears still come, flowing down Cogan's cheek, meeting en route the pallor that's rising up his body like a mist.

Slowly, a process that begins at an imperceptible moment, the head on Manu's lap starts to stiffen, grows cold, until all sense of motion has disappeared from Cogan's face. After a few minutes it takes on an ugly rictus, his mouth sloping down to one side, his jaw seeming to thicken into a lump of frozen meat. The eye's still open, but Manu can tell it's not seeing.

Finally, the police arrive in two cars, the *wololo* of their sirens sounding through the streets of the sleepy lakeside town. Once they see the flashing lights they've summoned, the *askaris* open the gates. Almost immediately, a doctor comes out. He rushes to the vehicle and, leaning over Manu, reaches a hand to Cogan's neck, placing a finger against his carotid artery.

He gives a little nod. 'Dead,' he superfluously adds, as if Manu, or the watching moon, or the waiting police, didn't realise that.

As the doctor's extracting himself from the Datsun, one of the policeman approaches, saying, 'Get out of the vehicle.' But Manu – still sitting there, immobile, pinch-faced, with Cogan's head in his lap – is remembering the moment Cogan came to his rescue at Rutshuru, saved him, basically. At first, stuck in shock, he refuses to budge at all from the blood-stained, fur-trimmed seat, moving only when the police take him by the arm and begin pulling.

'How did this man die? Who shot him? You?'

'No, no, he is a friend, and my employer, at The Passenger bar. One of the people who did this – his wife – will be there.'

The police know the bar, but they seem set on arresting Manu as the assassin. It is only when he begins confusedly explaining Cogan's theory, that Gerry and Aisha ordered the murder, that they start listening, though he's not sure they believe him at all. They put him in handcuffs.

He says, 'What about the body?'

Shrugging, one says: 'We will collect later. First we must check your story.'

He's put in a police car and driven to The Passenger. She's there all right. Sitting cuffed in the car, he glimpses the police pulling Aisha across the veranda, legs kicking. The police take keys from her handbag and clear the bar of customers, closing it up. Then, as one police car takes Aisha off to one station and him to another – separate places in central Kampala – twin sirens, mismatched in wail and fall, lament the progress of both vehicles over potholes and portions of lost time. Because as usual, even though it's by now well past 9 p.m., the Kampala traffic is as thick as treacle.

Manu spends two weeks under suspicion while investigations continue. They seem to believe him in the end, though, the Kampala cops, having spoken at length to Atul Khan, Cogan's solicitor; but there's still a little doubt, menacing away.

So now he sits cross-legged on the bare floor of the cell, waiting to hear his expected fate, as expected as the obese spider that, twice each day, progresses across the ceiling.

It's a different prison from that in which Aisha is being held. The forlorn tin particulars of bucket and bowl within the cell appear, across the hours, not like the inanimate objects that they are, but as the active agents of an unjust destiny. The bucket and bowl seem to move – in the indigent light that creeps through the bars, hardly enough to read the graffiti scratched on the walls – even when Manu doesn't kick them.

The graffiti, interspersed with images, is written in various languages. He can read the Swahili but not the Luganda, apart from a few words and phrases: *kafunda* (small hole-in-the-wall bar or shop); *nsenene* (fried grasshoppers); *jebale ko, polisi* (greetings and thank you, police, for the work that you do); *bambi, bambi, bambi* (my dear, my dear, my dear). There's one Swahili phrase, written in red, that says: *Mimi ni mlawimu aliestaafu* (I am a retired teacher).

The cell swarms with fleas and lice as well as language. They hop on his face, beetle through his hair, delve into the crevices of his body as he tries to sleep. Now and then he manages to catch one, squeeze it between finger and thumb. How does he feel? Exactly like one of these insects. For despite the police apparently believing his story, which is after all the truth, he still wonders whether he will continue to be accused of Cogan's murder.

Cogan's solicitor, Atul Khan, visits his cell. Dressed in a smart brown suit, he tells him not to worry. But Manu remains doubtful.

It's only when Gerry's picked up, during Manu's second week in prison, that the picture begins to clear. The assassins were two men on *boda* bikes, not Ugandans but Kenyans like Gerry, employees of a figure in the Nairobi underworld known as Hudihudi.

Atul Khan comes again that night and explains, covering his face with a handkerchief to mask the stench of the cell.

It goes like this. A few weeks prior to Cogan's death, Kenyan CID, after raiding a bonded warehouse in Athi River, owned by Hudihudi – apparently he's a big-time drug baron who controls much of Kenya's cocaine trade – inadvertently taped conversations between him and Gerry, in which the hit on Cogan was discussed. This Hudihudi is a Member of Parliament too – so it's whispered, though this fact hardly seems to come into the practicalities of the affair at all, as if there is a fictional world in which every super-rich Kenyan MP and even the President himself could be eating out of the same bowl, and it's just taken as normal . . . The Kenyan police eventually passed the recordings on to their Ugandan counterparts. Too late to save Cogan, but soon enough to save Manu.

Hudihudi ('the hoopoe' in Swahili) was not apprehended, and neither were his men, but Manu is at last let go, handed some possessions of Cogan's and some of his own, jumbled together in a plastic bag.

After Manu's release, Atul Khan drives him to a police garage where the Datsun is, Cogan's body having been removed to a morgue. Khan has had the car cleaned, thank God, but it still smells funny. Driving back to his flat, Manu is shaking, his hands so unsteady that he has to pull over and take deep breaths. When he does get back there, he spends a very long time washing, and longer sleeping.

Another day passes before he's able to pull himself together. Nothing seems real except the itch of the flea bites from when he was in the cell, and the memory of lice scurrying across his skin. The personal effects of Cogan's that he received from the police, collected from his person and from the Cherokee, seem the least real things of all: his lighter, a hip flask, his Stetson – not much else, certainly not his wallet. The idea of grieving for him, for all his faults, seems like something impossibly out of reach.

There are things to be done, all the same. Atul Khan helps by giving Manu a small cash float until the will is sorted out. He begins by getting the Cherokee towed out of the ditch by the side of the road, where it's remained all this while. Even though it's a much better vehicle than the Datsun, and still salvageable, he decides the best thing to do is sell it.

The next thing is to sort out The Passenger, which has been shuttered since Aisha's arrest. After collecting the keys from Khan, he goes to see the Ndere Troupe – whose dancing and flute-playing and pot-balancing doesn't seem so joyous to him that night – and after the show persuades his Banyamulenge friends, David and Matthias, to run the bar. Because he knows he can't, on his own, deal with both Normair and running a bar. In fact, he isn't sure that he can do any of it.

Chapter 10

In early June, what's left of Cogan is finally brought from the mortuary. A grim little funeral takes place at the Sacred Heart church in Entebbe. Manu, Atul Khan, a few nuns and the gravediggers (also serving to carry the coffin) are the only attendants besides the priest.

Manu has given the priest a bribe, using some of the money from the sale of the Cherokee, to allow burial there because he couldn't prove Cogan was Catholic; Manu's certain he wasn't – probably Baptist, or Episcopalian, he reckons, if he was of any denomination at all. He tries to think how Cogan would have liked such a ceremony to be, and the only thing he can think of (in the name of better action) is to throw his Stetson in, after the coffin has been shipped into the earth.

As he does so, Manu hears Cogan's voice: *Bullseye, baby!* A few dragonflies hover about the hat before the soil tossed by the gravediggers' shovels begins its dry rapping on the wood.

While he's walking back to The Passenger, it begins to rain; Manu speculates that the soil, back there in the graveyard, will quickly be turning to mud. And then realises that Cogan would probably have liked some music to have been playing while he was interred: that doleful song about cane-cutters on the Brazos River, Dylan's 'Leopard-Skin Pillbox Hat', or one of his other tunes. All that stuff he liked to sing, by turns bright and breezy, mournful and melancholy, whatever the weather outside the cockpit, reports on which the Texan told him not to trust. But it's too late now (as he also used to sing).

Manu also supposes, continuing to walk along, that he ought to inform Cogan's ex-wife and son in Carthage, but he hasn't a clue how to begin to find them.

A black Mercedes pulls up alongside him. For a second, his reflection sliding along its wing, it's like he's back in Lubumbashi, watching mining executives get into such vehicles. The passenger door opens, but it's not a businessman in the driver's seat, it's Brigadier Faithful.

'Get in,' Faithful says.

He does as he's told and shuts the door, the cream-leather seat sucking him down.

'Hello, Manu,' says Faithful.

Manu hardly hears it, because his eyes fix on the pistol propped in the cubby behind the gear lever.

'I was hoping to get to the funeral,' Faithful says, 'but I couldn't make it; did it go well?'

'Yes,' he whispers.

'Such a shame about Cogan. An entertaining man. Whipsmart sometimes. Other times . . . And what a silly fellow Gerry has been. He never could keep his trousers on; sometimes I wonder if all this unzipping simply happens because people are unhappy. Alas, I fear both he and Aisha will hang, but that is nothing we can get involved in because, as you know, the courts are extremely independent in Uganda.'

Manu sits there in shock. Faithful continues, as if what he has just told him is inconsequential. 'Now, there's something I need to ask you about.'

'Yes, Brigadier,' he replies, pressing his knees together. He's anxious Faithful's going to ask him about Edith, play the role of the angry father.

But it's not that. 'You were on the flight with Cogan out of Kilo Moto with those crates of gold, *ndiyo*?'

'Yes,' Manu replies, both relieved (because he hasn't mentioned Edith) and doubled down in anxiety (because of the crate buried under the *mvuli* tree).

'And you stopped and buried one of the crates at Kikorba?'

So that's it. There's no point in denying; Faithful obviously knows all about it, just as Cogan implied at the time. 'Yes,' he says again.

'Well, Cogan gave me the co-ordinates, so I know exactly where it is. He mentioned a *mvuli* tree. Is that right?'

'Yes, that's where we buried it.'

'Well, it's safe where it is – best place for it really – so we'll leave it there. What I need to know, my lad, is whether you yourself also took a note of those co-ordinates.'

Again Manu has a big decision to make, because he doesn't know whether saying yes again will put him in more danger or less. Before he can decide one way or the other, Faithful prompts: 'Cogan told me he asked you to do so, as an insurance.'

'Yes, that's right,' he says, leaning forwards and putting his head in his hands.

Faithful reaches for Manu's bowed head, and Manu fears he's going to hold the pistol to it; but all he does is rub his hair, like a father drying his son's hair with a towel.

'Stop worrying, this isn't about you. There may be a few monsters over the border, but we're not monsters in Uganda. What I need you to do is to take me where you kept the record of that location, yes?'

Manu sits up, takes a deep breath, 'OK, it's in The Passenger.'

'Of course!' he says. 'Well, let's go.'

Faithful starts the engine and drives there. There are only a few people in the bar when they arrive, and David, Manu's Munyamulenge friend – now his employee, in the new scheme of things – is serving behind the bar.

Everyone looks curiously at Faithful, a famous figure in the country because of his military exploits, as he follows Manu across to the little room where Manu used to sleep, now piled up with empty beer kegs and old crisp cartons.

Manu moves the kegs and cartons aside, points at the drawer in the chest. Faithful opens the drawer and, on seeing the piece of paper on which Manu wrote Anke's address, picks it up and looks at the writing on it, puzzled. 'What's this?'

'Not that. Underneath the drawer.'

Faithful puts the piece of paper on top of the chest, pulls out the drawer, turns it over. 'I see,' he says. 'Clever lad, aren't you?' He takes a small, black leather notebook out of the pocket of his uniform and checks the numbers written on the wood – against, Manu presumes, the co-ordinates that Cogan gave him.

'These seem right. *Sawa, twendeni.*' OK, let's go.

Before leaving the old, familiar room, its resident lizard still motionless on the ceiling, Manu picks up the scrap of paper with Anke's address on it and stuffs it in his pocket.

'What was that?' asks Faithful, who doesn't miss a thing.

'The address of a woman.'

The brigadier chuckles, then says: 'But I thought it was my daughter you were interested in?'

Manu gulps. 'So you. . . ?'

'Yes, the *askaris* gave me your messages.'

'I'm sorry,' Manu stutters, at a loss.

Faithful chuckles again, picking up the drawer. 'And I did pass them on to Edith. Look, I'd much rather she was going out with you than bringing home some American dude who doesn't understand our Ugandan ways. Not that she shows the slightest sign of wanting to come back here ever again – seems to want to become an American herself, like all our foolish youth. She's doing a course in communication analysis and practice, whatever the fuck that means. Don't get your hopes up.'

So that's that.

Manu follows him out into the bar, again with David's and the customers' eyes on the now even stranger sight of a UPDF brigadier carrying a small wooden drawer.

Outside, once they've got into the Mercedes again, Faithful passes Manu the drawer. 'Hungry?' he asks, as he starts the engine.

'Not really,' Manu says, still feeling very anxious.

'Well I am.' He drives on a little until they come to one of the street-side braziers selling roast maize and kebabs, chicken or goat. 'Come on,' he says. 'Everyone needs to eat.'

They get out of the vehicle, Faithful having grabbed the drawer from Manu's lap as they stopped. '*Mahindi choma,*' he says to the vendor, a young man of about Manu's age.

'Yes, *afande*,' the vendor replies, picking up a napkin to wrap the wooden end of a skewer of roast maize, which has been rubbed with chilli and salt.

'You're sure you don't want something, Manu?' Brigadier Faithful asks.

'I'm OK, really,' he replies, though the smells from the brazier are making him hungry.

Once the maize is in Faithful's hand and he's chewing on it, he says to the vendor, 'You're looking a bit low on fuel; take off the grill, my brother.'

The vendor does as he is told, using a long-pronged fork to lift the grill, on which pieces of stuck-on meat are still sizzling, with his other hand catching up as-yet-unsold skewers. The brigadier promptly tosses the wooden drawer with the co-ordinates on it into the brazier.

The confused vendor stands there with the grill still wedged on his fork, and the raw, skewered meat and maize in his other hand. The bulk of the drawer is in the iron frame of the burner, and the flames it's now drawing make it impossible for the man to put the grill back on.

Faithful hands the guy a few shillings and, after finishing his maize, nods at Manu to get back into the Mercedes.

'So you're probably wondering what that was all about?' he says, once they're both back in the car.

'Yes.'

'Well, it wasn't gold in that crate you and Cogan buried, it was a SAM-16 missile launcher.'

'What?'

'You remember how the plane carrying Rwandan President Habyarimana and his Burundian counterpart was shot down in '94, initiating the genocide?'

'Yes?' Everyone in the Great Lakes knows this story, which brought so much misery; it was uppermost in Manu's mind when the archbishop gave his talk back at the cathedral in Bukavu: two years ago, before *wazungu* came to woo him with their aeroplanes.

'So, that jet – a Mystère Falcon 50, really nice machines, they

223

are – was shot down by the shoulder-carried launcher you buried with Cogan. Well, by that one and at least two other ones, most likely; but the one you hid away with Cogan . . . that was passed from the RPA to the AFDL and used in some of the battles in the liberation of Zaire. We removed it from some dead AFDL on the way to Kilo Moto.'

'Why are you telling me this?' Manu asks, not wanting to hear any of it.

Faithful laughs. 'Well I have to tell someone, or it sits on my tits like a ten-tonne gorilla!'

Is it really that, though?

Because it seems unlikely to Manu that an older man in such a position would speak to him like this, just to admit his own anxieties. He wonders if, instead, Edith's dad actually just likes him, and is understanding of his situation . . . but is there something darker there, too? As if Faithful has calculated that the more Manu's trapped by de facto complicity, the more he's bound to keep his mouth shut.

But who knows?

'Some of these things even one's own president doesn't want to hear,' Faithful continues. 'The problem for us, by which I mean the UPDF, is that we supplied all those missile launchers to the RPA in the first place – because we believed in their cause back then, and they helped us get rid of Amin, Obote, the others after, when they were part of our own resistance movement. We'd bought the launchers from the Russians, you see – if your colleague Evgeny did the transportation!'

'So why's it so important, this weapon?'

'Look, we didn't know that Habyarimana was going to be shot down, we really didn't – the Rwandans started keeping things from us; they so like secrets, those people. The point for Uganda is that all the launchers used that day – and I think of it as the day everything began to fuck up, even though Habyarimana was a first-class shit – have numbers from the same series, beginning 048 or 049, and they're recorded in our own lists of officially purchased munitions. And now that the French and the UN and other busybodies are sniffing around Habyarimana's assassination, we don't want it all to come and roost unfairly on our doorstep.'

He's really going into the detail on this. Manu wonders if it's because he's genuinely patriotic and just wants to tell the truth to someone about that feeling. Simply proud about serving his country? Maybe it's indeed so, because overhearing other senior UPDF officers in the bar, especially those who were directly involved in overthrowing dictators, Manu has experienced this before. Even if it came in some cases with graft and abuse of position, and all the other things that happen when a small, elite group run a country – partly serving themselves, partly staving off a likely return to the chaos from which, as young men (and young women too, such as Edith's dead mother) they emerged – there was a time when that group did truly free Uganda from earlier tyranny. Many of the army's top echelons still believed in the noble ideas that made that happen, even as others in the country, mainly not soldiers but some soldiers too, restively wished for democratic change. If it wasn't going to happen soon, when? Museveni and the other resistance fighters who took part in the wars against Amin and Obote have been in power for – how long? Manu does a quick mental calculation – over twelve years already.

Faithful, one of the same band of partisans, has already continued blithely on about the weapon that shot down Habyarimana's plane, revealing an obscure future journey that's never got even three lines in history books. 'So when I got hold of that one missile launcher on the way to Kilo Moto where I saw you – it came from an AFDL outfit shot up by UNITA, us attacking just after – I thought well, it would be a good idea to put it in a secure place, and I asked Cogan, bless his soul, to do so.'

'Why didn't you just destroy it?'

'Good question . . . Manu, as you probably know, there are many theories about who killed Habyarimana, it's still, what's that phrase my daughter brought back from Britain – a hot potato? I'm not going to say directly what I think, but you can maybe work it out yourself when I tell you the reason we kept it, and why I asked Cogan to bury it.'

'I'm sorry, I don't understand.'

'The way things are going, Manu – not a good direction, sad to say – we may one day need leverage against the Rwandan high command. As I've said, the RPA used to be our friends, but now they too often act like the opposite.'

A chill flows through Manu, draining down his body into the leather seat of the Mercedes. None of this is information he wants to know.

'Now listen here,' says Faithful, 'I'm assuming you can't remember all those strings of numbers we just burned, unless you're some kind of genius memory act?'

'No.'

He picks up the pistol from the cubby and Manu lets out a deep breath, as if he's now finally going to meet his end, after all the other times it has nearly happened. But all Faithful does is use the trigger guard to itch the side of his face, before chucking the gun back into the cubby again, a movement that makes Manu jump in his seat.

'Relax,' Faithful says. 'It's just my scabies, which all we army fellows get, whatever our rank. If we wanted to rub you out, it could have happened as easy as it happened to Cogan. You're apparently a good pilot and we may need a few. More than a few. What do you say to coming into UPDF service?'

'I'm hoping to pull back from military work,' he says.

Faithful sighs. 'None of us *want* to fight, it's just the duty life throws at us. You're afraid of the violence, is that it?'

'Yes,' Manu replies, though it's so much more than that.

'I'd make it a good contract, paid in dollars.'

'It's not about the dollars, it's just I seem to have been pushed around by war, one way or another, since almost the day I left school.'

This statement seems to have a powerful effect on the brigadier. He lifts his big, scarred hands, which have been resting on the steering wheel, then rubs his eyes. 'Christ, boy, do I know what you mean. I've been where you are since I ducked out of secondary. Over twenty years! Doing O-levels, I should have been, not training in Mozambique or helping to kick Amin, Obote and the other dictators out of my own country!'

He laughs again, now lifting up his big hands in the air in front of the windscreen. 'All right, I surrender! Off you go, but it's quite likely I might have to ask you to do a few jobs for us; we're running out of options, since all you pilots seem to be hellbent on getting yourself killed or jailed. Or running off to the Emirates like Evgeny.'

'OK,' Manu says, speaking like a robot as he gets out of the car.

Faithful seems about to drive off, but then rolls down the window, saying, 'You know, I like your style, Manu, you're a good boy, and so many aren't. I'll let Edith know I've met with you.'

Once the Mercedes has glided away, Manu stands immobile on the street, thinking about Edith in America, his hopes of something evolving between them (stalled as they were by fantasies of Anke) now resting with her father, hardly the best sponsor for a suitor. And he isn't really a suitor, anyway, having done nothing more strenuous to pursue her than leave a few notes at the gates of Faithful's mansion. Sometimes he hates his own passivity, and he knows it's not good enough to simply blame it on his past.

Putting away these thoughts, simply feeling relieved that Faithful seemed willing to let him go, despite the dangerous knowledge he'd put in his head, Manu returns to The Passenger and orders a double whisky from David.

'So what was all that about?' the Munyamulenge boy asks.

'What?'

'The famous brigadier coming in here and marching you through to your old room, coming back with a piece of furniture?'

'You really don't want to know,' Manu tells him.

Chapter 11

At first, the business with Faithful doesn't preoccupy Manu as much as he first thought it would. There are many other things to worry about, after all. As Cogan indicated as he was dying, however incoherently, the new will did indeed name Manu as his inheritor: of both The Passenger and Normair.

Getting across the detail of these two businesses takes a lot of time and mental effort. What takes more of both is dealing with his own sense of isolation; it's like there's no one left to lean on now.

One morning in late July, after Atul Khan has finally sorted out the paperwork to do with the inheritance, delaying charging his fee on the basis of future business, Manu is sitting with Cogan's solicitor in The Passenger, drinking coffee. Dressed in his usual brown suit and a striped, school-like tie, the solicitor seems as thin as Papa, and just as full of advice.

'So what are you going do now?' he asks.

Inert, unable to act, paralysed; how can Manu tell him? If he could, he'd like to still this conversation, land it like a plane. But what he says is: 'Carry on as Cogan would have done.'

'I would not fully advise that,' Atul Khan replies. 'Cogan ruined himself by playing too many hands at the same time. I continually warned him about the dangers of military work, but he took no notice.'

Khan's words, or maybe the coffee, stir Manu to action at last, even if he knows it's likely impossible to avoid flying for the military, Normair being on such a shoestring. Later that day, he goes through Cogan's ledger for the company, working out what's booked.

Hardly anything. But then – the radio being on in The Passenger – a boon of sorts drops through the ether. The news is that Kabila has demanded that Rwandan and Ugandan troops leave Congo at once.

The very next morning a call comes through from Faithful, asking if Manu can help pick up Ugandan officers and equipment stranded at airports all over Congo. He feels he has no option but to assent; the firm will go under otherwise.

As Manu flies over the next few days, following Faithful's orders, he misses Cogan – misses his voice especially, misses those jokes and songs and the gruff, gravelly tone that graded over difficulties. *Shit's about to hit the fan again. At least this pull-out has brought in some business we can snap up. Paardy!* He wants the Texan here in the cabin beside him, like his father was once beside him, at the forge or on the maize plot.

Back at the bar, he imagines – here comes Cogan, rolling into The Passenger like a peal of thunder. It's always someone else. But Manu doesn't grieve as much as he expects to. It's the surest way to know that something's really wrong, not grieving; but why should he weep for Cogan, when he wept so little for his mother, his father, for Beatrice? It's all been stuffed tight as a tick with blood, this history of loss, and now it seems like it's sitting in his soul, waiting to explode.

At night in the flat, he lies in bed plagued equally by throwbacks of memory and half-baked future plans. How he wants to lay all his freight lightly down and jump forwards to a moment when everything is settled.

But . . . *I can only fly like that in my mind*, which is of no practical use at all. He already knows he'll get no further unless he jumps for real, takes action. But where, what, how?

Penetrating his bedroom, the rhythmical *tok-tok-clink*, *tok-tok-clink* of reed frogs, down in the wetlands by the lake, rattles in his head as he tries to sleep. It's like the sound of ice cubes being tipped into Cogan's glass of Johnnie Walker, but incessantly so.

As he sits in The Passenger a few weeks later, the sound of the zinc-framed clock in the bar almost imitates the frogs he's just left behind at the flat, and the ice cubes they imitated in turn. Another morning in this period of his failing to become the person he wants to be, now that he's truly on his own, and there's no one left to imitate. He's eating bread and honey again, puzzling over the schematic for the hydraulic system of the Cargomaster, which has gone wrong, meaning he has to cancel some of the UPDF extraction jobs for Faithful.

He sorts out the mechanical problem later that day at the airport, is justly proud of himself for that; but the hydraulics on the Cargomaster break again almost immediately; it's like a curse has fallen on him, he feels, as if all these events – in fact, separate events – are conspiring against him, making themselves seem more consecutive than the singular episodes that they really are. He has to pay for an engineer, who produces exactly the same paper plan of the aircraft's pipe system that Manu has already looked at, marking what's wrong with an X.

Very expensive X, written in felt-tip.

As for Manu, there is no recognised schematic for what he's suffering, because suffering is not really the problem. The absolute worst thing, he realises during these last days and nights of the interbellum, is not feelings but a *lack* of feelings.

Most often he feels only numbness. At best, it's as if he's been experiencing, in these two months after Cogan's death, something more like a summary of emotion than emotion itself. And what he knows, what he truly knows, as he does his best to continue dealing with the practical matters of Normair and the bar, is that these unfelt emotions are storing themselves up to ambush him in the future, like Recognition did up on the mountain. He wonders whether Recognition died of the wound he had made in his shin. He wishes he didn't give a shit, but part of him at least wants to know what happened.

It's during this time, too, more or less, that a second war suddenly starts, nipping at the hindquarters of the interbellum – the

Rwandans and Ugandans reinvading Congo with the aim of overthrowing their former proxy, Kabila, almost as soon as he has chucked them out. A much bigger and bloodier war it shall turn out to be, too – a dog that *really* hunts, as Cogan would have put it, hunts so well that the sound of its victims' dispatch remains largely unheard by the world; whole villages, whole towns being left silent and desolate, with not a soul to tell by whose hands they have become such wastelands. It will be chaos and complexity all over, with Rwanda and Uganda fighting Congo, Zimbabwe, Angola and Namibia – and sometimes each other. Chad and Sudan, they'll be in there somewhere, too, along with many militia groups with multifarious aims, and some with no aim at all besides rape and plunder.

As for you, Manu, says the clock on the wall of The Passenger, you might have passed your exams but you remain a candidate, subject to tests on your talent like us all, even us clocks who can't keep pace with all the other clocks in the world, who can't keep pace with the bends that time and its little sister history are making, all across this crooked universe. And even that, the whole interplanetary shooting match, the whole empire of light, is subject to tests too, expected to whip itself into shape, into form, *seeking structure every outpaced millimetre, every already spent second.*

IV

Fighting Fire, Treading Water

August 1998–February 2002

Chapter 1

As the second war begins, Manu is at Goma Airport in east Congo, on another small job for Faithful. About ten other pilots are with him, each with their own contracts to fulfil. They're all trying to ignore the chaos going on in the city by means of copious ingestion of caffeine in the pilots' café, a dismal place with a dirty tiled floor and – displayed in a greasy glass case – the usual dog-eared samosas.

The pilots look up from their polystyrene cups of coffee as Major Rusyo sweeps in, surrounded by gun-toting troops from the RPA's High Command Unit.

Manu last saw Rusyo at Kamituga with Cogan, picking up that generator, almost two years ago. Despite the odds against, he had hoped never to see him again.

'Hello Manu,' Rusyo says, shaking his hand with disconcerting enthusiasm, as if he's suddenly become one of the major's most valued business associates. Manu's simple uniform of black trousers and white shirt, without epaulettes, has not disguised him one jot.

'Sorry to hear about Cogan. Too bad.'

How did he hear about Cogan's death? Spies, probably. The Rwandan intelligence service is superb. But Rusyo could have heard in other ways. There's plenty of traffic of information between Uganda and Rwanda, those uneasy allies – Faithful himself could have been the conduit, despite his dislike of Rusyo.

'Good afternoon, gentlemen,' Rusyo announces to the other pilots, who include Dami Adedoyin, a well-built, middle-aged

Nigerian, a Zambian old-timer called Percy Phiri, and others of different nationalities.

'What's going to happen today, do you think?' Rusyo adds, his voice echoing off the walls.

No one replies. 'Well?'

'What?' Manu says in the end, crossly; the only benefit of his post-Cogan numbness is that he's lost most of his fear of this man. But he has to comply – for by now one of Rusyo's soldiers is coring the muzzle of a gun into Manu's kidneys.

'I'll tell you. Today, you are all going to fly me and my troops to Kitona Airbase.'

'You've got to be kidding!' says one of the other pilots, an American called Tim St Ville, known across the circuits for his button-down shirts, often pink or mauve, and much-thwarted sense of punctuality. 'I'm due in Dodoma first thing.'

'No, I'm utterly in earnest. Your flights to Kitona leave in thirty minutes!'

'I absolutely refuse,' says a young Scottish pilot called Nigel Paterson, shaking his head. 'It's illegal to hijack us like this.'

'Don't blame me,' Major Rusyo replies, in an oddly craven tone, bending his tall body and head towards the Scotsman, seeming to Manu like a wind-swept palm on a lakeshore as he speaks. 'It's my boss, General Kabarebe, who's in charge of this operation.'

'That may be,' says Paterson. 'But it's an impossible plan, all the same. Kitona's the most defended airbase in the country!'

'Shut your talking,' Phiri whispers to Paterson, bowing his grey head almost in imitation of Rusyo's posture.

Paterson ignores him. 'The Congolese will fight you to the end; they'll never betray the freedom that Kabila has brought them from Mobutu.'

'Tell me,' Rusyo asks, straightening up and gazing, as if absent-mindedly, towards the apron on which the aircraft of the becalmed pilots are parked. 'Which is your plane?'

'The Beechcraft.'

'Quite easy to fly?'

'Easy enough.'

'Good, because then we'll able to find someone else to fly it,' Rusyo says, taking out his gun and shooting Paterson in the head.

They all look at the Scotsman in stunned silence, as if expecting another rejoinder; but he's dead as stone already, his blood converging in the runnels between the tiles.

Kitona is in south-western Congo, lying at the mouth of the Congo River where it joins the Atlantic, near to the places (as Don Javier once explained) where the first European explorers and traders came into the region, with their steamers and their smallpox. It's now enemy territory for the Rwandans, though telling who's an enemy, who's a friend, is for everyone becoming as difficult as distinguishing between different types of yam.

The Nigerian guy, knowing a yam from a yam through being a veteran of multiple coups in his own country, assents to Rusyo's request with his best Ibadan beam. And then skips out. It's simply masterful, the way he pretends he's going for a piss then runs for his plane, taking off for Lagos in a rain of Rwandan gunfire.

Good work; Manu wishes he'd done the same. But the Rwandan soldier next to him has been waving his sub-machine gun over him the whole time, so it was never an option. He's trapped here, there's no getting out of it.

Rusyo, fuming about the Nigerian's escape, shouts at everyone, 'And don't get any smart ideas about the radio. Our signalmen are monitoring everything – any unauthorised transmissions and you'll be shot too.'

He singles out the soldier who keeps plugging his gun into Manu's body. 'You! Watch that one, he's slippy. Keep your eyes on him and don't leave his side.'

Stranded in Goma, disaffected Congolese troops have joined the Rwandan operation, turning against Kabila. They pile into any plane available, many into Percy Phiri's Boeing 707. The Rwandans – berets on, rifles and sub-machine guns at the ready – keep a close eye on these Congolese deserters before they themselves board. Manu's designated to fly ammunition, dozens of dark-green metal boxes, loading the Cargomaster to its limit.

His guard joining him in the cockpit, Manu flies over 1,500 kilometres and four-and-a-half hours from Goma towards Kitona, the plane's cabin filled with all these boxes, plus more in the hold. All the while with the same Uzi-waving RPA trooper that Rusyo told to keep an eye on him, sitting in the co-pilot's seat.

Manu's hands shake as he follows in the wake of Phiri's Boeing – albeit much more slowly, as the 707's cruising speed is as least twice as fast as that of his own plane. The Cargomaster passes over the winding grey waters of the Congo River, along which, he notices, long islands of reed are moving . . . until Kitona airbase materialises beneath him like another island, but massive and man-made, its runway flanked by hangars and barracks.

Later he'll hear how Phiri landed the Boeing, every second expecting it (as now Manu also expects) the Cargomaster to be brought down by a MANPAD. Somebody shot out the front tyre of the Boeing while it was touching down. Phiri landed it, though; the Rwandans and their Congolese allies reportedly poured out of the bigger, half-crippled aircraft, and after a short firefight secured the base.

As Manu himself lands, his guard – gun across his knees – jolts up and down beside him. There seems to be none of the protracted resistance predicted by the young dead Scot, Nigel Paterson. It helps, of course, that the RPA has already done a deal with the commander of the airbase at Kitona, persuading him to desert, Manu learns later. With the handover of further suitcases of dollars, the allegiance of the few Congolese officers unhappy with the arrangement is successfully secured.

How's it ordered, this new schematic of living, during which Manu's effectively a prisoner, flying under armed guard? Like this. Flies straight out of Kitona for a jungle airstrip, and another, and another; crashes for a few hours under canvas, pooped out on weed and beer, static roaring in his head. Next morning, tries to rouse himself with coffee and amphetamines. Breaking *all* Papa's rules now. Fear of getting in the airplane. Doesn't move. Gun at his ear. Moves. Wakes up a little in the cockpit. The cycle continues, more ammunition being loaded or unloaded at every point.

After a few days of this, joining Manu's almost-permanent minder, a semi-mute man he now knows is called Zachariah, other Rwandan soldiers begin getting on and off the Cargo-master like it's a bus. In mid-flight they open the doors without asking and fire down at Congolese below, using the plane like a gunship.

He hears Cogan's ghostly voice. *Paardy!* Not any more. Not ever.

He didn't sign up for any of this. It wasn't in the manuals, those well-thumbed volumes sitting on a shelf in a flat in Entebbe that he dare not hope he'll ever get back to. He feels helpless, angry, vengeful.

Outgoing, incoming, quake all the time. Something explodes very near on one trip, making the fuselage shake.

Fresh clip, fresh clip, and the troopers carry on firing. Funk of these sweating soldiers coming through from the passenger area: swamp of groin, swamp of armpit, harsh tobacco, booze. He's sweating all over, too, all the time. What *is* the time? Mumbling, groaning, tears as he takes off; mumbling, groaning, tears as he lands, sinking with what seems like a failing engine into the ground.

It's not failing, thank God, just overloaded. But how can he distance himself from them now, these men hooked on death?

Through it all, RPA officers, every stripe, bring on board cargoes of gold, diamonds, coltan, even sacks of coffee beans. It's a swipe; it's anything you can lay your hands on; it's sell any place there's a trader, someone who'll lodge your money in an account in Dubai or Mumbai, London or Zurich, no questions asked. Oh yes, *afande,* looky here, it's one colossal breakdown, one mother-fucker of an eruption, this massive, multi-country conflict . . . Manu feels borne along by it, like a lump of rock in a lava flow.

Now and then, during the next weeks, prisoners are brought on board, mostly local politicians or captured high-ranking members of the Congolese Army who've refused to come over to Rusyo's side. There's nothing Manu can do. Fear of getting in an airplane at all becomes fear of getting in the airplane to find one of these prisoners already inside, wrists bound by cable ties, only to notice he's not there at all on landing – tossed out earlier, over the Congo *fleuve*.

And every time, on getting down from the aeroplane, the troops who do the tossing-out, they look at the pilot with expressions of ghastly obeisance, eyes rolling upwards as they stagger past the front of the aircraft in their battledress – as if Manu himself, sitting up in the cabin, shoulders hunched under his stained white shirt, is being exalted as the god to whom their sacrifices are offered.

Troops, troops: 3000 more Rwandan troops and unpaid former Mobutu soldiers land in flights from Goma and Kigali to swell RPA forces in the west. They capture Moanda, the country's petrol refinery. They capture the Inga Dam, which supplies this part of Congo with electricity – promptly turning off the supply and plunging Kinshasa into darkness. They capture the small Atlantic port of Banana; they capture Congo's second-largest port at Boma; and they capture its largest at Matadi . . . they capture all these places in an area where the merciless dance of imperial commerce, trading under the name of civilisation, went on for over a century. Raiding banks, breaking into warehouses, prising open shipping containers, the officers fill their coffers, just as their colonial forebears did. As Manu slips deeper into despair, Zachariah the guard is by his side every minute.

The worst is what happens at Boma, where the younger women of the district are rounded up and taken to the Premier Bassing Hotel, which has been established as the Rwandan headquarters. Sitting in the hotel bar, in a huddle with other kidnapped pilots – including Percy Phiri, whose front wheel has been replaced by one from another Boeing, abandoned years ago at Kitona – Manu watches like an automaton as these poor women are paraded past him and upstairs. He's unable to say a single word, unable even to move as Rwandan soldiers constantly keep their guns on him and the others.

The troops aren't just using hijacked planes, they're also stealing cars, lorries, even a train one time, the passage of which Manu is ordered to fly ahead of, radioing back Congolese positions along the line.

In Kinshasa, he hears, rich people are packing up their belongings ready to flee, like they did the last time the Rwandans came in the first war. In the streets there, it's said, Banyamulenge and other Tutsi-looking people are being hunted down, burned alive by mobs, on the pretext of them being secret agents passing information to the RPA.

And this is in some cases probably true, but as Phiri says to Manu, as they sit like two stooges in that horror show of a bar at the Bassing Hotel (the third stooge, button-down Tim from Minnesota, already having suffered the same fate as Paterson, on account of too much complaining): 'Kagame's people are not so stupid as to only pick Tutsis as their spies!'

'Yes, but that's Kinshasa,' Manu says, 'look what's happening here.' As two more women are shepherded through the hotel's entrance door, he finally stands up and shouts, 'This can't go on!'

'You sit down at once,' urges Phiri — this wise old Zambian, who's ferried mining engineers and equipment between Joburg, Ndola and the Congolese mines for over thirty years, the full term of Mobutu's own terror, and logged nearly 30,000 hours. 'It makes me want to vomit too. But you'll get us all killed! Look what happened to that Scottish fool, look what happened to the American. So sit back down and see it out.'

Seeing Zachariah's rifle lift slightly across near the entrance to the bar, and how the violence-dulled eyes of all the guards fall on him, Manu does as the Zambian says.

The anger oozes unwillingly out of him as he settles back into the plastic seat — leaving behind only a feeling that would be sick, that would be sorry, were his mind not so numb, so blank, so unable to distinguish between one episode and the next in this stream of awful events.

The RPA capture Congolese tanks, repair them, roll into the next town, wallow in ruts of mud on the way out . . . Manu flying overhead all the while, landing, taking off – delivering shells, delivering spare parts, collecting goods, collecting strongboxes of cash in different denominations, moving officers about, moving prisoners about. In time, seeing even worse atrocities than those committed against the women of Boma, Manu realises that there's always something worse than what he thought was the worst before.

At first, it seems as if providence too is on board with all this, and that the RPA's blitzkrieg will succeed. Too bad for Kabila. But slowly the Rwandan advance grinds to a halt, as Zimbabwean and Angolan forces, supported by heavy airpower and artillery, bulk up Kabila's defences – which otherwise would be as flimsy as Manu's own. Even his name has gone, being referred to now simply as 'pilot one' in RPA radio transmissions.

In late August he's pinned down at N'djili Airport, on the outskirts of Kinshasa, with little chance of survival, he reckons. The Cargomaster is at the western end of a 4700-metre runway and he's sitting in the cabin, still under Zachariah's impassive eye, fairly large artillery shells and missiles being tossed at them. The Zimbabweans are the ones throwing this stuff across, along with the rockets that their compatriots in the air are raining down. It seems only a matter of time before the Cargomaster is hit.

There Manu sits, all the same, amid the crump of fire, watched by the dull-faced Rwandan trooper whose mum, whose dad, whose uncle and aunt were all probably murdered by Hutus. Not that Manu cares about the history any longer. Stinking, having not been able to wash properly for weeks, he just wants to go home – back to The Passenger, his flat, the Datsun, the new life he half made out of the bonfire of the old, which now seems as if it too is going up in flames. He feels very alone.

Hungry, too. There has hardly been time to eat, so intense has been the flying and the fighting. As other RPA soldiers carry ammo boxes and weapons on to the Cargomaster, in case they have to make a quick exit, and the few remaining Rwandan tanks square off with enemy tanks at the other end of the runway, and Zimbabwean Hawks and Lynxes and Alouettes strafe their positions, Manu tries to work out what's going on by listening to the airbands.

What he eventually establishes, through the crackle and squelch of the radio, flinching as weaponry explodes all round, is as follows: protected by a convoy of Zimbabwean armoured cars, Kabila himself is in the process of being brought to the other end of the runway and flown out to Lubumbashi.

Trench warfare develops over the next few days, across the middle of that very long runway at N'djili – so long it was once deemed a possible landing site for NASA's space shuttle – its edges littered with abandoned aircraft from previous eras. Although the Cargomaster has so far avoided a direct hit, there seems to Manu no chance of him escaping alive, as the RPA infantry begin to slip away . . . but eventually an order comes on the radio, from Rusyo as a matter of fact, already miles away.

'Take off! Take off! Pilot one, all of you. We're pulling out.'

It's a bad take-off, all right – *last I'll ever make*, thinks Manu – as Zimbabwean tracer bursts round the aircraft. Almost reaching altitude, he sees the burst of a MANPAD missile far below. There's only one thing for it, for pilot one.

He does the *pantsula*: Cogan's jinking, swivelling turn that causes a feeling of falling right when you're turning left, and is followed by the seeking of cover – a hill, a mountain, even a building.

It doesn't work, the missile's still heading straight towards the Cargomaster . . . Next to him, Zachariah starts up and rushes to the back of the aircraft, as if that would make any fucking difference.

The plane starts to autorotate, spinning round on itself like a globe on a spindle, and Manu's not sure he has the acceleration to come up out of the dive. Suddenly the Belgian girl with golden hair, and the show-off stunt he pulled for her in Lengai crater, bounces into his mind: he sees that a way to get the missile off his tail might be to combine the Anke move with the *pantsula* . . .

Toggling the controls, he uses the same pattern he deployed over the volcano in Tanzania, dipping up and down again with great rapidity. At the end of each cycle of these – banging his feet on the rudder pedals – he deploys the swivelling turn of the *pantsula*, directing the nose cone of the Cargomaster straight at the missile, making tighter and tighter turns . . .

Highly risky as it is, the trick works. Its guidance systems confused, the missile spins down over the airport. The double series of moves also has the effect of making Zachariah, who's rushed back into the front cabin in the midst of all this, fall over and bang his head. *Please let him be knocked unconscious . . .*

But could Manu actually do it, what the RPA did to others – put the plane on autopilot, tumble the guy out, at last go home?

Zachariah gets up in any case, rubbing his temple and looking angry.

'*Fusée sol-air*,' Manu explains, thinking of the one in Faithful's crate at Kikorba, held as a sometime threat against Zachariah's superiors.

The guy doesn't understand. Most of the time until now Manu has spoken to Zachariah, when he'll converse at all, in a mishmash of Swahili and English; in the fright of the past few minutes he's forgotten that Zachariah doesn't speak French, being one of those Tutsi Rwandese brought up in Uganda.

'Rocket,' Manu sighs, finally saying it in English, before adding: 'OK, what's our destination?'

'Maquela do Zombo,' intones Zachariah. 'That is where the major said to go if we had to withdraw.'

'What?'

Because Manu just can't believe it, if this really is the RPA's next move. Kitona, Boma, Banana, N'djili itself – these are all plausible places to fly to if you're trying to effect a military takeover of Congo.

'You are sure?'

'Yes.'

Maquela do Zombo? It even sounds like something out of the horror videos Manu and his schoolfriends sometimes used to watch, back in Bukavu, involving zombies, chain-saws, or children of the corn.

For one thing, Maquela's over the border in Angola – nominally enemy territory, since the Angolan government, having been on the Rwandan side in the first war, are now aligned with Kabila and Zimbabwe.

Manu flirts with the idea of flying somewhere else, but there's not that much fuel in the tank – certainly not enough to get back to Entebbe – and putting down in some random Congolese airport, maybe held by Zimbabweans or Angolans, or by Kabila's own Congolese forces, would be more dangerous than going along with Rusyo's instructions.

Setting the course – staring cheerlessly at the instrument panel – Manu slowly tries to work out the plan. The part of Angola that this whole, failed, misbegotten invasion force is now headed for lies within the rough territory of UNITA insurgents, who've been fighting for years to dislodge the generals and business-people who run Angola. UNITA now, it appears, has switched sides to ally with the Rwandans – *is that it*? he's not at all sure – mirroring in reverse the switch of the Angolan government to support Kabila, who they opposed in the first war.

As Manu filters all this, flying south into Angola, he remembers a time when Cogan tried to elucidate some detail of the first war to him, ending with these words of wisdom: 'In a way, kid, there ain't no point at all in explaining as it's so confusing. But in another way there is, 'cos just trying to explain, seeming like a dunderhead as you do so, makes clear how goddam complicated it is.'

Even the simple part that Manu has been told to play, in support of one side of this complex, shifting set of affiliations, doesn't stay simple. For as he's about halfway to Maquela, another message comes through from Rusyo on the radio. It supplies the co-ordinates of a smaller, more remote, UNITA-controlled bush strip where he's to put down and wait for further instructions.

The wait turns out to be a fortnight in duration, during which not just Manu but also Zachariah are guarded by grizzled UNITA veterans. They speak only Portuguese and Ovambo, so communication is difficult. Manu spends most of the time sitting under a large tamarind tree next to a couple of shacks. From one of these, at mealtimes, a half-dressed woman, a camp-follower of these almost geriatric rebels, regularly appears, carrying a purple plastic basin of half-fried *frango*, as chicken is called in those parts.

Starving, Manu gnaws these scant offerings down to the very bones, though he's outstripped in this process by Zachariah, who carefully splits the bones with his bayonet and sucks out the marrow, before crunching the gristly end-joints.

After the first week, Manu begins to follow Zachariah's example, borrowing his bayonet. He tries to talk to his minder, but he's not very bright, Zachariah. All this while, all this time of torpor and fried chicken, Manu visualises ways to escape, like that Nigerian pilot did at Goma.

No chance. They might have wrinkled faces, these old UNITA guys, but they're as watchful as spiders.

Finally receiving an order to fly, Manu lands at Maquela do Zombo to find that 3000 RPA troops have taken control of the airstrip there. The runaway Rwandan army has spent the intervening time – while Manu's been waiting in the bush – marching from N'djili. On arrival, they defeated Maquela's Angolan government defenders, the strip apparently not being as squarely in UNITA territory as was believed at the outset, when the RPA began that long trek from N'djili.

In many ways, even though they are losing now, what the RPA has done is quite impressive. But because he's angry, and because he's the senior pilot now (poor Phiri having bought it at N'djili, he's learned), Manu demands a meeting with Major Rusyo. He doesn't really care what happens; he knows Rusyo can dispatch him – like he has dispatched Nigel Paterson, Tim St Ville and countless others – but Manu believes he can't go on. He's reached another limit, like he did back in Bukavu, at the start of the first war.

The meeting goes like this: two voices, both full of anger, speaking under the sagging canvas of an army tent, lit by a Tilley lamp hanging from a cord and sour with the smell of unwashed bodies.

'When're you going to let me go home?'

'When we are done here.'

'When's that going to be?

'When we've extended the runway.'

'What do you mean?'

'We are extending the length of the runway so your friend Evgeny can send in big planes to pick us up. I've spoken to him in Dubai, it's all sorted out!'

'I thought he was working for Kabila and you'd cancelled his Rwandan contracts?'

'Well, let's say we've forgiven him. Evgeny works for everyone, as I guess you know. But the main thing is, he never lets a client down. You aren't planning to do so, I hope?'

'You were never my client. You haven't paid me anything.'

'But you're one of us! A Tutsi.'

'That tribal stuff is so much shit, no different now than when you and Recognition spouted it back in that camp in South Kivu in '96, or the Hutus on the radio in '94.'

Rusyo shakes his head sadly, and in an instant the force goes out of his speech, as if he were a balloon that has been popped by a needle. 'You're just wrong to make that comparison. Our idea of solidarity in Rwanda . . . it is completely different these days. We're rising above the past. Perhaps not here, right now, but at home we are.'

'Well I hope that's true,' Manu says, suddenly not sure what he thinks, because the major genuinely appears to believe that progress is being made. 'What happened to Recognition, anyway?' He doesn't say anything about his own encounter with that man on the slopes of the volcano with Anke, wanting to hear what Rusyo knows.

'That guy, why are you asking about him? Maybe he was involved in some of the risings against Kabila at the Banyamulenge camps in Bas-Congo? Or he's still causing trouble in the east, thinking he's a leader of men? A lot of you Mulenge fellows were killed, anyhow, by people in Kinshasa. You should have stuck with us. But to be honest, I've got no interest in your friend. As you've maybe seen, I've got much bigger things to worry about.'

'Recognition isn't my friend. Look, Major, I just want to get out of this.'

Sitting on his camp stool, under the hiss of the kerosene lamp, Rusyo appears extremely depressed, his voice dropping to a whisper. 'That's all I want, too. Just give me a bit more time. I'm serious, I promise you'll be paid.'

More time? Extending the runway takes, astonishingly, a total of nearly four months, which feel like the longest of Manu's whole life, making the torpor of the *frango* camp, or that other period of limbo after he fled from Bukavu, seem like nothing by comparison. But it's a period of immense tension, despite its extent. All the while, Manu and the other remaining pilots of small planes, only two or three, are under watch, like prisoners in a labour camp; and meanwhile the RPA's perimeter guard is itself on edge for an attack by Angolan government troops: this does happen several times, but they are repulsed in each instance. Rusyo makes Manu join in with the runway work, as he does everyone, whatever their rank or job. The digging blisters Manu's hands.

Once the runway is finally long enough, the planes that Evgeny has organised begin arriving, almost thirty flights, mostly Lets and Antonovs. They go straight out again, each taking what it can hold of the 3000 RPA troops back home to Kigali, and all by night to avoid being intercepted by Angolan or Zimbabwean MiGs.

With each flight, Manu looks to see if Evgeny is on board. But he never is; the pilots are other Russians or Ukrainians. Manu assumes Evgeny to be sitting in Dubai, pulling the strings. One of the flights brings fuel for the Cargomaster and the other small planes which escaped the fiasco at N'djili.

At last, the day comes when Manu himself flies out – Wednesday, 23 December 1998, he'll never forget it – with Rusyo and the last other remaining senior Rwandan officers on board. They leave in a shower of mortar fire as a mass of Angolan government troops begin to close in on the airfield – Luanda finally having decided, but too late, to deal once and for all with the Rwandan cuckoo in its nest.

When they finally land at Kigali, Manu says to Rusyo, 'So what about my wages?'

At this, gathering up his kit, the major just laughs. 'You really are extraordinary, the trust you place in people. Whatever made you think I was serious?'

'Because you said you were. It seemed a fair enough assumption, given what we have all been through. You promised.'

'Rather than whining about wages, you should count yourself lucky we're not just shooting you, now this has at last come to an end. Go back to Entebbe, before I change my mind. Anyway, from what I hear, you own an air cargo firm and a bar. What the fuck more do you want?'

Chapter 2

What he wants, Manu decides on landing at Entebbe with only just enough fuel, is to get out of this crazy situation completely; just as Papa was advising when they said goodbye, and Atul Khan too really, more recently. He should have kept utterly away from it, this second war, or 'polywar', as the few journalists covering it are now calling what's happened, struggling to explain it to their editors and the wider world. Does the Rwandan withdrawal mean the violence has exhausted itself? It's not yet clear.

Manu, at any rate, is definitely exhausted. He lurches from the Cargomaster and through immigration, holding his Ugandan passport to his chest like a badge of woe, only to find his woes added to when he reaches the airport car park. The Datsun won't start, having been sitting there so long.

He has to get a *boda*. From the dead zone, Aisha jabs him with the fingernail that used to itch her burn, or prod Cogan when she needed help. As he sits on the pillion, careful of his own calf on the hot exhaust despite his tiredness, encumbered by the battered flight bag on his knees, he imagines her as just another person tipped, like I was, into the cauldron – in her case on account, innocently enough, of a pair of lycra leggings.

When he gets back to The Passenger, the veranda outside is covered with streamers and lights. It's Christmas Eve, he realises – suddenly shocked that two years have passed since he met Edith on the beach, and played football there with the other Banyamulenge exiles.

He goes inside. Immediately David, the one he left in charge, rushes through the throng and embraces him tightly, seemingly immune to the human stink of his friend.

'*Afande*, you are back! We were getting worried. Very worried!'

Manu drops his flight bag on the floor. He's trying to avoid weeping.

'Come, have a drink,' says David, taking him by the arm and pulling him, half stunned, towards a bar stool.

The familiar old radio's on, and from the tannoy speaker a DJ announces: 'And next in honour of our father, that fallen elephant, the giant with a gentle soul, who died last month of a heart attack in Kinshasa, here is Pépé himself and the Empire Bakuba band, with his song about absent fathers, "Dadou"!'

And then at last they come, the honest tears, squeezed out by music that prompts memories of a group of friends, Jerome and Emile and Clement, messing around in a dorm in Bukavu, all those years ago.

Later, when Manu's ready to reseal his emotions, he and David go through the accounts for the almost five-month period that he's been away. He's amazed at how well David has done. There's a bit of money missing, he reckons, but much less than he would have expected. The bar is thriving. As he sits there, watching, it seems like a similar crowd to that of the old days, with the major difference that there are no pilots here now, just local folk from Entebbe and a few UPDF officers, none of whom he recognises.

He sends Matthias, David's lieutenant, down to Guchina's restaurant to buy him a fish supper. He's flaked out, and wants glucose, he reckons, but he doesn't drink too much as he waits for the food, being determined not to go the same way as the other freight dogs who – it now seems to him, excepting Papa – deliberately starved themselves of discipline, integrity, honour . . . all the other virtues he'd been taught were important, before he got drawn into their world.

The fish and chips arrive. Watching David, Matthias and two new Banyamulenge, Karl and Palatin, whom they've recruited in his absence, serve drinks to revellers as he eats, he becomes aware of how much they remind him of . . . *me, only a few years ago.*

He sees this recognition as a sign to straighten himself out; he has responsibilities now. These young men have no one to hang on to but him, just as he used to have no one to hang on to but the freight dogs, however badly that turned out. They might not be fliers but they, like him, have fallen out of the sky and been thrown into the world.

Once he's eaten, he picks up a bar chit and a biro and makes a list of the things he will do and the things he won't do, hoping to turn off the warning siren in his head that if he doesn't make his resolution now, it won't happen ever.

WILL DO: ORDINARY CARGO, TOURIST STUFF, TRANSPORTING EXPERTS LIKE ANKE.

WON'T DO: ANYTHING TO DO WITH FIGHTING, SOLDIERS, WAR OR CRIME.

He's at last certain of this, hating the lead-like weight of these conflicts – even sitting there in the jolly atmosphere of the bar he senses their burden – hating these wars that bring nothing about, except for killing many, enriching a few, and leaving those that survive with a sense of death-in-life that's hard to shake off.

Feeling grimy in soul and body, he says goodbye to David and the others and goes outside, flagging down another *boda* to take him back to his apartment. All through the period that he was in the war zone, the keys to the flat have been rattling around in one of the compartments of his flight bag. The day the flat was gifted feels, now, like a very long time ago, the time in between seeming to have folded into itself, like one of those origami tricks Cogan did with dollar bills.

This sense of spent time – disappeared time, distorted time – creates in Manu's mind an evocation of his family compound on the outskirts of Pendele, one which he associates with the smell of the woodsmoke that he now senses in the air whisking by the motorbike, the product of family suppers across the town.

The apartment, by contrast, smells stale, but everything is in good order otherwise. He takes the longest shower, throws himself down on the bed – his own bed again, at last.

In the morning he's woken by the kingfisher's call, its tone dipping one way and another. He decides, it being Christmas Day, that he will go to Mass again, like he did in '96 before the trip to Brno. The one in between he didn't go, Christmastide '97 having passed oblivious, like a drunken maniac's face in the street. Once more he joins the parade of frocks and suits, braids and *busutis*. After the Mass he makes his way to the beach, wanting to be alone.

And there, on the sand, Manu witnesses something he has heard about but never before seen. Heralded by a haunting cry as they fly in formation, wings in perfect unison, a flotilla of crested cranes, over thirty strong, are coming in low over the water. Landing on the beach in front of him, they arrange themselves in a circle, beginning an elaborate mating dance.

The plumage is mainly grey, though the wings are white, with occasional feathers of other colours interspersed. What stands out, in these big birds, is a bulbous black patch at the top of what would in humans be the forehead – but it competes for attention with a crest of stiff golden quills, white cheeks and a red throat patch.

All these features help animate the dance, which involves jumping and jinking and honking and booming, as the cranes bow or jiggle or open their wide wings outwards. He watches all this for nearly an hour. One by one, the birds begin to pair off and fly away. He has heard it said that this ritual by the Ugandan national bird involves each pair falling in love with each other for the rest of their lives.

A pretty story, he thinks. But, walking to The Passenger to get some lunch, he's determined that he won't let the seeming impossibility of any permanent pairing for me (as he thinks of this paradisal moment of integration), get in the way of his new resolve to keep his soul clean: as clean as if it had been sprayed and wiped and disinfected with Twinkle, with Jireh, with Spic-Span, those products with which he used to clean the bar.

As he enters The Passenger, David and Matthias are hard at work serving beer and club sandwiches, sodas and samosas to Christmas Day customers. The sight of food and drink being served to ordinary people – mostly Kampala businessmen taking their families for a day out in Entebbe – helps Manu feel anchored, tied down. But how long will I be able to stay like this, he wonders?

Chapter 3

Manu will pass, in fact – three years, is it? – in this mode of better adjustment, steadfastly keeping his resolution to avoid military flights – taking, in their place, tourists from Entebbe to Bwindi to marvel at gorillas, to Mahale to gawp at chimpanzees (inevitably the tourists say how fundamentally human the apes are), and on to Zanzibar, so they can press their own fundaments into hot sand. That too is marvellous, so they say.

Or he carries frozen fillets of tilapia to Mombasa, bringing back cheap electronics off Chinese ships for Suraj; or transports round Uganda bundles of market goods wrapped in plastic tape by enterprising women traders who drive a very hard bargain. He also makes friends with some people who run farming companies, again finding high-value agricultural crops to be a good line.

The dollar goes up again, which is good for revenue, as he's paid in that currency, and fuel's cheaper in this period too, so it's just easier to stay steady. He might feel like a dog chasing its own tail, but he doesn't even on financial grounds have to turn back to military work.

The temptation is still there, however. For although the Rwandans and Ugandans, and the Angolans and Zimbabweans too, have mostly – though by no means completely – withdrawn from the rest of the country, war has continued sporadically on in eastern Congo, the death toll rising as endless-seeming militias sprout up, most proxies of withdrawn forces or responses to them.

Sometime in summer 1999, Manu hears through pilot gossip

that Evgeny has been arrested, not by the Americans – his most recent employers after the RPA – but by the British, of all people, on a charge of money laundering. It turns out that all this time he has had a bank account in London, in which he was salting away his cash, then using it to buy properties. Manu imagines his poor wife – Maria, wasn't it? – presumably still in Dubai, waiting for her man to come home.

One morning further on in this period of steadfast resolution – a Saturday in mid-December 2000 it must've been, almost two years after Manu's return from Maquela do Zombo – David's mopping the floor of The Passenger, just like Manu used to, and Manu's doing paperwork. David chooses this moment to tell Manu a strange story about some people who came into the bar while he was away on his most recent flying job to Mombasa.

'I forget to say, *afande*. Some whites entered the bar last week, two men dressed in blue and grey suits and wearing lace-up shoes, and a woman in black with a zipper-sack round her middle.'

David pauses to squeeze the mop in its metal bucket, Manu watching as he sits smoking on Aisha's old stool, looking up from the contracts and flight plans strewn across the bar.

'Yes?'

'They began asking questions about the *muzungu* pilots who were here before, and about you as well.'

'What nationality were they? American?'

'No. European.'

'British?'

'No, I don't think so. Maybe from Italy, or Spain; I couldn't tell.'

'What did you say to them?'

'We said we didn't know much about the *muzungu* pilots as they are all gone now, but that you were our boss. We didn't say much – they seemed a bit like police or journalists, writing down our answers in notebooks.'

'You did well,' Manu says, stubbing out his cigarette. Must be something to do with Evgeny's case . . . though it puzzles him because that's a British matter, and these were apparently people from sunnier parts of Europe.

Though David's account returns him a little to the atmosphere of mistrust and unease that hovered round The Passenger when the freight dogs were there, Manu doesn't set much store by this tale of inquisitive visitors, not least because Europeans as a tribe, if that's what they are, don't hold so much sway in Kampala these days.

He has, by now, bought goods from one of the new Chinese shops in town to refurnish his apartment. Lying on his new bed there, listening to the kingfisher the Sunday after the exchange with David, Manu recollects Edith. Having heard nothing from her, he has made some discreet enquiries, learning that she has decided to stay on in the US and do postgraduate study. There seems no point in trying to contact her, but still he pines, despite a strong suspicion that they will never be reunited. It's high time to find someone else to think about, probably, but he keeps wanting to renew the memories of his attraction to her.

No good, *no man of feeling ever does jack shit in the real world*, Cogan huffs in his ear.

As for her father, Brigadier Faithful, he was arrested earlier this year – and then released – by the Ugandan government's Directorate for Ethics and Integrity. NGO people, speaking casually in The Passenger, said this was just to get the World Bank off the Ugandan government's back, in order to keep the aid flow coming. But those sorts of *wazungu*, Manu's learned, are always shouting their righteous mouths off about things they don't understand.

The kingfisher's still pipping away. He gets up from the new bed, goes to the window to look for it in the trees by the stream, but the bird stays hidden, like a lot in this region, he's found.

He maintains silence on politics these days, keeping his nose clean, banking green whenever he can. He's still a foreigner, after all, a stranger in a country that could turn hostile at any moment. He listens for the signals of that now, among the talk of the Ugandans at the bar and the news from the radio sitting above it.

On a day just over a year later, in the middle of January 2001, he's listening like this in The Passenger to the Africa service of Radio France Internationale when there's a newsflash informing listeners that Kabila has been assassinated. Like the death of Pépé Kallé, it seems like the end of something . . . looking into the foam of his beer glass, Manu sees Kabila again, back up in the Kivus, bullying the soldier who killed his father.

But who killed Kabila? That's the question being asked on the radio. *Un vrai mystère*, says the announcer, speciously comparing it to the assassination of President Kennedy.

According to the *New Vision*, the main Ugandan paper, an edition of which Manu buys a few days later, the suspects for Kabila's death include: a cabal of Lebanese diamond dealers; Kabila's personal bodyguard (conveniently shot in the immediate aftermath); a top aide-de-campe and cousin of the deceased (as the paper puts it); other senior figures in Kabila's orbit; agents of the Rwandan government, said still to be smarting from the failure of the second war; and rogue Banyamulenge, marooned and brutalised in Kinshasa, abandoned by their one-time mentor.

The last idea is a constant thread in the winding narrative of the other theories, suggesting perhaps that Banyamulenge were involved in some way, maybe employed by more powerful forces.

Dupes, Manu hears Cogan say. *Catspaws*.

Whatever the case, Kabila's son, Joseph, is almost immediately appointed president. Manu wonders if Recognition was involved in the assassination, if he survived the wound he gave him – it surely wasn't fatal? – and the various theories about Banyamulenge involvement are correct; but none seem proven in any way whatsoever.

His thoughts are prompted to drift in this direction because, not long after the assassination, he gets a series of calls on the Normair landline. Nothing's said, there's just boops and static on the line. Happens again and again.

At first he wonders if it's Recognition, soliciting once more some kind of rescue or help on a bogus basis of Banyamulenge solidarity, despite what happened on the volcano; then, ditching this idea (he shot Recognition, after all), starts to fret that the phone in The Passenger is being tapped: something to do with the investigation into Evgeny, or that visit to the bar from the Italians, Spaniards, whatever they were?

Chapter 4

Another year turns, time's bullet shooting across the threshold, into 2002; *stick 'em up, Manu! Time's got your number, but put your hands in the air and you won't get hurt.* But at first it's looking – during this new, freshly issued January – like his life will retain the same dormant, lonely pattern as the past three years, when the phone rings once more in The Passenger.

'Normair, how can I help you?' He answers all his calls like this, as Cogan did. But there is no answer at first; he wonders if it's a resumption of the strange, silent calls that he received in the early months of the previous year that spooked him so much, then suddenly stopped.

A female voice eventually says, 'Hello, is that Manu?'

'Yes, that's me.'

'I don't know if you remember, but it's Anke Desseaux here. You flew me from Arusha in 1997 and then we went up Nyiragongo and—'

'I certainly do! How are you?' He doesn't say anything about the refund Cogan didn't pay.

'I'm sorry I didn't contact you, but . . .'

'It's OK, I feel likewise.'

There's a slight pause, as if she's absorbing what he's said, before saying herself: 'The point is, there are some signals coming through that Nyiragongo might be waking up, so far as we can tell with inadequate instruments. I'd like to go see for myself.'

'I thought you said you never wanted to go back there.'

'I got over myself – I'll explain when I see you. So, could you pick me up at Entebbe in three days' time, fly me to the volcano?'

Manu gathers himself. Since the second war – which, although principally over, is dribbling on in multiple small but brutal ways, one peace agreement after another failing to hold – he's avoided Congo, his old homeland.

'It's still not very secure there, you do know that?' he tells her eventually.

'Yes, I know, but all I want you to do is fly me over the crater. I'm well aware of what can happen on the ground.'

She speaks in a slow, clear voice but he hears anxiety underneath it.

'Well?' she says.

Again he pauses, looking at the ashtray on the bar. The same one Aisha used to use, his own cigarette smouldering in it now. He considers the attack on Pendele and his compound, events in Bukavu, Bunia, Boma . . . *all the things that have happened to me in Congo, all the things I've seen happen to others* . . . none of which he wants to go back to, in any way at all.

And then, darting into his mind like the kingfisher diving into the stream by his flat, comes an image of Anke, her smooth shoulder blades, the heavy fluidity of her blonde hair; as when he first approached her at Arusha, his hand seeming to reach out in spite of itself, as if she were summoning him to her likewise, without even needing to turn round.

'OK,' he hears himself saying, with the awful automatism that's got him into trouble so many times before. 'That should be all right, I guess.'

'Fantastic.'

'I hope so.'

'What do you mean?'

'It's just . . . all these places are much harder for me to go back to than they used to be.'

'I know. I feel the same way, believe me. I won't ask you to do anything unsafe, Manu. Anyway, I have to fill in risk forms, ethics forms, all that stuff, for our research programme.'

He wants to laugh – as if all this form-filling made any difference at all, but says only – 'What time does your flight get in?'

'Sixteenth January; KLM539; 22.35.'

As he notes it down, he remembers her exactitude. 'That's clear enough,' he says.

'OK, great. See you on the sixteenth.'

'So what happened when you got back home?' Manu asks, driving Anke to her hotel, having picked her up on the night of her arrival and exchanged more than enough pleasantries. The Datsun has filled with the smell of her perfume, drowning his senses.

'It was terrible at first,' she says, looking guardedly across at him as he drives. 'As I said, I'm sorry I didn't contact you. I just couldn't think about nearly dying up there, and you got associated with that, even though it wasn't your fault. How did you know that man, Recognition?'

'I'll tell you all about it sometime,' he says, easing the gear lever into fourth. 'Not now, though. I want to hear about you!'

'Well, at first I tried to push it away, what happened on that volcano. But that didn't work, so I tried meditation, yoga, going to the gym – all useless. Then I went to a therapist called Thea Schaepdrijver . . .'

'Thea what?'

'Schaepdrijver – it means "sheep driver" in Flemish, and that's a little like how I felt, actually – like I was being goaded in a direction I didn't want to go.'

'How do you mean?'

'She didn't want to talk so much about our experience on the mountain, just about childhood trauma – the stuff that meant I couldn't deal with what happened there, so she said, as if anyone could deal with it.'

'That sounds like rubbish.'

'Maybe, but she had a point in a way. My father left when I was quite young. She said this meant I wasn't prepared for the challenges of life, because I was always expecting him to come back and help me sort them out. Maybe she was partly right, but nothing in our consultations really helped. I did it on my own in the end, through my own discipline.'

'How, by more yoga?'

She laughs, looking out of the window at the tangles of lights in the townships along the airport road. 'No, I mean the discipline of my work as a scientist. I realised that I'd been hiding from what was right for me. I basically needed to get back to being an Africa-focused volcanologist. So I started doing research projects in other African countries with volcanoes: Tarso Voon in Chad, Erta Ale in Ethiopia, where I'd been to before, other places too. Doing these trips has helped conquer my fear of going back to Congo . . .'

'And now you're ready?' Saying this, he wishes that he himself was ready to go back, had done the same emotional work of preparation, rather than the work of avoidance, as it seems to him the past three years have been.

'Yes,' Anke says, slapping her knee as if to send any last doubts on their way. 'It's like I've inoculated myself. I didn't really have much choice, anyway, in coming back here. In the last few weeks, we've been getting quite jumpy readings from the last few monitors still working in the Virungas – not all were destroyed, or lost their solar – and, well, the project leaders in my scientific consortium, they said I just had to come. All middle-aged men, of course, mostly too lazy to come out here themselves, but that's how it is. They were angry your firm didn't return some of the cash for that aborted expedition, by the way. Is there something we can do about the cost for this trip?'

'It wasn't my firm then.'

'So you own it now?'

'Yes, and a bar.'

'What?'

Approaching a dangerous intersection where cows, grazing at night on the grass in the inner circle of a roundabout, tend to wander on to the road, he wonders how much to tell her. 'Sadly, the owner died; he owned both a bar and an air firm, left them to me.'

'That's quite a legacy.'

'There was a lot to do. I'm not sure about any refund, can we see how it goes?' They pull into the car park of her hotel, one of the new upscale places by the lake, mostly used by tourists. It's late now, past midnight, and the *askaris* are dozing in their booth.

He helps her get her bags out of the boot, after which she stands looking at him under the portico, bats flitting to and fro under the conspicuous yellow light of two big lamps.

'Thank you for doing this for me, Manu.'

'That's OK.'

'But, about the money?'

He can't help sighing, irritated by her insistence. 'Yes, maybe. It's just an overflight of Nyiragongo, right? Not that crazy itinerary you came with last time.'

'Yes.'

'Well, see you tomorrow, 5 a.m.'

Chapter 5

The next day, as soon as they approach the crater in the Cargomaster, he suspects that they will be unable to fly over it – suspects, also, Anke's original description of Nyiragongo as only just 'starting to wake up'. The volcano's massive cauldron of lava must already have begun to erupt, because the sky is filled with just such a gas-laden plume of which she once warned him. Vegetation on the mountainside is burning, its smoke mixing with ash and the fire fountaining from the crater. With visibility reduced, he has to rely on his instruments, with which electrical discharges in the gas cloud are in any case interfering.

The Cargomaster lurches, yaws, pitches, its turbo struggling with the particles of ash. It appears, too, as if the updraughts from the eruption are determined to overthrow not just the aeroplane, but also the compass, which is giving confusing indications because of electromagnetic disturbance. He remembers Cogan once saying something about this, and checks against the heading indicator.

The dense fumes, uplit from the lava below, at first give the impression of a burning cloud. As he struggles to maintain level flight, the column of fiery air changes its shape into the outline of a vast broom, which begins to sweep towards the nose cone of the Cessna.

His attitude towards Anke changes too, flipping over like one of the needles on the instruments, which are going wild, ticking back and forth. He's aware of the internal process of becoming angry with her, cross that she should have warned him better of the risks. But it's all on him now. He tastes the same fear of losing control of the aircraft he had when taking off from Ndjili.

The volcano makes him feel powerless. It's as if this geological upheaval is nature's way of giving individual human efforts a searching appraisal. And Manu's not sure his own efforts are up to the test, given that he must now untangle complexities of flying practice that he's never faced before. As he tries to do this, pulling the plane away from the billowing cloud, a burst of transmission from the radio speaks of mass evacuations from Goma.

'Why did you make me come here?' he shouts at Anke through the roar of the intercom, once he finally gets to a spot of relatively tranquil air. 'You knew this was going to happen, didn't you?'

'I didn't know for certain. We have to make a judgment based on data, and the data's not very good round here. There were only two seismic stations left, none on Nyiragongo itself . . . and we need three to accurately locate the source position of any volcanic event.' Anke's starting to talk more quickly; she's obviously frightened too. 'So I had to come and see for myself.'

'There were some warnings!'

'You knew that yourself this morning,' Anke throws back. This is true; they both heard the first report of increased rumblings from Goma tower while he was doing his pre-flight checks, but there was no sense at all of the scale of what was going to happen. He took off at 06.30 and the eruption proper started at 08.25, just as they were arriving. Partly, perhaps mainly, this was his own fault.

'I knew, yes, but I didn't know it would be as bad as this! The science is your fucking department.'

Her hair – those strands of his concupiscent dreams of the past, which blew in reality into his face when, thigh to thigh, they were looking into the very crater that's just voided its contents – is now all cracked out at angles, by the electrostatics of the eruption, probably, or even sheer nerves.

He banks away from the miasmic, static-filled cloud, which has hunted closer again. The windows of the aircraft are becoming coated with a sticky, green-looking film. It stinks inside the cockpit now. Fine particles are lisping through the rubber seals, stinging their eyes, affecting their breathing. He begins to get seriously worried about the algae-like slick collecting on the windows; it's almost as if the green film is etching the glass even as it fogs it.

'What's going on with those little marks?' he asks Anke.

'The fume is acidic,' she explains.

'For fuck's sake,' he says, echoing Cogan.

Below he glimpses for a second the orange tide of lava rushing towards Goma.

He hears another distorted, white-noise-heavy update from Goma tower, then changes the frequency to Kigali, which is reporting the same news more clearly.

'Lava's heading for the airport,' he says, making a decision. 'We can't land at Goma; we'll have to go back to Entebbe. If we stay near here even a minute longer, our lives will be in danger.'

'Really?' Anke asks, as if she still doesn't believe him.

'Really. And I'm not sure we'll make it, hadn't counted on coming here and back on one tank of fuel.'

Chapter 6

They do make it, but only just. By then Anke's in quite a state herself, shaking her head from side to side as if she's trying to avert something. When the steps go down and she's about to exit the plane, she stumbles. He catches her by the arm. Righting herself, she does a strange thing, squeezing his hand – so hard he can feel her nails – as if to say thank you, or sorry, or maybe even please.

It almost makes him want to forgive her, this action; but then he sees that the outside of the plane, originally white, has turned green from the effects of the volcanic fume. Inspecting more closely, he realises that the window glass, and the whole paint surface in fact, is covered in tiny scratches from the acid she talked about. It's going to cost him a fortune to put right. As he looks the plane over, he remembers cleaning it when he first met Cogan.

Sulking, he doesn't speak to Anke as he drives her back to her hotel. She goes at once to take a shower and, she says, to get the money to pay him; he's determined now to give no discount on the basis of the previous, aborted expedition.

Once she has handed over the dollars, however, he has no immediate compulsion to leave, desperately craving release from the anxiety that this flight has caused. He wants to drink, drink in the same furious, almost suicidal way that the freight dogs did.

So he sits on a banquette beside her in the bar, drinking Nile Specials all afternoon, both not talking (though acutely conscious of each other), just watching looping reports on CNN about the eruption. Flows of lava into Goma itself, swallowing buildings in their intense heat, seemed to have stopped by now; but it's still pouring down another flank of the mountain into Lake Kivu.

That lake, by which he used to sit with his Bukavu school-mates, is furiously bubbling as magma hits the water. Now there's danger of an explosion of latent underwater gas, the reporter says – the same risk of which Anke warned on the mountain, before they were ambushed. Over 100 people are already dead.

'I'm going outside for a cigarette,' Manu says, almost making Anke jump from the force with which he grabs his packet of Sportsman and beer bottle off the table.

Sitting at a wooden table and bench on the beach, he watches a slight breeze off Lake Victoria tussle the palm trees that fringe the hotel – this other lake in the Rift, so calm and tranquil, in the very last minutes of civil twilight, even as its Kivu sister is still swallowing down gobbets of fire from Nyiragongo.

He's increasingly aware of how, like the two wars, the volcano has affected every aspect of life in the region. Events at tectonic level are the essential cause of all the mineral riches everyone was really fighting for, whatever politics they espoused. Even the fertile soil that once nourished his own family's crops and cattle comes from the same source. And now, it seems, the volcano has dealt a sudden and catastrophic blow to humans and animals alike.

The fate of the cattle especially pains him. He knows in his heart that Joséphine must be dead by now; but the idea of her, of any cow, being burned up in lava is just too terrible to retain in his head. Somehow it seems worse to him than the same thing happening to humans, even though he knows this is morally ridiculous. He thinks of the ad for powdered milk that he saw on that shopping trip with Anke on her previous trip, how they could both have been turned instantly into powder if caught in the furnace of the volcano, like these cows I'm imagining . . .

Maybe I'm not normal in caring about cows, he wonders, sucking at his teat-like Sportsman, supping on his udder-like Nile . . . then reflects that this feeling of non-normality, this feeling of a very specific individuality that can't be appropriated, however much others try, must itself also be a typical human condition. Just as flickering solidarity with other humankind also is; even if, in his own case, it has so often been betrayed by others, ruined by events, or damaged by ethnic labels that limit by defining.

As he smokes his cigarette now, a waiter comes and turns on some lamps under the thatched umbrellas above the tables, including his own – asking, as he does, if Manu wants another beer.

'Get me a whisky instead. Red Label, if you have it.'

'Yes, *afande*.'

He can afford it, but knows he should hold back, fearful of becoming like those drunk white pilots whom he used to call *afande* in the same fashion, all terminologically mimicking those dead souls in colonial armies, addressing their superiors, also dead, or at best suffering diseases of the elderly in English shires, now and then bothering carers or loved ones with tales of exploits past. If I drink too much, maybe I will bang my head like Cogan did . . .

The sun drops quickly towards the horizon, then just as quickly below it.

But alcohol wasn't always the only cause of harm in that wild, wired personality that he misses so much: if Cogan hadn't lived so much in the immediate present, not thinking of consequences . . . if he'd thought of her just a little bit more, maybe Aisha wouldn't have started fucking Gerry? Yet it was also true that alcohol blunted him, stopped him extending his understanding – over time, and to other people in the spaces around him . . . including me, Manu thinks, bitterly remembering the Texan's lack of concern after the ambush by Recognition's men.

The lamps at the table are fringed with a yellow underwing of decaying palm fronds, he notices with regret – as if this eventuality, perfectly natural, were somehow a comment, rushing in unwanted upon consciousness, upon his own talent, marred and wasted as he thinks of it now. He lights another cigarette, watches the moon rise through the whorls of his smoke. How pathetic it looks, the ash on the cigarette, waiting to fall again from its own end.

Hearing a noise, he looks out into the lake. A flotilla of fishermen in canoes are drifting past the shore, singing and calling to each other as their oars turn the water or clatter on the sides of their boats. Clouds of lake fly are swarming to hurricane lanterns mounted on prows, their light gleaming on the fishermen's skin like flakes of fire.

After a while, Anke comes out and joins him, sitting on the opposite side of the table, with her back to the lake.

'I'm sorry,' she says.

'You should be.'

'Will you let me explain?'

'OK.'

'I've been having a hard time, more than I let on to you when I arrived. I mentioned I'd been having therapy. . .'

'Yes.'

'I guess I just felt I needed to do what we did this morning.'

'So? You're not the only person to have suffered, you know?'

'Please don't speak to me so harshly.'

'We could have crashed today.'

'You have made me well aware of that.'

He looks at her across the table, still feeling as if everything has gone to ashes.

'Tell me about the man who tried to kill us. Recognition.'

The table, the whole lakeshore, seems to flood with silence. It's as if all the piled-up events of the past have reared up, like a cobra waiting to strike . . . but he says nothing, his smoke still rising to the moon, obscuring its lucid outline with dim curls.

Anke's watching him. 'Are you all right?' she says after a minute or two, maybe longer.

'Yes. Look, I'm sorry I've been so bad-tempered. I do understand why you had to go. I've had similar experiences myself.'

'Can I have one of your cigarettes?'

'Help yourself.'

'Why did you go silent on me like that just now? You looked like you'd seen a ghost.'

He doesn't reply.

'Tell me, Manu,' she says, with some force, though her being so direct oddly creates a more relaxed atmosphere.

So he tells her – about his parents, sister, Recognition, Cogan, all of it more or less, except the part about the archbishop and Don Javier. She laughs as he lists the idiosyncrasies of the freight dogs, then looks solemn when he says: 'Most of these guys gave me gifts in a way, and I've often wondered for what reason. But of all of them, Papa Chénal was the most genuine.'

'Why?'

'Because his gift was the advice to take care of myself, whereas the others were all self-serving in some way, mostly assuaging their own guilt, I think.'

As he describes his life since she was last in the region, her gaze seems to penetrate the fortifying layers that he has built up around his personality – for so many years, it seems like, even though he's still only twenty-four at this point. She announces, 'I'll come and sit next to you, I can hardly hear what you're saying, you're whispering so much.'

After she has placed herself by him on the bench, and he has come to the end of his story, Manu finds himself leaning over and kissing her. She responds, then seems to draw back, doubting herself.

'Can we?'

He nods, albeit uncertainly. Her eyes widen, soften, an anxious smile appearing on her lips – and then she kisses him, taking the initiative herself.

As he smells the shampoo in her hair – it has a more subtle scent than the perfume he remembers from her arrival – he senses the tension flooding out of him. Her kiss is an endorsement that he didn't know he'd been waiting for, but as it happens, he realises that he has wanted it so much. Her lips on his feel like the beginning of the end of his uncertainty and his loneliness, and all the terrible things he has seen.

They walk back, hand in hand and in silence, through the languid night to Anke's room. With every step, his cock stiffens. Inside, they hurriedly pull off each other's clothes. She sits on the bed but hesitates again when he places himself next to her. But as he turns and touches the side of her face, running his fingers down her cheek and neck, she rolls back on the bed and allows him to kiss her.

Lying alongside her, his fingers brush her stomach and breasts, then move in slow circles about her thighs. Excited by the tremors that rise to the surface of her skin, he soon begins kissing her again, her tongue encircling his, in a way that makes him understand something he'd remained stupidly unsure of up till now, which is that she wants this as much as he does.

'I love kissing you,' Anke confirms, before adding in French, '*Je suis si chaude*.' I'm really turned on.

'You're so wet,' he says, as if in confirmation, which produces from Anke an embarrassed giggle.

She touches his face with her fingertips, then squirms away from him. With her other hand she reaches for her handbag, pops it open and scrabbles around till she finds a condom; he's surprised she has one.

In future years, whatever's happened to him by then, he'll retain – more than these other details – an image in his head of Anke's black knickers on the white-tiled floor. When he comes, it's like the wheels meeting the earth on a hard landing, driving sparks into his brain.

They do it again later, after she has snoozed against his chest for an hour and woken to find the sheet poking up in front of her. Now he's the one to be embarrassed, but she makes a friendly joke about it, before beginning to tease him with her fingers.

Sitting afterwards on top of him, her back to his face, she pushes against him as she comes herself for the first time, tightening as she cries out. It is the first time, too, that he's experienced this reversed position.

For a second or two he's concerned that it's because she doesn't want to look at his black face, or that there's another lover she's imagining, waiting for her back in Belgium; but then he realises it was simply because she wanted to increase her own sensation, rubbing herself hard on him, the chill of her pleasure releasing on to his balls.

He comes soon after, knowing even as it's happening

– consciousness crash-landing again, undoing its own obliteration – that he will never forget this, no more than her touch on him, and the taste of her kisses, and the faint sound of waves, worming in through the curtains.

Afterwards, as they are lying in the bed, each on their side, face to face on the pillows, she asks him more about his family, and then Recognition. He tells her a little more of the same sad story.

'He's one of the bad guys,' he says of Recognition at the end. 'Not entirely, but mostly.'

'Are *you*?'

He's shocked by this question but tries to keep his voice calm.

'No. Keep trying to lift at least one leg out of the toilet of these wars. Sometimes fail, but I'm always trying my best.' He hears Cogan's voice speaking through him as he says this.

'I'm sorry. You must have suffered so much.'

'I was still a boy, really, when all this began. I'm not that any more. Though it still pains.'

But now, as she talks to him, it doesn't seem to him as if he's suffering any more, which is a great relief. Experiencing a deep, quiet peace, there in the bed beside her, he closes his eyes, as if this action might allow him to stay in the unquestionably good place a little longer.

Their two heads are very close together, foreheads touching. Even her skin feels intelligent to him right now. Deep within his skull, he suddenly sees a shape made of light, a shape like two ellipses crossed over each other, such as Don Javier sometimes made the class draw in maths.

And then, causing his eyes to open, she asks him a question, one that seems to him a strange one to ask right then. 'If you had a child yourself, what would you call it?'

He studies the slice of starlit sky between the curtains. 'Maybe Max, if it was a boy.'

She laughs, he guesses because he assumed a gender, then says: 'Why Max?'

'It was the first name of that pilot who was good to me: Max Chénal, Papa Chénal.'

'Those others sound grim, though. Sunshine crooks the lot of them.'

'What do you mean?'

'The type of men who think morals don't apply just because the sun's shining. My father used to have an old cigar box with that on the label.'

'Was he like that?'

'A little, maybe.'

There's a pause, and he can tell she doesn't want to say any more.

'Max was different. Used to play Beatles songs as he flew. He's from your country, actually. He has a farm in Flanders, on – the crest of the Messines Ridge, I think he said, though I didn't know quite what that meant.'

'It's a place in Flanders that saw a lot of action in the First World War. Why was he called Papa anyway?'

'He used to be a priest.'

'OK. But all the others, from what you say, they're like those that take gold teeth out of the dead on battlefields.'

'You're very certain of everything, Anke. What I have learned is not to judge so quickly, as the moment oneself is to be judged is always about to arrive.'

She raises herself up on one elbow, her slightly freckled breasts moving as she punches him playfully on the shoulder. 'Listen to yourself, won't you? I'll miss you, though.'

'What time's your flight back?'

'Eleven-thirty p.m. tomorrow. I wish you could come with me!'

He laughs. 'Maybe I'll come and see you in Belgium sometime. But you'll be back here again, won't you? You once said you wouldn't ever, but here you are.'

'Definitely. I'll have to come back anyway to study the effects of the eruption. And we still have all those monitors to install, if we can ever get to the sites.'

In the morning, when he wakes, he watches her for a few minutes while she still sleeps. Filaments of hair move over her face as she breathes. He notices – for the first time – small, silver-stud earrings, and the slight down on the lobes of her ears. Wondering how he'll feel when she has gone back to Belgium, he gets dressed and, leaving her sleeping, goes for a walk along the lakeshore, thinking about the direction that his life might now take.

At some point on this walk, summoned by the lapping waves, he experiences a need to go for a swim: to immerse himself, to wash off the grime of the enormous world, in which after a night with this magical woman (so his thoughts run, though she is, perhaps, just a woman, not a magical person at all), he no longer feels so alone. He slips off his shoes, his trousers, his pilot's shirt – dives into the lake in his boxers. There's a strong current, streaming from the south, moving over his body as he swims.

He glides between two buoys – stops, treads water – thinking: I don't want her to go away from me, like Edith did . . . but at the airport later that day she does just that, of course, gingerly releasing herself from his tight hug and disappearing through the departure gate.

Clack clack, goes the vintage airport sign soon after, dispatching her flight, dispatching Anke herself, *clack clack* – dispatching everything, it seems to Manu, just as the turning earth dispatches the passing landscape into darkness on his drive back to town, swallowing the last of sunlight in a single gulp.

V

The Lights of Europe

March 2004–December 2006

Chapter 1

The chance for Manu to see Anke again came about two years after her departure from Entebbe; in the intervening period, his life settled back down into that largely uneventful, now familiar pattern characterised by ordinary commercial work. He enlivened the boredom by getting type ratings for a few other aircraft, including Dakota DC3s, thinking he might one day buy one for Normair, in order to carry heavier freight. The good fortune came from an unexpected source: none other than Brigadier Faithful, father of Edith, who was still in the US. Now very much back in control after his brief run-in with the Directorate for Ethics and Integrity, Faithful called Manu to his office one day, without preamble demanding that he go fetch from Kikorba the crate containing the missile launcher, formerly thought to contain gold, that Manu and Cogan buried there in January 1997.

'But why now?' Manu asked, sitting in Faithful's office on the top floor of the Ministry of Defence in Kampala, not understanding how something that happened so long ago could be at all relevant.

'You don't need to know why.'

'I'm sorry, Brigadier, but I do. I'm not getting into stuff I don't understand any more. I've got myself into lots of trouble before by doing that.'

Faithful looked angry at first, but then his big, friendly face burst into a grin. 'You got shat on by Rusyo at Kitona back in '98, is that true?'

Manu nodded, uncertain which way this was going. Yes, on a flight for you, he feels like saying, but doesn't.

'Well this is the moment for you to get your revenge,' Faithful said. 'You know in Uganda we had some difficulties with Rwanda at the end of the second war, including fighting pitched battles with each other in Kisangani? Since then we've backed different factions, even though we're meant to be on the same side.'

'Yes,' Manu replied, though long ago he'd sickened of the ever-ramifying details of the faction-fighting back in his old country.

'Well let me tell you, the Rwandans are still playing messy, even more than before, so we've decided to teach Kigali a lesson. We're going to release the missile launcher that you and Cogan buried into the custody of a Dutch academic.'

Manu sat up straighter in his chair, unable to follow.

'Professor Alphonse Strijbosch. He's busy writing a report on the shooting-down of Habyarimana's plane that started the geno-cide in Rwanda. Well he is, this Strijbosch, a *sort* of academic; he works closely with the Dutch and other Western intelligence services that have an interest in the Great Lakes. Poking around really, releasing info to the media when the people who pay him tell him to. Few of the real spooks have much idea what they're dealing with over here, so European intelligence services sometimes turn to one of these professors or journalists, so-called "regional experts" for help. They could ask actual Africans now and then, but they don't, mostly.'

'Why do you want to do this?'

'It's simple enough. We want to pressure Rwanda. We're just sick of them drawing us into their intrigues. They do stuff we Ugandans would never dream of, having had quite enough of that in our own history. And we, well, our top intelligence guy General Kunyaza – not his real name, we call him that because he has more side dishes than the *à la carte* at the Sheraton – thought the best way to put some heat under them was to bust open the idea that they're ethically clean. You know, post-genocide mentality – all that.'

Although he was still struggling to keep up with what Faithful was saying, Manu didn't interrupt, as the brigadier continued: 'By using PR and hoodwinking Western observers, Kigali has sold that Twinkle-clean story fairly well. But now they're getting cocky, starting to interfere in Ugandan affairs more and more. Encouraging Europe-based bodies to think that the Tutsis did indeed shoot down Habyarimana can help us take them down a peg. So – what I want you to do is go get that crate, fly it over to this Strijbosch fellow in Amsterdam. The Dutch intelligence service will be there with him to meet you: they'll formally receive it on behalf of the Netherlands government. But you'll still need to get end-user certs to get it there. Go see Suraj, he'll fix you for that.'

'If it's a legal export, why use Suraj at all?'

Faithful let out a boomy laugh. 'You know as well as I do that if you try to get the certs downstairs, you'll be sitting in a plastic chair for three months outside someone's office and have to pay a bribe. It's quicker for Suraj to do his normal thing. I'll pay him, except that this time he'll be making false certs that are real ones! In a way we're telling the truth through a lie here, so all's good, right?'

'I guess.'

'You've got a couple of days to decide,' Faithful said, reaching out to grab his hand. 'When you've made up your mind, I'll give you the co-ordinates. Shall we say eighty kay US, plus costs?'

'OK,' he said, still not sure what to do, though it was plenty enough for the job.

'And Manu?'

'Yes.'

'Don't make the wrong decision.'

In the end, it didn't take him long to decide – not because of the money Faithful offered, or the potential threat maybe contained in the brigadier's parting words (if he heard them right; it could have been something else). He agreed because he wanted to see Anke, and to experience other excitements now that his life had become so humdrum. And, he rationalised, this wasn't military work as such, just a job of transport – one that might even do some good.

When he collected the crate from Kikorba, Cogan came to mind as he dug it up. 'OK Manu, so now we dig a hole,' said that laughing, cynical voice again as he did so, though he himself was soon laughing cynically at his attempts to skirt over the fact that he'd again broken his commitment to renounce mercenary employment – for here he was, falling back into a hole, and this time he was digging it on his own.

That was three weeks ago. Arriving now, at Schiphol Airport in Amsterdam, after a long flight with refuels in Khartoum and Athens, Sarajevo and Nuremberg, he signs over the crate to Professor Strijbosch's intelligence-service friends. Strijbosch himself is an intense-looking, bearded man with thinning curly hair and a large nose.

Strong face, Manu thinks, sure now that Faithful's right about Strijbosch basically being a sort of spy, despite his university credentials. The professor doesn't say anything much to Manu, however, as the Dutch intelligence operatives – one a heavyset white in a blue suit, the other a dreadlocked black in a sweatshirt and trainers – co-sign all the documents like it's nothing, what's happening. The black guy does raise his eyebrows as he looks over the document Suraj has produced.

'OK, can I go now?' Manu says, once everything is signed. He's desperate for a beer and bed, having booked into a little hotel on the Herengracht in central Amsterdam, his plan being to take a train to Belgium in the morning and look up Anke.

'Sure,' the agent with the dreads says, in answer to his question, a slightly pitying look seeming to enter his eyes as he speaks.

Why this man's looking like that only becomes clear fifteen minutes later, on the way through Immigration.

The border official takes Manu's passport, looks him up on the computer – looks him up for a long time, then makes a phone call, speaking in Dutch, so Manu doesn't have a clue what he's saying. After some minutes, the official says, in English: 'I'm sorry, sir, please stand to one side, one of my colleagues needs to speak with you.'

Manu swallows his irritation at this, thinking – despite the happy diversity of state authority in the Netherlands, as manifested by the black intelligence operative – that this is a race thing. Hardly a few seconds have passed, anyway, before three Dutch police arrive in navy-blue uniforms and thick-soled shoes. They bundle him into a brightly lit room, plant him in a chair.

'Emmanuel Kwizera,' one of them says. 'We are arresting you on an Interpol Red Notice issued by a Spanish judge, Rafael Escondido, on the charge of the murder of Don Javier Mendía, SJ, a Spanish citizen, in Bukavu in November 1996. Plus an ancillary charge of the killing of a Congolese archbishop, Christophe Munzihirwa, at the same occasion.'

He almost falls off the chair in shock; so here's the dog of history, taking his balls in its jaws. He can hardly absorb what they next tell him, which is that Spanish judges can issue independent arrest warrants, and that these cases can include crimes against those of other nationalities, because Spanish law assumes universal jurisdiction in human rights cases.

His own prosecution, they tell him, has been initiated by a group of Catholic activists based in a village on the Costa de la Luz in Andalusia, who've taken a number of Hutu refugees under their wing, one of whom – apparently the principal witness – was at Nyamwera market when he and others fired at the car Don Javier was in, and the archbishop was shot, after the RPA had abused him with their bayonets.

'You'll be taken to a holding cell tonight,' the other policeman says, 'and then tomorrow, or the next day, or the day after, depending on how things go, there will be a hearing under Dutch law to determine the legality of your transfer to the Spanish authorities.'

'Do I get a lawyer?' Manu asks.

'Of course,' says the cop in an offended voice. 'This is the Netherlands!'

Manu protests that he has just delivered an item of importance to the government of the same country, with the full knowledge of its intelligence service, but this cuts no ice at all with the police. 'We simply have to oblige when an Interpol notice is issued, and yours has been out for over two years. Whether you've had dealings with other parts of our government is beside the point.'

They put him in handcuffs and transport him, in a closed van, to the penitentiary zone of a court in central Amsterdam. It's hardly like a Ugandan jail, with its wood panels and neat basin and shower, and pressed sheets – more like the hotel he stayed in on the trip to Brno with Evgeny.

He remembers the enormous grey handbag of one of the women the pair of them spoke to, after a fashion, in the hotel bar there – sees her open it again, turning the brass clip with lacquered fingernails. However comfortable the unit he's being held in is, the lock on its door cannot be opened so easily.

The authorities do not allow him to retain his luggage, money, passport or pilot's licence, but they do give him some new clothes to wear, neatly folded in cellophane wrappers: underpants, blue shirt and nylon tracksuit, grey socks, black slip-on shoes (too tight) and also a green plastic anorak with a fur-trimmed hood. It's not a bad deal being a prisoner in Holland, but still Manu's utterly crushed by what has happened, thinking now of the hole he dug to unearth the crate at Kikorba, and the entry of bullets and blades into the body of the archbishop, as the same cavity: an abyss that he has been forced to give his name to and is now waiting to claim him as its own.

The next morning, the lawyer who's been appointed for his defence, a man called Schoonraad, comes to see him. He tells him more about the indictment. It's not just Manu; he's part of a much bigger case initiated by the small Catholic group that has taken in the Hutus, a case accusing forty people in total, including Rusyo, a number of other senior Rwandan officers and some AFDL, for several counts of genocide and human rights abuses. There's no mention of Recognition.

As well as Don Javier, the case names seven other Spaniards, health workers, missionaries or teachers who died during those turbulent years in Congo, of whose death Manu is not accused. It's the fate of all these Spanish nationals, including Don Javier, Schoonraad says, that has prompted Escondido's investigation, a reponse to a complaint lodged by this Andalusia-based Catholic group at Spain's National Court in Madrid; adding that that's where Manu will be going, in a few days, if the Dutch court grants extradition.

'It's partly political, all this,' Schoonraad explains smoothly. 'There's a whole lot of left-wing judges in Spain who began investigating crimes by the Franco side in the Spanish Civil War, and then started looking at other human rights violations against Spaniards, during past military regimes in Chile and Argentina mostly. Congo and Rwanda were at the bottom of their list, but it looks like they've got there now. So, the million-euro question: did you do it?'

'I was one of those who shot at the car Don Javier was in, yes,' Manu says, 'but I had no choice.'

'What about this archbishop?'

'Again, I was under duress. I think I missed anyhow. He'd already been stabbed several times, and then the RPA shot him after.'

'OK, well, you should know that I personally don't care whether you did or not. But don't admit anything at all in the courtroom, yes? That's where things count.'

Chapter 2

The extradition hearing begins the following day. The court has testimony from a single witness stating that it was Manu who shot Don Javier, and the archbishop too. He protests that this can't be possible to prove, it being a very confused situation, with lots of guns firing out of the Rwandan personnel carrier as well as him firing from the Land Cruiser; and a very confused situation, too, when the archbishop died. How could any witness even have known his name, anyway, if they weren't in the vehicle, or by the fence of SINELAC? Surely these fellows in black robes understand it was an official Rwandan assassination team?

'Say again what you claim were Major Rusyo's actions the night before these shootings . . . You were beaten?'

'Yes.'

'But not on the morning of the shooting?'

'No. But again afterwards.'

'Where had you slept the previous night?'

'In Recognition's tent. Well, outside it . . .'

'Who's Recognition?'

He explains.

'You say you slept both inside and outside his tent?' one asks. 'Which?'

'Both. I slept on the ground outside in the later part of the night. I had to get out of there. I was scared.'

'Your testimony is very imprecise, Mr Kwizera. Where there are details, they strike me more as factitious than factual.'

What the fuck? as Jerome used to say.

'Let us start again at the beginning. You went to the market of your own volition?'

'Recognition said I would be killed if I didn't behave properly. By then I was a soldier under orders, so my own will did not really come into it.'

Two of the judges look at each other; the third writes down a note.

'What do you think he meant, this individual . . . Recognition?' says the one who's writing.

'He meant I must kill when told to do so.'

'What did you intend, in going with the AFDL from your family home in the first place?'

An odd question, showing how little they understand – to which his reply is: 'I wanted to be free of danger. My parents had just been killed by the opposing forces, so naturally I thought the AFDL were people who might protect me.'

Someone in the gallery gives a perplexing, outraged laugh at his reply. One of the judges commands silence but he – like the laugher in the gallery – has a look of what Manu deems white accusation. It hovers like a dragonfly, this look of denunciation, above the man's pinched forehead. He suspects that this frowning judge envisages him, a black man, to be up to his neck in all of this, and simply for that reason. Higher than the neck. Higher than the top of his head. The attitude of the other two judges seems more kindly; but about judges, who knows?

It's absolutely true he was in the midst of what happened – there's no holding clear of that fact, or of its tragic consequences, however he might wish otherwise.

He just tells them the truth. 'I was there, and I shot, but under pain of death. I did not really know what I was shooting at or whether I hit any target.'

'Thank you. You have nothing to add?'

'Not now.'

'You may be seated.'

He sits, looks at the floor of the little box he's being held in. Patterned tiles; but what he sees is Joséphine's tessellated hide, as she breaks free from the other cows, moving through weeds to the edge of the path and going a little down, into the turned earth of one of the terraces on which his father grew cassava.

Later that afternoon, the judges start asking him further questions, a few about Rusyo, but others about Recognition – a lot about him, in fact. It's exhausting, because Manu doesn't know what to say; he tries to keep his answers truthful, all the time worrying how it will affect his case.

Then he slowly realises something, which is how strange it is that there are all these questions about Recognition, because he isn't mentioned in the indictment as one of those charged. It slowly dawns on him that Recognition must be the witness they keep talking about. In a break, he mentions this to Schoonraad.

The lawyer looks at him in astonishment. 'Yes, he's the source of the written testimony. I thought you knew?'

'No. He was the main one who made me do it!'

'You should have told me before.'

'I didn't even know he was the witness. They just refer to "the witness". Are you telling me these investigators went to Congo and spoke to him?'

'He's in Spain, they saw him there.'

'Spain?'

'Yes, he's become a friar – part of the extremist Catholic group on the coast of Andalusia that brought the case, provoked into doing so by the Hutus who've sought refuge there. The leader of the group, Monsignor Amado Muñiz, was once a missionary in Zaire.'

'Recognition's no more a Hutu than I am. Nor a friar!'

'Well that's what it says in the court documents – a "Hutu friar" – one who knew you in the past, was at the market, and recognised you when you shot from Rusyo's vehicle. Apparently now working as a cook for these Hutu-supporting Catholics. They live in a castle, all these old priests and nuns. They're mostly former missionaries in Congo and Rwanda, employing the Hutus they've helped gain asylum as people to cook or clean or do their laundry.'

It's so unreal, so preposterous, that Manu wants to laugh, but it's nervous laughter that eventually comes, subsiding as he sits down to tell Schoonraad the truth about Recognition. On going back into the courtroom, the lawyer at once gives a version of what Manu's told him to the judges, who swiftly adjourn the case to the next day.

The following morning, Schoonraad makes an argument that because the witness is not present, is in fact implicated in the case himself, and his written witness testimony has anyway not been properly verified, Recognition's deposition is inadmissible in its entirety. This causes a shock, a flutter among the black robes at their angled bench, and a deal of procedural discussion.

Much pressing of Manu's palms into his eyes during all this. A lot of visualising of good things to keep out the bad, good things like his flute in his hand as he follows Joséphine, her dinging bell, and the rest of the herd along a path, his father's sure fingers at the forge, his mother's delicious fish. Now and then, too, a hoarse, repeated drawing-in of breath, as if he has asthma and each intake of air will never be enough.

It goes on and on, the essential legal drone. All the real thoughts and emotions, and all those very human physical and mental experiences past and present that the law is squashing away, are too much for him to process; it's as if the court is trying to throw a net over a tree full of bees.

He tries to remain rational, to anchor himself in a logical train of thoughts, each one a tie-down block, ranged one after another along the edge of a runway.

But, standing there in the dock in his prison shoes, he begins to think of himself as barely alive. Through these proceedings, it's like something's been sucking out his human juices, and all that's left is the rotten idea of the accused, this abstract *thing* against which society must be defended, as if he's some kind of creature from a swamp that can have only heathenish hope in his heart.

They are not his own ears any more, listening to the arguments, nor his own feet in these prison shoes that pinch his toes. It has become something else, his body, something apart: a drying cowskin strung on crossed sticks, as he saw at Kamituga on the first trip with Cogan.

At the end of it, this discussion about whether Recognition is a viable witness in absentia, one of the judges announces, 'The case will proceed.'

Finally, rage surfaces in Manu. He shouts, *'Écoutez, bon Dieu!'* There in the courtroom it echoes about, and then he falls back on to his chair, utterly spent. The atmosphere in the court shifts.

The lead judge says he is again postponing the hearing till the late afternoon, and that in the meantime the accused should be taken outside for some air. As if that, so kind, might help fate to better unwind!

Manu has to wear handcuffs, of course, feeling the scrape of them on his wrists as he's taken out by the constable, a fleshy man whose pistol bounces on his hip with every step; the butt of this side arm jingles against the keys of the handcuffs.

Again it rings in Manu's head, Joséphine's bell, the sound commingling with a visual image that also fizzes through from the past: his father quenching one half of a cow bell – hot from the forge – in a trough of water, in order to harden it.

Chapter 3

Although it's nominally a spring day, Amsterdam is grey and gloomy, fog enfolding its tall buildings, which are packed as tight as too many cattle in a *boma*. Manu, Schoonraad and the fat constable stand together on the steps outside the courthouse. From a distance, drumming and chanting and a hooting of horns can be heard.

'There's some demonstration today,' Schoonraad says.

Manu's wearing the shiny, fur-hooded anorak that has been supplied to him by the authorities. He stands there, mute and fuming, angry at how the law is beating him into submission, like the wings of a great bird that obscures the whole sky.

Schoonraad and the constable light cigarettes, appearing to Manu as matched automata, reaching into their pockets for lighters at the same time. Having lit them, they each brandish their cigarette like the sabres of the gigantic Moorish statues pictured on a billboard erected opposite. It's an advert for an exhibition of Spanish art at the Rijksmuseum.

Fucking Spain; fucking Spanish judges interfering in African business. Who do they think they are? The clothes and armour of the Moors in the billboard poster – their black-marble faces, their rearing arms and advancing legs – are reflected many times in the shiny cladding of one of the buildings nearby.

Schoonraad begins speaking with the constable in a tangle of Dutch: a glottal knot that Manu can't unpick, instead watching tourists as they move about in little groups in the square below the courthouse steps. Mostly Japanese, they're sipping coffee or chocolate from corrugated cardboard cups, some taking photo-graphs with fancy electronic cameras.

A man in an off-white mackintosh moves forwards up the steps, holding a recording device out in front of him.

'So what's the news on this feller?' this guy says in English to Schoonraad, whom he appears to know. 'Can I do an interview?'

'This is Mr Desmond Fingler,' Schoonraad explains. 'A corres-pondent for *Africa Confidential*. It's up to you whether you speak to him or not.'

'O'Fingle,' the man corrects him, naming the letters and apostrophe in a strong Irish accent, as if adjusting the answer to a crossword clue.

Manu shrugs, not even looking at the man.

'Well?' the journalist says, slightly aggressively.

Schoonraad says: 'Hearing postponed until four o'clock.'

'Who is he?' the man asks, but his attention then turns to the digital recorder in his hand, which he begins to look at it in a puzzled way, pressing buttons.

'Manu Kwizera,' Schoonraad replies, looking as bored as a sheet of paper. 'Accused of murder of a Spanish priest in Congo, plus a Congolese archbishop in a secondary count.'

'And did he?' Manu hears the journalist say, 'Kill the priest and the archbishop?'

'You know I can't speak too much about cases in session,' Schoonraad answers wearily. 'I've said enough already.'

'Will you speak yourself?' the journalist asks Manu directly.

When he doesn't reply, the journalist says, 'My name's Des O'Fingle,' as if Manu didn't hear before, and being on familiar terms would make a difference. 'Well?'

'My lawyer,' Manu mumbles.

Taking a step down, Schoonraad says stoutly: 'His defence is that, as a teenager, he was abducted by soldiers. He had to follow their orders or die.'

'It's an old defence,' returns O'Fingle. 'Tomorrow we will hear it again.'

Appearing to misunderstand, Schoonraad counters, 'The case is postponed only until later this afternoon.'

'So can I get an interview?' O'Fingle asks again, then looks at his recording device more closely. 'Feckit, the batteries have gone in this yoke.' He waves the machine like a wand. 'I'll have to change them first.'

'Up to you, Mr Kwizera,' Schoonraad says, brushing down his suit, to which some flakes of cigarette ash have attached.

Shaking his head, Manu looks once more at the billboard. Spain! What has that place got to do with him or his life? And how did Recognition get to the Costa de la Luz, anyhow?

'You speak for me,' he tells Schoonraad when O'Fingle asks again, but the lawyer says nothing.

By now, anyhow, O'Fingle's busy changing the batteries in the device. It's one of those in which the battery compartment separates from the main section, revealing a steel USB connector that can be plugged into a computer to download files.

The journalist sits down on the steps, laying out next to his wallet on the damp concrete the two components of the recorder and its padded leather case. He struggles to get a pair of triple-A batteries out of their tight plastic wrapping.

Manu has no time to weigh up the pros and cons. Flying in combat has taught him that sometimes one just needs to act. He squats down and, in the same movement, scoops up the steel part of the journalist's recorder with one hand, with the other grabbing a hank of his thinning hair. Jumping a few steps down, he pulls back O'Fingle's head and applies the steel plug of the USB to his throat, wrenching his body in front of his own. He smells, thinks Manu, now curiously separable from himself, faintly of urine.

O'Fingle issues a loud, unmanly shriek; Schoonraad and the constable stand apparently frozen, cigarettes in mid-air.

The constable pulls his pistol out of its holster. He points it at Manu, who jolts the journalist's squirming body in front of his own, pressing the metal harder against his throat.

'I will shoot,' announces the constable.

'You will not,' Manu says, calmly. 'I'm pressing against his carotid artery. If I cut, blood will flow.'

'Don't do this!' Schoonraad pleads. 'It will affect your case.'

'What do you want?' asks the constable, still pointing the gun at Manu.

'Lie down on the steps, both of you,' Manu shouts. 'On your backs!'

Schoonraad obeys, but the constable stays put, so Manu starts twisting the steel plug into the journalist's throat, making him squeal.

'You, policeman: slide your gun on to the next step, or this gets worse.'

A stand-off. There's a shout of alarm, Manu isn't sure from where. Behind him, too, whispers in Japanese, the sound of cameras clicking.

The constable seems about to shoot, but then obviously thinks better of it. He puts the gun on the first step, next pushing it slightly with his foot, so it chunks within Manu's reach. Then he lies down on his back, like Schoonraad. Manu grasps the pistol, releases his captive member of the press.

'Lie down with them,' he orders O'Fingle, pushing him away, then reaching down to pick up the wallet and the other part of the recording device. He slips them into the pockets of his fur-trimmed coat. Holding his bleeding neck, O'Fingle does as he's told.

Manu levels the gun at their bodies, which are disposed over the steps of the courthouse like figures in a painting.

'Don't,' pleads Schoonraad, in the tone of an exasperated parent.

Manu ignores him, directing his remarks at the constable. 'Now the keys.'

The constable unhooks the keys to the handcuffs and tosses them towards him.

Too far, that bunch of keys goes. But it doesn't matter because it's the right direction for Manu to run, the gun still in his cuffed hands as he scoops up the keys and puts them in his mouth. Sour taste of metal, though he's not sure if it's that or blood, as the keys might have cut his lip.

He dodges between the tourists, hearing a cry in Dutch: '*Grijp hem!*' Seize him.

Very soon – the constable having scrambled up the steps to press a button in the lobby of the court – a siren starts. Half shrugging off his coat to cover the gun and cuffs, Manu runs on to a busy pavement, then crosses a concrete-flanked highway, dodging cars.

After running a bit further, not sure if he's being immediately pursued, though sure it will happen soon, he slips into an alley, disturbing a pigeon that's pecking at the contents of an upturned garbage bin, making it flit off; it cautiously returns a few seconds later.

By then he's spitting the keys out into his hands, fiddling them round until he is able to unlock the cuffs. The gun he puts into the pocket of the parka; on putting the coat back on, he senses the weapon's weight.

About to throw away the cuffs, he suddenly wonders if they might come in handy too, so drops them into the other pocket, next to O'Fingle's wallet and the component pieces of the recording device. He pulls out the wallet, sees there is a quite a bit of cash in it.

He hears more sirens; also that chanting and drumming of before, a din of horns, protesting shouts . . . all getting louder. The pigeon rises once and for all, heading for the far end of the alley, the beat of its wings chiming with his beating heart. He sees a police car pass by, very slowly – moving across the narrow gap at the end of the alley, lights flashing . . .

The police car is followed by, in sequence: policemen in matt-black body armour, running at a jog-trot with truncheons in their hands, groups of shouting people carrying placards, some beating kettle drums or sounding hooters, and then a truck, decked out with drapes, upon which an Arabic-looking man is standing, speaking into a loudhailer.

Must be the demonstration Schoonraad mentioned, and a good place to hide in, he reckons.

The crowd thickens in the wake of the truck, but only when he's slipped out of the alley into the demonstration does he realise how large it is; there must be over 500 people gathered here, moving haltingly forwards, some carrying Palestinian flags, as well as those of other nations, and the banners of unions and other political groups.

Many in the crowd are dressed in brightly coloured clothing, despite the apparent seriousness of the subject of their protest, which is the wall between Israel and the West Bank. A fair number are wearing masks bearing a cartoon face of the current US president, George W. Bush; others wear caricatures of the Israeli prime minister, Ariel Sharon.

Manu weaves deep into the shouting mob, seeking out other black faces. What he has in mind is that he needs cover, for he's wary of standing out. He needs to change his appearance, too, thinking he might use some of the money in the journalist's wallet to do so.

He finds a young man in a Castro-type military peaked cap and a red, black and green liberation jumpsuit. Seeing more police ahead entering the crowd and blowing whistles, trying to split it, or search for him maybe, Manu remarks to this studious-looking fellow black man, as casually as he can, 'Cool cap, can I buy it?'

But the man frowns and says, 'No way.'

At which moment the noise and jostling from the crowd grow louder and rougher, to a point of fury. Clearly having been alerted by the court, the police are now actively picking out black faces and isolating them. This is disturbing the dynamic of the crowd, with unintended consequences for the authorities, however they may be characterised.

As white men with truncheons, probably. For with every black person that the police apprehend, seeking an individual, Manu himself, among an assumed type – pinning them down, pushing them roughly against walls – the crowd whirls in fury round the police, pushing against them in turn and attempting to release those whom the police are trying to detain.

From each of these encounters, successive movements spin out in a violent spiral, like the untidy writing of which, once one had one's pen licence, Don Javier used to complain in class. Next to Manu, the man in the Castro cap is shaking his head in disapproval at the action of the police, as the two of them are jostled to and fro by the movements of surrounding people. Picking up a streamer and an abandoned Bush mask, Manu pulls the latter over his face and, seeing an entrance to the subway, filters down into its comforting den of smell, where piss and tobacco contend with freshly baked rolls and coffee.

The noise of the protest above begins to drift away but there are, among the travellers, many coming to the protest, some already wearing their own masks of Bush and Sharon. Boarding a subway train, he judges that he's able to keep his mask on for a while, attracting only cursory looks until, after a few stops, he abandons it, leaving President Bush to continue his worthy service on an empty seat.

Chapter 4

Hardly two hours after escaping the court, he's staring from the window of an intercity express. The low-lying Dutch country-side speeds by, curtained now in wet fog. There's a woman with a baby in the carriage near him. She greeted him with a nod when he got on.

The intervening time has passed in a blur. He left the subway at Amsterdam Centraal and examined the departure boards for mainline trains. He bought a ticket for Brussels, via Antwerp, using some of the journalist's cash. The train stopped briefly at the Belgian border, but there was no police check there.

Rain's now streaming from the sky, supplementing muddy puddles on the ploughed fields, making rents in the fog, which drapes itself like damp cobwebs on lines of tall, thin trees. Inside the moving carriage, the lozenge shape and lemon-coloured glass of the light fittings remind him of the cabin lights in the Cargomaster, though these are much cleaner.

Too many memories. He tries to stretch back: just relax, whatever the past says. But the velour of the seat itches his neck. If he pulls up the hood of his coat, the fur of that itches too. The intercity train is hot as well, and the prison shoes seem to pinch even more than they did in the court. Impossible to be at ease even in his body, never mind all the rest.

He looks at his fellow passenger, this woman with blonde hair who raises, now, memories of being with Anke; how relentless, how merciless it is, this recourse to the past, always mending its pace, always preying at his heels; even when the memory's welcome, the close-nipping character of retrospective mental process discomfits him.

And perhaps that's why, thinks Manu now, Cogan chose, so far as he was able, that other tyranny of living only in the present moment. He didn't like backsliding, whether on Manu's account or his own; in fact, the only times Manu can remember him talking about the past involve the violent incident near the airbase in England that caused him to be ejected from the airforce, the early days of his first marriage to that woman in Carthage, and the circumstances which lead him, against his best judgement, to marry Aisha, following seduction, one by the other or perhaps both, there at the photocopier in the flyblown, bullet-scarred offices where Manu began learning how to fly, his lost craft as he now thinks of it. And, yes, Cogan's sundered son, back in America, probably the most important past factor of all, a bottomless sadness.

But in his own case the memory provoked by the woman on the train points Manu forwards, too . . . what was that place Anke said she worked? A museum in Tervuren; but residing somewhere called Leuven – neither that far from Brussels, if he remembers rightly.

The woman begins feeding her baby, cowling breast and child under a lacy shawl. He recalls with great tenderness his mother coming to him, kneeling down next to the pallet, lifting the mosquito net to caress his face. It might have been a mud hut but we had mosquito nets, he silently tells the ghost of Cogan, as he once told that living, breathing, itching-himself man about cleaning his nails.

Manu keeps his eyes on the sliding doors at each end of the carriage. His full bladder is pressing now, but he dare not move. He has some notion that he might find a hiding place before any checks are made, or that, if challenged, he will jump from the train, a prospect that makes him shudder with fear. He feels too weary to do either, though, should the need arrive. As if all he has left is his own restless, judicially pursued body, now refusing to move at all.

But there seem to be no guards on this train. He puts his hands into the pockets of his anorak, touches the handcuffs – what did he think he was going to do with those? – the gun of the constable, the two parts of O'Fingle's recording device, his wallet. The cash in it was reduced by the purchase of the ticket. There are some credit cards, but he knows too well to use those.

He finally succumbs to the pleadings of his bladder, goes to the toilet. While on his way back, he stops in the gap between two carriages.

Putting his head out of the window and seeing that the train is about to pass over a river bridge, on an impulse he quickly reaches into his pocket and tosses out the handcuffs. The manacles clack like castanets against the outside of the carriage, then flick off a girder of the bridge before spinning into the chasm below. The train is passing too quickly for him to see any splash.

On returning to his seat, he drowses. No dreams at first, no thoughts, nothing but the penal body, the surrounding, over-warm air of the carriage, and the gentle sounds of a baby as it settles to sleep against its mother. Which eventually give him a slight milky sense of hope, and the bounty of sleep for himself.

The doors slide open, and he wakes up with the backward start of one on the edge of a gyrating vortex, the kind of place where you'd think yourself a fool for harbouring any hope whatsoever. But it's just a guy with a wooden guitar strapped to his back, moving gingerly through the swaying carriage with a plastic cup of coffee in his hand.

Phrases in Dutch, resistant to Manu's comprehension until they turn to French, issue from a grille in the roof of the carriage. They announce that the train's approaching Antwerp, before continuing on to Brussels. He expels a loud, tense breath.

The woman with the baby looks up at him. He closes his eyes again, trying to withdraw into the seat, glad of the concealing shadows of a tunnel; it has the effect of reducing the light in the carriage to that of the lozenge-shaped lights alone.

He looks at his own face in the window above the woman. *What am I going to do?* He pictures a line of black-uniformed figures with semi-automatic rifles waiting for him on the platform in Antwerp, or the platform in Brussels. He stands up, feeling the weight of his own weapon in the pocket of the coat. More or less useless in these circumstances, he reasons, unless he was to take a hostage. And he couldn't do that again.

He makes his way out of the carriage, into the area between it and the next one, thinking again – as the sliding doors hiss shut behind him – to find some hiding place. He opens the door of the toilet a second time and looks in, hoping there is some way . . . but it's a very modern train and every panel in that toilet is sealed shut.

He goes back to the door in the area between the carriages, looks out of the window again. The train is now passing through an industrial area, with old warehouses of grimy red brick on one side and large steel silos on the other. Then come concrete embankments.

It would be deadly to jump. Useless.

But as he's pondering these options, the train slows down to pass into another tunnel. The light becomes meagre again. Now is the time, whatever the danger.

Pushing down the window, he gets a leg out and then, with great difficulty, for it means bending torso to hips at almost a right angle, extracts most of his second leg and upper body into the dark, rushing air.

For a few seconds, exhausted and terrified, he hangs ridiculously like that, with one foot on the narrow passenger step and another still hooked up on the window, as the train gathers speed to exit the tunnel.

Chapter 5

Four days later, a figure in a parka is trudging beside the road from Leuven to Tervuren. Johnnie Walker, and how he wishes he could have a drink right now, to revive his flagging spirits. It's very early in the morning, and one of Manu's ankles is still hurting from when he jumped, collapsing on a pile of stone chips and accumulated muck by the side of the track; the rest of the train rushed by so close it sucked out his very breath.

Now, when the pain gets too much, he stops to observe warblers, flycatchers and swallows swooping under telephone wires, scything over hedge tops – here by this road to Tervuren, on the outskirts of Brussels. Some of these birds seem similar to species that he knows from home, ones he used to shoot at with his catapult.

He figures that perhaps he too strikes the motorists as some kind of migratory creature, tramping doggedly along the verge of the road as they drive past. This seems unlikely, overrating the capacity for imagination in commuters on their way into a city of Western Europe, and underrating their mistrust of anything out of their ken. Their eyes, anyway, would mostly be on their dials and gauges.

All the same, the stream of vehicles make him anxious, as if the thud of each one presages the sudden approach of a police car, from out of which authority will once more appear to take him back into its grasp. But he tries not to turn his head, reasoning that drivers will take less interest in a random pedestrian who takes no notice of them than in one who does.

In the pockets of the coat remain the pistol that he had from the constable, and the two parts of the recording device and the wallet that he took from the journalist. The money left after the purchase of the train ticket is now all but gone. Some of it he spent replacing, at a shop in Leuven, the pinching prison shoes with a pair of white trainers. More comfortable . . . if again not the Nike Airs I'd wished for shopping in Entebbe . . . for someone doing a lot of walking: it took him a whole day to walk from Antwerp to Leuven; this journey he's now on, thank God, is much shorter.

But he has kept the prison shoes nonetheless, carrying them in a bag along with a loaf of bread, some cheese, apples, a bottle of water and a map. It's a plastic, tartan-patterned bag that he also picked up in Leuven: a small version of what is often referred to as a 'Chinese laundry bag', perhaps erroneously enough, or in West Africa, a 'Ghana Must Go'.

He spent two days in Leuven looking for the home of Anke – to no avail. There were many *Desseaux, A.* in the Leuven telephone directory, and he soon grew tired of hovering outside people's houses and crossing them off the page of the directory that he'd ripped out in a library.

Finding newspapers to cover his body, he slept under the porticos of office buildings. In one newspaper, *La Libre Belgique*, he saw his own face and read a story about 'an African war criminal on the run', as it described him.

Once he was moved on by the police, but there was no sense in which he felt pursued or suspected in particular, as himself. Here, he was just yet another African migrant, of which there appeared to be many in Belgium.

He talked to one other in this category, a Senegalese who told him he'd heard that there were plenty of migrant hostels in Brussels – adding that, if he wanted work, or a place to stay, the Bar Maïs in Matongé was said to be a good place to begin looking.

On the second evening, Manu foraged for food in a rubbish bin outside a McDonald's. That night, he was unable to sleep – in the doorway of a bank – owing to the lights and unbearable bass music from a nightclub opposite; the sound reminded him of heavy munitions. So he stood up and began walking, away from the boom and the neon towards the limits of the town and darkness, having in mind to make his way to the museum where he understood Anke worked, at Tervuren.

The road he's now on takes him through low, half-flooded fields, the water lying on them like sheets of metal. In the chill, early light, cows are standing motionless in the fields. It is all he can do to stop himself from climbing over the barbed wire and going to them, cradling their heads like he used to cradle Joséphine's.

As he walks, he ruminates, too, on Anke, of her snoozing on his chest in the hotel in Entebbe, and of the light-filled ellipse that came into his mind when they lay head to head after making love on waking. So much time has passed, but he's sure she must have seen it too, that shape in his head: that this, in fact, is what's drawing them back together, two lodestones of feeling, operating telepathically.

The pylons in the fields next to the road stalk him like giants. He wonders how the bases of the pylons can be fixed at all, amid these fields as waterlogged as swamps. Curls of mist, ascending from the sodden turf, make it seem as if each steel structure might also rise into the lightening sky.

What do rise and much plague him are midges, climbing in spiralling clouds out of the opaline haze above the marshy fields. They bear down on his neck, his cheeks, his eyebrows, raising welts.

As the commuter traffic begins to concentrate, he arrives at the edge of Tervuren. Signs start announcing his destination, which is the Royal Museum of Central Africa, where Anke said her volcanic consortium was based. He passes through a large area of parkland before coming into classical gardens containing a lake, then sees an imposing edifice rise before him.

Chapter 6

The Royal Museum reminds Manu of pictures that Don Javier showed him – and Jerome, and Emile, and Clement, and all the others in those long-lost lessons – images of the Prado and the Louvre and suchlike palaces of Western culture. And perhaps the visitors that he sees now, stepping out of cars and coaches in order to visit this museum, are indeed the same cosmopolitan types, well armoured in camel-hair coats and Hermès scarves, who might visit the Louvre and the Prado. People who know their wine and who would – he senses it with certainty from his tongue to his toes – consider the *terroir* of Congo and Rwanda to be the soil of barbarism.

Manu stands out – of course he has this hunch again – with his black face, but after paying a small entrance fee he passes the security guards without any obstruction, them perhaps thinking, so he speculates: *Here's a national of our former colony, Congo, come to give a supreme adieu to the country's past glories under Belgian rule!*

The rotunda at the centre of the museum is dominated by large allegorical statues. One giant golden statue shows a European missionary with a Congolese boy clutching his robes, above a plaque reading: 'Belgium brings civilisation to Congo'. Another, showing an Arab slave trader forcing a Congolese woman into slavery, while planting his foot on the neck of her dead companion, is titled simply '*L'esclavage*'. A third, titled 'The Artist', shows a seated, half-naked man drawing in the soil between his splayed legs.

Manu has a sense of dizziness, unsteadiness, like he might

topple over any second – whether this comes from the disturbing artworks, from his long walk, or restless nights on the street he cannot tell. He reaches into his Ghana Must Go for an apple; takes a bite; savours the sugar seeping into him.

Looking for authentic images of the Congo that he knows, he passes through other rooms and halls. The first ones are stacked with rows of stuffed birds and game – giraffes, kudu, hippos, many large snakes. The embalmed pythons and cobras are artfully displayed, entwined with hanging coils of raw rubber vine and processed latex.

Standing slack-jawed in front of a stuffed bush pig, the unpleasant smell that comes when one singes these animals, to prepare them for eating, returns to him. He recalls a hunting trip with his father and uncles: and afterwards the blackened tail of the pig sticking out like a small piece of plaited rope, hard and charred, ticking back and forth as it was swung over glowing coals when they got back to Pendele.

He steps into a further hall, a half-lost world of pith helmets, canes, officers' uniforms, heavy leather suitcases and weapons, including the double-barrelled, heavy-bore shotgun of the explorer Stanley, and other items of regard.

Exhausted, he sits on an upholstered chair. Facing him now is an ivory sculpture by the name of *Aequatoria*, its cracked surface plugged with pieces of gold and other metals. He stares at its subject: a colonial official, as corpulent as Cogan. One of the man's podgy, statue-frozen hands is beating ineffectually at the air with a rolled-up copy of a magazine, the other is holding a dripping shaving brush which appears to be made of silver.

The official has evidently missed the insect that must have been bothering him, for, constructed from a greenish jewel, it's sitting incognito on the crown of his fallen hat. This headwear lies at his feet along with his abandoned razor, also silver, and another crouched Congolese boy holding a bowl of water.

There's something sickly, but also inexplicably splendid about this exhibit. What was the intention of its creator? The closer Manu looks, the more it appears that the cracks in the face of the man, which he initially took for flaws, are deliberately intended to give him the look of a pig, specifically a bush pig, he reckons, just like the stuffed one.

The plaque on the base says KLEIN, COQUILHATVILLE. The date given is 1887. A wall text informs him that Coquilhatville was a town, once a centre for artistic pursuits and the production of political pamphlets, that after independence in 1960 became a city, Mbandaka; and that the sculptor, Klein, was an employee of the Brussels-based trading company *Société Anonyme Belge pour le Commerce du Haut-Congo*.

Manu has a funny feeling that this sculpture has a voice speaking to him from the past; or two pasts, to be exact: the colonial past of the sculpture's making, and his own. That it's a stump of time as well as of tusk; several tusks more likely . . . For Mbandaka was a place where many Hutus who'd fled from Rwanda were massacred by the AFDL and the RPA, after he started flying with Cogan. He saw the bodies there, piled like sacks by the side of the river.

It now makes him sick to the pit of his stomach that he helped haul the arms that contributed to killings. But he cannot organise it into the idea of an offence: something inside him is still keeping at arm's length the direct relationship between transporting arms and their use.

He tries to focus on finding Anke, wanders about till he eyes another chair and, feeling exhausted, sits on it. Almost immediately, a security guard enters the room, coming across to say that these chairs are only for guards.

'It's an ordinance of the museum,' the man explains.

'I seek Anke Desseaux,' Manu says in French, standing up, because if it's an ordinance, well . . .

He has a moustache, this guard, and a short leather coat with a sheepskin collar. The collar of the flying jacket Evgeny gave him was like this, Manu remembers; attacked by moths, its structure breaking down – coming out in tufts – it had eventually to be thrown away.

'I'm here to see Anke Desseaux,' he repeats. Putting his hand into one of the pockets of the parka, he feels the stippled handle of the constable's pistol. 'I met her in my own country. I believe she works here.'

Looking at him like one of the judges, as if his only deeds could be crimes, the guard repeats mechanically, 'Your own country?'

Manu decides simply to nod.

'Follow me,' says the security guard, who then surprises him by reaching out his hand, making an open palm to indicate direction.

The guard leads him through a maze-like series of halls and rooms until, after passing through a large hall of elephant skulls and tusks, and another smaller one containing photographs and models of volcanoes, including Nyiragongo and Nyamuragira and others from his region, they come to a door of dark wood.

'What's your name?' asks the guard.

He gives him a false one, though evidently Congolese. 'Max Kongolo.'

The guard knocks and goes in, closing the big door behind him. Spotting another chair, Manu sits down, so tired he has forgotten already about the ordinance.

A few minutes later the guard reappears. 'I am afraid that Mme Desseaux is occupied.'

He says this – his tongue giving his moustache a tiny lick as he speaks – in a way that implies she will be occupied for a long time, perhaps forever. Manu's again suddenly reminded of Evgeny.

'Well then, I will wait.' He's walked a long way to see her, this woman on whom he's pinned all hope, and there's no going back now.

'She will be busy all day,' says the guard, bluntly.

'Days come to an end.'

'That is true,' replies the guard, looking down at him on the chair, 'but what do you plan to do?'

'Sit here?'

'That is not possible. And as I said, these chairs are for us.'

What a prick. 'OK, I will wander the galleries some more.'

The guard's moustache twitches wetly again, and then he

shrugs. As the man shows no intention of moving off, Manu stands up and, giving the guard a firm nod, strolls back into the volcano hall, and then the one filled with elephant crania. He hovers next to one of these – well it's a pair, the skull of a baby elephant with nub-like tusks sitting atop the skull of a vast bull – and becomes even more determined to see Anke.

When after some minutes the guard walks past him and on to some other part of the museum, Manu goes straight back to the door of Anke's office and, without knocking, opens it.

Chapter 7

She's wearing a bright-green dress and sitting at a desk littered with books, papers, jars of pens. There's also a small musical instrument, made of wood and metal – he recognises it as an *mbira*, a type of thumb piano – and a small, horseshoe-shaped magnet, painted mainly red. When she looks up and sees his face, she gives a gasp – one so large that the noise of it seems to spiral through the whole room.

'Manu!'

The colour of her dress reminds him of a particular species of cricket that used to gather in large numbers at home on mornings after nights of heavy rain. The light of a lamp catches her ash-blonde hair, one or two strands of which are falling slightly over her face.

She does not stand up. Her face is slightly obscured by a computer screen. As he moves round the table she shrinks from him, moving back her chair.

'That was you, who asked to see me?'

'I assumed you'd know it was me. Max! Like the child I said I'd have.'

She shakes her head. 'I forgot. But I remember now.'

'You do? You remember?'

He can see her properly at last. Her shoulders seem rounder than before. He waits for her to speak. The lamp makes a clicking sound, as if she's only just turned it on and it's heating up.

She looks at him nervously. 'I'm shocked you're here, to be honest; I read about you in the newspaper.' Her voice seems indistinct.

'I was wrongly arrested,' he says, not knowing what to say. 'There was nothing I could do – I did not want to involve you.'

'The Dutch police came and asked me questions.'

'What did you say?'

'Just that you flew me. They laughed at that. It was humiliating.'

'I'm sorry,' he mumbles.

'Why have you come here?'

'I need your help.'

She releases a wordless remonstration. Then, seeming to need to act, reaches out, bends down the lamp. 'They said you're a war criminal.'

'And you believe them?'

'I came to believe the person I slept with was pretending he was someone else.'

'That's not true!'

'Then I saw the article in the newspaper – about your escape. What you're accused of . . . it's horrible. I'm sorry, but I just want you to leave, and never to contact me again.'

'What I am accused of, it's not simple. In my mind, I am innocent.'

'That's what most criminals say.' A jigger of panic passes over the skin of her forehead, before tumbling into those eyes that were once so soft. 'You coming here, it could cost me my job! You have to go, at once.'

'Please, Anke.' He tries to conjure the light–filled, elliptical image that came into his mind at the hotel in Entebbe.

'I don't want to, I just can't even listen to you!' She looks down at the desk.

'When we were together, you did listen.'

He wants so badly to touch her, to hold her; to say please again, sorry, something – all in a form of words that he cannot begin to find, but words that would, in a better place, another time, appease her, placate her, cause her to be how she was before.

She repeats, very slowly and deliberately, 'You have to go.'

The sureness of her tone causes him to move backwards, to feel the fishtail of the parka swaying obediently behind him, though his emotions don't want to obey the downward pressure he's trying to keep on them. In this moment, he wonders if he has become abhorrent to her and that this chance of love, perhaps his only chance (as he then presumes; fatal error of all disappointed in love!) has been blown entirely.

Another silence. In her nervousness, Anke picks up the thumb piano, passes it from hand to hand. 'Please go,' she says, eventually. She puts down the *mbira*, as if to signal that his agreement is already a given.

He sits on the edge of desk, gently moving aside papers, then suddenly reaches over for the instrument, making Anke jump.

'Sorry. It's just . . . I remember these.' He laughs and, trying not to sound too angry, says: 'About the first thing in this place that I do remember!'

'Manu, I can't do this. You can't be here.'

She pauses, looks at the desk again, stricken. A range of feelings seems to pass across her face, before she lifts her head to speak. 'This is my whole world. You even being here threatens it. Don't you understand that?'

He presses one of the metal strips on the *mbira*, then another, and a third. The notes merge, vibrating in the room.

'Hard to tune, these,' he comments in a harsh voice, putting the instrument back on to the desk.

'Have you listened to a single thing I've said?'

'Yes. And of course, I understand. It just makes me very sad. I thought . . . I thought you were a proper person, someone who follows through on their true feelings.'

'That's not fair. You just need to go, Manu.'

'I need some cash.' He's aware that he sounds like a sulking child now.

Sighing, Anke reaches under the desk for her handbag. 'I'll give you what I have, but you need to promise me some things.'

'Yes?'

'That you will go from here quietly. That you will never contact me again. Not ever. Like I said, you could lose me my job, ruin my life – invading like this.'

She takes out a purse from the bag and removes all the notes that are in it, puts them in front of him. About 100 euros, it looks like. Resting on the desk next to the little magnet, one of her hands, he notices, is clasped tight, but shaking slightly.

He wants to reach out, to calm her, but knows that the best thing is not to touch her at all. He looks at the red-painted magnet, trying to remember where he has seen one of these before. Must have been in Don Javier's physics lessons.

'Anke,' he says. 'Please don't be like this. What they say I did, to my teacher and that archbishop, it wasn't my fault. None of it happened through my own free will.'

'You also transported lots of weapons,' she says, her eyes flashing.

'I'd stopped most of that by the time we were together.'

'You didn't tell me about it.'

'I didn't lie either.'

'Look, we were not "together". It was one night, a long time ago.'

How much nearer in my mind, thinks Manu, remembering now Don Javier's cane pointing across zones of Zaire in class, zones where so many got killed, pulled into the war, both wars, by forces beyond their control. Then she says something which shocks him, brings him close to losing his own control.

'Just a fuck. I enjoyed it at the time but don't make it into anything more, to solve your own problems. Please, just take the money and leave.'

'I hope I will be able to explain it all to you properly one day.'

She sighs again, shaking her head, as if she just can't believe how much he has overrated her feelings. 'That can't happen. Ever. I'm getting married, Manu.'

He feels crushed by this information, his confidence that he will be able to explain himself to her ebbing away. 'Who to?' he says dumbly.

'You don't need to know that.'

He snatches up the money, wondering if his thoughts about another man being in her head, when they slept together, were true after all. He hopes not, all the same. Mumbling a thank you, he puts the cash in the pocket of the coat, realising again there's a gun in there, too. His soul sags, heavy with shame.

He goes to the door, then turns to her.

'I tried to find your house in Leuven.'

Finally, Anke's anger bursts through in full, though she keeps her voice to an urgent whisper. 'Stop this! You've got your money, so just go now, will you?'

'But I love you, it's as simple as that.'

For a second, less than a second, she seems to experience a doubt.

In this tiny interval, during which she seems to waver, he wonders if what he's just told her is true. *Does* he love her, really? Surely it was just a transient feeling, brought on by physical desire, in what was maybe for her (if decaying palm fronds can be considered to produce exoticism) an exotic location? How can one gauge the difference between love and desire anyhow?

He just knows that he desperately needs her. But it's too late for all that, far too late, as he sees that she's put her hands over her ears, pressing them hard into her head. In this moment, she seems like a person trying to stop herself being engulfed in a despair that's nothing to do with him at all. The gesture makes him feel even more tender towards her.

Dropping her hands before she speaks, Anke will soon allay any fears that how she's been acting – during these last three seconds; or however long it is that her palms have been pressing on her ears – goes beyond his unwanted presence in any way at all. She desires him, in fact, to clear off, and now states her reasons why more strongly.

'You're not free to love me, because you're being sought by the police, even if you don't act like you are. Which is stupid of you, as stupid as escaping in the first place. This isn't Uganda or Congo, you know, you can't just do what you like. And also – I am not free to love you.'

'Why?'

'I just could not be . . .'

'What?'

'Apart from getting married, I just could not be with someone who has done the things you've done!'

This statement comes out in a rush, followed by – 'Don't

worry, I won't ring the police, but you can't, you simply can't, expect to walk in here and for me to treat you like I did before.'

He looks into her eyes and knows from what he sees there that there is, now, nothing he can say that will win her over. If she will not love him of her own accord, there is nothing, absolutely nothing, he can say that will convince her to do so. It's not like they're in court, after all, and he can argue her round to his way of feeling, like Schoonraad tried to with the judges, failing though he did, on the issue of setting aside Recognition's testimony.

But still he tries, telling her in one last-ditch attempt, 'That may all be as you say, but I *know* that you think of me when I think of you.'

What he has in mind, it's that light-filled, double-ellipse shape that first appeared when they were lying head to head in the hotel room in Entebbe, that on his trek from Leuven he fancied was a telepathic connection; as if this magical idea, purely internal and self-reflexive, as even he suspects it is, might nonetheless – if evidenced in the right way – serve as the best advocate for his suit.

Puzzlement rises in her face, like a ripple made by a hopeful fish. And then he knows for sure that it's sweet nothing, nothing but a fantasy – not something likely to project to another mind or transfer to another heart, as her next words attest.

They're spoken calmly, in a slow sequence, like she's reading out some text to him, in the way Don Javier used to in class. It's as if, in the careful evolution of these units of speech, she has caught hold of herself and wants to be just as firm with him, in the hope that he will finally grasp her meaning. 'I don't know what you're talking about. Not at all. Go somewhere safe, Manu, but don't ever come near me again. Forget me.'

Is that it, then? 'I'll try.'

'Where will you go?'

'I heard people like me can get work in Matongé,' he says, clinging with mental fingernails on to this question about where he'll go, with its suggestion that, despite her instruction to forget her, he himself might not be forgotten.

He looks again at the magnet. *L'aimant me réservera peut-être une surprise*, he thinks. Maybe the magnet's got a surprise in store for me.

'If you want to get a job, you should have a wash.'

The almost casual cruelty of this forces an ending at last.

Not just clear off; get clean.

In silence, persuaded finally of the futility of his illusions, he turns away from her, opens the door, walks through it, closes it behind him, all very quietly.

He tries not to weep as he goes through different halls, taking another route out of the museum from that which he came in, passing a line of spiders in cages and, outside a cafeteria, a statue of Tintin from the comic books.

Already already already, with each progression of his steps, the interchange with Anke seems like a dream, one that's begun dispersing the pangs of emotion that he was feeling just now (along with a demeaning sense of supplication) into a lingering mist of melancholy. Coming outside onto the museum steps, he puts his hand into the pocket of his coat, hooks a finger through the trigger guard of the Dutch constable's weapon. That's it. He knows what he must do.

As Anke says: forget her. Forget her voice, forget her body, forget her spirit. Listen only to the voice of the pistol that his hand now grasps.

But what the object says, wisest counsel he's ever been given perhaps, is not *shoot*, but *persist*.

Chapter 8

On leaving the museum, he boards Tram 44 into central Brussels. The weather outside remains misty and cold. Even with the parka and the enclosure of the tram, it's like he's experiencing Belgium as a collection of wintry sorrows, any benevolence it might offer obscured under a blanket of meteorological misery. Perhaps it would be the same if he had landed elsewhere in Europe. For already the business with Anke is starting to feel like just another obstacle in the arrival of a poor black man in a rich white country.

He wants to escape; but where to? It's as if there is now no circumstance under which he could ever be truly free or happy: as if all he'll have, for all time, is his itching body, wrapped in its judicial, spirit-reducing coat, from the shiny surface of which he imagines the glances of the *blancs* on the tram are bouncing off like drops of rain.

He tells himself to stay calm, as if he were flying. He develops a vague plan to find a hostel, a job, identity papers if he can get them.

On arrival at Montgomery, he realises that he's very hungry. A cart is selling hot sausages in rolls just outside the station. It's a clever contraption, a metal box that opens up into a stove, all pulled by a moped. An obscene pink tongue, curling on a yellow background, emerging from a grinning boy in a baseball cap, is displayed on the box's side. The impression of this licking tongue is dynamic, like it's about to lick Manu himself, as he reads the brand name written across its corrugated surface.

He buys a hot dog from the van, which does a little to restore him. After finishing it he wanders for a while, still carrying the woven plastic bag, until he's trudging alongside a busy road that bisects a Brussels park. The park contains a triumphal arch, grand arcades, more statues.

Also many tramps, dozing on consecutive benches. One in particular – Congolese like himself, Manu reckons, albeit with no evidence – catches his attention, skin dirtied by the city, droplets of congealed grime like candle wax on his beard, plastic bags lining his boots.

As he looks at this man, who is mumbling in his sleep, Manu imagines one day becoming one of these displaced black vagrants, human beings whose lives have been poisoned by the histories of violent empires and the regimes that followed, human beings resented by the country in which they've landed up – if that is indeed the actuality, in the case of this fellow.

He walks on, entering streets where modern skyscrapers give over to tiled buildings and cobbles before turning back again to modernity.

His destination is Matongé, a quarter of Brussels where Africans go for shopping and entertainment, and site of the bar that the Senegalese in Leuven mentioned. He remembers his 'pub crawl' with Cogan at the original Matonge in Kinshasa – a place doing well enough without an accent, before its story migrated north – that time when Cogan hit his head on the culvert. Drinking warm beer and cheap whisky in bars that played *soukous* tracks by Pépé Kallé and the Empire Bakuba band, the same stuff from his schooldays that they used to jive to in the dorm, listening to Clement's short-wave . . .

He mentally turns over a series of events – how the Empire band's performing dwarf, Emoro, supremo of the somersault, was after his death deftly replaced by three pygmy dancers. And how then the vastly fat, enormously tall bandleader, Kallé – bigger than Cogan, bigger than that other false *dadou* Kabila, his body somehow seeming to embody the resistance of Africa to all the bullshit flung at it – finally followed Emoro to the grave: that final injustice which all humans must suffer, whatever their origins.

He keeps on having to backtrack, going to and fro along Brussels's busy avenues, looking for where city maps are displayed, trying to commit their details to memory, then going back to find one when he forgets something.

Passing a vast, plate-glass, steel-beamed building, with four wings of unequal size projecting from a central core in the shape of a star, which a sign announces as the headquarters of the European Commission, he moves on south, gets a little lost again, crosses under the Chausée d'Etterbeek . . . before he finds the Rue de Pascale and is able to orient in the direction of Matongé.

He tries to tamp down anxiety about being hunted. But he can't really think about these very real dangers, because every part of his mind begins to fill again with the absence of Anke. He knows he's simply without her, just as he was without Edith earlier – without anyone really, trekking through the unforgiving city. This place of modernity anyway, it makes him feel as if he's only experiencing the surfaces of things; and that he, also – being occasionally inspected by unnamable passers-by, as his personality rattles on through the streets – is just another surface too. Was that how Anke saw him back in Uganda he wonders, something to be touched and stroked, but not truly known?

Might as well be in the Gauntlet, and not in the good way Evgeny liked to conceive of it. The radio's off, the radar's off, no way to reach her. You behaved stupidly, asking her to fill a gap in yourself that she could not, he says to himself. I was just an adventure she had with a black man in Uganda. And now you've got that gap again, that space which you think anyone could fill if they just loved you enough – anyone idealised as a special someone . . . the very 'one' that Papa warned you against, all those years ago, sitting in the close, hot air of Mama K's bar in Mzuzu, as the Omo ad jingled from the van outside.

Arriving at Matongé, he finds it to be a vibrant area packed with restaurants from different African countries, as well as grocers, hairdressers, record stores, places selling wigs and fabrics, dried fish and craft items, and many other products besides. At the tables of cafés sit Congolese men speaking Lingala, Swahili, French. Emboldened by the illusion of being at home, he makes enquiries until he finds a route to the Bar Maïs.

When he gets there, it's filled with a wider variety of Francophone Africans – Ivorians, Togolese, Moroccans – as well as more Congolese, most sitting on steel chairs drinking Pelfort beer. Some are reading newspapers. Some are playing chess. One, dressed in a fancy suit and crocodile-skin shoes, reminding Manu of Gerry, is striking poses on his bar stool.

He can see no drinkers with eastern Congolese features, though he knows not to trust those as a gauge of ethnicity. Listening to the people in the bar talk, however – about Joseph Kabila, son of the Kabila he met and now president himself, and the wider situation back home – he realises that most of these men are probably people exiled on account of one Kabila regime or another, or that of Mobutu previously. He'll have to watch his step: all these groups have reason to dislike a Tutsi.

He does a nonchalant-seeming tour of the tables, buys a Pelfort, sits on one of the chairs. Trying to blend in, he ostentatiously taps his foot to the *soukous* coming from a set of speakers.

Three Congolese men nearby are having a heated discussion about politics – specifically the ethnic divisions that have riven the Great Lakes in recent years. They're quite old, all of them, and two are wearing trilby hats. The third has a walking stick with a bone handle that he bangs on the floor, like a gavel, to make his points. He's drinking pastis rather than Pelfort.

These guys remind Manu of the old men of Pendele, who used to sit on stools at the barber's (in fact, the shade of a baobab on the edge of the village), talking aggressively as they waited to get their greying hair and whiskers trimmed.

Cars are passing in the street. How dark Brussels is! It's only early afternoon but some of the vehicles have already put their headlights on. He closes his eyes against them, thinking of Pendele, trying to be back in that other place in a time before war – leaving the meadows with Joséphine and the herd, walking down paths towards home and supper.

But every time one of the lit cars turns in the street, its beam strikes his closed lids, piercing them. The taste of bean stew, the feeling of *ugali* or Joséphine's hide under his fingers . . . it's all being swept away by the lights of Europe.

He looks at the trio of old Congolese men . . . The one with a walking cane seems to have kind eyes, despite his having just banged the cane on the floor again for emphasis. Manu edges his chair closer, asks in as neutral French as he can manage: 'My friend, I have just arrived in Brussels. May I seek your assistance?'

The old man gives a nod, then says, 'What're you after?'

'A hostel, papers, *travail*.'

The man laughs. 'Not much, then. I cannot help you with papers. You need to find Romanians; they are best at that. There is always work for us kind of blacks at the abattoirs here in Brussels. But you will only get six euros an hour. And there's a hostel for Africans in Schaerbeek: the Hotel Papejan, founded by some philanthropists. Though be warned, it's a rough enough place.'

He's thanking this man when one of the others at the table challenges, 'Why you helping this *mec*? Banyamulenge trash for sure. I can tell from his accent.'

'*C'est vrai?*' asks the man with the cane, the kindness in his eyes retracting instantly.

Manu nods. There's no point in pretending if they've rumbled him already.

The man with the cane says, 'Best you go, there's always broken glass when you Rwandans come in here.'

'I'm not Rwandan.' These points need to be made, whatever the risk.

'Still. You Banyamulenge helped them steal our country. Obediently sold it, to Rwanda and Uganda, too.'

He raps his cane on the floor. The bar falls silent. Everyone's looking at Manu, who says: '*Dans ce cas, monsieur, je ne suis pas dupe.*' Sir, I'm not deceived about this issue.

None of them reply. But as he makes to leave, he senses the eyes of the bar continuing to train on him, just as he felt the silent, accusing eyes of the judges in the court. At the door, something hits him on the shoulder.

'Cow shit,' laughs someone behind. But it's only an ice cube.

Once outside, he walks like an automaton past small shops selling counterfeit handbags and waxed fabrics, past food kitchens, tropical fruit stalls and stands selling craft items in ebony and ivory . . .

As he walks, he considers the man's accusation: about obedient Banyamulenge helping the Rwandans and Ugandans steal Congo. Considers also the way the others in the bar tilted and stared at him as this was said, squeezing him into a position where he had to be other, even though plenty of them were from diverse places enough.

This push and pull between different groups, though . . . it'll go on for eternity if people don't make an effort to understand each other, he thinks, while also conscious (more conscious: in sore calves, in an aching ankle) that he's really tired – one form of understanding, at least, that carries across ethnic and tribal and national divisions. All time, all geography, too. Because every human being knows what it is to be tired, that's one togetherness we can all really count on! The thought cheers him up. but only a little.

Continuing up this street of migrant businesses, he makes way for a North African man in a leather jacket carrying a shop dummy – it obstructs most of the pavement, as he's carrying the mannequin crossways, its bare sketch of humanity seeming eerily alive in his arms.

Back on the pavement, he next requests directions to Schaerbeek from a group of white Belgian teenagers. Jigging like marionettes to Congolese music blasting from the door of a record shop, they ignore him completely. Eventually, he come to a VOUS ÊTES ICI sign, and is able to orient himself for a further trek – down an avenue of boutiques and restaurants – to the street on which the Hotel Papejan, the hostel mentioned by the man with the cane, is located.

It takes much mental energy just to shackle himself to the present moment. He keeps thinking of his family, struck by dread that their faces will modulate in his memory to some edge state where he can't, in his mind's eye, properly see them any more.

The bovine visage of Joséphine too, he fears, will be subject to this key change; will also ebb from view like this, becoming almost irrecoverable as it reaches a limit of sequence.

Passing along the street of fashion emporia, passing by shops with names like Zadig & Voltaire, Hobbs, and Princesse Tam-Tam, and more periodically eateries dubbed things like Café K, Le Réalisme and La Voie Royale – he conceives, as one foot follows another, across pavements that still cover prehistoric rock and the accidental crypts of hunted bear-dogs and hunted aurochs and other hunted animals whose time will never come round again, that the history of mankind, the history of all living beings, perhaps of the earth itself, is one of sequential absence.

He wonders what other beings are waiting to be summoned forth, into the negative. Not me, he braves, figuring his own character now as that of a wily Odysseus, seeking a harbour at the western edge of the world.

Then pulls back to sense, reckoning he should look lively, being a hunted man, *un homme traqué*, as he puts it to himself.

And so, and so, at one street corner, a spot when there's patent, positive danger, he's as ready for action as he was in the air above Congo in wartime. His heart begins to whop like the music from the record shop as he notices a group of police with sub-machine guns. But through sheer force of will he passes them by, trying to look calm. The policemen's cigarette smoke merges with clouds of moisture in the mist-charged air. He slips his hand into the pocket containing the constable's gun, so its outline will not show. A cold wind blows down the street, making him long for warm skies, but he's not challenged.

Chapter 9

Announcing itself with a small brass plate, the hostel in Schaerbeek is not quite what he's been expecting. Were it not for the sign, from its exterior the Hotel Papejan would appear to be a five-storey, old-fashioned residential house, between a shoe shop and a Turkish grill, albeit in an area of Brussels that seems to have its seamier side, even though it's only 3 p.m.. Going into the lobby, he finds the front desk to be a modern, stainless-steel affair, despite the plaster of the walls and ceiling being dirty and crumbling.

Although there is a smell of tobacco, there's no one behind the desk, on which stands – in the place where one would more likely imagine a computer screen – a small television and video player. The sounds from its speaker suggest some kind of sporting occasion, but Manu cannot see the picture.

The only sign of the true nature of the establishment is disclosed by a shelf above the desk, on which are lined up six ebony statues. Geometric and unnaturalistic in design, they're coated with a thick layer of dust, revealed intermittently by a fluorescent tube that flickers from the ceiling.

Hearing a noise, he turns to see a man hovering behind him, his face full of cheerful mistrust as he takes in Manu's green parka coat, blue tracksuit, white trainers and the Chinese laundry bag. The man's a plump, middle-aged *muzungu* wearing an indigo shirt covered with seemingly random phrases in French. One catches Manu's eye: *La vraie vie est ailleurs.* True life is elsewhere. They're all written in an opulently baroque script, full of curls that recall the pythons and rubber vines in Anke's museum.

Is it poetry on his shirt? Manu wonders. It's something.

'Are you the owner?'

'I am.'

'I seek accommodation.'

The man asks how many nights.

'By the night.'

'Sharing or sole? Own berth, it's sixteen euros; sharing, it's eight.'

'Sharing?'

'Some of our guests share beds with others, who work night shifts, or vice versa. Night side, day side, it's the same.'

'My own berth, night and day.' If I can get work, he reasons, Anke's money should be enough to see me through, though to what outcome, what border, he does not know.

'OK,' the man says. 'Fill this in.' He passes across a form with boxes to fill with passport number, address, occupation.

'I am sorry, I am not able to do all this.'

The man's expression momentarily creases, then relaxes again. 'No problem. I can do for you.' He lowers his voice. 'You need ID, passport?'

'Yes.'

'Belgian passport is four thousand euro; ID and work permit two thousand.'

There is something wrong with one of the man's ears; it's crumpled up, like an old flannel that's been left on the edge of a hotel bath: consequence of an injury or some peculiar disease, perhaps.

'Well?' he says.

'Not yet. Too much money. But I look for work. Somebody mentioned slaughterhouses.'

The man smiles, showing nicotine-stained teeth. 'Some of our guests do work in those places. It will be fine for you, my friend. Come, I show you the dormitory, then I give you directions to one of those abattoirs. I am Carolus, by the way.'

Manu follows the owner upstairs. On the first floor, he glances into a room filled with iron-framed beds, some covered with canvas, haphazardly draped, or surrounded by makeshift curtains. As well as cigarettes, disgustingly strong even to a smoker, there's a smell of spicy food, mixed with alcohol and male sweat.

The next floor is the same, and the next two. On the fifth floor, the owner – Carolus – beckons him in, past a hanging metal chain. Dim lights affixed to rafters illuminate further lines of old-fashioned iron beds. It's some operation, this place.

'This way,' says Carolus, the fragmentary words on his shirt illuminating with each successive bulb.

They pass sleeping men, mostly sub-Saharan Africans or Maghrebians, together with a few Eastern Europeans. Some still have their boots on. One man is moaning and mumbling to himself in his sleep; Manu recalls the tramp he saw in the park.

Each bed has a two-door metal locker next to it, and there are cigarette butts all over the floor. Some of the occupants have set up cubicles of plywood around their beds – through the gaps in which he can make out slices of empty faces, sometimes glancing up as he and Carolus pass. All these men (he can see no women) appear to him as creatures of permanent *dépaysement*, disoriented denizens of alien domains, who once likely had ID cards, passports, stamped papers *etc.*, in their source countries; but now possess nothing, no form, no *acte de naissance*, no documented origin, no official shape or substance, being without even the bare substantiality of ghosts, for ghosts at least bear their stories.

And now I, he thinks, am in the very same little boat.

'Here you go,' says Carolus, presenting Manu's berth with a chivalric flourish. It's a dark, low, stifling box, piled with musty blankets. The previous occupant has done the thing with wooden sides, hammering nails into splintered ply. The mattress is stained and the floor inside the cubby strewn with empty bottles of cheap spirit and food cartons.

Manu sits down on the low bed, looking at his trainers as he clutches the plastic laundry bag on his knees. He still has a few apples in it, and the end of a loaf.

Carolus says, 'It is not safe to leave belongings here, but . . . well, you are not unlike many of our guests in having very few.

I will leave you to collect your thoughts, and when you come downstairs, give you directions to Anderlecht.'

Once the owner has gone, Manu remains sitting on the bed. He's feeling even more tired, if that were possible. He wonders what to do about the pistol, still sitting heavy in the pocket of the parka. Best thing is – hide it in one of the empty takeaway food cartons and push it under the bed.

Having done this, he walks a little beyond his cot to the end of the dorm, where most of the beds are empty. In the end wall, integrated into the brick of the gable, a large black-metal fan is turning. Through the moving blades of the fan, shafts of crossed light from outside fall, making rippling patterns on the dusty floorboards.

Manu looks at the fan, feeling as if he is going to faint. It's as if the strength that has carried him this far is now being chopped up by the blades.

A voice behind him says, in English: 'I too stared at that damned thing when I first came here.'

He turns to see a tall, brown-skinned man, about whom hovers a strong smell of fish.

'It makes you think too much, you see, and we cannot afford too much thinking. All we must do is work and pray. Do you want some coffee, my friend? It is the best, from my own country.'

'That is very kind.'

'Come, sit.'

He follows the man over to a cubicle, where the guy squats down and begins brewing a pot of coffee on a little burner stove that runs off a gas cylinder.

'My name is Abdi. I am from Somalia. You?'

'Congo,' Manu says, over the hiss of the flame. 'Via Uganda . . .'

'I know, I know,' Abdi says, chuckling. 'Many other places also. It's the same for most of us. What's your name?'

'Manu.'

'What did you do, before?'

'I was a pilot.'

There are fish scales, like the fingernails of a child, all over the floor and stuck to Abdi's boots, as well as the bottoms of his overalls.

'Haw – big man. You were a captain?'

'Kind of, in the end.' He watches Abdi pour the boiling water over a filter full of sweet-smelling coffee granules.

'Me, I *was* a captain – no kind of! Here.' He hands over a small cup of steaming black liquid, creamy brown froth on its surface.

'Thank you.'

'Not a captain of planes. Boats. Before I became a victim of crimes.'

'How so?'

'I was a fisherman in my village, near Kismayo. Then, because of war, it became harder to sell fish. Trawlers came from other countries and took even the fish we would catch just for eatings. So we turned to piracy, and in time I became the king of the pirates in our region. We took many ships and won many ransoms. Then one day the Royal Navy of Britain came and made a bombardment of my village. All of my family, dead. Everyone should know that British people are thugs underneath, even as they pretend to be gentlemen on top. Only the Russians are worse. No! In some ways they are better, because at least they don't pretend.'

His fingers dart into the blackness under the bed and, taking hold of a cockroach, squeezes it. 'One day I will have my revenge on those British. You?'

'It's a long story.' Manu doesn't say any more, feeling he should guard against self-disclosure.

'Don't worry, you don't need to tell! We are all long-storied here, and fuck those who want the whole story. Some hope that one day they can go home, be whole people again, so the story can finally end. But I tell you, my friend, most of the people in this hostel will never do that. The idea of return is an illusion. All we can do is dream our best dream of the present.'

'You said we should just work and pray before.'

'Eh, you try to catch me out! True, I said that. But when I am working, you see, I dream. When I bend over the conveyor – I work in a fish-processing plant – I'm a young boy in Somalia again, way back before I shifted to this stinking, evil place.'

'Why do you say "evil"?' Don Javier always used to advise, be very careful in describing someone as evil, because only God can make that authorised judgement.

'Carolus, the owner.'

'He was friendly enough to me.'

'I bet. He fucks the young boys here. You're quite handsome yourself, so watch out for your arse.'

'I knew one like this. One of the other pilots in Uganda. But he was a good man. This was his country, he came back here.'

'Well, I don't like those gays.'

'He was kind. He didn't drink – only milk. He played Beatles songs while we flew.'

'That is all as may be, but the one downstairs is not a good man, that's for sure. If they cannot pay, he makes them do it with him. There's another, too, Klungel his name is, who makes films of their filth. They dress up boys from this place in different costumes and take them to the countryside. Policemen, players of team sports in striped shirts, priests; once even the Pope of Rome, with his triangular hat. I tell you, if I can ever leave this place, I will slice them both before I go.' Abdi sighs. 'Or do something, anyhow. Have you got a weapon?'

Manu shakes his head, not wanting to reveal the pistol. It worries him, still having it. Not good enough, that hiding place in a food carton.

'I have this,' Abdi says, proudly. Standing, he pulls up the trouser of his overall to reveal a long, thin-bladed knife strapped to his calf. 'You do need a weapon here, or people will rob you. Sometimes you just need to stab him, the other guy.'

'I'm not into that,' Manu says. He has to hide the gun better, though. But can he trust this Abdi? Who seems like a gangster, maybe, but has held out the hand of friendship.

'Brother,' Manu says finally, touching Abdi's arm, 'I do have a gun.'

Abdi stares at him.

'But nowhere to conceal it,' he continues. 'It is a pistol.'

The Somali gives a low whistle. 'You look like a boy. Tall as a *timir* tree, but a boy all the same to the eyes. But I see now that you are actually one serious motherfucker underneath. Come, I show you.'

Looking around to make sure no one is watching, Abdi goes over to the fan, which is still slowly turning, casting its bars of light over the fish-scale-strewn surface of the floorboards. Kneeling down, he removes two bricks from the cracked wall beneath it. Behind, in a space where the structure of the fan is fixed to a steel bar bolted into another course of bricks, is a recess in which are stored several small packets, apparently wrapped in clingfilm.

'Go, get your weapon,' he whispers.

When he does not move, Abdi speaks with strident insistence, gesturing at the recess. 'Put him here. Quickly!'

Manu turns round, makes his way back to his billet, trying to seem unremarkable as he walks past occupied cubicles.

Reaching his space, he bends down and collects the pistol, now sticky with the residue of takeaway meals, dropping it once more into the pocket of his coat, where it rattles against the parts of the recording device that he took from the journalist.

He walks back to the end wall, where Abdi's waiting to stow the gun. 'Nine millimetre,' he says approvingly as he handles it, having first taken care to cover his palm with a rag. 'In Somalia we used Star, a Chinese brand. Rubbish. This one's better.' He clicks out the magazine, looks at the rounds and some writing on the casing before adding: 'Czech.'

'I should get rid of it.'

'Probably, though you might regret it. I will hide it for now, anyhow.'

'Thank you.'

When the gun is hidden, Manu goes downstairs to get from Carolus the address of the slaughterhouse and a map. Carolus's sidekick is with him now, his bum pressing like dough on the metal desk as the pair watch a rugby match on the television. It really is sport, he is able to ascertain for sure this time, not one of the bizarre outdoor orgies Abdi described and said were filmed; he wonders if his new Somali friend is just one to make mischief.

Carolus introduces the other man as René Klungel – the

second man Abdi mentioned – who's heavily built with rings on every finger, metal piercings plugged into his face and wearing a leather jacket and jeans; he gives Manu's anorak an appraising look as Carolus writes down the address of the abattoir on a scrap of paper.

'It's called Weill Viandes,' Carolus says, his balding head bent as he adds a rough map to the address. 'There's a whole street of slaughterhouses near there, so if you don't hit a vein of gold in one, try another.'

Klungel's still looking at Manu, suspicion passing across his metal-mangled face. 'Where d'you get that coat?' he asks, his voice tinged with threat.

Manu shrugs, although his heart is beating hard. 'Why do you want to know?'

From between Klungel's studded lips a snicker sounds, jangling Manu's nerves. 'Seen 'em before. Those are the coats the Netherlands courts give to prisoners. Lose it! We don't want any trouble here.'

Giving him the map, Carolus allows his hand to rest too long on Manu's. He moves it away with a sickly smile. Maybe, after all, Abdi was right about these men.

Earlier, he anticipated going to the slaughterhouse that day, but looking now at the clock in the lobby he realises it's probably too late. So he goes back upstairs, into his cubicle, eats the rest of his bread, some cheese and one of the apples as men clump in and out.

It's hard to sleep in such a public place, but eventually he drifts off – into a strange dream in which two small, colourful birds are fighting and then one of them is suddenly in his own hand . . . before escaping through a window, which it somehow seems to open with its beak, before flying off into the sky.

Chapter 10

The following morning, he's jolted awake by the sound of men entering the dorm. Heavy boots – but those of workers, not police. He eats another apple and goes downstairs into the street. It's cold outside. But, remembering what Klungel said, he drops his incriminating coat into a rubbish bin. He begins to shiver soon after, but almost convinces himself that he's a brave explorer, prospecting Darkest Europe, going at his new life as it comes, needing his wits more than a parka, his perspicacity more than warmth.

As he walks across the grey city to Anderlecht, he has to take the map out of his trouser pocket several times to make sense of where he is. After a number of wrong turns, he arrives at the large factory site of Weill Viandes, where trucks are coming in and going out in adjacent roadways, leading to stockyards or the outlets of freezer units. Waiting in these lanes, the truck drivers have laminated cards on lanyards, which they hold out towards an electronic reader at the gates.

Offered a job that very day, not half an hour after going into the factory, he's given an induction to working in an abattoir by a hoggish, breathless man with jaundiced eyes. Announcing himself to be Willem de Zwaan, chief foreman, he seems happy to learn that Manu's from Congo. He informs him pleasantly that among the Africans of his experience, many of whom he finds idle, Congolese have always made the best workers, despite the troubled history of their country, which he knows a bit about from his wife.

At first Manu infers from this that the man's spouse might be Congolese; but he can't square this with the racist statement about the idleness of Africans in general. Probably it's more likely, he reckons – as de Zwaan wheels him back outside, saying it's important that he understands how all the stuff, as he puts it, comes in – that Mrs de Zwaan is from colonialist stock.

De Zwaan gestures at the incoming lorry drivers queuing in the roadways, telling Manu, '*C'est injuste que la loi européenne sur les tachygraphes numériques l'emporte sur la loi Belge,*' some reference to disliked European Union regulations, Manu presumes, though he doesn't know quite what a tachograph is, Congolese and Ugandan trucks not being known to carry these instruments.

Calling jovially to the drivers, de Zwaan then takes Manu back inside, to get a white coat and hairnet from a line of pegs and some boots from the storeroom. Remarkably, they seem like the same Bata brand of gumboots the Rwandan Army gave the AFDL, but the rubber of these has been dyed white rather than green. Pulling them on, he briefly recalls the rubber vines at Anke's colonialist museum. It's like history's making a double joke of him, being forced to wear these things again.

He has to sign some personal-risk waivers, but there's less formality than he expected. It's clear there's such a demand for labour at Weill Viandes that work permits and such like are readily overlooked, at least in their finer details. It's a strange place all right, Europe; was there ever anywhere like it?

Next de Zwaan tells him about lunch breaks and toilet breaks and the pay he'll receive. 'Cash at the end of each week. If you miss a shift, you can kiss goodbye to the envelope.'

Then he takes Manu on a tour of the slaughterhouse. The smell of the place is extraordinary, not just the smell of blood and shit (both of which are smeared on the walls and floor in various places), but also a vapour that Manu can only describe to himself as the smell of death, perhaps something to do with excretions from the glands of animals suddenly experiencing fear. It reminds him of the smell of human sweat during war, which is different from ordinary sweat – not just stronger, different, closer to the smell of sweat after sex.

'The purpose of an abattoir,' de Zwaan explains breezily, nudging him to point out how even bristles are being swept up, washed, bagged, 'is to extract the final per cent of value from the whole; each stage in the journey of the animals who enter this place is designed to help achieve that monetary end.'

They cross a lofty balcony, over the rail of which de Zwaan extends a commanding arm. 'Everything you see here leads to the development of a foodstuff or other product of use to human beings . . . less so than before, perhaps, now there's plastic, but still basically true. I bet you have combs in Congo that might have come from this very place, years ago. Do you?'

'What?'

'Do you have bone combs in your country?'

'We have combs,' Manu concedes, wondering what the hell he's going on about. De Zwaan's French is atrociously accented, which he puts down to the foreman being Flemish.

'Well, there you are. We don't make bone ones any more, but Weill's has significant plans to develop bioplastics from animal fat. Some of these will even carry an electric current! Can you imagine?'

'No,' Manu replies, in all frankness.

'Don't worry, you'll soon understand just how up to date we are here at Weill Viandes.'

They walk on, their feet moving like those of skaters, but on a sheen of blood rather than ice. There are little boxes on the walls, from one of which de Zwaan deftly extracts a pair of thin plastic gloves as they pass, telling Manu to put them on.

'Be very careful of skin,' de Zwaan informs him, as they pass over another red puddle. 'Most of our workplace accidents happen when people slip on a scrap of hide lying on blood like this. You slide like on a banana skin.'

He gives an obscene hoot. 'But I guess you know all about bananas! Look at this machinery, amazing really − when I first came here, even younger than you, we did all of this only with knives.'

Above their heads, wheels and chains are moving, carrying the swinging merchandise of Weill Viandes; Manu thinks of an army of hanged persons, marching on pure automation, but upside down.

Under this chainwork are men, mainly brown men or black men, each with a specific task, employing chopper or scraper, steam jet or electric saw. To Manu they don't seem in the least bit idle, contrary to de Zwaan's opinion.

He sees a calf hit on the head with a hammer. He sees bones split, offal slopped into buckets, knots of gristle tossed into plastic bins. He sees horns cut with angle grinders and cows being flayed, workers putting a boot up on the wall to get a better grip on the stiff hide as they pull it off.

It's disgusting, but Manu can't help but give a nervous grin when de Zwaan tells him that his particular job will be to strip the colons out of pig carcasses, then wash and trim them, ready for making sausages.

'Why are you smiling?' de Zwaan demands, the buttons on his white coat straining as he speaks. 'A slaughterhouse is not a smiling matter, and this is a model slaughterhouse.'

'Nothing, sir. Just pleased to have my job.'

What he can't tell him is that, in Congo, those white colonists who remained after independence were referred to as *colons*, as in fact they were before independence, when they were much greater in number. But if de Zwaan's wife really is from a family of former *colons*, he'd know that anyway.

The stripping-out of the other type of colon Manu will do with a plastic-handled knife – *erg scherp*, de Zwaan says, nicking into Flemish – which, when it's not in the hand, he cautions, should hang from a little sheath on the operative's belt.

After getting one of these knives from another storeroom, they reach a place separated off by lines on the factory floor, where lambs are being strung up by the legs. He watches blades being drawn across their throats by men with indifferent faces. The blood of the lambs pours down into foaming steel collectors. Nostrils dilating, the waiting animals are shrieking, their noise mixing with a constant banging sound, like rifle shots.

'This is the halal zone,' continues de Zwaan, having to raise his voice. 'The rest of it we do by the humane killer, if it's cattle.

Electric shock if it's pigs. The humane killer has a bolt action, powered by compressed gas. That's that noise you can hear. Of course, Muslims don't eat pigs, so there's no need for halal in that case. You're not a Muslim, are you?'

'No. Catholic.'

'Good, because you're on pigs, like I said. Take my tip. You'll always get a job at an abattoir if you're able to accommodate yourself to pigs.'

De Zwaan takes him to his actual station, which is nearby. It surprises Manu that the profane pork is so close to the sacred lamb. The Belgian then goes through the procedural motions of making sausages, saying: 'When you've filled the tray, send it down the line to be stuffed, right?'

'OK.'

'And look, this is very important, as you're right on the edge of the halal zone. See that white line?'

'Yes.'

'I guess you would. Well, that marks the square of the halal area, which you absolutely must not cross, as there'll likely be pig blood on your boots. Understand what I'm saying? Took me ages to explain the rules to that bloke.'

He gestures at an operative in the halal zone who's splitting lamb carcasses with a cleaver. 'Name of Raed, but unfortunately speaks no French, despite being a Christian. Doesn't speak at all in fact – has to write everything down – carries a notebook for the purpose – some other Arab translating. We've got a lot of them here, lots of Arab customers too. I didn't even know they had Christians over there . . . Raed's a very hard worker, anyhow. Not like some.'

With that, de Zwaan leaves Manu to get on with his job. The racism is his problem, not mine: Manu tries to hold that thought steady as he unsheathes the little knife, pulls down his first entrail; but – fuck you, *colon*, what it would be to stick this in yours!

Later that morning, after reaching a rough total of seven metres of sausage casings, he places a tray of them on the conveyor belt that goes to the sausage-stuffing zone. There the open ends of the casings are rolled on a nozzle and squirted full of sausage meat, before the open end is sealed up and each sausage is complete.

Once this tray of casings is on its way, he presses a button – at which point an upper conveyor, carrying the grisly line of pig carcasses on hooks, jerks forwards. The next carcass appears in front of him, swinging from side to side. It feels as he could just as adroitly be hoisted up there, just as easily be another keyboard of pink-and-white ribs, waiting for more entrails to be tinkled down by the *erg scherp* knife.

At lunchtime he goes to the refectory, buys a cheese roll, looking about at the other workers in their blood-stained coats and overalls. On breaks, most of the employees of Weill Viandes appear to separate into national or tribal groups. Mindful of his uncomfortable experience in the Bar Maïs, Manu keeps well away from the Congolese and Rwandan workers, the latter mostly Hutus, so far as he can tell. Once he's finished eating, still having some break time left, he takes a different route back to his station.

On the way, he passes a vast render tub. Into this the severed heads of pigs are being cast, for boiling down; further along there's another of these pits, into which the severed heads of cattle are being tossed. Reminding him a little, as he watches, of the lava lake of Nyiragongo, yellow steam rises from these render tubs, their brothy surfaces occasionally punctured by a protruding ear or snout.

Steel pipes snake across the simmering tops of these pits in order to pump off fat. And not even the cooling of this hot grease is the final stage of de Zwaan's journey of the animals. Their complaining clamour has long ceased, but their bones are yet to be ground, and by now Manu's due at his station.

On the way, he glimpses a man stroking the ears of a calf that's still alive; is it the same man he saw hit another calf with a hammer earlier? He's not certain, but what he feels is the velvety touch of Joséphine's hide against his face, the drub of her heart in his ear as he milked her – and what does it count for now, that closeness he once had with an animal?

337

As the carcasses jerk forwards above him, he again senses the rub of history, of past events – personal events and public events, recent ones and ones long distant – jointly seeking form, seeking a stable meaning that's immediately altered by further lapse of time. Time, time, he thinks, hooking me up two ways, altering the past even as it recedes. Time, time, time, speechless as a statue, but speaking all the same.

During the afternoon, Manu now and then glances at the silent Iraqi man on the halal station nearby. Raed has thick black eyebrows and eyes no less black. He hits the lambs very forcefully with his cleaver, as if he has a personal vendetta. Occasionally, bits of the bones that Raed has split fly over into Manu's area. He has to pick them out: hard, as the thin latex gloves he's wearing prevent the use of fingernails.

As he works on, he considers the value that his labour represents to the owners of this factory, whoever they are, and how this in turn is translated into euros, which so far he has only come by through theft or borrowing. What's happened to me, he thinks, can't be cut as cleanly as the edges of a banknote, instead clumping together like the dark-green, blood-flecked, half-absorbed pig nuts that he washes out of the intestines with the steam hose.

At the end of the shift he joins the flood of departing workers, who're gliding away like ghosts to mingle with the larger mass of commuting Bruxellois.

Stopping in the flow, he turns to look back at the abattoir, which is pumping out waste steam, noticing in the apex of the roof what he did not see on coming in: a large industrial clock with the brand name SIEMENS printed across the face. The clock is very corroded round its edges and he realises that this whole jungle of an abattoir is much older than he first thought, bamboozled by de Zwaan's proclamations of modernity.

This factory clock causes him to remember the much smaller one on the wall in The Passenger; ticking on, at least he hopes so, as David and the other Banyamulenge guys serve drinks, wash glasses, mop the floor. He knows that he should contact them, explain what has happened, but it seems too risky, the Dutch authorities still being after him.

Back at the hostel that night, Manu's lying on his cot when Abdi comes over and invites him to eat. They sit next to the small sun of the Somali's Primus stove as he makes a modest flatbread made of flour and water, topped with sliced boiled eggs mixed with cumin and chilli, and a small mess of spinach.

They eat, and it's delicious.

Abdi says: 'I have something to tell you.'

'Yes?'

'I sold your gun today. Too dangerous to keep it here. Sometimes there are raids.'

'OK.'

'I will give you half the money.'

'That would be good.'

'Did you kill someone with it?'

'No. I haven't killed anyone here. I ran away from a court in the Netherlands.'

'They're after you?'

'Perhaps. My picture was in a newspaper.'

'Don't worry. It doesn't make much difference. In this big city, we might be different kinds of black to each other, but we're all the same to those who hound us.'

Opposite Abdi's cot, a man is sitting cross-legged on the floor. His fingers are continually clicking through a rosary. Manu realises it's the Iraqi fellow on the next station to his at the slaughterhouse, the one who chops with a vengeance.

He raises a hand in greeting. Raed's head moves, nodding almost imperceptibly.

'What's that?' Abdi asks, watching.

'That man, he works at the abattoir where I got a job.'

'Yes, his name is Raed.'

'I know. I would talk to him but I was told he speaks no French.'

Abdi nods. 'It would be Arabic, but that's right. He's a mute. Once, another Arab and I pieced together what happened to

339

him; he wrote some stuff down, on a scrap of paper.'

As the subject of this discussion continues clicking his rosary beads, Abdi tells Manu that Raed was once in Saddam Hussein's army and then deserted. When he was caught, officials took him to a hospital, stuffed cotton wool in his mouth, and pulled out his tongue with pliers.

'He fled to Saudi Arabia, worked there as a labourer, then came on foot to Europe. Jordan, Syria, Turkey, Bulgaria . . . finally here, as if this fucking place is a paradise worth heading for. Had a very bad time in Saudi, too. Raed really hates Saudis. I suppose it must have been more torture, maybe them thinking he was some kind of fundamentalist, even though he's Christian.'

The sound of the beads moving through Raed's fingers forms an image in Manu's mind. It's of his dead mother performing the same action when alive.

Abdi gathers up the dishes, afterwards giving him his share of the money from the sale of the pistol. It's 120 euros. A lot of money. Better than shooting anybody, too, if the police do eventually catch up with him.

Chapter 11

A few weeks later, after fitful sleep, Manu's making his way to Weill Viandes when he spots Raed further ahead. Running to catch up with him on the pavement, he makes the double sibilant noise that people of the south know as the sign of wanting someone's attention. Hearing, Raed turns his head and nods at him.

They walk together. Like all guests of Hotel Papejan, they both smell very strongly of sweat, standing out from the mass of commuters, each of those transient beings seeming to be slathered in their morning of roses, their morning of jasmine, their morning of sandalwood – all products likely grown, as were this pair of men, on southern soils.

Falling into step with Raed, Manu has an urge to talk to this man who cannot. Letting go of self-consciousness, he begins to speak without rational order, like someone whose personhood is being tipped out, in the manner of marbles from a plastic cup – speaking first in French, then English, finally babbling melodiously on in Swahili.

Manu relates here a proverb he remembers, there a snatch of lyric from a favourite tune. Plus half-remembered fragments of schoolbook translations, mixed in with the names of famous men and women. It was a game he used to play with friends in the schoolyard in Bukavu, reformulating their English lessons in accordance with what they heard on Friday nights, when Don Javier permitted them to watch television:

Sikujua kwamba siyo Mike Tyson aliyekuwa mkarimu kwake. I didn't know that it was not Mike Tyson who was kind to her.

Snoop Dogg hana budi kwenda, na Madonna hana budi kwenda naye. Snoop Dogg should go, and Madonna should go with him.

Christopher Columbus, nimekuja kukushukuru kwa kuniponya ule ugonjwa uliotowesha nguvu zangu zote. Christopher Columbus, I've come to thank you for having cured that sore which totally incapacitated me.

Naam Robinson Crusoe, lazima nirudi nyumbani; nawe ushikwe na ugonjwa unaoponyeka. Well Robinson Crusoe, I have to go home; may you be curably sick.

All those schoolfriends with whom he used to do this – where are they now? he asks as he paces the pavement alongside Raed, who suddenly lets out a ciphered sound, half a shout of joy, half a groan.

He cannot understand, Manu knows, but he intuits that Raed gets it all the same, perhaps recognising those Swahili words which derive from Arabic, or responding to something in intonation, in sound alone. They both halt anyway, after Raed gives out this strangulated noise; and then Raed turns to him and smiles. Somehow or other, understanding has happened.

They resume walking, these two translated men, eventually arriving at the slaughterhouse to begin their shift.

At about half-two, three men in Arab gear and expensive shoes come in with de Zwaan and begin looking over the halal zone. Very soon, the visitors start remonstrating with him, telling him in broken French that the restricted area is not fit for purpose and will not pass certification of the Halal Research Council of the Kingdom of Saudi Arabia.

Raed hears the word 'Saudi' all right; or maybe he can tell the visitors' nationality from how they look. He at once comes over to Manu – gives his shoulders a sharp downwards wrench . . . at which point the lights go out.

In the darkness, a roar of sound issues from the workers – obscenities, harangues, yelps – and then something strikes Manu on the back. He understands only then what Raed meant, *Get down or you'll be hurt!* – for there's now a shower of joints and bones flying through the air.

Emergency lights pool from the walls of the slaughterhouse, showing men's arms windmilling as they toss ragged bits of flesh across the factory floor. Some of them keep to their knees like Manu is now, to make a lower target, but not so low as not to be able to throw meats.

Hunks of shank, slices of jowl, handfuls of jelly, coils of rind descend — elastically athletic, the rinds stretch out in flight, contract on landing, bouncing along . . . Pig tails, pig ears, cuts of beef, backs of bacon, lumps of mutton — all type of wet, bony debris drops round Manu, landing on his head, his arms, his legs.

In a pause, he hears de Zwaan shouting commands; then someone else call in reply: '*Vous avez vos règles, ou quoi?*' You having your period, or what?

And another: '*Les anglais ont débarqué!*' The English have landed!

And someone else, '*Et ils niquent ta mère!*' And they're fucking your mother!

Manu thinks of his own, not mumbling on about the Chwezi on a moonlit night, but in the storehouse; was that what happened to her there?

The insult to de Zwaan is greeted by the laughter of 300 men, speaking knowingly or unknowingly to the troughs of blood hidden when slaughter saunters out into the world, tricked out in plastic packets in supermarkets or laid out enticingly on butchers' counters; or (Manu thinks) the horrors that happen when soldiers, English or Rwandan or whatever, invade a place, wrapping their violence in necessity or duty or honour.

And then the barrage begins again. Meats that miss their targets slide down the slimy walls, the fattest nuggets glistening in the fuzzy blue light like jewels.

Manu watches a few staggering, white-coated men circle each other, slashing with the same little blades as he has on his belt. Settling buried scores, it seems like. As these men fight, their white coats redden — seemingly the origin of the jokes about the English and de Zwaan's period. He wonders how much longer this can go on before someone gets killed.

343

A whistle blows. Somebody screams. Chickens flap across, released from their cages.

He sees other men spinning round like hammer throwers, in order to achieve the momentum to heave bigger pieces of meat up into the air. Some are whole ribcages, like those out of which Manu has been stripping viscera, the cut ribs sticking out of them like teeth. One of these heavy pieces strikes de Zwaan, felling him in an instant.

Manu spots Raed, not at his own station; he's cutting at a side of pork outside the halal zone, removing double sets of chops and shooting them in the direction of the Saudi inspectors. The visitors crouch beneath a suspended lamb, trying to dodge Raed's missiles.

A siren moans. It slowly rises, then cuts out, as if acknowledging its belatedness. As the last tones of the siren reverberate in the girdered roof, a few chicken feathers flutter down.

The big brown double doors to the stockyards push open, bringing a widening slice of daylight – and the sight of milling cattle, sheep, pigs, each in their corridor of steel-rack fence. Between the fences, Belgian police are running, nightsticks in hand, radios squawking at their hips as if they're responding to the noises coming from the beaks of the escaped fowl.

As the police boots slide on the strewn arena, a few last bones spin through the air. One of these cracks de Zwaan on the forehead, just as he is standing up in recovery from the previous blow.

Whoever threw that is a master at this game, which, unanticipated although it was by Manu, has obviously happened many times. This eruption is not fuelled by anti-Islamic feeling, he reckons, not least because many of the workers are Muslims. It's more a sort of macabre carnival, expressing the rage of immigrant vassalage, the bitter furies of dispossessed people turning on themselves as well as the authorities.

But it really is ending now, with the entrance of the police. The Saudi inspectors flee towards the gates, one of them turning to stare balefully, from under his blood-spattered *keffiyeh*, at Raed. Employees return to their stations, many swaying, as if shocked by the excess of brutality in this rough communion that they've shared with each other, and with the parts of dead beasts that they've turned into projectiles.

Some continue lying or sitting on the floor. One of the seated men, as if roughly recowled for a second birth, has a white, rubbery membrane draped over his head. He's trembling, from laughter or from fright. Forbearing to touch the wobbling caul, turning his face to one side in revulsion, a policeman lifts him to his feet. Another policeman assists de Zwaan in getting to his feet.

Manu is also trembling as he stands up, gazing at a surreal carpet of flesh. He steals a look at Raed, who's now returned to his station in the halal zone, methodically resuming the rhythms of his ordinary work, as if that too is a way of recalibrating justice.

Was it Raed who extinguished the lights? It does not seem so, for he wouldn't have had time before giving Manu his mimed warning. It must have been known by many beforehand, this thrashing-out against the bosses. But in searching for clues as to who planned it, passing among dazed, bloodstained faces, the police are on a hiding to nothing.

De Zwaan's voice comes on the tannoy, ordering an emergency end of shift for all workers except cleaners – vassals to all others, lowest caste of all, still having to labour after this riot of meat: *cette émeute de viande*, as Manu couches it in mental language, walking back to the Hotel Papejan, trekking through the fetish country of bars, illuminated massage parlours and late-night foreign-exchange bureaux.

Chapter 12

Two days later, life at the slaughterhouse has returned to what counts as normal in that place. Nearly everything is back in line, workers and beasts alike stuporous and docile, de Zwaan keeping a closer-than-normal eye on everything, plodding to and fro. A large, pewter-coloured bruise has bloomed on his forehead. Although the floor has been mopped, several times, there are still pools of reddened water here and there.

Manu desperately now wants out of this hole, to break free to some other way of living. But what's he to do? The sale of the gun hasn't generated enough money to buy a new ID, and he believes there remains a strong probability that the police will find him.

As he strips down intestines in the slaughterhouse, he's super-conscious of an itching patch of athlete's foot. Since the evening he walked back from the riot it has got steadily worse, the stipples on his sole seeming (when he inspects in the toilet on breaks) to have both risen and widened, making him limp. Standing up all day in rubber boots doesn't help, of course.

About lunchtime, de Zwaan approaches him. 'You're African, aren't you?'

'I'm Congolese. You know that, boss.'

'And you're fairly poor?'

'Yes.' He grits his teeth.

'Well, you know that I am your friend?'

'Yes, sir.'

'That is why I am offering you an opportunity to see more of your African chums.'

'There are many Africans in the slaughterhouse, sir.'

'This is different. You'll really feel at home. Ever heard of the trade show AGRIPA?'

'No.'

'It's one of the largest agricultural trade shows in the world, held here in Brussels. This year there's a theme of African cattle for the livestock competition. You know what I mean by theme?'

'A special focus?'

'I suppose,' considers de Zwaan, as if there were twenty-nine other answers. 'Anyway, the organisers have asked for a loan of one of our men, to do a demonstration of the preparation of sausages.'

'OK.'

De Zwaan seems overexcited. 'Are you game?' he asks. 'It's in a fortnight's time – look.'

He holds out a sheet of paper on which a date and other instructions are typed in French.

At first, Manu doesn't look at the paper in de Zwaan's hand. He puts down his knife, studying where it lies at his station, a ribbon of blood trickling off the blade on to the steel of the counter. 'There's extra money?' he asks, unrolling his latex gloves.

'Thirty euros.'

He takes the paper from de Zwaan's hand. 'Then I will do it.'

'Good! You will need to get yourself to Brussels Expo, which is a big exhibition site in the north of the city, near the Stade Roi Baudoin. You can do that?'

'Yes.'

'Take a coat, gloves, hairnet and your knife, and a crimper. Everything else will be provided. You will have to do the stuffing of the sausages yourself, by hand. We can't haul machinery over there or spare another worker. That OK?'

'I will do my best.'

'It's not hard; go check the stuffing station here, make a study. At the Expo, you'll need to get to stand A45, like it says here. That's Hall A. I'll have the materials delivered for you . . . and collected too. And Manu?'

347

'Yes?'

'This is an important expo for our company. You realise that I am giving you a special chance by choosing you to represent us?'

'Yes, sir,' he says, weighing up his value in euros.

'Well don't fuck it up.'

When the appointed day comes, he makes his way across the city, passing shops and stores different to those he sees on his normal route, continuing until he arrives at a complex of modern industrial warehouses where large flags announce the entrance to the trade show.

Many of the visitors to this expo look to be farmers. They're mostly men, with such a uniformity of wide jowls, facial hair and coarse, over-red skin that it would be easy to count them as relatives of each other. If they notice him at all, they look at him as a foreigner – 'Black as my grandfather's hat,' one comments to another – their antennae-like whiskers seeming to twitch in search of the history that has brought him here.

His troublesome foot itching, he makes his way into the lobby area, and, after some difficulty with registration and navigation, finds his bearings. Hall A, where he's bound, is dubbed 'Work and Food'. It's too brightly lit, full of confusing corridors in which stalls – selling fumigants and feed, pesticides and biostimulants, milking machinery and bovine medicines – are signed with sequential numbers and letters.

Breaking the pattern of these corridors is a series of gated pens containing various species of well-primped farm animals, including the cleanest cows Manu has ever seen, pigs with metal tags in their ears, and horses with plaited manes. The Belgian Blue cattle are particularly fine: huge, pied-skinned, extremely muscled.

The animals in the enclosures blink under the artificial light as they champ on bright-green foliage or tug at bales of hay. Many of these creatures are already shitting away so merrily that it seems like the highly illuminated, white-panelled modernity of this high-roofed, technically confident place is being punctured by the rising of irrepressible organic smells.

Some of the aisles contain agricultural machinery, such as tractors and ploughs. Painted in primary colours, these machines seem both toy-like and epic in the harsh overhead lighting. The brand names of these vehicles – DONG FENG, PACKO, KRAMP – mean nothing to Manu.

Indeed, as he tries to find his own stand, it amazes him in what ignorance he has lived, while there are such agricultural riches in the world. If all these things, not just tractors but the whole commercial panoply of sacked fertiliser, vials of flea poison and endless varieties of feed, were themselves to drop out of the clouds above the Kivus, farmers there would have to pinch themselves to convince themselves it was not a dream.

Looking as instructed for stand A45, he continues through the crowds till he finds it. Two vacuum chillpacks, one of sausage meat and one of casings, await him in a refrigerator, along with labelled wrappings for individual packets of sausages, and steel trays on which to stack the packets. De Zwaan has told him to fill the fridge with finished sausages, offering them free to anyone who comes to watch him work.

Noticing that he seems to be in some sort of area for craft foods, between a beer seller and a stall piled high with pickles and mustards, Manu puts on his gloves and hairnet, unpacks the sausage meat and begins stuffing it into the translucent casings.

Farmers continually pass to and fro in front of him, but none of them looks much at the work that he is doing, or at the sign, WEILL VIANDES, which gives the address and telephone number of the slaughterhouse. De Zwaan has also given him a little cache of business cards to give out, but so little interest is shown in his activities that he doesn't even bother to open the packet.

Many of the visitors to the expo have large trolleys, which they push spasmodically down the aisles. After several hours more, during which no one stops to watch him apart from a small blond boy who picks his nose in front of the stall for a few minutes, he has used up the supply of meat and casings.

There seems no point in hanging around for the rest of the day, despite his being on a whole-day rate, so he starts cleaning up the counter. He wonders whether to take some of the sausages back to the hostel, but many of the people there are Muslims, and he knows he cannot bring himself to eat them after handling them. Never again, he vowed, soon after starting work at the abattoir, will he eat a hot dog like the one he bought off the cart at Montgomery metro-stop after being sent packing by Anke.

He tries not to think of her, knowing that he must forget her, just as he's had to forget Edith. But he still can't help thinking of the soft light that came into Anke's eyes, and the smile to her mouth, before she kissed him – it now seems so long ago, he reflects, what happened by that gleaming lake where islands stud the water and the crested cranes fly free.

No good, all this: past happiness that must be wiped away.

He throws his cloth in a refuse bin, slams the door of the refrigerator. Leaving the useless meat inside to be collected by De Zwaan's men the next day, he takes off his hairnet and white coat, puts them back in the Chinese bag, and walks off into the revolving crowds.

He leaves Hall A and bypasses Hall B, walking to Hall C, drawn by the signage that promises an 'Africa Zone'. He moves under industrial arched rafters, swooping from the base of the building to the top, as if to suggest an infinite curvature of space. But the space is finite, of course: ending on the floor, where the arched rafters are embedded in blocks of concrete like giant arrowheads. They make him think of the tie-down blocks at airports with which, in times gone by, he anchored the Cargomaster.

Mustn't go there . . . knowing too well by now that piling memories on top of a present experience of being lost in another way simply makes everything worse. But even the wisdom which he knows he needs to get through it, this next stage of existence – the wisdom of separating out categories, of dividing aftermaths from the events that precede them, of not mixing up the different stories in his life so far – itself seems to blur into the familiar mental mess, staggering backwards, even as it tries to walk forwards in the corridor of the mind.

The gallery through which he's making his way is devoted

exclusively to African cattle. Stall after stall, each containing a single penned cow or bull from different African countries, line the aisles. Most of these stalls have a flagpole from which listlessly drape the relevant national colours.

He passes in a daze between Abyssinian Xebu, Nigerian Adamawa, Sudanese Abigar, Malawian Angoni, Ethiopian Arado, Togolese Aventonou, Malian Azaouak, Eritrean Baherie, Cameroonian Bakosi, Ivorian Baoule, South African Bonsmara, Tanzanian Boran, Zimbabwean Tuli, Rwandan Watusi, all noisily chewing fodder . . . Inexplicably, too, in the stall for Equatorial Guinea there's a donkey with a pendant squiggle of dried drool in the corner of one eye.

Walking between those stalls is like a descent into another world, a journey that wrenches him back to some of the very memories he's been trying to banish, for many of these cattle are versions of the same general Sanga group to which his own family herd belonged: cattle with wide, lyre-shaped horns and cylindrical torsos, all harking back to some *ur*-species, before the differentiation caused by breeding and territory.

Unsteady, he wavers in the aisle, with people passing by either side, jostling him under the lights and curving rafters. It causes a ripple of panic in him, the mixing of the crowded, jarring modern atmosphere with the ancient Sanga profile. His panic is intensified by a rhythmic sound of consumed cud, oscillating between the stalls – flowing like a gathering chorus, moving from one to another, it's a sort of *chwah chwah*, seeming to increase with the force of a propeller on an airfield, before an aircraft takes off.

By each of the stalls, handlers for the national breeds hang about, or sit on plastic chairs. While some are in national costume, others are in suits and clutching briefcases, as if they're the waiting substitutes of the businessmen, politicians or other big men who steer the show back home. But there are also some handlers who move like real herdsmen, Ethiopians and Kenyans and Sudanese mostly. Manu sees in their postures something that's the likeness of those who graze their cattle on the Kivu meadows, like he once did.

351

Watching these people, he gets a glimpse of what he might have become had he not been snatched from meadow to cockpit to slaughterhouse. An immense wave of woe washes over him, not just at the thought of his originary herdsman self being ripped away, but also at the loss of the peace-loving version of a freight dog that he tried to develop after Cogan's death. All past conjecture now, more untimely even than it was in the moment.

Driven to find something that can link him to some idea of home, the best he can presently throw together, he goes in search first of the Congolese stall, then of the Rwandan one, meaning only to spy them out and not show himself. But the Congolese stall is empty, and the Rwandan handler has deserted his post, leaving the Watusi specimen there to join the chorus of the cud. Rusyo, Kagame, the grinding machine of state power back in Kigali, would (Manu surmises) chew the fellow out if they knew.

He makes his way over to the Ugandan stall. There is no cow in this one either, but it is at least attended – by a woman with a jolly-looking face who wears a traditional Ugandan dress. He starts a conversation, in English. It turns out she's a Teso from Tororo.

'Tororo: the town with the Rock!' he says, referring to the landmark of eastern Uganda that Cogan once told him to be careful of. 'I used to fly planes and we had to watch out for that. There was a warning light on top, but it often didn't work.'

As he speaks, he becomes aware that it might be unwise to mention his past in this way, for how many central African pilot fugitives from the law can there be in Brussels?

'What's your name?' she asks, while gesturing that he should sit down on one of two plastic chairs to the side of the stall.

He gives her the same false name he gave the security guard at Anke's institution: Max Kongolo.

The Teso woman says, 'Max, that Rock can be seen throughout our whole district. There's a legend among our people that it is what made us know we had reached the Promised Land. The Rock was its sign, the sign of the one God in whose name Jesus came, extending his promise of redemption by being revealed in human flesh!'

He realises that he's in the presence of a Born Again, and that he could be here for hours, days, more, if he lets this woman keep talking. It's a shame, because she really does have a pleasing face, one that reminds him of the Ugandan women who sold goods at the market in Entebbe. But the Teso lady launches into an enthusiastic explanation of the divine plan, as laid down before time itself, she says, and proven by matching phrases from different parts of the Bible; from which she then produces numerous citations, as if doing so calls forward all prophesy to an end-point right now.

'So you've met my wife,' an approaching voice says, with a hint of embarrassed reprimand. 'Enough, my dear,' continues a bearded man in blue overalls. In his early fifties, he's leading an Ankole cow by a rope towards the empty stall.

Manu's patch of athlete's foot erupts into itching again, its explosive pulses almost in time with those of a roof light above that's gone on the blink.

As for the animal being conveyed towards him, it's so distinctive – with large, upturned horns, over two metres long in total span and white-on-brown markings – that he almost convinces himself it could be Joséphine. As it waits to enter the stall, it even assumes one of her postures, which was to slightly lift the weight off her right foreleg (it was once sliced by a piece of volcanic rock as sharp as a scimitar; he had to bind the wound with a piece of his shirt, never fettering her again on that leg, which remained sensitive).

But this animal at the Expo is much older a beast than even Joséphine would be now, her brown fur silvering, her hump and dewlap shrunk, her limbs sagging, her eyes dull, like cataracted moons seeking in vain the gravity of earth: that force proven by Adam's vaulting ambition to get on his own two feet, in Don Javier's opinion.

Unsettled by a feeling of being into too many places at the same time, Manu gets up off the chair. The light from the huge lamp affixed to the top inner curve of the arch above – it's flickering with chaotic exorbitance now, outstripping in its oscillations the itchings on his foot, outstripping even the pernicious groping for coherence between past and present that his mind has been undergoing. One second the lamp – not even at airports has he seen so monstrous a light – floods down on him theatrically, makes a sharply defined circle, the next he's in shadow.

He says to the Born Again's husband, 'Shame to see a noble breed, pride of the Ankole and my own Banyamulenge, so brought down.' Once more he's aware of having dangerously misspoken, of not keeping his identity a secret, but he's simply overwrought by the sight of this cow, the poor image of Joséphine.

The man, who's now putting the degraded beast into its arched stall – a hard job, with those wide horns – replies matily, having been apprised of Manu's familiar origins, 'Well, you speak true, she's not the best we could have brought, but the president said, we're not going to ruin any of our best beasts by sending them all that way just to be gawped at by a few *wazungu*! So we brought this old dear, a beauty in her day but looking the worse for wear now.'

Manu goes over to the cow and, putting out his hand, strokes her on the nose, saying, 'Good girl, good girl.'

Says the man: 'She can hardly stand; the flight was very bad for her. I've just taken her to the vet here. Apparently she has a bad heart.'

Manu remains silent, caught in wonder as he continues calming and relaxing the cow by stroking. 'You flew a single cow, all the way from Uganda to here?'

The man shakes his head. 'No, these Belgians sent a big plane, a converted Airbus, to each region of Africa and picked up cattle from the different countries, except for those idiots in Malabo who sent a donkey.'

'Yes, I saw that.'

'Like a taxi for cows it was, us handlers all sitting up front, in what would have been the first-class seats!'

At that moment the cow reaches out violently, pushing her wet nose towards Manu. Again he strokes her nose, whereupon she immediately collapses with a clattering thud against the side of the stall.

'Shit!' curses the man. 'I think she's had it.'

'It's dead?' says his tiresome wife, looking on. 'Does this mean we can go home?'

The man opens up the stall – a difficult manoeuvre, as the corpse of the cow is pressed against the door. Manu tries to help him, holding her head, pulling her dripping nose and rheumy eyes towards his stomach, cupping his arms under the boat-like curve of her horns.

And then, letting go, he just begins weeping, leaning on the edge of the stall, looking at the man who has his ear against the cow's chest, listening for her heart. It's not Joséphine, Manu knows that, but this cow so reminds him of her. But now, more than ever since he trod them, the meadow paths through which Joséphine used to follow him, or he her, seem vertiginously high, definitively away: a separated world, voided into mental darkness by a stream of events that are ever threatening to, but never do, reach their crisis.

How he wishes it was her that was spared, rather than him. Notwithstanding full feeling for the past loss of relative human life, that of his father and his mother and his sister and his uncles, whose mourning he has consumed inside himself, almost like those pygmies of the deep forest ('*autochthons de la forêt profonde*', as he puts it in his own interior voice, that voice we all hear when we speak to ourselves), who weep as they place hot coals in the carcass of elephant they're cooking, he deeply loved that animal.

'I'm so sorry,' says Manu, pulling himself jerkily back into joint and wondering if this bizarre episode is a conclusive rupture with the past that has been plaguing him: is in fact the very crisis, the moment when one thing becomes something other.

'It's not your fault,' the man says. 'The vet said it could happen anytime now.'

Anytime now – but what Manu thinks of, right then, is something his mother once said about the Chwezis, which is that the start of the collapse of their empire was marked by the death of the sacred cow Bihogo, in fulfillment of a prophesy that their empire would crumble if it died.

The Belgian farmers continue to pass by, mitigating the challenges of their wobbling trolleys with curses. To these challenges a horn of the dead cow, still protruding from the stall, has been added, but this too is met with a grim detour. Gloomy triumph over practical obstacles is said to be part of the tribal character of northern Europeans, prosecutors themselves of many a crumbled empire, and perhaps this is an example of it.

The Ugandan handler says, 'What the hell am I going to do with the body?'

'There must be a procedure here,' Manu says, but knowing in his heart that it's likely to be delivered into a furnace or disposed of in a place like Weill Viandes.

Having spoken, he becomes dimly conscious of a thin, white-haired Belgian standing nearby. The man is looking in puzzlement as much at Manu as at the corpse of the cow; no doubt another person, Manu surmises, who has satisfied his desire for agricultural merchandise, judging by the pile on the trolley in front of him.

Manu doesn't look properly at the man's face, but takes in the fact that he is wearing a yellow T-shirt, on which is printed a list of names in black, connected by ampersands:

John &
Paul &
Ringo &
George.

'I guess I should go and find someone to help with this,' the Ugandan says.

'We should bury her,' Manu says, still moved by the sight of the cow's corpse, around whose protruding horn farmers continue to steer.

He kneels down, places a hand on the soft brown hide, thinking of the cigarette-packet marks on Joséphine's flank. 'We should bury her,' he says again, hearing his poor mother cry out.

Still he watches and listens, the thin Belgian man who's now leaning on the steering bar of his own trolley as if it's a farm gate.

Through his glasses, sharp blue eyes are drilling into Manu.

At which point a security guard appears, wearing an orange hi-vis jacket too tight and short in the sleeves, and clutching a radio. 'What you going to do about this, then?' he demands, nodding at the corpse of the cow.

'We are going to drag it out,' Manu says, in a voice clogged by grief. It's as if he's reached some final limit of horror that cannot be overreached but can't be explained either. Why should the death of a random cow affect him so greatly, when he's seen so much death before?

'Not while the expo is still going on you aren't,' says the guard, whose portly shape and half-threatening attitude remind Manu of that other guard, the one in Anke's museum.

He begins lifting his radio when another voice, that of the thin, white-haired Belgian standing by, says: 'No need for that, officer, I have an estate car and trailer. If you radio me a pass to drive through to the back of the hall, we'll get it out that way.' He points at the back of the stall. 'Those are doors there, are they not? Manu, you come with me and we'll get my pickup.'

Chapter 13

Still weeping, he follows in the wake of the man with the Beatles T-shirt whom his tangled senses are struggling to accept is really, actually here . . . just a few steps ahead of him in this strange, artificial place. The imperium of all things is slipping away in the same sideways movement as the veering trolley full of farm-related matter that Papa Chénal is busy trying to steer towards the car park, his manoeuvring not aided by his occasionally turning to Manu and smiling, his blue eyes now lit with pleasure.

The two of them get into Papa's muddy pickup, which passes through two checkpoints at which stewards radio the security guard in the orange hi-vis back in Hall C to check it's OK for Papa to drive the vehicle to the back gate of the hall. It takes a while, the aggregate of all this business. As they're kept waiting, Papa takes one of his hands off the steering wheel, places it on one of Manu's own, and squeezes. 'We'll talk later, yes?' he says, before returning his hand to the wheel.

Still in something of a stupor, he helps Papa find and open the back door of the area of Hall C, where the Ugandan stall is located, and, with the help of the blue-overalled handler and his Born Again wife, haul the dead cow up on to the back of the pickup.

Then suddenly they are driving, about to get on to the ring road round Brussels, when Manu remembers his scant possessions at the hostel. A slight return is made to the Rue des Croisades, where he picks up his prison shoes, which have inexplicably come to seem important to him, even though they are uncomfortable and not things he chose to wear, and also the two bits of the recording device stolen from the journalist on the steps of the court and a few other small items he has bought over the months of employment at Weill Viandes. The value of these things he cannot calculate – probably they're not worth the return – but he hasn't much left to hold on to.

And all through this process of collection of objects, another process of collection or recollection is still going on as he hears his mother cry out again, and then his father and his sister, Don Javier and Cogan too. All the voices coalescing as if in one citation, a monologue of the dead. He looks around in the stalls for Abdi but he's nowhere to be seen, and so tramps downstairs.

In the lobby of the hostel on the way out, having recovered somewhat, he quickly settles up with Klungel and Carolus, those apparent preyers on people of the abyss. What Abdi said might about them might be true, might be not, but the condescending way they look at him as he leaves, as if they're on the top of a mountain and he's at the very bottom, makes him want to chop them with the side of his hand.

And so, finally, as moonlight slowly begins to whiten the office blocks of the city, the two of them, Papa and Manu, are soon again approaching the slipway of the Brussels Ring. They're heading towards West Flanders, to a place in the countryside which is, Papa tells him, near the Ypres Salient and other historic sites of the First World War.

As he speaks, Manu remains silent, tracking the lights of the oncoming vehicles, still in a daze. Papa reminds him that he has a potato farm, La Fosse, on the Messines Ridge. He talks casually about how he has supplemented his income with tours of the battlefield areas on the farm, showing tourists abandoned trenches, huge craters, old artillery shells, other odd things he's dug up. He says that he does not neglect to mention to these visitors ('*touristes sombres*', he calls them, dark tourists) his discovery on laying a new floor in his barn of a much larger example of ordnance, still unexploded. Lying ten metres below, it's a British First World War mine.

'I just covered it up again. Doesn't stop me sleeping at night – why should it, after what the two of us have seen? It's been there all this time. There's no reason it should blow up now.'

And then Papa begins to describe the old plane that he has inside the barn, the Dakota DC-3 which he once or twice mentioned when they were together in Uganda.

'Unable to resist, I bought it here at an auction while on holiday, then went back to Entebbe,' he says. 'I was a fool – had no idea how long it was going to take me to do up. I'm nearly there now, though. But what about you, Manu? How did you end up at that expo?'

He tries to give Papa a concise account of all that he's been through, at the end of which the old man says: 'Well, I guess your eyes have been fully opened now.'

'But I think I've failed in my life.'

'There's no shame in failure. Sometimes the opposite.'

The entrance of Papa's farm lies on a bend of country road. Protected on one side by a windbreak of poplars – whose treetops the moon has, by now, tipped with silver – the house seems very old, with a thatched roof and irons in its brickwork. Manu enters a large, warm kitchen. Papa gives him a glass of beer, pours himself a glass of milk. Seeing Papa's signature drink unlocks something in Manu. He grabs the thin old man into an urgent hug, and holds on tight; after a few seconds, Papa spins the two of them round so he can put his glass down safely on the counter.

'Never thought I'd get a dance out of you, Manu,' Papa laughs, shrugging him off with a consolatory pat on the shoulder. Sipping the beer, Manu realises that the only example of ordinary human hospitality he can remember since escaping from the court is Abdi sharing his food with him in the hostel. He tells Papa about the Somali's Primus stove and the old man smiles, saying, 'Well, I think we can go one better than that.'

Papa starts preparing a meal, a process that Manu watches with fascination. First, he turns on a kettle. He next seeks out a hessian sack of small potatoes and, taking out four or five, begins to peel them; the falling peels remind Manu of the scales he noticed around Abdi, back at the hostel that first night.

Papa places the peeled potatoes in a pan. He pours the boiled water from the kettle on top of them, throwing in a few pinches of sea salt. He then retrieves a white plate from the fridge, on which sits a fillet of fish. He cuts it into two with a sharp knife. As the potatoes boil in their salted water, he scatters a handful of flour over the two pieces of fish.

'This is toasted flour,' he explains. 'Everything tastes better if you toast your flour.'

Sitting on a wheelback chair, drinking the marvellous beer, Manu watches Papa turn over the pieces of fish in the flour. After washing his fingertips under the tap, the old man turns two grinders above the fish, one containing salt, one pepper. He takes another dish out of the fridge and cuts off a slice of butter. He melts this in a heavy iron frying pan on the stove. When the butter begins to foam, he places the two pieces of fish in the pan and cooks them for three or four minutes on one side, filling the kitchen with delicious smells. He then turns them over with a spatula and cooks them on the other side, before turning off the heat.

By now, the potatoes could be nearly boiled. Papa prods them with a fork and comments that they need a touch longer. He pours Manu another bottle of beer ('this stuff won best beer in Belgium') and starts chopping some parsley on a board. Next he cuts a lemon and squeezes half of it over the browned, sweet-smelling fish.

After this, he removes the potatoes from the stove and drains them, looking through the shroud of steam at Manu. Being studied by this slight, smiling old-timer, who half belongs to that world which he has left behind, he realises that it's OK to stop pretending, and that he might now start to be himself again: be individual, like Cogan once advised, so many unforgiving skies ago.

But how? How, after being in the netherworld of war so long, and materially benefiting from it? How, after defying good for so long, and suffering the relentless dents of conscience, which signals itself like a disease? How, after being in a factory which collapses human and animal destinies in a terrifying way, reducing both to a rough, denatured design of what they should be?

Papa brings to the table the potatoes and the fish, over which he throws a garland of chopped parsley. He serves the fish with the potatoes and pours the remaining butter over them.

The two of them eat, and afterwards Papa says: 'I expect you are very tired, poor boy. Well, you've found your foxhole now.' He's speaking French and the word he uses is *tranchée-abri*.

He takes Manu up some stairs edged with a wobbly banister, shows him to a room with a large wooden bed, and bids him good night.

In the morning, before Papa wakes, Manu gets up and goes outside, into a small garden. He sees that the house sits above the floodplain of a small river, which he then walks down to, crossing a long, green lawn on which three polythene tunnels are pitched, held up by ribbed supports. A clump of willows hangs over the river, in which small black fish swim, darting to and fro under a bridge wide and strong enough to bear a tractor. On the other side of the bridge is a large potato field, another of ploughed soil, with oak trees at its edge – and a third, untended field, which is full of brambles, dilapidated concrete structures, pieces of rusted metal and very large holes.

Coming back up the gleaming green road of the lawn – on an edge of which tall poles carry a telephone wire, leading through the garden to the farmhouse – he stands in the sun, leaning against the wooden wall of a dove house that's in the garden. He continues like this, hardly moving, almost pitched back into that precious monotony that he knew as a cowherd in the Kivus, until Papa appears and calls him in for a bowl of milky coffee and croissants with jam.

Bent over the bowl at the kitchen table, white hair hanging down, Papa looks much thinner than he used to, and now has more than one black spot on his face.

While Papa's washing up, Manu wanders through the big

old house. There are large fireplaces in several rooms, a square television in one (surrounded by tatty armchairs), and polished floorboards throughout. On a windowsill in the hall, next to the stairs, a kind of doll made of straw sits in a chipped mug; the figure's outstretched arms reach over the edge of the mug, and her lace-crowned head is covered in dust.

Later that day, in the middle of the ploughed field, the two of them dig a pit with a mini-excavator and bury the cow from the expo. Manu does not weep any more for this corporeal symbol of his old life, this model of what Joséphine might have become, all these years later, because it's an oddly happy occasion. For this episode of interral, while practical enough in its details, feels like a new beginning as well as the surrender of something.

In the late afternoon, Papa takes him to the barn, the sliding doors of which present a fairly large and ancient aeroplane, its fuselage glittering (as Papa turns on the lights) under suspended lamps. The wings of this craft, the same Dakota that Papa talked about, seem almost too big for the building, only just fitting within the space. The hull of the plane is patched with oval pieces of aluminum, riveted at regular intervals round their perimeters. Well, not so regular in some places, Manu thinks, picturing unseen, hearing unheard, times when Papa was gunning in the rivets . . . their relentless sound, caught in a twisted manifold of memory and imagination, recalls that of the so-called humane killer, back at Weill Viandes, the sight of Edith swimming in shampoo foam at Aero Beach and distant, so distant now, the workers at Bukavu docks, up to their waists in frothy water.

On either side of the plane are items of heavy old furniture covered with tools. In one corner of the barn there's an oil-stained sofa, its fabric of the same pattern – once, maybe – as the armchairs in the house. There's also a miniature yellow crane and, in another corner, a long, rectangular cardboard box; above this receptacle, a protective black rubber mask hangs from the apparatus of an arc welder.

Seeing him look at the welder, Papa says: 'I hope you'll allow me to teach you how to use that one day.'

Lying in his bed in the farmhouse that night, Manu considers the utter coincidence of Papa coming along yesterday at the expo, down that particular aisle, where, again by chance, he was transfixed by a cow that was not Joséphine.

He considers also, now, the divisions between persons and acts that the Dutch judges were trying to gauge, and all the interactions between individuals and groups that rained such hell down on Congo; and feels that he'd quail under the complexity of it all, were it not for this comforting sensation of cool sheets; which, he reckons, any human person might appreciate touching their body.

But how can one ever be certain about these matters? These matters that assume universality among human beings . . . might he just as well assume kinship with those pigs that he eviscerated at Weill Viandes? He knows one thing, though: he's not Rusyo, and not Recognition either. Whatever they are, and it's probably quite different in each case . . . *whatever I have done, whatever I've been accused of* – those people, I'm not like them. He weighs in his mind, all the same, the nature of likenesses, and wonders if the elders at his initiation ceremony were right after all, about the danger of copies.

Is Recognition really in Andalusia, living a false life in a fortress full of former missionaries, working as a cook, like Schoonraad said? It seems utterly impossible on the surface of things, but Manu's aware, well enough aware by now, that deeper down the world can act in strange ways, its chains of causation moving with all the mystery of magma in the bowels of the earth. What's Recognition calling himself now, he wonders? Brother Something, probably.

He imagines him limping along the sunlit battlements of his fastness, friary, abbey – what did Schoonraad call it? – on the way back to its kitchen, a bunch of onions in his hand as he plans what he needs to say next to his hosts in order for them to keep believing in his story.

And then his thoughts turn to where someone else might be: Edith. Probably head down over a pile of books, at the library of her university in Ohio. Forgiving her departure and silence (was there ever anything to forgive?), he pictures her fondly, eyes shadowed by too much study, perhaps doubting whether she can make her grade, just as he used to doubt whether he could pass his flying exams.

Chapter 14

Over the next six months, he works hard – on the farm and on the Dakota. Papa, who's taking a lot of pills – sleeping pills, pills for blood pressure, pills for what he mysteriously terms 'other illness' – describes manual work as the best medicine that someone like Manu could possibly have, and Manu reckons he's right.

He learns to drive the tractor and how to pull behind it the double-action cutaway harrow. He learns about the potato harvest, about earlies and main crops and rotation. He learns about ploughing and ridging, about sowing and spraying with dithane. He learns about clamps. He learns about seeding on wooden trays, in the polythene tunnels on the greensward.

He learns about packing in burlap bags. He learns about blight and black leg and brown rot and ring rot. He learns about scurf and mosaic. He learns about skin finish and rust spots and slugs.

He learns to distinguish between different varieties of potato, able to pitch them in his hands, telling at a glance from the texture of the skin.

He learns about trueness to type and frequency of eyes. He learns about the influence of light on yield and that the object of tillage is to increase it. He learns that the best distance to plant apart is sixty centimetres.

He walks among the kneeling pickers, hired just for the harvest fortnight, many of them immigrants, and learns how to manage them. He waits at the farmhouse while Papa makes trips into Ypres to see his doctor. Thinking of Edith, in this period, more often than Anke, he listens to the pair of collared doves that clatter under the eaves of the farmhouse, flitting between there and the dovecote proper.

In the evenings, he dons overalls and helps Papa to restore the plane in the barn, piece by piece. It seems an unending job, full of difficulties, but it's so good for the head, this screwing-in of new spark plugs or wielding of the arc welder: it produces when touching metal a sparky orange light, but left to burn alone is the sharpest blue, like Papa's eyes used to be, though they're dimmer now, Manu reckons.

Papa still has the old cassette player he used to bring into the cockpit when they flew together. He puts on his Beatles albums in the barn, almost getting through the whole catalogue. His favourite song nowadays is 'Revolution' rather than 'The Fool on the Hill' – because, he says, you get grumpier the nearer you are to death, less willing to accept more bullshit, as he puts it. He sings along loudly, nonetheless, to the chorus about how it's going to be all right, and sometimes Manu joins in.

There's a lot to do. They have to crane in two second-hand engines, rebuild the cockpit and make a variety of repairs to the fuselage, with plenty of engineering compromises – *pis allers*, as Papa terms them – along the way.

Now and then, as the two of them work away, Papa wheezes heavily, sometimes having to go and lie on the grease-stained old sofa in the barn, clutching his ulcerated stomach. The old British bomb, he tells him one evening, is right under this sofa, so if it does go off, 'I shall rise to heaven like a pasha ascending.'

'What is it you want now, Manu?', Papa then asks.

'To go back,' he says, sure of that now.

'Congo?'

He shakes his head. 'Entebbe. There's nothing left for me in Congo.'

'Quite right. Home is where you turn to, not where you're from.'

'But I don't know how.'

'You'll work it out.' Papa coughs so much that Manu worries that he's going to vomit. 'Oh my,' Papa says, waving a hand at the long cardboard box in one corner of the barn, 'Looks like I'll be in that thing sooner than I was thinking.'

Manu asks Papa what he means and is shocked by the answer, which is that the long cardboard box is a coffin, even if it looks more like something in which goods would be delivered. Manu tells him it's time to stop working and helps him – Papa's body is pencil-thin now – back to the house, where Manu makes him some supper, and they watch the news on the television, sitting with trays on their laps.

During this meal, Manu demands, 'So what's wrong with you, then? Why are you coughing so much? And why have you got a coffin in the barn?'

Papa just shrugs and says: 'When I was a young man I was a smoker and, well, it's played havoc with my lungs. And that coffin's saving me a few euros. I saw this ad in the paper that talked about how expensive funerals were – going out in a cardboard box felt very sensible, so I thought I'd buy ahead.'

Within a year of Manu's arrest at Schiphol – during which his sleep is still much troubled by bad dreams, despite the relative peace of daily life at the farm – he becomes a Belgian citizen. This is achieved through a series of bogus formalities that would be termed corruption in another country. Belgium might be about number 15 in an index which ranks countries by their perceived levels of corruption and Uganda about number 151, but everyone knows, Papa says, that those lists are all bull.

'I'd trust a Ugandan businessman over a Belgian lawyer any day,' he says.

Nationalisation as a Belgian citizen happens with the help of the mayor of Ypres, who's an old schoolfriend of Papa's; and, Manu suspects, possibly a former lover. Mayor Perse tells him that if Papa adopts him, naturalisation will follow, and he aids the old pilot in filling out, not entirely truthfully, the myriad of necessary forms.

After this is done, Papa explains that he has informed Mayor Perse of Manu's real life story, including the business of his escape from the court. He assures him that the mayor can be trusted . . . 'as if he were myself'. But as Manu sits next to Papa in the pickup on the way back from Ypres, worrying about the old man's erratic driving, he wonders what that would mean in his own case, which feels more like a collection of personalities than a single self.

He takes Papa's surname and becomes Adamu Chénal, *réfugié orphelin que M. Chénal a sauvé de Congo déchiré par la guerre*, as it's put to the authorities. A refugee orphan that M. Chénal saved from war-torn Congo. Acting a role; but what could be more real than the official description?

After he has his new passport, Manu sleeps a little more peacefully and his inner life becomes less disturbed, but he still harbours a suspicion that there's something else awaiting him in the future, something that will, one day – like the *erg scherp* knife, with which one of his former selves used to cut out intestines – tear open the past and allow it to come tumbling into the present.

The improvement in his official status coincides with a deterioration in the physical state of his protector. For as time goes by, Papa's 'other illness' discloses itself more truthfully as AIDS. He grows so weak that Manu has to help him out of the bath, putting his arms round his skinny white ribs and lifting him up. There are lots of visits to hospital in Ypres, but he's too far gone for the doctors to do much good.

On the way back from one of these hospital visits, Papa chooses a route that briefly brings them alongside the Leperlee, a canalised river that flows into the Yser at Fort Knokke. Manu (now driving himself, Papa being too feeble) parks the pickup by the river when Papa tells him to pull over. They get out, Manu helping Papa to a bench at a spot where there are high, grey houses on the other side but a green, willow-veiled bank on theirs. It's almost dusk when Papa informs him that he's going to die very soon.

The two of them sit in silence, watching a barge pass by, the reassuring clank of its diesel engine oddly adding to the tranquillity of the moment – which is anyway soon broken by one of Papa's coughing fits, loud enough to startle a moorhen out from some weeds.

'I could do with a rest from all this hacking, anyhow,' he says, when he's done.

Manu doesn't know what to say, sitting there like someone in a trance as Papa tells him that he has arranged to be buried on his own land.

His face is very pale now, like he's already a shadow in the living world, one whose visage Manu fears that he will soon begin to forget, like those other faces of loved ones – his parents and sister, Don Javier, even Cogan – all of which, against the best efforts of the will, have indeed begun to resist exact definition in the mind's eye, just as he countenanced while walking down that fancy avenue – Avenue Louise, was it? – on the way between Matongé and the Hotel Papejan. The dead go away like smoke, squeaking under a door.

'Buried on the farm?' Manu asks in bewilderment.

'It's legal; I checked with my friend the mayor. The law on burial in your own plot is quite clear.'

'I don't want to think about you dying.'

'I *am* going to, silly boy, and it's best we think about what happens when I do. Look, even when I said goodbye to you in Entebbe, I knew I was going to die, so I have made preparations.'

'That cardboard coffin?'

'It's perfectly sensible – biodegradable, of course!'

'What do you want me to do?'

'I want you to dig a pit with the digger and put me in it, like we did with the cow from the expo.'

'Where?' Manu can hardly believe what they are discussing.

'I don't mind. Not too near the river, though. You'll get the digger stuck. Maybe near where we buried the cow. Not too near though!'

'Why not be buried in a churchyard, properly?'

'I don't believe in God any more, at least I think I don't, but he does keep pulling on me a bit. Besides, it could draw too much attention. You might be legal now, Manu, but we still have to be careful.'

'I don't care. I don't see how I will be able to live in Belgium if you're not here.'

'You'll get along fine. I have left the farm to you.'

Another gift. Manu wonders if this comes with a reciprocal obligation, as he has suspected in the past of the other freight dogs, so he says: 'I'm grateful, but why, Papa?'

'Why? Don't be an imbecile – it's because I have no one else. And I have always admired you.'

'But . . .'

'You're ready for some good luck, that's the most of it. You've learned the means of earning a livelihood, whether as a pilot or something else.'

'We haven't finished the plane.'

'No, but you will. Watch out for metal fatigue in the nose.'

Manu promises to get the Dakota flightworthy.

'And what about flying our big old bird, then? I've already got it a call sign! You know you said you wanted to go back to Entebbe?'

He's mentioned this idea to Papa a few more times now.

'Yes.'

'Well maybe that's possible. I've done a bit of homework on your behalf . . . I spoke to our local airstrip manager and filed draft flight plans in my name; they're to Entebbe with enough stops en route. If you ever want to activate them in your own name, the door is open, but you'll have to find a way of sorting your licence. Maybe get it sent from Uganda? Actually, if I'm well enough tomorrow, let's go to the airfield at Moorsele and you can meet some of the people there.'

He is well enough, just about, and the visit to Moorsele goes well, too. In the pickup on the way back – ruthlessly practical in his conversation now – Papa announces, breathing hard: 'You'll have to get the plane transported to the airfield, and that's not going to be easy. But there's plenty of money for it. Sell the farm if you want to, I don't mind about that – maybe you'll want to buy one in Uganda, set up your own place? Anyway, whatever you decide, my friend the mayor will help you.'

Chapter 15

It happens one morning. The doves are cooing outside Papa's bedroom window, and now the breath in the old man's chest is slowing, stint by stint, as his illness comes to a terminus. In his own anguish, Manu grips Papa's hand so hard it makes the old man cry out in weak protest. His last words are, consequently: 'Don't do that, Manu' – in essence the same cautionary advice that Papa has been meting out to him ever since they first met.

Afterwards, Manu shuts his friend's eyes with careful fingers, thinking it's more than anyone did for his family. Nor for Cogan, who went to his grave with a single, frozen eye staring just as starkly as it did at the moment of his death in a Datsun, the other being as closed as the gates of heaven.

Sighing, he fetches the cassette player from the barn, puts on 'Revolution' – lays his head down on the pillow next to Papa's, so it's like they are listening together. Long after the song has finished, and after Manu seems to have slept for a while, he goes downstairs and calls the mayor, and together they work out a suitable day for the burial that Papa has requested.

When that day comes, as instructed, Manu uses the mini-excavator to dig a pit – like the one in which they buried the cow from the trade show. The cardboard coffin has the consistency of an eggbox. Quite a few tears fall as he and Mayor Perse manoeuvre it, with far less ceremony than should obtain, into the hole; they're lucky to have the help of a few mystified labourers who are working on the farm at the time.

Manu's lonely in the months after Papa is buried, working in the barn on the Dakota now that the potato harvest is finished. Memories fasten their talons into him once again, scratching across the roof of the barn, but he tries to fortify himself with notions of grit, pluck, hardihood. The countervailing memories are made worse when the battlefield tourists turn up, in parties or sometimes alone. First World War tours of sites on the farm make up a large part of its income, so these people can't just be turned away. Manu is used to it, having accompanied Papa when he gave the tours, but it's different doing it on his own.

These visitors are probably good for Manu, nonetheless, as he sees so few other people during this period, apart from occasional tense encounters with neighbouring farmers. He tells the tourists things he has read in the red-bound history books that he's found in Papa's bedroom, whose damp, curling pages are full of inky black-and-white photographs, including ones of the Messines Ridge itself.

The tourists are more than surprised to see a black-faced farmer in West Flanders, some being unwilling to accept the substitution of an African for the white son of the soil they were expecting on making the booking. A few treat Manu very rudely as he shows them the holes, pillboxes and pieces of weaponry, and the remains of the old German foxhole still covered with rusty barbed wire.

Occasionally the visitors are themselves German and he tries to mollify them by using another word for this cavity that he's learned from Papa's books: *Schützenloch*, slit-trench. With Francophones, he tries out, as well as *tranchée-abri,* the marginally less inspiring *trou individuel*, individual hole (yes, that's my situation, he thinks); but this multilingualism he has developed, building on earlier facility, wins him scant favour. They're all just judgmental *wazungu*, when all is said and done, to whom he's all *schwarz*, *noir*, negatively implied, he rants internally once they've left, feeling racist himself even as the loaded words repeat in his head . . . The tourists' only half-whispered implication of a black Belgian farmer just being wrong and a white one somehow right he hates, wishing there was some way out of the impasse, the *trou* as he says to himself again, but knowing already that's also kind of wrong, because are holes are black too.

Like those ones Don Javier used to speak of, in his God-filled forays into astrophysics? It's as if the whole conceptual structure of western language, science too, is against him; that's the kind of shape his thoughts take after these tours, as he sits at the kitchen table drinking Belgium's best beer, leaving only the sulky realisation, like the foam at the bottom of the glass, that it's all a job for someone cleverer than me.

Well, maybe, but he still has his own voice and it can do things. For even the most suspicious visitors are amazed when standing at the edge of the great craters opened by exploded mines – in which, he has read, and eloquently tells them, German troops lay dead or wandered round the margins of the holes . . . stunned, dazed, horror-stricken. It's as if his vivid description of this disorientation stuns the dark tourists out of their own entrenched selves, forcing them to recognise the universal plight of a traumatised person, a human being, irrespective of one's group (*tribu*, *gruppe*, *kundi* – what horrible words they are, he feels).

Kind, he contradictorily thinks, during one of these tours, and Joséphine comes duly to mind, suddenly so much more exact, so much more individual in remembrance than life that he almost jumps out of the *bottes de caoutchouc froid* of Papa's that he's adopted for these tours, these cold Wellington boots that feel heavier with each step through the muddy earth.

The edges of the craters have the same awful verticality that he had seen flying along the edges of the Rift. Sometimes, as he's giving his spiel to the tourists, pointing at the rust-stained metal sticking out of the sides of the pits, he has to turn away, imagining his own body being flung down like the merest apostrophe (such as Don Javier used to correct, especially on its), into one of these holes, the precipitous descent and heightening terror only redeemed by a curious suspension that halts the plunge just before he hits the bottom.

One night, this moment of near-death creeps into Manu's dreams. It wakes him in the early hours, and after lying awake for a while he goes downstairs to find some of Papa's sleeping tablets.

He knows that they're in a chest of drawers. The drawer sticks halfway, then reluctantly opens fully to reveal handkerchiefs, odd keys, cardboard or foil packets of pills of various types. There's a smell of mothballs, too. What Manu notices, though, are the black plastic parts of the recording device that he stole from the journalist outside the court, about which he'd totally forgotten. He now remembers that he'd put them in the drawer himself, the morning after arriving at Papa's farm.

He takes out the parts of the recorder, fits them together and presses PLAY. But there's nothing to hear, just static. He foresees pouring a furious, leapfrogging story into his own ears, into those of others too, perhaps listeners full of suspicion, just as he always is, these days, of himself.

He presses RECORD and speaks into the little grille of the microphone: '*C'est la fin de la nuit et je viens de trouver l'appareil d'enregistrement que j'ai volé à cet espèce de pisse-copie blanc.*' He listens to what he's said a couple of times – 'it's the end of the night and I've just found the recording device I stole from that white hack journalist' – but doesn't get any further, feeling incredibly self-conscious (despite there being no one to listen) about 'speaking of myself' in this manner, in the first person, with a voice mediated by technology; especially when types like that felt so free to write such lies about him. And as he clicks STOP he feels like he's back before the judges, and will be evermore.

The following evening, just in from harrowing the fields, darkness already having fallen, he receives a phone call.

'Manu,' says a voice, one that he's relieved is not that of another battlefield visitor, or worse, some spectre from his past, come to hunt him down.

'Mayor Perse here, I've got good news for you.'

'What's that?' Manu says suspiciously, resting a hand on the wobbly banister of the stairs.

'I've made some enquiries – very discreetly – and I'm delighted to say that the Spanish extradition case against you was dropped . . . six months ago! They have lost faith in their main witness, that chap called Recognition.'

'Really?' This is such good fortune that he can't believe it, though the next part seems believable enough.

'However, the charges of assault and absconding still stand in the files of the Dutch national constabulary. But there's no sense, at least so far as I can find out, in which European authorities are actively looking for you; I suppose it was reckoned that, given the original case against you has collapsed, the matter no longer has urgency; or perhaps there simply aren't the resources to look for you with any energy. Often the case.'

'Thank you, Mr Mayor, for letting me know.'

While he's sure the mayor would not betray him, Monsieur Perse's kindness makes Manu feel peculiar, like this is yet another entry in his mounting account of debts to *wazungu*, as he figures it. He grips the banister harder, wondering if he's ever going to escape such traps, mental and emotional and historical, that entangle people in relations of power.

'My pleasure. I know Max would have wanted me to tell you. I miss him so much, Manu . . . Adamu, I suppose I should say!'

The mayor gives a little laugh about his joke on Manu's new name, and Manu says thank you again. Then the mayor asks about his plans for the future. 'Max said you wanted to go back to Africa, in that jalopy of a plane, is that right?'

'Yes – I think that is what I want to do.'

'Selling the farm?'

'Yes, I'm afraid so.'

'Well, let me know if there is any way I can help. I'm always here.'

The phone goes down at Mayor Perse's end. Afterwards, one of Manu's hands is still gripping the banister, static hissing in the ear to which his other hand continues to hold the phone. He stands like this as if he's a statue, looking at the corn dolly in the chipped mug on the windowsill that he first noticed when he came here.

Months' more dust have covered its straw head and body since he last noted its presence, but this fragile little figure seems to him, right now, just as full of protective magic as any amulet he saw back home. He finally puts the phone down and crosses to the window, picks up the scratchy figure. Holding it, he looks up out of the window into the cluster of stars now hanging over the farm and thanks them for what the mayor has told him.

And then, perhaps because such amulets can summon bad as much as they call down good, Recognition gathers into the compass of his thought. Hope that bastard is, at the very least, pulling up onions for the rest of his whole fucking life! And weeping evermore. Unlikely, but Manu knows now the horrid wonder that a man's own soul might become, when examined by himself.

Welcome as it is, it's not the mayor's news which gives Manu the final impetus to start planning his return to Uganda, but a documentary that he happens to catch, a few weeks later, on Papa's old television. The documentary's subject is the resurgence of the Rwandan economy in the years since the genocide. Mentioning a joint US-Rwandan project to pipe methane from the depths of Lake Kivu, the camera cuts to a familiar face, subtitled as 'Rwandan Minister for Wealth Creation'. This person is saying: 'The objective of this project is to encourage foreign investment into the country and assist in the environmentally friendly reduction of wood-based fuel in cooking.'

The face of the speaker, to Manu's great bewilderment, is that of Major Rusyo. Dressed in a suit and tie, he has clearly retired from the army. Manu watches the rest of the programme, which outlines other impressive developments in Rwanda (implying en route, as Europeans so often like to say, that too much of Africa has been economically immobilised since colonial times, or even gone backwards); but Rusyo doesn't appear again. Manu turns off the television, feeling angry that this man, who's done him so much harm, is obviously thriving, then goes for a walk to settle himself, trying to stop hate rising in him like the fiery springs that feed volcanoes.

He passes through the farm gates and into the field where Papa and the expo cow were buried, at the edge of which a stand of oaks has released a volley of acorns. They crunch under his feet. Thinking of Papa's mollifying spirit, and the more troubled ones of Cogan and the other pilots – who Manu now hopes are all now moving in pure air, beyond the bounds of sky, in some super-ethereal version of the Gauntlet – he does his best to think of Rusyo with a generous spirit.

For surely even Rusyo, like Manu himself, and the whole choir of peoples who live by the Great Lakes under the shadow of violence, deserve understanding, some kind of communion, however uneasy, having been through collective horrors – all now become formless, unable to be pinned down in time and space, even though they happened. Committed by particular hands, in particular places, on particular days, they happened all right.

This day by now is waning, following the familiar course of all days. The whole flat, *polder* landscape of West Flanders, which once rang with the war that was meant to end all wars (as Europeans also like to say), is being ravished by a winter sunset.

As he crosses the yard on his way back, his eye is caught by a large, pinkish worm, seeking to nourish its blind life. It's wriggling across the corrugated concrete with unrivalled fury, guessing its way home (maybe the field from which Manu has just come?), but is frustrated by the lumps of mud and shrunken, half-rotten potatoes that obstruct its path. It gives him pause, watching that worm struggle: he half wants to tread it underfoot, end its travails like an angel of mercy, half wants to cheer it on to conquering triumph. But he doesn't do either, and knows anyway that the worm is just a self-curated mime of his own being, that one who must go now, however complicated it will be, whatever the challenges he'll face.

Chapter 16

There will, in fact, be so many obstacles before Manu even gets into the Dakota that he almost loses heart. For it takes more than a few months to sell the farm, despite the assistance of Mayor Perse, and to get the old plane through exacting formalities of air-safety certificates, transit visas, other difficulties. He also has to have his pilot licence sent from Uganda, as Papa suggested: that wager-won, acetate-covered document that he strived so hard to get and which has brought him, perhaps, equal measures of risk and reward.

But how, in the end, are those two quantities to be measured? They certainly, he's sure of this now at least, cannot be totted up like the sums he used to do in pencil under Don Javier's instruction back in Bukavu, either to be retained or erased depending on a right or wrong answer.

In securing his pilot's licence he's helped by Suraj, the Indian trader for whom he did so many flights. When he rings him – he doesn't know who else to ask – Suraj, accommodating as always, says no problem, then tells Manu that his Banyamulenge boys, David and Matthias, have managed to hold on to The Passenger and are running it very well, so far as he can make out.

Suraj has some news about Evgeny, too. He tells Manu that the Russian's return to Dubai didn't work out after his release by 'busybods in Britain', as Suraj terms the British authorities that hauled up Evgeny on a money-laundering charge. Suraj explains how, having lost nearly everything, including his wife, Evgeny relocated to Congo and set up a passenger airline there. But during a flight that he himself piloted, to Kisangani, the plane crashed, with no survivors.

One theory, says Suraj, is that a live pygmy crocodile which was in someone's luggage that day might have escaped, causing passengers to surge in panic to the front of the aircraft, putting it into a hard-to-recover dive. 'Bad way to go,' says Suraj, 'but I guess he'd lost practice in flying, spending too much time on *biznes* . . . like I always said, Manu, Cogan was definitely the better pilot.'

The eventual arrival of the licence that Suraj has winkled out of the Ugandan Civil Aviation Authority, and kindly sent by DHL to the farm, throws Manu into a panic: a fear that the Manu Kwizera whose name is on it and the Adamu Chénal who now owns the plane, and has a Belgian passport, will be fingered as one and the same, in too tight a circle. But, thinking about his own experiences, he remembers that the moments when a flying licence is checked (surprisingly rarely) and the more customary moments when a passport is checked (on passing through immigration) are quite separate. And anyway, there's no immigration control at Moorsele airfield, so far as he could tell on his visit there with Papa.

He deems it wise, indeed imperative, to take the Dakota for a test flight, and gets permission to do this from the officials at Moorsele, who are intrigued as the place is generally used only for parachuting and leisure flights. But they all knew of Papa and his project, which has been holed up in the barn for so long, and they remember Manu from his visit there with Papa, a couple of days before he died.

With all this in hand, Manu organises for the plane to be mounted on a low-loader and taken to the strip at Moorsele – a difficult and (as Papa predicted) expensive procedure. Albeit somewhat mitigated by the shortness of the journey, which is only about fifteen kilometres, all this is made more difficult than it might otherwise have been by the fact of a December snowfall in Flanders.

Doing the pre-flight checks, that familiar litany which Cogan taught him so long ago, Manu recalls his Banyamulenge boys, whom he imagines chucking out the last, drunk customers and sweeping up broken glass at The Passenger. It is, perhaps, a case of how, at times of extreme stress – will this old thing, the dream of my dead friend, so much repaired, actually get into the air? – the mind switches attentional focus so the executive task that needs to be accomplished can actually happen.

These thoughts make Manu realise, anyway, as he opens up the engine, frees the brakes and (aligning the aircraft with the runway centre, its outer edges banked with light snowfalls) begins the take-off roll for the test flight, that he needs to let the guys in The Passenger know he's coming.

No time to think more about all that, though, as he moves the throttle levers forwards and the fine old bird, patched up yet still magnificent, trembling like there's signs of trouble . . . just how it is with old planes, Manu says to himself, half convinced, as he checks successive decisions against the instruments . . . picks up revs and speed across the 500-odd metres of the take-off and, lumbering slightly – bit of a taildragger this one, rough in response to controls, but there's not too much to worry about is there, *what about that metal fatigue Papa mentioned*? – lifts its nose and 7,650 kilograms, the weight of the empty plane, into the winter sky.

The plane climbs at a positive rate, altitude and speed still increasing, and he soon has enough confidence to retract the landing gear and rise to cruising height, not too high as this is just a few go-arounds, and he needs to keep to the flight plan that's been filed; but high enough to reveal the snowy landscape below, its frieze of white and green, interrupted by black roads and clumps of town or village.

There are certainly niggling problems, the engine's spluttering a bit – are the carburettors still clogged? – and there's a slight smell of fuel in the cockpit, but it's too late now. And everything seems, doesn't it, to be going OK now?

He gives a whoop of joy and banks the aircraft – all those nuts and bolts and struts and spars over which they spent so many hours and so much care – in the direction of Papa's farmhouse, having to circle a little until he finds its thatched roof half laden with snow. He resists the temptation to do the *pantsula* over it; not sure the Dakota could take that, but despite this nervousness, it's a pure joy to be back in the air again.

This is, he's suddenly aware, the very first flight that he has made for his own purposes. Rather than carrying out orders, he has made his own plan and realised it, clasping the clouds, it seems like, as his own. He's at last no longer in the allegiance-less world of the freight dogs; instead he's in his own world, master of his fate, even if the body of the Dakota is shuddering like Joséphine shaking off a fly. It's an odd mixture of feelings, all right, like he's finally killing a beast held in view for years, at the same time trying to find (in a sunset? it hasn't come yet, there above Flanders) something to replace that homestead torched at Pendele.

For all that, on the way back to Moorsele a few tears come, a whole tide of held-back emotion in fact, as he imagines how wonderful it would have been for Papa to have been below, looking up when he flew over the farmhouse; or, better still, to be beside him in the cockpit now. His mind traces the features, too, of a more extensive fantasy – some idea, impossible in reality, that he could have been in authentic solidarity with the freight dogs, rather than the asymmetric union he now knows it was. What they did every day was wrong, and they all ran their bodies right into the ground.

As for Anke, he has (against his own past conjecture) almost forgotten her; but how could we know them, those shapes of the unfinished past that might throw themselves again across our mental path?

There are, of course, a few technical difficulties with the plane to sort out after the test flight, but he has the cash now to get those fixed by maintenance engineers at one of the companies at the airfield. Mostly old-timers, they tell him they're delighted to work on the kind of craft, now vintage, such as they first worked on as youngsters in training, for Sabena or KLM, or the Belgian Air Force.

So different, these people, with an international outlook from their experiences in aviation, to the racist farmers who are his neighbours, or the tourists who come to the farm. The retired engineers help him, too, with the business of refiling a flight plan from Moorsele to Entebbe in his own name. EBMO to EBB, he's amused to discover, but it's quite complicated to work out, with new circumstances demanding different fuel stops, at locations en route, from the ones Papa put in the draft.

When the repairs are finally done and the flight plan is sorted, thinking of Papa's suggestion that he might buy a farm some-where in Uganda – there's still more than enough money left for that – he loads the pickup with as much agricultural equipment as he can and drives it to the airfield. He makes another couple of trips like this, adding in seed potatoes, thinking that he might be able to plant these in Ugandan soil – plant 'Irish', as he remem-bers potatoes are called there.

He doesn't have much idea what to expect when he reaches Entebbe; but has by now taken the precaution of letting David and Matthias know that he's on his way, and will again be arriving at The Passenger on a Christmas Eve . . . Of course, they're delighted (as well as being very surprised) to be hearing from him, after all this time of being apart.

Having found his satphone number in an old address book of Papa's, he also rang Brigadier (now General, he discovers) Faithful to give him the same news, and more specifically to ask a favour.

'You!' said Faithful, once Manu explained who he was. 'I've been feeling guilty about you for ages. Obviously, I heard the reports about your arrest, as I was following what happened to the missile launcher, but at the time I was scratching my head to know what to do, as the reasons for your arrest were not related to Uganda or the UPDF. But then you disappeared! Where are you now?'

Manu told him, and Faithful said: 'That's a good story, and I should thank you for what you did for us; but what do you want to do now?'

'To come back to Uganda . . . and this is the reason for my call. I was hoping you might get me cleared in terms of landing permits and a visa.'

'Why do you need a visa? You became a Ugandan citizen, didn't you? I seem to recall Cogan telling me that.'

'I had to change my name here, became a Belgian.'

'Ha! So what're you called now?'

It felt strange telling him, and then relaying the call sign and other information about the Dakota that needed the landing permit. But he was determined to do it, this flight home as he thought of it, as much by the book as he could, despite the difficulty of the mismatch of name and nationality between his passport and flying licence.

As he took down the details, Faithful didn't seem that surprised about any of it, which was perhaps a simple matter of age. But there also sounded in his tone, as he asked Manu a few more questions over the crackly line, a sense that here was someone else who'd been in conflict situations, who'd sat in the saddle of contingencies for many years, just understood that such turns of events happened; and also that the decisions and emotional trajectory of adventurous individuals – people like himself, people like Manu – did not occur in an expected or natural pattern.

Or maybe it's rather a mutual understanding that peace lives nowhere, not even in death. 'Nta ho bucyikera n'ikuzimu baraganya,' Manu thinks, as General Faithful continues speaking, which proverbial declaration in Kinyarwanda amounts to the same. Meaning that it wasn't finished, there was always another last outrage to be revenged, by another outrageous solution; but perhaps, too, that the dreadful calculus of revenge could never be the answer, which would leave only the always inadequate mechanisms of reconciliation and, at best, a respectful reckoning of history.

The Banyamulenge boys at The Passenger had come out of conflict, too, but they had not been so long in it, and so deliberately (for Manu was able to admit this now, on his own account), as had he and Faithful. There was also, under the exchange of words between these two men, younger and older, an awkward feeling that while their shared experience of the past might make the present easier to live with, problems would continue to manifest, in unexpected ways, within the ambit of their region (unexpected ways, new ways, but sometimes also reformations of old archetypes), and perhaps even between the pair of them, too; for it was Faithful, after all, who'd sent Manu on the mission to Amsterdam which had caused him so much trouble.

Faithful seemed to acknowledge this at one point by saying: 'I just want to say again Manu, I'm so sorry about what happened to you – it wasn't right.'

But the event of his arrest was, by now, just another backwash of the past in Manu's mind; he didn't blame the old soldier. As they continued talking, Manu in the farmhouse in Flanders, Faithful in his office in Kampala, or at his house by the lakeshore in Garuga (Manu presuming one or other of these locations, seeing in his mind's eye the brick of a satphone in the general's hand), there was no consciousness of the dominance that he'd sometimes experienced before in his encounters with Faithful.

They also spoke a little of the current situation in the Great Lakes. Manu mostly felt these days that he wanted to disclaim any link (though he knew well enough that there was one, whether he liked it or not) to the world of politics and power there. The upshot of this part of their dialogue – cheerless enough in its way, and however deplorable in the progressive view of the NGO people who used to come into The Passenger – was that there would be no resolution, all very perfect; only, at best, a new equilibrium.

Or as Faithful put it: 'East Congo's still in a tug of war, just now it's lots of little strings rather than big ropes.'

At the close of this conversation, almost offhandedly, as an aside or irrelevance (but he was a cunning old dog), the general also mentioned, and in a more ebullient tone, that Edith was back in Uganda.

'She finally finished her studies in the US and came back here. Wants to make documentaries, which seems to be a very expensive business. As if studying in the US wasn't dear enough!'

The news of Edith's return lifted Manu's heart more than

he thought might ever have been possible. In receipt of this information – it hit his synapses like blinding light – he at once told Faithful that he hoped to see her.

'Of course you do,' Faithful chuckled, seeming to understand, and then said goodbye.

Standing under the beams of the farmhouse, having put down the telephone, Manu's eye was caught by the sight of a crow on the top of a telephone pole – in fact, it was one of the series of posts on the lawn which supported the wire down which this conversation, this dialogue he'd just had, connected to the local and the national Belgian exchange, before being beamed up into space and bouncing down from a satellite into Faithful's handset in Uganda. The crow's head and open beak were pitching up and down as it cawed.

It perversely seemed to Manu, as he watched, that this crow was trying to hoist his own freight – all the load of humankind, perhaps – and failing. Of course, he knew there was no reason at all why a crow, of all creatures, should bear that weight. Better it lifted its wings and fanned its flight elsewhere, with some more natural goal in view, unable to hinder human crimes, or mend the monstrous times that humans caused for all.

His own monstrous times – so he hoped, throwing himself on his mattress that night – were over at last; but just as hope in that matter sprung, he heard another bird. A pair of owls, in fact, calling to each other outside, roosting in Papa's poplars probably. And he just didn't know whether to make, of their *hulule, hulule*, a good omen or bad – settling in the end, as he finally dozed off, for going at life as he'd learned, show of omens or not.

VI

The Deconfliction Zone

January 2007

The football landed on the tin roof of the veranda, making Manu look up from his accounts, which he was writing in pencil in an old exercise book. A spider's web, under the eaves of the bungalow, caught his eye. Very big spider, its mottled thorax the size of his own fingertip, and a large web, too – moving as the spider shifted position.

As the ball rolled off the roof and some of the kids came to collect it, he thought about everything that had transpired in the past year or so . . . bowing his head over the sums again, but no longer really concentrating. A lot had happened in Uganda itself since he'd left, and in the Great Lakes generally; but he was happy to let history pass him by nowadays, content to breathe his own air only.

His homecoming was not entirely favourable. In the end, though most of the flight was uneventful, the Dakota didn't make it to Entebbe, crash-landing in some hills near the western Ugandan town of Mbarara after one and then the other engine failed. He survived all right, but there was no chance of getting the plane back into service.

He put down his pencil, flashes of the flight coming back to him. The sequence of revs and magnetos, the business of refuelling at different stops, of keeping the yoke steady, pressing pedals, companionless and uncertain of success, was exhausting . . . It was a bumpy flight, and uncomfortable – cold in Europe, hot when he got to the tropics, as the heater and the gasper vents weren't working properly, despite his and Papa's best efforts. Fear came when the engines finally guttered, the plane slewing over green hills, more fear when he was pulling the throttle rearwards and lifting the nose cone to mitigate impact; then came the horror of impact itself, weak metalwork at the front – just as Papa warned – pushing into the cockpit, narrowly missing his own body.

The controlled way in which he'd hit the looming hillside – using its slope to absorb momentum – was the only reason he'd survived. It could easily have been otherwise, and he knew that he had his training, those seven missions to heaven, to thank for it not being so. That and his own determination (now and then he allowed himself congratulation on this) had carried him through; against probability, against possibility even, he had powerfully delineated his own objective and reached it, give or take 300-odd kilometres, the distance from Mbarara to Entebbe. Yet still he had the occasional sense of being a translated man, a double man, or even triple – part in Congo, part in Uganda, part in Europe; for, after all, that continent too was in the magma of his make-up now.

The children bundled past the veranda, fighting over the football like puppies. Manu watched them tumble, remembering when he'd seen – joined in with – a similar, informal, pitchless game on the beach back there in Entebbe, with the Banyamulenge boys.

Astonished when he really did return, making a first trip from Mbarara to Entebbe – looking at him like someone come back from the dead, despite the warning call he'd given – David and Matthias were still running The Passenger on his behalf, splitting any profits; but his heart wasn't in that place any more: too many memories . . .

A memory he did hold, willingly kept, was one of Cogan's little origami sculptures that he found perched behind the bar on that trip to The Passenger: the winged man, it was.

Now he was here, in Mbarara, and it felt like a good place to be. Although definitively part of Uganda, it was also an interzone between Rwanda, Congo and Uganda itself, a place where refugees gathered; that was how he saw himself these days, though he knew well enough that others collected under that category had had an even worse time of it than he had. Aerially speaking, it was in the old deconfliction zone that he had flown through on one of his first flights with Cogan, on the main corridor in and out of Congo from Uganda.

The Dakota was now on the other side of the compound, beyond the football-playing kids. Its propellers were immobile and its undercarriage buckled, the two main wheels half crumpled into the hull, the tail wheel twisted like a broken leg. Beneath the wings, chickens were pecking about in the dust. Sunlight was bouncing off the riveted fuselage. On an engine cowling was painted, very neatly, in large black letters: GOOD FOOD WORLD CAFÉ.

Thinking perhaps of Aero Beach, he'd set up a restaurant in the old plane. Using some of Papa's money and fees owed him by General Faithful, who'd lived up to his name, he'd also bought land around the crash site, the local farmers being only too willing to sell. He'd built this concrete bungalow, a few mud-hut storehouses, a latrine and another concrete building that served as a kitchen and dormitory. Using the seedlings carried on the plane, he had planted potatoes in some nearby fields – fulfilling some of Papa's suggestion that he set up a farm on his own; though it was, in truth, a very modest affair, agriculturally a far cry from the glories of that expo in Brussels.

The restaurant was for tourists, mainly, on their way to or from seeing gorillas in Bwindi Impenetrable Forest. The so-called impenetrable forest, as Cogan once said. There was a party in tonight, an American family, so he'd better get moving.

The football that the children were kicking about flew through the air towards him, landing almost in his lap. He held it for a second, looking at it in wonderment. Then threw it back to them, their joyful, liquid voices resounding in his ears like the sound of his old, lost flute, or an echo of fairyland; the latter was a fanciful notion, despite the tranche of territory that his new homestead looked over actually being known locally as the Bachwezi valley, in honour of the Chwezi kings who once might have reigned here, in the days of legend of which his mother used to speak, that he now thought of as mainly nonsense, refuted by many historians, though not all. Their disputes (he had gone into this a little) created a division in his own mind about how he felt towards those old tales; but he was able to live with divisions these days, even those with a few townsfolk of Mbarara who spoke against him, referring to him as 'that weird man on the hill who locks children up in a plane'. This was laughably far from the truth, as it was hard to keep the kids out. Samuel in particular liked to go into the cockpit and mess about, reminding Manu of Cogan and Evgeny, those two overgrown children, when they showed him round a similar hulk at Aero Beach.

He'd got a new flute by now, a pale imitation of the one he used to have, made by a master flute-maker, but since the inadequate instrument lay beside him on a table on the veranda he picked it up, began playing an old air, just as if he were still as free as Joséphine and the other cattle, on a mountain top at sunset.

As he played – thinking of the pauses that came in the presently unsung words which commonly went with the tune – he heard Edith's voice calling: not the Edith of distant, idealised fantasy but the real Edith, who'd come from the city to join him once she heard from her father what had happened. It was a passionate reunion, but now her practical, insistent voice was shouting, 'Come on, will you, Manu? The visitors will be here in less than an hour. I can't get everything ready on my own!' She'd changed, was no longer the girl who didn't care about tomorrow.

They were not yet married, though this too was planned – a big affair in Kampala, if Edith's stepmother was to have her way. Putting down his flute, Manu went into the house to wash his hands, and don his apron and chequered chef's trousers, in order to prepare food for the tourists.

At around one the American family appeared, in a pearl-grey Toyota people carrier with a driver. They were very loud, full of valiant and victorious tales of trials undergone earlier in their safari (they'd been to Queen Elizabeth National Park as well as to Bwindi). Having greeted them, Manu organised one of the boys – Samuel – to get them sodas or beers as required, and they sat down next to him on the wicker benches that he'd procured for the veranda.

The family's name was Himmelman. The father was a compact, hirsute fellow who owned a chain of urology clinics in Texas (very different from Cogan, except perhaps for a slight grouchiness). The mother was one of those lovely, birdlike ladies whose smile alone might have carried her away from evil as fast as an express train.

There were two Miss Himmelmans, one blonde, one dark, Keren and Danielle, both wearing sunglasses and cosmetics. Unmarried New York professionals in their early thirties, he gathered: Keren ran a pet-grooming business, Danielle was a lawyer. There was also a son, Barry. He was some kind of financier, sharp as a porcupine's quill. Wearing the most expensive safari kit money could buy, he also sported the largest camera Manu had ever seen.

'We should have something on Wall Street called the Himmelman index,' said Barry, after telling Manu more details of supposed dangers experienced in the park and before, which included: a wheel falling off their vehicle and rolling down a hill; being charged at by a bull elephant and having to reverse at speed; and (when they first arrived in Entebbe) getting caught up in a political riot. 'An index of volatility in emerging economies.'

'Well, it was you kids who wanted to come here,' commented the father in gravelly tones. 'I've been coming to Africa for fifteen years, because of your mad mom and you children, and this year I just needed a break, guys. I actually wanted to go to the Amalfi coast again – that place in Italy where we dove in green pools off the cliffs when you were all little kids, before we got so safari bold.'

'Hotel Miramalfi!' chorused the daughters, two American songbirds migrated to a spot of East African hillside, surrounded by acacia and mopani trees, and a few acres of potatoes. 'But this meal in the aeroplane sounds fun, Dad,' said Danielle, cajoling him.

'Maybe,' he said.

'It will be!' said Manu, amused by this voluble bunch. 'Fish and chips OK?'

'Perfect,' said the dad.

'I'll see what I can do.'

Manu raised two fingers to his mouth and gave a shrill whistle. Leaving their football, the ragged boys and girls immediately ran to the other concrete building near the plane.

'Make Max's fish,' he called to them. 'And chips!'

Lights came on inside the building (it had no glass in its windows) and as the visiting party went towards the plane, the children lit gas burners and began cooking the food that Manu had prepared. They knew the drill by now.

In the old Dakota, the remaining passenger chairs had been rearranged in fours around communal wooden tables. Edith joined them, Manu poured more drinks – beers for the father and son, Diet Cokes for the mother and daughters – then began telling the Americans the story of how the plane they were inside of had ended up here, along with a little (not too much) of his own life story. He'd learned the importance of storytelling when showing those tourists round Papa's farm.

As Manu spoke, the visitors looked in wonder around the interior of the old aircraft; they seemed almost shocked by its basic, bare structure, and the metal-and-oil smells that still permeated it.

Later, a train of children began bringing in plates of fillets of crumbed fish and rough-cut fried potatoes, newly harvested from the surrounding fields.

The Himmelman son asked the kids their names as they put down the plates on the makeshift tables in the aircraft. They said Miriam and Michael, Vincent, Charity, Fidèle, Callixte, Patience, Roger and Samuel. Charity was a little older than the others, about sixteen maybe, the trauma of whatever she had experienced still showing a little in a stoop; whether of physical or psychological origin it was impossible to tell.

During the meal, Barry wielded his big camera and began taking photos.

The boy called Samuel – who had round and questioning

eyes, and a head so beautifully shaped that it would make any human in the whole world want to pay attention to every hair on it – asked the young American, 'Why is one part of your camera black and the other part grey?'

It was true: the main camera was the normal black, but the lens part was off-white, putty-grey.

The son said: 'Good question, and I bought it just to come here. Lenses contain glass which expands with heat, distorting images and this, it's the new Canon L series, stops the glass overheating, as white surfaces deter sunlight.'

A faint smell of piss wafted over from the latrine and Manu saw the financier's nostrils mushroom – ever so widely, as if the pleasant occasion of a meal had been robbed away in some still greater larceny than this basic reminder of other facts of the body besides ingestion.

The dad said, 'Sounds like bullshit to me, cameras have got along well enough being black for as long as I can remember.' He looked at the children crowding round. 'These can't all be your kids?'

'They're orphans from the war in Congo,' Edith said.

'Some were near this spot when I landed, they really spooked me, coming out of the maize like voodoo children,' Manu explained. 'More came later. Refugees, like I was once myself I suppose, and for them this *is* a place of refuge.'

'He's teaching them how to cook,' said Edith.

'Really?' said the blonde daughter, Keren.

'Yes, and to farm,' Manu said. 'I realised that the thing to do was to stress the value of work. When everything else has been taken away from you, you need to find something you can take pride in. And hospitality is what's most needed when people have lost their homes or been moved about against their will.'

'Don't play the martyr, Manu,' said Edith. 'It makes you sound like a dweeb.' This remark made the Americans laugh; they laughed even more when Edith explained that she'd picked up this word in Ohio.

'What about you?' the mum asked Edith. 'I hope you're not going to sit by the side of Manu, enabling him? I work in museums to avoid that with this old sourpuss.' Referring to her husband, who just gave a cryptic smile.

A little thrown, Edith replied, 'Well, my father always wanted me to go into politics, but I want to make documentaries, that's what I studied in my communications course at Ohio – tell the truth about this part of the world! – but, well, it's not easy here.'

'More interesting, though,' said the mum. 'I wish you the very best success.'

Manu decided that he liked this group of people. They had none of the fragility that some *wazungu* exhibited on coming to the restaurant in the plane – fretting about getting tetanus from the jagged pieces of metal in the aircraft interior – sometimes displaying similar outright racism to that he remembered from those other tourists, the ones who came to Papa's farm, who visibly blenched when they saw his black face, and then made pointed comments.

Charity asked the visitors, 'How did you find the meal?'

'Great,' the son called Barry said, and the mother and daughters agreed.

'What did you think, boss?' Charity asked Manu.

'Good.'

'Not great?' she said, sorrowfully.

'Near. Chips slightly undercooked.'

'And what about you, sir?' she asked Mr Himmelman.

'I'm with my family for once,' he said. 'I also thought it was great.'

She grinned, showing nearly perfect white teeth; the complexion of the face around them, as smooth as the surfaces of the lakes Manu knew from his earlier lives, on days unruffled by wind, was more perfected still. Only life, experience itself, subject to its own description, could ever tell what happened to her next, though Samuel had a few ideas.

'Please, can we go and play football again?' he asked, as if pleading to regain a kind of paradise, which in a way it was, evening sport being not that unlike the trance state which fled from me . . . Manu suddenly thought . . . so many meadows ago.

'OK, but clear the table first,' he said, more abruptly than he meant.

'I didn't think of it at first as a restaurant,' Manu said later, once the kids had gone. 'In fact, I'm not sure what it is!'

'A social enterprise,' ventured the blonde daughter of the Americans.

'Something with social goals as well as business ones,' added the other. 'We should make a donation, Dad.'

'Maybe,' he said again, more gruffly than before.

Manu shook his head, not wanting to claim their pity. 'There's no need, you already paid for the meal when you booked.'

But they insisted, and quite a generous donation it was, too – Mrs Himmelman saying, as her husband handed it over later: 'Look, we can see that you're standing on your own two feet perfectly fine. This is for the kids, and only because my parents, Zvi's too, were refugees in their time . . . people who had to flee, or be trodden down by the stronger.'

Holding the cash, Manu thought about all the gifts he'd received from *wazungu* in his life. This felt different, for these people had nothing at all to gain from him; and as she said, it wasn't about him anyway. He decided that he would put the money towards fees for the children, so they could go to the school in town, which he and Edith had not so far been able to afford.

The American family stowed themselves in their vehicle, ready for departure. As they did so, Manu thought about the images stored in the camera of the Himmelman son, waiting to be downloaded tomorrow, or more likely another day, or another . . . another day, as humans have been saying since the time of the ark. The sun was pouring out its almost last tot of light, making the air tremble, like Cogan's hands sometimes did, when he needed a drink. It struck Manu that, in his old homestead at Pendele, now would be about time for the cattle to be put away.

The kids came out and waved. As soon as the people carrier containing the Himmelmans began moving, the children ran off, shouting at each other, determined to get in the last of football before it got too dark and the form of the football itself became resistant to sight.

Manu watched the vehicle weave down the sandy track, on its way to Mbarara and then to the airport at Entebbe – from where the Americans would lift off into the golden sky, just as he had done so many times in the past. Maybe it was time to begin that again, to stop being a landsman – Cogan's term . . . should he be setting up a flying school, teaching others to soar as he once did, rather than to cook and hoe? But he wasn't sure if flying was real gold any more: it had brought him a fair bit of grief, that bet the freight dogs made. Even that wonderful feeling he'd had, on the test flight out of Moorsele, of at last clasping the clouds as his own, had lost its gloss. Not one cloud, after all, was his alone; more to the point, and something else, none of them owned by will the name of *cloud* or *nuage* or *igicu* or *wingu* that humans gave it. But he'd tasted the burning light clouds must feel and that, that too was something.

And now, afterwards, at least he had some autonomy and wasn't, he felt, in a world directly full of massacre and murder and wrong.

The Americans' vehicle continued winding down the track towards town and the big tarmac road east, the road that one way or another had existed for centuries, bringing in its days as a simple path, explorers and traders back from Congo, a thin and weary line of carriers or captives behind them, all en route through Kampala – where obeisance must be made at the court of a tall king in a palace of polished reeds – then on to Mombasa, the coast and other authorities. The government had recently announced plans for the road to be better paved and made safe; this road which he knew well from his own trips on it to The Passenger, or to see Edith's mother for councils of war, that to his repeated amusement (repeated because it was always there), passed by a sign that said SIGN NOT IN USE.

Not yet having reached this sign of contradiction, the Toyota's pearl-grey shape fell away until it was obscured by the pattern of the hills, which rolled in great waves to the horizon. The fluid contours of the landscape – brown and green, green and brown, glowing under the libation of the declining sun – were punctuated by scats of smoke from smouldering bush fires, rising into the stillness of the sky.

He caught another glimpse of the people carrier, further down on a bend of the track, and was surprised how small it seemed, suggesting (as it followed the direction in which it lost itself) the end of a view in a painting. Lord, Manu thought, what a long way I can see from here.

What he at any rate next saw, but only in his vicarious mind's eye, was a little black obelisk: that recording device into which he'd once tried speaking the unspeakable cargo of his life, back in Papa's farmhouse. He hadn't done it. Shuddering now, he again felt like some rascal trying to stitch together a story before the law, or that time he had tried to explain himself to Anke in the museum, failing miserably. The load of the past began to sink into him again, as if a hatch had been opened in the top of his head and an oil-like liquid, gravid with unease, was being poured in.

So it was lucky that Edith came to him right then, there on the periphery of his own property, as the sunset flattened – trod lightly over the sandy soil, put her arms round his waist, gave him a touch of her lips on his neck – saying, because she so liked a plan these days: 'What's happening tomorrow?'

'I don't know,' he replied, turning to take hold of her in the recovered richness of the moment, and it was true. Deep in the valley in front of them, as the sun stood its very final round – a frothing bar of zodiacal light – the hoot of a flight of cranes could be heard. Soon after, they appeared, flying in integrated formation.

Manu imagined the cranes flying further, just like he had, over the pages of the earth; flying over the village and the jungle and the booming surf, flying over container ships, flying over dhows, over the city and the country and the zooming times, over the iron years and all the oppression that's done, flying through night and flying through day, flying further and further, trumpeting, bugling, whooping as they went, summoning all who would listen, summoning us and carrying us, carrying us away to where we can all sing our own note together.

But they'd long ago gone, lifted into the real horizon, those cranes, way before he got to the end of this meditation.

Edith squeezed his waist and he heard the remote thudding of some good mother in the nearby village, pounding maize or millet to feed little Rukidi, Nuhu or Irene in the morning; as if to say, *life still goes on, life still takes place . . .*

Acknowledgements

I'd like to thank the following for their invaluable help and support, of many different types, during the writing of this book: Alex Kerridge, Alison Porteous, Ally Ireson, Andrew Cowan, Belinda Glover, Chris McGreal, Christine Odeph, David Pyle, Elias Mutani, Elkyn Ernst, Gloria Mwaniga, Ian Pindar, Jake Rollinson, Jay Parini, Jenni Barclay, Jeremy McElvie, Keith Tutt, Kirsty Dunseath, Lois Rose, Michela Wrong, Miles Morland, Natasha Fairweather, Otosireze Obi-Young, Peter Simmons, Phoebe Batchelor, Rebecca Baccarat, Rowan Whiteside, Sam Kiley, Sam West, Stephen Romer, Tony Farrell, Troy Onyango, Victoria Evans. Thanks also to my agent, Jim Gill at United, and to Lettice Franklin, Sarah Fortune and all the wonderful team at Weidenfeld & Nicolson.

The primary historical source for this novel is *From Genocide to Continental War: The 'Congolese' Conflict and the Crisis of Contemporary Africa*, by Gérard Prunier (Hurst, 2009). I am also indebted to the poet Don Paterson, for an adaptation of one of his ever fabulous, always appropriate aphorisms, as collected in *The Book of Shadows* (Picador, 2005).